THE
SPEED
OF A
FLAME

THE
SPEED
OF A
FLAME

SIXTUS BECKMESSER

Copyright © 2024 Sixtus Beckmesser

The moral right of the author has been asserted.

Apart from any fair dealing for the purposes of research or private study, or criticism or review, as permitted under the Copyright, Designs and Patents Act 1988, this publication may only be reproduced, stored or transmitted, in any form or by any means, with the prior permission in writing of the publishers, or in the case of reprographic reproduction in accordance with the terms of licences issued by the Copyright Licensing Agency. Enquiries concerning reproduction outside those terms should be sent to the publishers.

This is a work of fiction. Names, characters, businesses, places, events and incidents are either the products of the author's imagination or used in a fictitious manner. Any resemblance to actual persons, living or dead, or actual events is purely coincidental.

Troubador Publishing Ltd
Unit E2 Airfield Business Park,
Harrison Road, Market Harborough,
Leicestershire LE16 7UL
Tel: 0116 279 2299
Email: books@troubador.co.uk
Web: www.troubador.co.uk

ISBN 9781805144458

British Library Cataloguing in Publication Data.
A catalogue record for this book is available from the British Library.

Printed and bound in Great Britain by 4edge Limited
Typeset in 12pt Adobe Garamond Pro by Troubador Publishing Ltd, Leicester, UK

Matador is an imprint of Troubador Publishing

To my late wife Jennifer, my fellow lover of Florence and Tuscany

CONTENTS

1	Homecoming	3
2	A Sword of Compassion	24
3	The Swans	44
4	Rapita	55
5	Dungeon	83
6	Lawrie	100
7	Runes	127
8	The Bunkers	147
9	Dead Souls	167
10	The Flame of Torches	189
11	The Prisoners	213
12	The Triumph	233
13	Ein Ritter nahte da	257
14	The Patriot Game	281

LIVONIA

PART THREE

1
HOMECOMING

*E già, per gli splendori antelucani
Che tanto ai peregrin surgon piu grati
Quanto tornando albergan men lontani,*

Dante Purgatorio XXVII vv 109-11[1]

She didn't notice him. Why should she have done? She was late. She had had to collect some work from her tutor, which had taken longer than she had expected. At last, she had been able to grab her bag and had dived into the U-Bahn station heading for the Hauptbahnhof with her mind only on catching the train. Momentarily, he had been in front of her as she crossed the concourse but he didn't stand out in the crowd, he was just another man dressed in the impeccably clean overalls of a German workman. He was carrying a bag of tools and there was nothing to suggest that he was anything other than a carpenter or a

---

1 Tr: Mark Musa
   And now, before the splendour of the dawn
   (more welcomed by the homebound pilgrim now,
   The closer he awakes to home each day

plumber about to catch a train home after a day's work in the centre of Munich.

She just made it and she settled into her seat on the IC to Berlin. She thought about recent events. Her father had spoken to her on the scrambled line from home two days ago. He was worried about the recent, apparently inexplicable, explosion in the new Dutch-Livonian joint venture electronics factory at Königshof. This was one of the key plants, which would advance the Livonian industrial and economic base, prior to joining the European Union. Mara understood how important this and similar ventures were to their future. She wondered whether the outrage might make her father insist: once more, that she took a private detective with her when she returned to Munich. She didn't see why it should. There had been no motive or explanation for the explosion, although the police seemed certain that it was deliberate. Probably it was some lone crank.

She pulled herself up guiltily at thinking so selfishly about a matter of national importance but she did hope her father didn't change his mind about the detective. She was grateful that he had allowed her to come home this term without him. It was not that Ilya himself bothered her. He was as kind, pleasant and as unobtrusive as he possibly could be. Student life had, however, inevitably been massively compromised by his presence. She had argued with force that he would not be able to prevent any real threat to her and just made her more conspicuous. She hoped, by this continuing pressure, to get her father to allow her to dispense with him altogether. Being able to undertake this journey alone was a step in the right direction. Her father was too concerned about her safety. It was ridiculous. Where could a threat come from? Stefan Travsky and Konradin were securely in an island jail and the support that they had once enjoyed had melted away. Although it was known that some of the new soi-disant democrats had served in the dreaded National Agency of Security (Nazional Agentur Sicherheitpolizei), the present Government had granted an extensive amnesty, which seemed to have been highly successful in uniting the country.

She put security out of her mind. She was looking forward to the next few days. There was so much going on. She was most excited about seeing Detti again, and then there was the wedding to look forward to. At the same time, she was a little apprehensive. She found the change back from being a university student amongst thousands to being the first lady of Livonia always a bit daunting. The change of role was so dramatic, so complete. It is true that a few of the more popular magazines sought her out in Munich and produced nauseatingly sugary articles about her. One German piece had even been entitled *Die Schülerin Prinzessin* which had infuriated her, striking as it did at her very youthful appearance, which she still found embarrassing. On that occasion she did get a stiff letter of protest written from the Livonian Embassy in Berlin pointing out that Livonia was a republic and that Frau Tamara Oblova was certainly not a schoolgirl. It probably didn't achieve much but it made her feel better.

She leapt out of the train at the Berlin Hauptbahnhof and guiltily took a taxi to Kranzler. The station was only just open and the U-bahn connections seemed impossibly complicated or non-existent. As she got a chance to look around, she felt again so strongly her deep love for this rough, rugged, modern metropolis that her Munich friends found so hard to understand. Few of them realised however that it was the city that had saved her life and given to her her first taste of freedom after the dreadful Farm days. She was too shy to explain to them these real reasons for her love of Berlin.

When she had threaded her way through the crowds and entered Kranzler, she caught sight of a young woman with a mane of shining chestnut hair glinting red in the bright lights of the café. A black velvet band held her hair back but it still fell well below her shoulders. At first, the other girl had her back to the entrance but as Mara pushed through the doorway on the second floor Rotunda, hanging on to her grip for dear life against the afternoon Ku'damm crowd, she turned round to search the entrance. Their eyes met and Bernadette Niamh O'Neill, Gräfin von Ritter, Komturin of the Hanseatic Order of St Nicklaus quickly relinquished a huge half-demolished slice of Sachertorte. It left considerable traces of chocolate on her face as she leapt up in unleashed joy, at the same time uttering a rather unmusical shriek of welcome from her normally musical larynx:

'How's Marc and how did you find Manchester?' Mara asked breathlessly, in well-rehearsed English, whilst hugging her friend and acquiring some of the Sachertorte at second hand.

'The first's grand, the second's wet.' replied Detty 'The music is incredible but it's the weather – you'd not believe it – even after Ireland. Will ye not have some coffee and Torte?'

'It looks very good. I'll get some.'

Mara disappeared to the counter to choose from the massed array of different flavours and returned carrying a plate of almond and cream layered cake and a cup of coffee. Having demonstrated her newly acquired English skill to Detty, she used the break provided by her trip to the counter to change gratefully into German. It was the first time that they had talked together. Detty sensed her pride in her improved English, but also her relief when they could revert, without any loss of face, into German to chatter about their experiences since they had last seen each other. Mara had found her psychology and political science course absorbing and had been surprised that she had done the initial assignments easily. There had been time for parties and concerts; it had all been '*herrlich*'.

'Have you seen anything of *mein Schwager*?' asked Detty innocently.

'Yes – from time to time – in a group of friends, you know.' said Mara colouring deeply, which belied her studied nonchalance.

'Give him my love.' Detty didn't want to embarrass Mara further so early in their reunion but privately she shared Marc's reservations over his brother's relationship with Mara. Bill von Ritter was the younger brother of Detty's husband Marc and he was studying for his doctorate at Munich. He was great fun but far too attractive to women and he had a track record with girls that didn't inspire confidence when your closest friend was involved.

'Now tell me about Manchester and Eileen Vaughan. All about it.'

Mara had hurried to move the conversation away from Bill:

'They must have thought you were marvellous.'

Detty laughed:

'Not exactly. They have had more young women who think that they have got marvellous voices in that place than you could dream about. The first job is to cut them down to size.'

Detty had arranged to go to the Royal Northern College of Music for a year after a lot of discussion with Bernhard Meisl, the chorus master at Bayreuth, who had been teaching her. She was to study with Eileen Vaughan, who had the reputation of being both the most formidable and greatest coach of dramatic voices in Europe. Detty had leapt at the idea because it provided the opportunity for a period away from the limelight. She had wanted to study hard with the best and allow her voice to mature completely, whilst learning more repertory and improving her stagecraft. There was no problem with Eileen, who she found a fierce but inspirational teacher and with whom she immediately formed a close relationship.

Apart from the work, it had been hard going. The weather was dreadful and although she was no older than many of the post graduate performers' diploma students, there was a gulf between them, which she found it hard to bridge. She was married to an absent husband, which isolated her. She was also a public figure of some notoriety after her exploits of the previous years. Worst of all, she had already sung a leading role at a great festival, which was the sort of opportunity that many of her would-be companions could only dream about. Some jealousy was natural but the worst part was that it was assumed that she would be stuck up and arrogant. She worked hard to correct this, allowing her friendly relaxed humour to show as often as she could. Quietly she also sometimes avoided entering collegiate competitions for which she was qualified. She was aware of her unusual status and didn't want to hog the limelight. A few nights with her banjo singing Irish songs in The Salutation, the pub behind the College, began to melt the ice, particularly amongst the men and the instrumentalists. She was still, however, looked upon with a mixture of envy and suspicion by the other female postgraduate voice students.

This suspicion had not lessened when she was given the part of *Palmyra* in the College production of Delius' *Koanga*. Detty knew that Eileen had pushed her to audition for this to test her pupil's newfound dramatic skills in a part with a background that was completely unfamiliar. Detty had found the opera beautiful and moving and had enjoying singing opposite the Barbadian baritone whose glorious voice was clearly heading straight for stardom. She wondered how much he would resent a white singer being given the part that had formerly been an Afro-American preserve. After a rehearsal, which had gone well, Detty felt bold enough to tackle him on this sensitive subject.

'It was written by a white, Detty, wasn't it? As long as you can sing it, and you certainly can, it doesn't matter a damn to me.'

After that they had got on well, and Detty had enjoyed the opera more and more. She began to reflect that, in spite of Eileen's efforts to make her do something different, in the last analysis the part was not so far from her previous life-experience. After all, Palmyra is supposed to be half European, and, at one stage in her life, Detty herself had been virtually a slave, which was certainly not an experience shared by her fellow students. She even thought that Simon Perez, the evil overseer in the opera, bore some resemblance to Konradin with his odious mixture of sadism and lust. The performances had gone well and, to her surprise, she had received a second plaudit from Sir Henry Knight, the doyen of English music critics, in the London Times. He seemed rather impressed that she had been prepared to descend from the dizzy heights of the Bayreuth Festival to go to college to perfect her art.

In reality, she had understood, that after the extraordinary events of the year before, her singing career was in danger of running ahead of itself. She had been catapulted from a small solo part at Bayreuth into the limelight of a great soprano role through a very strange series of coincidences. That was nothing however compared with the extraordinary set of circumstances surrounding the Königshof Fidelio, many of which had nothing to do with music at all. She never doubted her voice or her musicianship but she was painfully aware that she had a severely limited and rather unbalanced repertory, virtually no previous training in stagecraft and only a rudimentary knowledge of Italian. She felt that she was in grave danger of becoming a sort of infant prodigy or nine days wonder. After consulting with Bernhard Meisl and Haydn Roberts, she had therefore decided that a postgraduate course of study at a Conservatoire was essential to give her some dramatic training and the chance to study more roles out of the limelight. The decision to go to Manchester rather than Munich was partly due to Eileen Vaughan's high reputation and partly to the fact that she would see at least something of Marc who was now with the German Military Attaché in London and working for NATO. At weekends, despite the distance, she had usually been able to return to Henley, where they had kept their house, and be with him, albeit for only a few hours.

She recounted all this to Mara as they talked and the chat continued in the taxi to Schönefeld Airport to catch the plane to Königshof. In less than an hour, they tumbled out of the Lufthansa flight on to the dark, chilly Baltic tarmac. It was strange to be back. The obvious scars of last year's fighting had been cleared with remarkable speed, but the contrast with the airports of Berlin and Munich was still striking. There were no automated landing facilities yet and, even as VIPs, they had to walk the two hundred metres to the terminal now accompanied, unobtrusively, by two security men. Detty watched bemused as Mara entered the VIP lounge as Anna Weber, student from Munich, and emerged as Tamara Nikolaevna Oblova, first lady of the Hanseatic Republic of Livonia.

The official car swept Mara away amongst the smiles and applause of the late-night airport passengers. Mara, still not used to playing the *Grand Dame*, stuck her head out of the window to remind Detty that she was expected at the Hansehaus the following Friday for dinner before the wedding on the Saturday and the parade some days later. Detty herself had been offered an official car and driver/private detective but had declined both and had negotiated a small hire car through the normal channels. She had done this in order to try to avoid some of the attention and adulation that now surrounded her in Livonia. Fat chance, she thought, as she went to collect her car past groups of people suddenly recognising her striking and well-known features then blowing kisses and calling *'Herzlich zuruck Wilkommen'*. [2]

Eventually she reached the hire car office and proffered her credit card only to have it brushed away and be informed that 'the Hansehaus has looked after all that'. Protest at that point seemed useless and after thanking the clerk, she collected the car and drove out through the southern suburbs, retracing the route of Malinov's and Marc's heady,

---

2 Welcome back!

final advance from the *Zehnheiligenweg* to the Winterburg. The streets were now quiet on the late winter evening. There was little traffic compared with Berlin or Manchester. She reached the rolling forest with the tracery of the trees etched silver-tinged and black in the headlights. The bitter cold of the evening began to bite, as it got later. It reminded her of her first visit a seeming age ago. After an hour or so driving away from the city, she turned in by a bright new notice in gold on blue on the gates of *Schloss Krenek*, which read '*Schliessen O'Neill Hochmusikschule*', and underneath 'Visitors are requested to enquire at reception.'

She squeezed to the side of the narrow drive to allow a service van marked 'Plumbing and Heating' and obviously in a hurry, to overtake her before the point where the drive narrowed. Must be an emergency she thought for a call out as late as this and hoped she wouldn't arrive to find darkness, then she forgot all about it. She passed the abandoned lodge, which was surrounded by building works preparing for its re-birth as the college library. As she did so, she thought about the history of the place.

The original buildings at *Schloss Krenek* went back beyond the Hanse to the days when the Teutonic Knights had built a Commanderie on the small knoll, which dominated the surrounding forests and lakes. The ruined site had been rebuilt in the seventeenth century as the country house of the Graf von Krenek, a successful soldier of fortune, who had developed the estate and built the elegant Baroque *Schloss*. Prussian aristocrats had occupied the house and fished and shot on the adjoining lake until the fall of the German Empire when the house had been used by successive regimes for various purposes and had fallen into disrepair.

The most recent history of the *Schloss* was well known to Detty who, herself, had been wounded taking part in the defence of the lake against an attacking force of NAS commandos. When he heard that his wife had asked for it as the site of the new national conservatory, Marc had teased her, unmercifully. At the purchasing ceremony, he had declared that it was appropriate that it had passed from one soldier of fortune to another. Detty had scandalised the on-looking Livonian dignitaries by punching her husband hard in the midriff. She replied that, with his record, he was a fine one to call her a soldier of fortune. Anyway, she liked soldiers of fortune, and had fallen in love with the story of Sir John Hawkwood, who seemed an interesting and unusual sort of Saxon, when she had been in Florence on their honeymoon.

The first voice competition of the new College had been set for the following day. The date had been arranged in consultation with Detty so that she could attend to award the prizes. Unfortunately, Hank Schliessen, world famous American Heldentenor and the Conservatoire's co-founder, had an engagement to sing Aeneas in a new production of *Les Troyens* at the Metropolitan, New York and so couldn't, to his distress, be there. Detty, however, had been able to persuade Eileen Vaughan and Bernhard Meisl to join Helge von Grunstrand, the Director of the School, to form a distinguished panel of judges. Hotels in rural Livonia were next to non-existent so Bernhard and Eileen were staying at the *Schloss* and had also, to Detty's delight, agreed to give masterclasses to the students that day. Detty herself had taken the opportunity to pay a flying visit to her parents-in-law in Franconia before coming on via Berlin. She felt that, much as she would have liked to attend the masterclasses, this might be the moment to stand back and allow the students to have unimpeded access to the visiting teachers.

Helge was in the front porch to greet her:

'Detti, it has been *schon lange*. Wonderful to see you! How was Manchester? No, tell me over dinner – it's so late and it's all ready. But first you must meet the students.'

Introductions followed. The school had been founded the previous autumn with money provided by Henry Schliessen and the Wurzburgfranken Bank. The Schliessen Donation was public knowledge. The one from the German merchant bank, however, had been channelled privately through a gift to Detty's fund for the re-establishment of musical education in Livonia. After the Freiheitsfest performances of *Fidelio*, there had been no difficulty in getting distinguished musicians, both Livonian and foreign, to serve on the board with Detty as president. Such was the extraordinary atmosphere in the country and the reverence lavished on Detty that nobody thought it at all unusual to have a twenty-four-year-old woman, herself about to become a student again, as President of the Conservatoire's Board of Management. Helge, the obvious choice as Principal in spite of his commitments with the Königshof orchestra, had been willing to serve and was duly appointed. With the help of the board, this time without Detty, who was in Manchester, he had selected his music staff, initially small but with plans for the future. To the amazement and gratification of all concerned, there were eight hundred initial applications for places on the first undergraduate course and, whilst inevitably not all had exceptional talent, extremely promising youngsters filled the available fifty places.

This evening Helge had arranged a reception so that all the students could have a chance to talk with the distinguished guests before dinner, which was to be followed by a chamber recital, sadly short because of the lateness of the hour.

It gave Detty quiet pleasure to see the great drawing room of the *Schloss* filled with relaxed laughter and musical gossip. She remembered the quite different feeling that it had had during the anxious, exciting days of the previous year when she herself had narrowly escaped with her life after being wounded by a fascist sniper. Only for a few minutes, after they had sat down to dinner, did the cheerful atmosphere become more sombre. Helge mentioned the explosion at Königshof. Miraculously nobody had been killed but there was considerable damage to the delicate installation and two Dutch engineers had been injured and were in hospital. Bernhard asked Helge whether he thought it was the act of an isolated fanatic or represented something more serious.

Helge thought for some moments while the others, including Detty, hung on his answer. At last, he said:

'It's really very hard to tell. There has been nothing else like it – yet – but there is supposed to be a Ukrainian group who seem to have got mixed up with some old NAS and there may be something more serious going on. There are rumours of an attempt to de-stabilise the country but not much hard evidence. Many NAS escaped to Belarus after the capture of Königshof last year. It was about the only country that would have them.'

'Surely they won't succeed?' asked Detty feeling an involuntary shudder as the thought of the old evil passed through her.

'They won't succeed – no- but like all terror groups they could be hard to pin down. They may do a lot of damage, particularly at a critical time when the political stability and economic progress of the country is so important for our future.'

The serious moment passed and the talk moved on to next year's *Freiheitsfest*. This was to be held in December around the National Day, the Feast of St Nicklaus on December 6th. They discussed how they should celebrate it. Helge favoured a performance of Waldhuter's *Hanse* together with the Beethoven Choral symphony, as a patriotic European celebration of Livonia's intended application to join the Union. Detty had at first favoured *Die Meistersinger*, pointing out that it involved a lot of minor parts as well as the major ones and would give a splendid challenge to the country's burgeoning musical life.

Helge laughed:

'You haven't of course considered the major roles, Detty?' he asked slyly.

She laughed back:

'I thought that you would suspect hidden motives. Of course, I have thought about it. To get one thing out of the way, I would love to try *Eva* before I get too long in the tooth but I don't think my voice is ideal for it.'

She raised an eyebrow quizzically at Eileen who nodded.

'Equally' she went on 'I can't see Hank singing *Walther* although I know he has reserved time to come back here then. The home team could, however, be really strong for several roles. What about, for instance, Martina as *Eva* and Lev as *Walther*?'

Martina Schlerova and Lev Forjela had been the *Marzelline* and *Jacquino* in the previous year's *Fidelio*. Detty warmed to her task:

'and Dieter would be a superb *Pogner*.'

There was some nodding round the table and a moment's silence broken by Helge.

'Don't think I am backing out' he said 'every conductor worthy of his salt wants to do *Die Meistersinger* but I think, realistically, we might be talking about two years' time not next year. I would be quite prepared to start planning it though. Do you have the time to help find a producer and try and help book the other soloists, Detty? We will have to find some that we can afford and it will have to be done well in advance.'

'Sure, I will' said Detty. 'If Eileen will let me.'

'I might even be able to help. How do you fancy a black *Beckmesser?*' said the latter.

'That is a grand idea! As long as no fool thinks it's racist.'

Detty leapt up in excitement knowing that Eileen meant Hartley Thomas, her partner in the recent Manchester *Koanga* who she knew had leanings towards comedy roles.

'So, this year we stick to the original plan. Say we do the Choral Symphony alone as a main piece on the opening night, and the Hanse tone poem with a concerto as the second concert. Then, we really need another choral piece for the third programme to give the chorus enough to do. They are coming on well and we have a spring season with *Carmen* and *Onegin* planned.

After coffee they listened to a delightful performance of the 2nd Rasumovsky quartet from the students and as the applause died away, Helge turned to Detty.

'We cannot let you leave here without hearing you sing, Detty.'

'What – in front of my teacher at this time of night?' she said in mock horror 'but yours to command, Herr *Generaldirektor*, what would you like?'

'Anything – we will leave it up to you.'

There was a murmur of agreement.

'OK, it's always good to have a free hand.'

She thought for a moment and then walked over to the College's treasured Steinway that always sat in state in the corner of the grand drawing room, until it was needed in the still unfinished concert hall that was being built in the grounds.

'Do you need an accompanist?' asked Helge.

'I am going to try and find something new for Eileen who knows most of my repertory backwards and beyond, so I don't think even you will know these. I haven't a score and although I can vouch for the vocal line, I think that I will have to try and improvise an impromptu piano accompaniment from memory.'

They all looked fascinated but puzzled. Her voice filled the old hall with a beautiful lilting melody in a strange language, which was followed by a piano intermezzo and then a second swirling song. At the end, they applauded and looked at her for an explanation.

'Well. How was that? Does anyone know it?'

Eileen Vaughan said:

'I've never heard it sung before but I've heard about it and I think that I recognised the Irish language. Is it from Patrick Cassidy's *'The Children of Lir?* It suits your voice – Handelian, but none the worse for that' she added.

'Never try and fool your professor.' Detty laughed 'Indeed it is – they want me to sing it at the Kilkenny Festival next year. Those were the two soprano solos from the middle section where *Fionnuala* and her brothers have been changed into swans and must spend three years each in ever more terrible places. The first is *Fionnuala's* Farewell to *Lough Derravagh* and the second her lament in the northern sea. It's quite demanding – needs a good orchestra, traditional instruments, and a chorus and, of course, soloists who can sing in Irish Gaelic. I love it. The story gives me goose pimples and makes me cry. It comes straight out of the bogs of my roots.' she laughed.

'It was wonderful' said Helge thoughtfully 'Thank you for letting us hear it. Can you tell us the whole story?'

Detty duly obliged adding something of how the cantata had come to be written.

'Presumably, you – or somebody – think they can assemble the correct forces for Kilkenny. Would they be transportable here for the *Freiheitsfest?*'

It was Detty's turn to look startled.

'I don't see why not. The inspiration behind Kilkenny is Adele O'Mara who taught me in Ireland. I will talk to her.'

Helge looked excited.

'If we are doing the Beethoven and Waldhuter from local resources we could spend a bit more on the third piece. It would be a very suitable European gesture and the piece is lovely from what we've heard tonight – as well as coming from the homeland of our local heroine.'

Detty pulled a rude and not very heroine-like face at him:

'The programme for Kilkenny is probably not complete yet. There's a lot of traditional and chamber music apart from one or two big pieces like the Cassidy. I suppose there would be no chance of an exchange with your orchestra doing the *Waldhuter* there – if it would be feasible?'

'Of course, there might be – but bluntly somebody would have to pay and as you know transporting and housing a symphony orchestra, even a poorly paid one, is far from cheap. You realise only too well that Livonia does not have any funds for this sort of thing.'

'Still, it might be possible. There is quite a lot of Irish money these days if you can winkle it out and we might get a bank, and an airline might provide transport free as publicity. If the grand scheme for the exchange does not work then perhaps your orchestra could play the Cassidy and we could just bring the traditional instrumentalists, chorus and soloists.'

'That might be fun' said Helge 'Good for their experience.'

'I heard the recording of last year's *Fidelio* and I thought that they were miraculous and so was your orchestra – the more so given the circumstances.' said Eileen.

'Thank you.' Helge was obviously pleased 'I hope that we are better now. I take it that you would be free Detty?'

'Surely. I have kept it clear. I am giving this year up to study so I only have *Woglinde* at Bayreuth and possibly a *Tatiana* at St Petersburg, if they can be persuaded to let a foreigner in, in early summer. That is together, of course, with whatever my disciplinarian voice teacher finds for me in Manchester. It's rumoured that she thinks it would be good for me to sing *Sarastro*.'

'No, it was actually *The Queen of the Night* that I had in mind.'

'I think I might prefer *Sarastro*.' said Detty laughing and pulling a long face at the idea of getting her big dramatic voice round those impossible coloratura runs although she was aware that the great Birgit Nilsson had said that she often sang it for practice.

They said their goodnights. Thoughtfully Detty walked down the same corridor to her room that she had travelled the year before. It was in those dark days of the war in this very same place that the idea of the music school had first come to her. Music had always been close to her heart. However, even she had been surprised at the electric effect that the song that she had written to the theme of Waldhuter's *Hanse* tone poem had had on the dispirited army. She reflected ruefully that her career as a patriotic songwriter, although it had worked beyond her dreams, depended largely on plagiarism. For the *Freiheitslied* she had at least written the text and adapted the melody but later, however, she had shamelessly used anything that came to hand to serve the insurgents' cause. Irish rebel songs and German volkslieder were all grist for her mill and had been remarkably successful. It was the reputation that she had gained from these troops' concerts that enabled her to embark on the mad escapade that had turned the course of the war. That was all behind her now and she was profoundly grateful that peace had enabled her to promote the cause of music in her adopted second, or was it third, homeland.

She slept well, waking as she usually did at the glimmers of winter's first light. She turned on her travelling radio just in time for the news. Livonia seemed quiet but the main item was an explosion on the late-night train from Berlin to Munich that had derailed the train and killed sixty people. The reasons for this awful disaster were not at all clear but sabotage, possibly from an extreme right-wing group, was suspected. Detty wondered if she knew anybody who might have been on the train. Marc was still in England, Bill in Munich and she had seen Mara safely in Königshof but she wasn't sure about her father-in-law who, she knew, occasionally went to Berlin by train. A quick phone call to Oberdorf produced the reassuring voice of Hildegard telling her that Graf Max had left that morning for Frankfurt and had not been to Berlin. She had a quick gossip with her mother-in-law, Sophie, and felt a bit better. She was however still sad and a little cross. This was to have been a perfect day and she had looked forward to it for some time. Now it was overcast by this news. She told herself not to be selfish and wondered how the people who had relatives or friends involved were feeling. Suppose Mara had been on that train instead of the earlier one in the opposite direction. She shuddered and wondered for an instant whether it could have been the same train returning. To put the thought out of her mind she leapt out of bed and across to the window.

The lake was much the same but it seemed smaller than in her memory. She could see the ruined summerhouse, which had been Liese's command post and the spot, fifty metres to the right, where she had been wounded. This morning all was calm with the long shadow of the house striking westwards across the frosty grass at the first pale rays of the chilly sun. It was going to be a fine day but bitterly cold. She seized her dressing gown and towel and went down the creaky corridor to the bathroom. For the rest of the day, she forgot about war and disasters and immersed herself in Schubert, Waldhuter and Mozart as the contestants presented their lieder and arias.

It was satisfying to concentrate on other people's music for a change. For Detty the most impressive performance was by a young baritone called Leif Rohren. His grandfather had come from Norway as a dairy farmer and the family had remained in Livonia, caught up in the subsequent convulsions. Leif was now twenty-five and started with a Grieg song followed by a dramatic account of *'Eri tu'* from Verdi's *Un Ballo in Maschera* which had the entire audience, judges included, on the edge of their seats. His main rival was Olga Forjela, the exceptionally talented soprano younger sister of Lev Forjela, the singer of Jacquino in the Königshof *Fidelio* the previous year. Her contribution was a stunningly accurate *'Gretchen am Spinrad'* and a *'Come scoglio'* which Detty had to admit she would have been proud to have sung herself. The first prize went to Olga but Eileen in announcing the winners said that the standard was incredibly high for a Conservatoire in its first year and that she hoped to arrange some exchanges with Manchester.

Feeling a glow of satisfaction for all concerned at how well it had gone, Detty said her goodbyes and, explaining that she must leave for Königshof early, went to her room.

*

At first, she was so stunned that she could only stare at the echelon of broken glass at her feet reaching across from the shattered French window while her ears rang with the roar of the explosion. Gradually, fearfully, she looked up and out onto the drive and the lawn. There was a heap of twisted metal that had once been the little hire car, which she should have been driving back to the capital. What was left of the engine was upside down across the grass pointing at her like a stubby accusing finger.

The howl of the police siren roused her from her daze. The Commissar was a balding, fatherly man in his fifties who tried to find the right words to express his outrage at this act of violence. It was sadly easy to see what had happened. Joe Mysarek, the young handyman from the village, had kindly offered to save Detty a bit of time by driving her car round from the garage in the old coach house at the back of the *Schloss* while she had a quick roll and coffee. It had cost him his life and saved hers. The car had exploded as he backed it alongside the front porch and all that was left of him was a severed limb on the grass and pieces of flesh adhering to the tangled wreckage.

It was clear to everybody that the bomb had been intended for her. The staff and visitors assembled in various dishevelled states of dress and even more chaotic emotions. There was relief at Detty's escape, shame that the college should have hosted, however unwittingly, this terror and overwhelming sadness and horror that a decent young man with a wife and new baby should have been slaughtered so wantonly.

By mid-morning, Detty had told the Commissar all that she could, which was little enough. She knew of no reason now why anybody should want to kill her. Travsky junior and Konradin were still in their island prison and she had not received any threats or other evidence that his associates were active and pursuing a vendetta against her. The Commissar looked puzzled and said he must consult with his Chiefs in the capital.

'You must be very careful. Where will you be staying for the rest of your visit to Livonia?'

'The Hansehaus' Detty replied managing a smile.

'There, at least, you will be safe.' The Commissar seemed relieved that his responsibility for her safety would manifestly end when she became a personal guest of the President, saying that he would arrange for her to be taken there at once.

'There is something I must do first. Nobody has spoken to Joe's wife yet and I would like to break the news to her.'

She was firm and the Commissar, seeing that argument was useless, told his Marshall to drive the Frau Komturin to the Mazureks' bungalow.

The next three hours were some of the most difficult that Detty had ever spent. Irina Masyrek's initial pleasure at receiving a visit from Livonia's legendary heroine quickly turned to desolation when she knew its cause. Detty did her best to support her knowing that comfort was impossible. Both devout Catholics, they were able to pray together. Afterwards Irina stood up, saying through her tears:

'It was kind and good of you to come to me. I think Joe would have been proud to save you and I will come to take pride in it too. But not now---for now I cannot feel or think-- it can't be true.'

She wept again.

By mid-afternoon, the family had gathered round, allowing a humble and guilty Detty to take her sorrowful leave promising to come again. As the police car drove her to Königshof, she reflected that bravery was sometimes easier to achieve than to witness. She had missed the ceremony at the University where she was to have received an honorary degree and wondered how she would cope with Masha's wedding on the morrow.

She arrived at the Hansehaus that evening subdued and gloomy. She hated the idea of the wedding the following day and was even anxious at the prospect of an evening spent with her dearest friend. All the pleasure that she had felt about being back in Livonia had vanished.

Mara had already heard about the explosion. She met her anxiously in the reception area and immediately took her up to the drawing room in the comfortable Presidential private flat on the fourth floor, above the offices and public rooms. The President was away at a European Union meeting in Strasbourg. Gradually, Detty felt less tense. Mara could always bring quiet resource to a crisis and it helped Detty to feel better. She remembered the first time that they had really met on the dreadful bus to the Farm and how immediately she had felt the strength of the young woman who had then been briefly her pupil. They had been through so much, good, and bad, together since then. As her hostess opened an old bottle of Jameson's that she had been keeping since her visit to Ballyinch, Detty found her voice.

'That poor woman, Mara, they had worked together for everything and then it was just swept away. It should have been me. I feel so much to blame. I had so much less to lose.'

Mara just listened. There were no platitudes. As they were alone, Mara cooked supper in the little private kitchen. She had planned the menu with care. Detty at first didn't feel that she could face food and started to eat just from politeness. Her appetite came back enough to please her hostess but she apologised for her mood and felt wretched that Mara had been to so much trouble. The home-made borsht and saddle of hare in horseradish cream had been so carefully and lovingly prepared. For the first time since they had been together in freedom, there was no music. Mara seemed nervous and anxious to say something but couldn't find a way to start. In the end it blurted out,

'Detti, you know you were puzzled when Masha was in hospital after her release and she kept having terrors shouting about a belt and then couldn't remember anything about it afterwards. You couldn't figure it out?'

'I remember very well – go on.'

'Well, I believe that I know what she was talking about. I think that I have always known really but I – I couldn't talk about it……'

Mara was pale and fidgety and looked on the verge of breaking down. Detty was still puzzled. They all loved Masha and had been horrified at her treatment but she felt there was more to Mara's distress even than that. She simply said quietly.

'Tell me'

'Well, I think that they used a thing called a stun belt on her. It was invented in America to control violent prisoners when they moved them around. They put it round the prisoner's waist and then the guard can activate it from anywhere nearby with a thing like a TV remote control. A huge electric shock goes through the prisoner's back and spreads all over the body. It doesn't kill but it causes agony then the prisoner passes out for some seconds and……. often… loses control of….well…. everything.'

Detty was quiet for some time, and then she asked hoarsely, already knowing what the reply must be.

'Mara, how do you know so much about this dreadful thing?'

The expected answer came in a hoarse whisper:

'Because they used it on me.'

Detty sat looking at her horrified despite guessing the explanation. She knew that they had used primitive electric instruments and shocks on Mara because of her terrible burns but she had never said anything about this ghastly refinement. Mara repeated, still in a whisper.

'I couldn't talk about it. They were kind at the de-briefing but the shame... Perhaps now I can tell you, as I am older, but for a teenager ...to describe what it did to you. I just couldn't. You remember that they took me away after I tore up the Governor's paper on the platform and he was so angry. Well, they put the stun belt on me and tried it out – several times. The shock goes into your side like a giant electric drill then you pass out and ....everything else happens. When you come to you are all stiff and in a terrible mess. They let me shower then put the belt back on under the kimono before I went back on the platform. That was the reason for the strange clothes. The long loose kimono was so that it didn't show. They said the Governor had the controller in his pocket and would activate it if I didn't do exactly as they wanted. If he used it on me in public, he would just tell the reporters afterwards that I had become severely epileptic – they seemed to think that all people with epilepsy were idiots – shows you the sort of people they were – are. What could I do but agree?'

She paused:

'Fortunately, they only had one belt then as they are very expensive but I suspect they used it thoroughly on Masha when they interrogated her as she was so important... before they shot her that is.'

Mara broke down in uncontrollable weeping and Detty put her arms round her and hugged her. The horror of this on top of everything else that she had suffered was so unspeakable that there were no words. Eventually they went to bed. Detty quietly left her door ajar so as to hear if Mara called in the night. She lay awake cursing herself for ignoring the clues, which explained in full the suffering of both her friends. She brooded gloomily on the task of holding back cruelty and horror, which kept reappearing with its Hydra's heads. How had she managed to think that she was coming back to Livonia for art and love?

2
A SWORD OF COMPASSION

Defend the poor and the fatherless:
See that such as are in need and necessity have right,
Deliver the outcast and poor,
Save them from the hand of the ungodly

PSALM 82

That night the horrors, so long absent, pursued Detty ferociously again. Joe had turned into the bleeding wounded ghost who became the Armourer and was pursuing her through the woods to the banks of the old warehouse on the Fojn. Suddenly her foot caught fast. She tried to escape and cry out. She couldn't move and the cry wouldn't come. Then she struggled upwards through sleep and she awoke screaming and struggling. Her feet were enmeshed in her quilt, which had twisted round her. She freed herself and lay, wide-awake, sweating and shivering in the cold of the northern night through her open window. She hoped that she hadn't woken Mara but in spite of her own distress of the previous night, Mara was still sleeping soundly. It was four in the morning. She turned over and passed into a dreamless sleep until the shrill of her alarm awakened her, startled and unbelieving, at six.

A quick shower, jeans, sweater and leather coat against the cold and she let herself out of the private flat. To save the noise of the lift, she crept down through the deserted public rooms and offices to the night desk. The duty officer, Falk, was the veteran FWL sergeant- major who had stopped her when she arrived at the war. He had never forgotten the incident when he had detained her as a spy and now treated her with a mixture of hero-worship, deference and embarrassment that she found amusing but a bit overwhelming. He leapt to his feet behind the desk.

'Frau Hauptmann, is anything the matter? – yesterday –'

He paused, not knowing how to put it then blurted:

'Are you all right? Is there a problem in His Excellency's flat?'

'No, Falk, I am just going to the airport to meet my husband who is coming over for Frau Hauptmann Masha's wedding today. Has the taxi arrived yet?'

Her question was answered by a buzz from the guard at the outer security gate. The taxi was on time. It was a grey morning with a fine cold drizzle. They turned out of the Hansehaus into the side streets, which lay behind it, to cut across town to the airport. In a small square, at the first winter light, the market traders were setting up their stalls and laughing and joking over steaming glasses of black tea. It was more cheerful and noisy than usual because, the night before, FC Königshof had achieved a surprising but highly creditable, away draw against the Italian club, Lazio, in the Champions League. Nobody looked over their shoulder or talked in whispers in this Königshof. This was the measure of their achievement, thought Detty, feeling more positive. It was worth the struggle. No bastards were going to wreck it now.

She paid the taxi and had a coffee at the airport. The Berlin plane had already landed but nobody had come through Arrivals. She stood craning her neck on tiptoe at the arrival gate like, she thought, a teenager waiting for her first date. Then he was there with a huge smile and a crushing bear hug, which drove the breath out of her body but that she wanted to go on forever. He had heard about the explosion on the news and also, fortunately, that she had escaped unhurt. He was understandably anxious. She must leave Livonia as soon as possible. She said that was rubbish. There was no motive for the attack and she was probably safer in Königshof under the protection of the authorities than she would be elsewhere. Eventually he gave up. He knew her too well to expect her to be deflected by mere reason.

As they went back to the Hansehaus to change, they talked through the explosion and its consequences. Gradually they were able to chat more normally and talked about the singing competition, army friends and the exercises. They were even able to plan the re-decoration for their little, seldom lived-in, English house. Detty was beginning to feel herself again but it still wasn't the right time to tell Marc her most important news.

Masha had telephoned Detty in England to ask her if she would sing at the wedding. It was to be a strictly civilian affair and the guests were mainly colleagues from *FreiSender Livonias* together with Masha's family and local friends. There was also a smaller party made up of Rudi's family from Germany. The religious ceremony was to be held in the little church at Masha's home village that was a few kilometres from Litovsk near the Russian border. Such was his regard for Marc, however, that Rudi had been insistent that both the von Ritters had to be present, even if the ceremony had to be held at four in the morning on a February Monday. Marc in turn had had to call in some favours from both the British and the German authorities in order to get there. To Detty's distress, he had to fly back to England the following day but she was comforted by the promise that there was to be some leave later.

Enjoying the rare privilege of a day with her husband, she drove out with Marc stopping for lunch at a country *Gasthof* on the way. After the explosion, the Königshof police had insisted that she had a security escort, which might have spoilt the one day that they could spend in each other's company. In the event, however, the two special policemen were ex FWL and had served with the Intelligence Corps. Detty insisted that they all have lunch together. It became clear that they were delighted to have been given the task of looking after Detty and Marc and even more pleased at the prospect of attending Masha's wedding. One of the young men looked up from his *Sledzie Nadziewane* and said:

'She was the bravest person in the whole army' then he looked at Detty 'except you of course.'

He had no sooner said it than he realised it sounded trite. He blushed deeply. Detty smiled and shook her head:

'I never had to suffer what she suffered.'

'It wouldn't be proper to argue with you, Frau Komturin,' said the young man.

Sensing embarrassment, Marc came to the rescue:

'She is quite right' he said, indicating his wife 'You have to have served as a plasterer's mate to get full battle honours in Livonia.'

Detty dissolved in mock rage and they laughed, breaking the tension. The story of Detty's cack-handed efforts to help re-plaster the Hoftheatre before her *Fidelio* had passed into Livonian folklore.

As they arrived at the church, miraculously, the rain stopped and a pale sun appeared. The security men faded quietly into the background. They took their place as unobtrusively as possible waiting for the bride, as was the custom, at the church door. Rudi came first. He was very slender but managed his artificial right leg effortlessly and was otherwise, seemingly, fit. They greeted them and did the rounds talking to the guests who did their best to keep moving in the bitter cold. Rudi was clearly delighted that Marc and Detty had indeed arrived and thanked them warmly.

Detty had not seen Masha face to face since she had visited her in hospital in those awful days of waiting before the final advance on Königshof. Masha didn't know then what Detty had just learnt from Mara but it was still obvious that she had been cruelly damaged by her unspeakable experiences at the hands of the NAS. Detty, with the help of her brother-in-law, Bill, had arranged for Masha to go to Munich to the Max Planckt Institute to see one of the leading authorities on post-traumatic stress. Detty had no idea how it had gone and just hoped that she had been able to tell her therapist everything. She didn't know how Masha would cope with this important day. She had seemed cheerful on the telephone but they had talked mainly about the service music and hadn't touched on deeper things.

At last, the bride arrived in a *Troika*, reflecting the Russian culture of this part of the land. She had lost a lot of weight from the chunky, boisterous, fearless captain of intelligence that they both remembered. She wore a full-length French grey silk sheath dress with a white crown of living camellias. It all set off her long dark hair to perfection and Detty immediately noticed her smile twinkling with real pleasure. As she was handed down from the *Troika*, she laughed saying:

'I thought we would need the skis this morning, it's so cold.'

She seemed at ease and was enjoying her day. The Mass followed the wedding ceremony, tranquil, solemn, and yet joyful. Afterwards while the couple embraced each other as husband and wife, the whole congregation looked on. They were all silently moved, as the two disabled heroic survivors enjoyed this quiet moment. They had found each other again, were alive and they rejoiced in it. At the same time, they suffered the deep injury of survival amongst the dead. Noiselessly, Detty and Helge von Grunstrand made their way to the altar steps. Standing at the side of the bridal couple, with a tiny signal to Helge Detty broke into Mozart's *Exsultate Jubilate*. When Masha had asked hesitatingly whether she would be prepared to sing at the wedding, Detty had agreed at once. It took her only a moment to decide that it had to be the Mozart with its appropriate *recitativo secco* and radiance after darkness and night. It was tricky for her voice however with its high coloratura passages needing lightness and accurate mobility. She anxiously muttered to Marc as she resumed her seat after the bright *Alleluia*:

'Was I all right?'

'You were fine – worth coming half across Europe for.' he whispered teasingly 'but you know I'm a bit of a fan.'

The eating and drinking featured a splendid Livonian country spread. There was laughter and dancing until late in the evening the couple set off for an undisclosed destination on the way to their Cretan honeymoon. As they drove back, Detty felt a sense of gloom and anticlimax. She hated Marc going. He would be in Turkey when she returned to Manchester and the promised leave wasn't for some time.

At the Hansehaus, they found that Nicklaus had returned from Strasbourg. There had been a formal dinner for some French industrialists who had come with him. Mara was, as usual, acting as her father's hostess. She had gone to the wedding separately, representing the President, so she could leave early for her diplomatic duties. She seemed fully recovered, looked stunning in an elegant black satin evening dress setting off her fair curls to perfection. She had clearly, and unsurprisingly, captivated the Frenchmen who were exhibiting a good deal of Gallic gallantry. Detty and Marc were introduced and, after having coffee, they gave their excuses on the grounds of Marc's early morning flight and went to bed. They made love hungrily and repeatedly and then lay exhausted listening to the city night sounds:

'Darling, I'm late' she said in English. It sounded bald, she wished she'd chosen German.

'What do you mean you're late, *Schatz*?'

'*Meine Tagen verspätung haben.*'

She wasn't sure that it sounded better in German but the light slowly dawned on Marc and a huge smile spread over his face.

'*Bist du ...wirklich*, darling?'

He mixed languages as he often did when he was excited or upset.

'Yes, I did a test in Berlin as I came through to make sure.'

'But that's wonderful-when?'

'It's very early. I wanted to talk to you first, so I haven't seen anyone but I think that it's the end of October.

Marc was still stunned but incredibly happy as he left for the morning plane. He kept fussing her about things she had hardly considered herself such as the country, the hospital, the doctor, what she should eat and do.

'You will be telling me what I ought to think next' she laughed as they stood outside the departure lounge.

She felt very flat as she turned away. The two bodyguards were, despite their tact and courtesy, proving a burden. She could see what Mara meant when she had complained about having to have one. She wished that she could go straight back to England but she had the Initiation Ceremony of the Order of St Nicklaus to attend and had promised Mara to stay for the week so that they could spend some time together before their ways parted for Munich and Manchester. It had sounded fun and she had been looking forward to it but now the fun had evaporated in the explosion and its dreadful aftermath. But stay she must for both these reasons and there passed through the gloomy depths of her mind something about rats and a sinking ship. Pull yourself together she said to herself – a couple of civic outrages won't destroy what they-we- have done. The police will get to the bottom of it, a few gangsters will be arrested and it will all be history. As she was trying to reason with herself, she realised that that wasn't all. She had been deeply disturbed by Mara's revelations about her own treatment under the NAS and insights into Masha's torture. Somehow, there seemed to be a connection between the present troubles and past terror. She told herself that it was ridiculous; the NAS was in the past. After all both women had found a life after their ordeals, although she realised that in each case it had taken help and courage. How lucky she had been to be able to take revenge for her own lesser sufferings. She now felt guilty about the triumphs of last summer, which had given her, and she had to admit, the nation emerging into freedom, so much satisfaction at the time.

After a couple of days of chat and visits to old comrades and friends with Mara, Detty was beginning to feel less gloomy. One day they visited the farmer who had sheltered Detty and arranged for her escape to Orianenberg. Ulev, the farmer, and his wife who was also called Mara were relaxed and hospitable. Katrina, the remaining daughter had been married the year before to a forestry officer. The wedding photographs were produced and admired. Mara turned on the car radio on the way home to get the weather forecast for the following day when they were to go riding. They just caught the end of the news. There had been a massive collapse at the site of the new *Hansestadion*. This was to be the pride of the re-emerging country. It incorporated the new Königshof velodrome, football, and athletics facilities. It was the most conspicuous symbol of awakened pride in the re-emergent democracy. The cause of the collapse was unclear. The opposition leader, Valery Tarin, was interviewed and suggested that the project had gone ahead too fast, that the terms of the contract had encouraged jerry-building. He claimed that men's lives had been lost because of the ambition and arrogance of the President and his government of cronies. Acrimony and dissension were growing. The honeymoon period was over. A week later, the police proved beyond doubt that the collapse was due to an explosive charge placed at a sensitive point in the half-erected structure. It had been detonated remotely at a time when the maximum number of people would be under the structure. There was no question of a structural fault. Public opinion was mollified to some extent but many of the hard things had been said and couldn't be unsaid.

In addition to the legitimate criticism of the official opposition, there was more than a hint of orchestrated unrest of an altogether more sinister kind. Detty was witness to enough Hansehaus soirees to know that the government were beginning to get more seriously worried, although the motives and structure of the nascent terrorism still were unclear. There were elements that suggested the tactics of the former fascist government and its agents. Against this, however, it had to be set the fact that the principal members of the old regime were either dead or in close confinement.

Detty visited the injured from the *Hansestadion* disaster the following day. The Livonian injured gave her the usual warm reception, as the local heroine, but one ward was, despite everything, particularly special to her. The patients included a cheerful black carpenter from Reading and four men from Roscommon, experts, who had been working on the metalwork of the Stadium. They had been told that there was to be a visit from a VIP and expected a rotund figure in a mayoral chain speaking a language none of them could understand. Worthy but boring they had decided and went back to watching the CNN news. Their apathy disappeared when a striking, tall chestnut-haired young woman appeared at the door.

'First of all, thank you all for your work here. I am so sorry it should have ended in your being hurt but, believe me, we, in Livonia, won't forget your help.'

The four Irishmen's jaws dropped at the soft but marked Irish accent in this strange land. One of them found his voice:

'You'll not be from here, then,' adding self-consciously 'originally I mean, ma'am.'

He wasn't prepared for the gusty ringing laughter from the vision:

'Athy, County Kildare. As if you couldn't have guessed it already.' she said and continued chatting for a few minutes first about Ireland then the Thames valley. Feeling much better and still laughing, she went on to continue her tour.

It was not until she left the hospital that the gloom descended on her again. She got into the car after looking carefully under it as the police had instructed her. She drove back to town ruminating on why ghastly things always seemed to happen to such fine people. At least there was the St Nicklaus initiation to take her mind off the present problems. It was her first official duty as an Officer of the Order, and, although she knew the procedure of Oath and Charge thoroughly, she still felt extremely nervous.

It dawned fine the following day. The chapel of the old Commanderie flickered dark and gold in the candlelight that thrust weird shadows over the stone relief carvings on the memorials to Nicklaus von der Fojn and Alexander Fieradin, the two founders and first Hochmeisters of the Order, massive alongside the central nave. First the falcon and a moment later the chalice stood out from first one tomb then the other as the light flickered, almost as if they were dancing a ghostly gavotte. Detty stood slightly behind Nicklaus Oblov who wore the current habit of Hochmeister of the Order. On the other side, level with her and darkly visible in the subdued light, was the burly figure of Sergei Malinov, formerly Commander-in-Chief of the FWL now Minister of Defence of Livonia. When Nicklaus had persuaded him to accept the other Komturshaft of the Order, Sergei had insisted, much to Detty's embarrassment, in being appointed as her junior:

'It's only right' he had said 'My contribution to the State came nowhere near to hers and anyway she was invested first.'

Detty, feeling strangely more nervous than she had at her own investiture, glanced down at her own white tunic covered with its pale cream cloak. The silk cloak was decorated on the left with the golden falcon while the right side depicted the Chalice of Zablovsk with the motto of the Order *Humanitas Ubique Est*, Humanity Is Universal, embroidered underneath. She reflected that it was serendipitous that the costume of the old Order was equally suitable for men and women. She wondered, though, what those tough old warriors would have thought about women wearing the full regalia of Komtur and Ritter of their Order.

Behind her was the Altar of the Chapel of the Knights of St Nicklaus. Formerly the Sacred Chalice of Zablovsk itself would have been unveiled for such a ceremony but the Chalice was gone, having disappeared during the convulsions of the Second World War. The altar was now symbolically bare of all furnishings. In front of it was a long low table with their three ceremonial swords with their blades chased with the *Humanitas Ubique Est* motto on one side and with the instruction, *Per Audaciam Providete*, Through Valour Succour, on the other. They had been lovingly made in the old foundry at Königshof by the great grandson of the man who had made the last swords of the original order over a hundred years before. All had their hilts towards the altar and their blades towards the world. They symbolised, as the Mottos that their blades declared, the oath to honour the rights of all, protect freedom, justice and faith. Detty's own sword lay on the right and slightly behind the Hochmeister's. She had had to wait to receive her own as it had not been ready for her ceremony at the Hoftheatre after *Fidelio*. She had returned to Königshof for the day of Sergei's lone investiture when, at the same time, she had been presented with her sword by the Hochmeister in this same old Chapel at Zablovsk. She remembered being overwhelmed by the power of her emotions. She left Manchester as a scruffy music student to be swept up, a few hours later, into this world of chivalry with its medieval associations. She wondered about the ritual and the emblems. When she talked to contemporary Livonians, however, there was no doubt that they saw the rebirth of the Order as a potent and comforting symbol of their integrity, history, and a protection of their own new liberty.

Now she was here again for the first full convocation of investiture. In front of her were the initiates, many as young as herself, all former comrades, and many close friends. These were the people who had led Livonia's struggle for freedom and today a grateful state and people were to do them honour as they deserved. On a lower table slightly in front of the other, were twenty new swords with their gilded hilts glistening. Each lay on a vellum scroll headed with the arms of the Order made up of the Insignia of the Chalice, formerly gold but sable since its disappearance, surmounted by the Falcon of Livonia, destra, and the three herrings of the Hanse on their ground of gold, sinistra. The citation of past gallantry and the Promise of Fealty above the Arms of the initiate Ritter or Ritterin was inscribed below the Insignia.

Nicklaus stepped forward, smiled, and read the mandate of the Order which Detty translated to herself silently:

'For thy power standeth not in multitude, nor thy might in strong men: for thou art a God of the afflicted, a helper of the oppressed, an upholder of the weak, a protector of the forlorn, a saviour of them that are without hope.'

The old order may have consisted of tough old knights, mused Detty, but the mandate showed that their hearts were in the right place and their mandate honoured the words of Judith, a woman warrior.

Nicklaus continued:

'We honour you all for your distinguished service to our country and our liberty. I am proud to greet you as a brother with the thanks of our free people of Livonia. The traditions of the order of St Nicklaus have been honoured in this land for over a thousand years and the refoundation of the Order, to live again in modern times is a symbol of our determination to be true to the spirit of the mandate, the traditions of humanity, justice and probity of the Hanse'.

'I shall ask you to step forward one by one to give the Oath of Fealty before me, as Hochmeister, and then you will receive the Dedication of your sword from the Senior Commander of the Order, Komturin Bernadette Niamh O'Neill who will deliver the Charge.'

Detty was struck by the strange sound of her Celtic name, accurately pronounced by the President, amid this very Teutonic ceremony. Nevertheless, O'Neill she had always been in the Livonian service and O'Neill she would remain, even if von Ritter might have sounded more in character on this day. After all, she thought, if this ceremony was not, amongst other things, about European unity its purpose was diminished.

Nicklaus was hearing the Oath from the first initiate:

> *'I will strive for the honour of the most glorious Virgin, for all the Saints*
> *and our holy Nicklaus,*
> *I will fight for the liberty of all people,*
> *and for the rule of justice in the light of charity.*
> *I will seek victory in freedom, compassion in strength and*
> *stand always, unto death, to defend the defenceless from*
> *exploitation and the tyrant's lash.'*

This was followed by the Hochmeister's response from Psalm 82

> *Defend the poor and the fatherless:*
> *See that such as are in need and necessity have right.*
> *Deliver the outcast and poor.*
> *Save them from the hand of the ungodly*

Detty was as moved by the words now as much as she had been that day when, in a dream of unreality, she had sworn the Oath herself. She was still miles away when she realised that the first initiate, a pilot from the air force was already kneeling in front of her. With a start, she grasped his sword, hilt towards the young man and began to recite the Latin Charge:

> *"Take this sword, its brightness stands for faith,*
> *It's point for hope, and its hilt for charity. Use it well...*
> *This sword is thine by valour. Its light is the future,*
> *Its guard is for freedom and its edge for justice.*
> *Arm thyself with its true virtues,*
> *Use its strength well for all humanity."*

After he grasped the hilt, still kneeling, she held her hand out to him and declared St Peter's biblical exhortation:

> *'Surge, et ego ipse homo sum.'*[3]

---

3 Stand up; I myself also am human Acts 10:26

As he bowed over his sword she reverted to German and said:

'*Meinen Glückwunsch, mein Bruder!*'

and kissed him on both cheeks.

She thought that the young man, who had knocked over a dozen fascist planes out of the sky without a thought for his own safety, was going to faint with the emotion of the moment. He gathered himself, however, and murmuring his thanks returned to his stall.

The next initiate was Liese Zahnsdorf, her friend and companion. She read the Charge remembering the day when, muddy, unkempt, and dishevelled, she had met Liese again after crossing into the Interfluss. She thought how situations changed in a seemingly brief time. After reading the Charge she grasped Liese particularly warmly and said quietly:

'*Herzlich Wilkommen und Glückwunsch, meine geliebte Schwester*'

Then she wondered guiltily, like a schoolchild, if this might be considered favouritism in this most solemn of moments.

She left Königshof the following week for Berlin, half-relieved and half sad. The deep pleasure of the Bruckner in the Philharmonie, where she spent her evening, was a dimension from another planet. She got on the train for Leipzig the following morning with the power of the music still filling her head. At the same time, she felt guilty, something dreadful was again brewing in Livonia and she wasn't there to fight it. She tried to comfort herself that she was doing her bit. She was indeed off to the *Meistersingerhalle* in Nürnberg to give a charity recital to raise money for *Livonian Hochmusikschule* but that somehow didn't seem to be enough.

The presence of her father-in-law, Max, at Leipzig station was irrationally reassuring. He had the same rocklike qualities of dependability and steadfastness, which she so much admired in his son and she immediately, for no logical reason, felt better. They stopped on the way back for her first Franken bier in months both feeling like truants from school. The old innkeeper in the Wald had clearly known Max since he had rambled those woods as a small child in the frightening aftermath of world war, while they waited for news that never came of Max's father, not seen or heard from since Stalingrad. The affectionate greeting between the merchant banker of the new Germany and the

Gastgeber, with more than a foot still in the old one, affected Detty profoundly. The peace of Oberdorf with its old friends, rushing water of the new springtime and still frosty pines completed the healing process. She found herself able to concentrate on Schumann and Wolf, as her morning sickness temporarily abated. There was the occasional flutter of conscience that elsewhere a people and a country, very dear to her, were troubled but, after all, she was a professional and singing badly in a prestigious charity recital at Nuremburg wouldn't help Livonia.

She had insisted on Trudi coming from Munich to accompany her. The reassuring presence of an extremely sensitive pianist and old friend gave her confidence in front of a sophisticated and critical audience. The recitalist is completely exposed and she had a tough and, in the event somewhat under-rehearsed, programme. She got a warm ovation, which was perhaps intended as much for Livonia as for the singer. She knew that it had not been one of her best efforts. The *Nordbayerische Kurier* said that it had been a remarkable evening of passion and maturity with two young performers from different ends of the continent joining together to aid a re-born land and symbolising the best in the new cosmopolitan Europe. The *Suddeutsche Zeitung* congratulated the performers on their motives whilst commenting that, at least in the present phase of her career, Frau O'Neill's remarkable vocal powers were perhaps more suited to the stage than the precision of Wolf. That hurt Detty who had always prided herself on her prowess as a lieder singer. The article ended dryly by saying that nobody could deny that Wolf's setting of Eichendorff's *Der Musikant*, with its emphasis on barefoot roving, might have been written specially for the evening's soloist with her remarkable taste for involvement in dramatic adventures. Even a disappointed Detty couldn't help a smile.

She had a final coffee with Trudi and thanked her again apologising for her less than perfect performance. Trudi told her not to be stupid and that she always aimed for the impossible.

She flew back to Dublin looking forward to a period of complete relaxation. Max had taken her to the airport and kissed her warmly on leaving:

'Look after Marc, Detty, he adores you and you deserve it.'

She was left wondering what she had done to deserve this consideration from such great people.

*

She had grown. She now filled her stall and looked imperiously over the mere humans below her proud head. The look of eagles was still there, flashing from her eyes. Detty stood in front of her wondering why it took a horse to teach her subservience and humility. Yet, this beautiful creature somehow also dominated the woman who was supposed to be her owner and her mistress. She turned back to Christy after staring at Firebrand for an age.

'She's done very well.'

'She has surely.'

'Where do we go from here?'

'I'd thought of a couple of bumpers in the autumn and February, then perhaps Fairyhouse and Naas, a small hurdle at Fairyhouse then perhaps Leopardstown and, if she does OK, then straight for the Triumph Hurdle at Cheltenham. She's an early sort and very fast but with her physique she will train on and I don't think that there is any harm in letting her take her chance in a big race early. Is that all right?'

'Of course, you're the boss.'

Detty was interested that he had used the human word physique rather than the more normal conformation.

'Yes, but you're the owner.'

'Don't be stupid, Christy, the day that I argue with you about entries, I really will be out of my mind. Can you get us tickets and a hotel for Cheltenham if she goes?'

'You'll be bringing himself along then?'

'You keep him away – unless there is a World War of course.'

'Well, you'll be getting tickets anyway but I'll fix a good hotel – full of decent Irish people – not one of those gin palaces.'

She laughed. It was good to see Firebrand and Christy again as a flash of sanity in a disturbed world. They went back for tea and barmbrack with Deidre and laughed at old racing stories and family jokes. Detty thought how she had once resented the narrow parochialism of her homeland that she had now come to love so much as an oasis of sanity amongst her worries.

She walked into the kitchen at Ballyinch when she got back wondering again whether she ought to tell her parents her news and deciding yet again that it was too early. Her mother was peacefully ironing. The television was on in the background. It was like any night that, as a child, she might have returned from the convent for the weekend. The item on the television news was broadcast in a matter of fact, routine way. It was the sort of piece of foreign news that was mandatory, but, as was well known to the producers, of almost no domestic interest.

Peggy looked up to find her daughter staring, fixed and horrified at the screen. All Detty could say was:

'Oh my God – no – it can't be true – not there'.

At that moment, the sound of Brian's car was heard in the drive returning from evening surgery. Detty rushed to greet him with more than usual urgency then said, breathlessly:

'May I 'phone?'

Without waiting for permission, she picked up the telephone and dialled the private security number of the Hansehaus.

'*Darf ich mit Ännchen sprechen?*' she said automatically using the old code of the insurgents. To her relief it was understood immediately. Tamara was on the line.

'Mara, what the hell has happened?'

'They have blown up the school at Sovils. There are about forty dead and nearly one hundred injured. Mostly young girls and boys.'

Mara's voice was flat – almost dead, with emotional and physical exhaustion.

'My father has gone there but I don't know whether he should have. The local groups – you know – are active. He isn't safe. This country isn't safe.'

She sounded tired beyond belief, so different from the laughing girl in Berlin.

'I must come back. I can't leave you like this.'

'No, Detty, even you can't sort this out. Finally, we must stand on our own feet-or find them feet of clay.'

She sounded hopeless.

'But Mara you people made me a *Komturin* of St Nicklaus, if I cannot stand by you in trouble, who can? I remember my oath even if you don't:

"I will seek victory in freedom, compassion in strength and will stand always to the defence of the defenceless from exploitation and the tyrant's lash."

She repeated the last words of her initiation oath adding:

'I shall come tomorrow or if that cannot be arranged the day after.'

Later she had to struggle furiously first with her parents, who found their daughter's continued involvement with this strange foreign country odd in the extreme. She then tackled the convoluted European air timetables, which provided flights from Dublin to the ends of the earth but not, by any means, to Königshof. Exhausted and depressed she gave up and went up to her room to try and think things out. She was in a turmoil, which contrasted starkly with her initial peace. Home was now a cordon, not a sanctuary and she could hardly wait to be free of it – like, she thought, so many of her fellow ex-patriots before her. Although, this time, it was not famine or brutality, which drove her forth but rather her passionate involvement with a distant land.

Marc had heard the news and rang her from London. He knew too well now to try to dissuade her from going to Königshof, although his unspoken concern for her and the baby was transparent. He promised he would try and sort out the flights and ring her back. For the next hour, she fidgeted and could settle to nothing. At last, the 'phone rang. It was now Thursday and Mark said that it was completely impossible to get a flight to Königshof until the following Monday morning and then she would have to change in Berlin. This meant either at least one night in England or in Berlin. The logical choice was to let Mark meet her from Dublin, spend two nights with him at their Henley home and let him take her to the airport at the crack of dawn on the Monday. She rang Mara again to let her know that she was coming and would be at Henley if there were any developments.

Her father produced a bottle of Jameson's and poured a round. Detty, calmer now everything was fixed, wondered whether she should be drinking it but decided that it would do her no harm as a once off. She started to tell her parents what had been happening in Livonia. She glossed over the first explosion, which had nearly killed her, as 'a minor incident' but she did explain why what had happened at St Paul's School at Sovils was so especially important to her.

'Are you sure these things are associated?' asked her father.

'We can't be sure of anything but it's stretching coincidence a bit far to believe that they are not connected.'

She was tense all the way to the airport and not helped by a text message from Marc to say that he wouldn't be able to meet her because he had an unexpected meeting in Whitehall that day. Detty felt cross but realised that Marc couldn't help it. Pentagon senior officers had a habit of arriving at short notice in London and expecting everybody to be available. This was probably another such event and that Marc in his overanxious state would be beside himself with fury. Anyway, it was a only a short taxi ride from Heathrow to Henley and presented no great problem.

The late winter day was brilliant with unexpected sunshine as the taxi took the road through the woods of Remenham Hill. At any other time, she would have delighted in the countryside at its most appealing, but the worry of Sovils gnawed at her constantly. She threw open the front door and was confronted by the slight abandoned odours of the little house chilled by its winter emptiness. Marc usually stayed in London during the week unless she was able to get home. She checked the e-mail and her heart raced as it retrieved a message from Königshof. After such a run of disasters, she could hardly bear the thought of worse to come. The message was to ring Ännchen as soon as possible. Trembling she dialled the private number.

'Frau Tamara has gone to Sovils with The President.'

Detty cursed first the information and then her selfishness. What could be more natural than Nicklaus Oblov and his daughter visiting the bereaved families?

'*Wann kommt sie zurück?*'

'They said about five this afternoon. Shall I ask Frau Tamara to telephone you.?'

'Please do'

Detty settled at the piano working on Amelia's *'Come in quest'ora bruna'* from *Simon Boccanegra*. She was offering this as part of her final prova for the *Concorso International 'Tebaldi – Gobbi'* which was taking place in Florence in two weeks' time. She had been encouraged to enter by Eileen Vaughan as part of her attempt to master the Italian repertory. The early rounds were held in London, Vienna, New York, and Tokyo as well as Florence with two contestants from each going through to the final in Florence. All the finalists qualified for an intensive six weeks of study at the Accademia Musicale Chigiana in Siena. This was followed by roles in a production by young artists at the Teatro della Pergola in Florence as part of the *Maggio Musicale Fiorentino* festival. It was an extremely attractive package. The rules stated that a Puccini aria must be offered in the semi-final and an Italian canzone and Verdi aria in the final. Detty, at Eileen's suggestion, had performed the less usual *'Senza mamma, o bimbo'* from *Suor Angelica* in the semi-final. This had suited her powerful voice and had produced a very positive reaction from the judges possibly bored by the two *'O mio babbino caro's'* and one *'Si, mi chiamano Mimi'* offered by the sopranos amongst her rivals. Anyway, she had been delighted to be selected for the final. She had at first considered offering *'Ecco l'orrido campo'* from *Un Ballo in Maschera* as her Verdi aria. Eileen had encouraged her to look again being afraid that Detty would give the impression of only being able to tackle big dramatic pieces. The gentle, supposed orphan girl's song at dawn had won the day. Normally the aria entranced her but to-day she found it hard to concentrate and her practice was passionless.

She got up from the keyboard with a sigh and made herself a cup of tea reflecting that with things the way they were she was unlikely to be able to attend the Florence final anyway. This was a secondary worry. In the past, her tutors at Oxford had been remarkably patient with her unscripted absences largely because they sympathised with her motives and approved of their intention. She realised however that understanding was not limitless and the situation was different at Manchester. She could hardly expect to retain the interest of the best available voice teachers if her presence was unpredictable. She had five days of holiday left before she was due back at the Manchester but that hardly seemed enough to return to Livonia and achieve anything worthwhile. It seemed that soon she might have to make a choice between Livonia and the career that, after some hesitation, was increasingly important to her.

At ten past four, English time, the telephone rang.

'It's good news as far as it goes.' said a breathless Mara 'the police rounded up fifteen people in a dawn raid in the docks here this morning. They included the Sovils bombers who also tried to blow you up. It also included the unit that caused the explosion at the Stadion who probably also exploded the Berlin-Munich train. It looks increasingly as if the train bomb was destined to get me but the device went off too late on the way back to München, so in a sense we have both been lucky.'

'But why, Mara? Why on earth?'

'It's not at all clear and I'm very muddled myself. The old regime got a lot of its finance from illegal sales of weapons and some from drugs. In its turn, Moltravia formed a useful halfway safe house for dealers. It may be that some of the more powerful east European Mafia groups are trying to destabilise Livonia in order to get their safe haven back. This is only a hypothesis and we don't have much in the way of firm evidence. Certainly, some of the old guard of the NAS are involved but they don't seem to be the leaders who are almost certainly foreign.'

She added hesitantly:

'There is really no need for you to come now although it would be good to see you again and Sergei asked last week if there was any chance of your being here for the Wild Cygnets' Passing Out Parade. He said that several of the graduate term had asked him particularly if you could be there.'

3
THE SWANS

Zogen einst fünf wilde Schwäne[4]

VOLKSLEID- VON ZUCCALMAGLIO

Amongst the many honorific titles that had been thrust on Detty at the end of the Civil War was that of Colonel-in-Chief of the *Frei Wehr Livonias* Elite Special Commando Corps. Before the battle of the *Zehnheiligenweg*, she had given a particularly popular FWL concert and had raised cheers singing the peace-loving folksong of the Five Wild Swans. The following day Malinov had asked for volunteers during the battle to undertake the difficult and critical river crossing. The volunteers had formed a unit that had become a permanent elite special operations corps, which in turn had developed a training college. The nickname of the unit, the Wild Swans, was never in doubt. The tune had been whistled and sung by the FWL and their supporters as another revolutionary hymn during that dreadful campaign. The shoulder badge adopted by the Unit was a wild swan with neck stretched in extended flight.

---

4   There were once five wild swans

It was inevitable that the trainees of the Corps College should be labelled the Cygnets. The first intake of Cygnets was having its graduation parade that day. The morning was bright but Detty felt the biting chill cut across her lips straight from the late spring arctic snows. It made her glad of her campaign thermal underclothes under the simple cut of her dress uniform and greatcoat. The Baltic cold and the knifing Siberian wind were icy but the sun and the excitement made up for everything. Detty wondered how the Band was able to play under such conditions, with frozen fingers and frosted lips. It seemed to make no difference and the music poured out as the first two terms of cadets paraded. Then there was an expectant pause before the appearance of the senior term. The graduate term, wearing proudly for the first time, their green and white cockades, marched into the parade ground. Feeling slightly old, Detty looked across the Parade. At the middle of the first column was a young woman, immaculate in her full-dress uniform, whose head had at first been hidden, being at a substantially lower level than those of her colleagues. A pang clutched at Detty's throat as she looked down at the wheelchair that was the cause of the cadet's low profile. She wondered about the girl's circumstances. Not for the first time, she felt proud of her adopted country with a mixture of emotions. To admit a disabled girl to an elite commando corps showed a rejection of conventions that many would be incapable of grasping. Perhaps this was true freedom. She was far away, lost in thought when the lilting tune on the fifes brought her to, with its unexpected familiarity. She found herself, almost unconsciously, singing the words of the new tune, *The Irish Soldier Laddie* which she knew so well, under her breath:

It was a strange experience to hear the old rebel song of 1798 and of the Easter parades being played by a band of faraway youngsters who had no idea of the events of '98 or even where Wexford was. Nonetheless, the compliment to her was touching and she smiled in appreciation.

She turned to Sergei Malinov who was standing next to her grinning broadly.

'Sergei, how on earth did they get hold of this?'

'I think that you once sung it at a concert during the war and introduced it by saying that it had to do with your family and family name. A bright soldier who was there never forgot the tune. He is now a Warrant Officer Instructor at the College and he suggested that they marched in to it as a special compliment to their Colonel-in-Chief at their first passing out parade. Once they knew that you could definitely be here, taking the Salute, it was finally settled. I think a certain Bundeswehr Major had something to do with providing the music and the details.'

'Oh, did he then?' said Detty 'I'll have something to say to that husband of mine when I can find him, which isn't easy. At the least he didn't tell them to play *'We're on the Road to God knows where'* which judging from the last week or two, might have been more to the point.'

'Don't start saying things like that, Detty, or the whole country will go into a decline. You know we'll pull through. We've faced worse.'

'I know – I'm sorry. I ought to be ashamed of myself.'

She sprung to attention to return the impeccable eyes right salute kicking herself for making a joke that was perhaps too near the bone on this day of all days.

She did not have too much time to consider as The Parade was drawn up for the inspection and award of the Sword of Honour and Prizes. The Sword of Honour went to a short dark young man whose father had been blown up in the front line during the first assault on the Interfluss. He had a particular look in his deep dark eyes and Detty wondered where she had seen it before. She realised with a start that it was the look of eagles that she had seen in the eyes of her own filly, Firebrand. He thanked her in a quiet firm voice before saluting. The Prize for Reconnaissance and Intelligence Studies went to the girl in the wheelchair. Detty felt inadequate when she could only say 'Well done' but there was so much more she would have liked to ask.

There was a reception after the Parade before lunch and Detty took the opportunity to ask Liese Zahnsdorf, who lectured on intelligence at the College, about the disabled girl.

'Her name is Tatiana Lobokova' Liese told her 'She had both her legs amputated above the knees after a landmine explosion near the Fojn during the first rebellion when she was ten. When she applied to join the Corps, we first thought that her application was a kind of black joke. Eventually, however, after a lot of argument we agreed to interview her. She was amazing. She produced well-reasoned arguments that half the Corps activities consisted of intelligence work and the Officers specialising in that, at least after their initial training, seldom got involved in other activities. She claimed that she had a special talent for deductive and inductive analytical reasoning, which made her suitable for this kind of work. In the subsequent aptitude tests, she made good in spades her claims in a most impressive style and came a clear top of the candidature. I knew that I could use her in Intelligence and argued hard for her acceptance. I got a surprising amount of support. We won and in spite of the logistic problems anticipated in training, she was in. Come over and I will introduce you properly.'

A crowd of well-wishers surrounded Tatiana who was standing, obviously on artificial legs, and leaning slightly against a balustrade. She was laughing and joking with them. Liese edged her way through the crowd to reach her and seeing her senior approach she straightened up to greet them.

'Tanya, Detty particularly wanted to meet you and talk to you – properly I mean.'

'As an intelligence amateur (retired), it is a pleasure to meet somebody who really knows how to do it and you clearly do. Congratulations again. It can't have been easy.'

'Oh, the lack of an undercarriage, you mean. It does create a few problems, Frau Komturin.'

'Please call me Detty. I am fed up with being made to feel like a grandmother and I'll remind you that I am not much older than you. It was only a year or two ago when I first got involved with this load of hooligans.'

She indicated Liese and towards the assembled top brass:

'I was only a poor little student teacher myself until they led me astray.'

'Yes, I've heard a bit about your activities as a waif and stray.' said Tatiana now smiling:

'I believe it was your husband who said that, measured in terms of strategic value in war, you were about equivalent to a battle-hardened Panzer division.'

'Well,' said Detty 'that does a lot for my feminine ego and anyway husbands are not always the most reliable judges.'

'All the same I guess that most of Livonia might reckon that an under-estimate.'

'OK, then enough about me. Tell me how you manage to do what you do with your disability.'

'It's quite simple – ninety per cent of it is low cunning. I have a problem in parades, as I can't march as fast as the others on my peg legs so I make them push me instead. To be fair, they don't seem to mind.'

'That simple, is it?' said Detty with a quizzical expression.

'Yes, it really is, honestly.'

'Don't you ever feel angry?' She asked more seriously.

'Yes, I do sometimes and then I tell myself to grow up.'

Detty left that evening to go back to the Hansehaus thinking a lot about Tanya. In many ways, she saw in her a mirror image of herself without, of course, the disability. At one level, the Tanyas of Livonia were the hope of the future but from another aspect, they represented a crushing responsibility to ensure that they were able to fulfil themselves.

The following morning, when Nicklaus was at breakfast, Detty found out more about the current political situation. As Mara had told her, fifteen people had been arrested. Amongst these was a low order Swiss hood called Gerti Neumann who had a thoroughly unsavoury reputation. He was known to be responsible for numerous small-scale drug operations and rather more extensive extortion rackets. With him were four German Swiss henchmen who appeared to be straight out of the drug scene in Zurich. It appeared almost certain that Gerti and his cronies had bungled the Berlin train explosion. This was possibly because they were too high on their own merchandise to know what they were doing. They had also been responsible for the Sovils school bombing which had, tragically, gone as planned. The connection with the explosion of Detty's car at the music school was less clear. The police thought that they had fibre evidence from an American with Mafia connections taken from *Schloss Krenek*. He had incontrovertibly been involved in the stadium explosion. The fibres from a fleece jacket collected from under the wreck of Detty's hire car were suggestive that he might be connected with the attack on her. They thought it was unsatisfactory to base a whole prosecution on this rather tenuous data. It might prejudice the conviction of the others for the stadium outrage where there was much clearer evidence. Many of the suspects were clearly minor players in the gang responsible for the explosion at the *Hansestadion*. In addition, there were, however, two Belorussian operators, who had been caught by sheer good fortune when they were found to have a command radio link to the bomb squad at the *Stadion*. These two appeared higher up the chain of command and were possibly more important fishes in the net. The police thought that even they were unlikely to be the real brains of the terrorist campaign. The trial was to be held at once.

Detty completed her stay and a tour of the sites of the renascent Königshof with Mara, stopping at a block of flats here and a factory there. One day they went out into the spring pine forests, fleecy coated and armed against the increasingly bitter cold – just two kids on an impromptu day's holiday. They stopped by a slow flowing stream, full of new broken ice, to eat sausage, drink beer and talk and laugh about the past, good, and bad, that they had shared. Detty was reminded of their idyllic few days in Kildare and Wicklow and wondered why life could not always be like this. Too soon, it was over. Detty clutched her score of *'La Wally'*, which all the finalists in her competition were expected to learn, headed for the airport. She was still accompanied by her discreet plain-clothes policeman.

She changed at Berlin and Munich and was delayed three hours at the latter. On the spur of the moment, she decided to go into the city to a Munich hotel rather than arrive in Florence in the middle of the night. She had wondered whether to go home to Oberdorf or stay in the rather uninteresting hotels around Freising. Eventually, feeling wickedly extravagant, she decided that she would book herself into the Vier Jahreszeiten for the night. She wanted to go and have dinner at Boettner where she had spent a memorable lunch with Marc and his boss after their escape from Moltravia. She telephoned Marc from the hotel, toasting him conscious of her pregnancy with *Orangensaft* from the minibar.

In the morning, she felt self-indulgent, consuming boiled eggs and smoked ham whilst skimming the *Suddeutsche Zeitung* for news of the Livonian trial. Eventually she found it and read:

'It must be allowed that Livonia has suffered grievously from internal oppressors and external conspirators in the past. The defendants in the present case, however, have claimed that they will not receive a fair trial at Königshof and, unfortunately, in the light of the very high emotions involved this may be true.'

Detty exploded, spluttering into her coffee, and wondering whether even-handed leading article writers had ever seen the sort of tragedy that she had witnessed with a good young husband and father splattered in pieces all over the lawn of a music academy. Then she calmed down, the *Suddeutsche Zeitung* was, however irritatingly, right of course. She and the others had fought the war for justice and the rule of law. It was desperately important for the new Livonia that these people got a fair, and transparently fair, trial. The article continued:

'The suggestion that the trial is transferred to the Netherlands would appear to be the best solution. It is to be hoped that the normally just and reasonable regime of Nicklaus Oblov will allow this to take place.'

She was just finishing the article when she was aware of somebody standing behind her and immediately an unforgettably rich voice with a surprisingly attractive South African twang said in English:

'Detty, how lovely! But what are you doing here?'

Detty swivelled round to find herself looking into the ebony smiling face of Almeida Tulla behind her. Almeida, the black earth goddess, freedom fighter and dramatic contralto was, amongst all the other things, the *Erda* in the current *Ring* at Bayreuth.

'I might ask you the same but I'm only passing through on my way to Florence and Siena to learn how to sing.'

Almeida grinned:

'Now I've heard everything. As for me, I'm singing *Ulrica* in *Ballo* here this evening. If you can break your journey for long enough come along, we can have dinner afterwards, as you know I'm only in the first act, so if you don't mind missing the rest of the show we could go quite early.'

Detty needed no second invitation. She loved Almeida both for herself and what she represented. She had arranged to spend a few days in Florence before the masterclasses started in Siena. It was just the case of telephoning to postpone her hotel booking by a day.

A day in Munich was never a penance. The weather was warm with a hint of spring in the air. At lunchtime, she sat in the Englischer Garten over *Käsebrot* and more *Orangensaft* writing postcards to Ireland, England, and Livonia like a true tourist. When she got back to the Hotel to bath and change for the opera, there was a message to ring reception. Apparently, a gentleman had called asking whether she had already checked out to go to Florence. The Concierge said that they were always wary of that type of enquiry. He had told the caller that they couldn't give any information but that they would try and contact Frau von Ritter to give her a message. The caller had said not to bother and, when asked, had just said to tell her that Herr Weber had called. Detty knew a couple of Herr Webers and neither of them were in Munich nor likely to want to contact her. It was also the Munich University alias of Mara but the Concierge was sure that this was a man and anyway Mara was in Königshof. Certainly, none of them knew that she was staying in the city after her flight delay. Weber however was a very common name. Although the incident puzzled her slightly, she was not unduly worried and soon put it out of her mind.

The re-built marble of the glorious theatre retained its special magic for Detty. It was a good performance. Almeida had sent a message to suggest that Detty should stay in the theatre for the short second act. They would meet at the stage door in the Maximilianstrasse afterwards. Almeida was in chillingly fine form as the fortune-teller with her superb contralto giving full measure to *E lui, e lui! ne' palpiti*. The young Russian tenor had a beautiful lyrical voice and did justice to his peach of a part. Only the Greek soprano was nervous and inclined to be sharp. Almeida said afterwards that the girl, Elena Staphylenous, hadn't been well and had a lot of personal problems. It was a shame because she had a good voice and it was her first big chance.

It had to be Boettner again for dinner and the short walk brought Detty's memories of her first visit there with Marc and his chief flooding back. This time the talk was all musical shop but the *Hechtsouffle* was as good as ever. She allowed herself a small glass of classic Krug champagne and looked on with envy as Almeida did justice to the Wurzburger Stein Trocken Spätlese. They talked and talked about Marc, their families and Almeida's new boyfriend, the Japanese racing driver, Ishotoko Tikinaya. Detty felt that she began to really know, as well as admire, Almeida. Then, inevitably, they got onto future musical plans.

They shared some gossip about the state of the Bayreuth *Ring* and the production modifications planned for the current year. Almeida asked about Livonia and afterwards Detty described, with pride, the progress the Conservatoire had made and the recent singing contest. She had no difficulty in getting Almeida to agree that she would be a judge in the next one. She then went on to talk about the half-made plans for the *Freiheitsfest*. She mentioned her excitement at singing *The Children of Lir* at home in Ireland and then in Livonia together with the great European anthem of the Beethoven's Ninth. She said that she still felt, however, that the programme lacked something, possibly only for Königshof, possibly for the Irish end as well. Almeida after a moment's silent thought said:

'Why don't you do *Alexander Nevsky* and I'll come and sing the Russian widow for you – if you will let me – no fee – put the fee towards your Musikschule. I'll do a couple of masterclasses with your youngsters at the same time if you like. I would like to do it for you and it would do your Russian people's morale good. I was supposed to go to the Malaysian Grand Prix with Ishotoko but this sounds more exciting and I expect he will forgive me if I make it up to him.'

She said this with a wicked gleam of laughter, half hidden behind the resolution of her eyes. Detty, startled, took only a moment to respond:

'You really mean it? You are certainly right about it making our Russian population feel valued.'

'Of course, I mean it.'

'Then you are on, and we will try and show you, and Ishotoko too if he is free after the race, what Livonian hospitality can really be like.'

The following morning Detty took a moment to 'phone Helge von Grunstrand to explain Almeida's offer, which he agreed immediately, should be accepted. She sent a quick card of thanks and acceptance to Almeida, which she dropped in at the Nationalstheatre stage door next to the hotel. Then, feeling happier than she had done for a long time, she got a taxi to the airport and boarded the morning flight to Pisa. The seat next to her was occupied by a lone Spanish nun, who seemed only to speak a dialect that made conversation difficult. Detty got out her *La Wally* score and went through the name part. At first, the Nun seemed rather interested in looking over her arm but soon decided it was not in her sphere and gave up.

She arrived at Pisa to find the thunder and lightning cracking over Michelangelo's quarries in the hills of Carrara and the rain teeming down. All the trains from the airport were cancelled due to *un guasto improvviso* and she cursed her decision to fly to Pisa rather than the nearer, but trainless, Peretola. She tried to get a self-drive car, which she could return on arriving in Florence but because of the train failure and a big pharmaceutical conference, all were booked. In the end, the best she could do was to employ the cousin of one of the counter staff of a minor car hire firm to drive her to Florence *abusivo*. As she anticipated it was not only abusivo but *carissimo*. It might well have been even more so had the driver not fancied the chance of an *incontro romantico* when he discovered that his passenger was a young and good-looking, long-legged red head. Moreover, he noticed, despite her wedding ring, she was without a man anywhere in sight. Northern girls, he knew, frequently sported wedding rings as transient, easily dispensable armour. Detty however politely but firmly fought off the suggestion that he should show her the nightlife of Florence that evening.

It was still raining heavily when they arrived in the city and feeling somewhat jaded, she decamped at the corner of the Via dei Tornabuoni. Her driver had said it would be better not to stop outside the hotel because of the *Finanza*. Detty couldn't really understand why the Financial Police should be hiding inside the Helvetia & Bristol Hotel. Possibly the narrow Via dei Pescioni made an unauthorised driver rather more conspicuous and a fast getaway more difficult. She decided that there was no point in pursuing the matter and dragged her large case the short distance to the hotel past the massively dripping walls of the Palazzo Strozzi. She was happy at last to be near to the warm and dry. The ritual of the extended bath was followed by dinner at the *Uomo di Galestro*. She felt slightly sad at dining alone and thought of Marc back from Turkey in his Norwegian fastnesses. The *risotto nero*, however, followed by a *cacciuco* of indecent proportions re-awakened her dormant hedonism. She crossed the Piazza della Republica to the Giubbe Rosse for a last coffee and then she retired to bed with her well being restored.

The following morning, she awoke to a blaze of sunshine across her room and the clatter of early morning in the street. She now had only three days in Florence before going to the classes in Siena and she was determined to make the most of it.

4
RAPITA

Ne andro sola e lontana[5]

LA WALLY ACT 1 T Luigi Illica

As she changed after the final performance, she was feeling satisfied, although she realised it was far from perfect. She sensed, however, that her Manchester training and the Siena workshops had given her command of a testing role. Her voice, already strong, was now furnished with a reasonably secure bel canto appoggiatura and legato. These, together with her improved Italian, had passed muster in front of the natives. It was, she felt, a special achievement to succeed in the city of the Camerata where it had all started. She was secretly pleased and relieved that her four-month pregnancy has caused no problems. She felt that she had cleared a major artistic hurdle.

Her '*Ebben? ... Ne andro lontana*' had stopped the performance for several minutes and more than one critical Florentine had remarked on the quality of the closing scene of *La Wally, facevano venute le lacrime agli*

---

5   I shall go there far away and alone

occhi.⁶ Further '*La Nazione*' had suggested that it was indeed gratifying to hear *un legato cosi schietto*⁷ from a young soprano. The critic could not resist adding the dig that it was particularly so when one considered that she had taken such risks with her voice by singing Wagner when still immature. The double-edged compliment made Detty, who felt she was beginning to understand Italy and the Italians, smile. *La Nazione* continued that the young singers' season at the Teatro della Pergola had proved a brilliant innovation to the *Maggio Musicale*. The quality was so high that the senior artists at the Teatro Communale should look to their laurels. The Marchese Seravalle, now in his nineties, had asked to meet her and had hobbled round to visit her dressing room especially to tell her that her performance was marvellous. He added that as a small boy he had heard her great compatriot, Margaret Sheridan, sing in the same role at Bologna. Detty found this gesture, by the kind, dignified old man, greatly moving and intriguing as a glimpse of the past which fascinated her. She had been enthralled by her brief conversation with him.

Now she looked forward to a few weeks at Oberdorf and even some days with Marc before going on to Bayreuth and the more familiar territory of the bottom of the Rhein and *Woglinde*. Bayreuth, she knew, must be her last engagement before she prepared to have the baby in the autumn. That day's performance had been the final one in Florence and, as was usual on a Sunday, had started early. It was still light when she had finished chatting with the last of the well-wishers and a few autograph hunters. As she left the theatre, she wondered yet again how a street as unprepossessing as the Via della Pergola could hide such a jewel of a theatre. It had once witnessed the premier of Verdi's Macbeth in the presence of the Maestro amongst other great occasions. It took her only a few moments to cross behind the Duomo, rather un-prima donna like carrying her own bag, and reach the Helvetia & Bristol. She was greeted by the concierge with his usual:

'*Buona sera, Signora Contessa*'

---

6   Made tears come to my eyes
7   So pure a legato

Followed by the less usual:

'e oggi, la rappresentazione, com'' e andata, mi scusi?'[8]

Detty was at first taken aback but then remembered the few minutes conversation which she had had with him whilst waiting for the taxi that morning.

'Abbastanza bene, grazie,' she replied adding with a smile *'meno male!'* then *'Sarebbe possibile di trovarmi un tassi fra un ora e mezza?'*

'Voluntieri, Signora Contessa, Lei vuole anche di tornare stasera?'[9]

She smiled broadly:

'I hope to come back sometime – no I'm joking- the Marchese has arranged a car back, I believe.'

She went to the lift for her room to change for the reception. She had time for a long soak whilst preparing to look the part for the evening. She had reserved the magnolia silk cocktail dress from Lanoure for the occasion. Marc had wanted to come but a last-minute NATO security meeting in the face of the deteriorating situation in the Balkans had stopped him. Uncharitably she thought again of Bismarck's much quoted remark about the Balkans not being worth the healthy bones of a Pomeranian grenadier. She stopped guiltily in her tracks and chided herself for her unaccustomed xenophobia. She realised too that some unthinking people might say the same about the Baltic States, which meant so much to her.

The farewell party was at the Marchese's villa the other side of the Arno on the Poggio Imperiale. Soft lights were beginning to shine more brightly from the hall in the short dusk. She paid off the taxi and was greeted by the over-dressed doorman. Immediately her mind flew to the *Haushofmeister* in *Ariadne auf Naxos* and she giggled trying to control herself. Worse was to come, she tried to look as dignified as possible as she climbed the stairs. The two Bernini marble statues which adorned the top had no time for her, the male eyeing the female with an indolent lasciviousness, as they gazed across the well at each other, each propped

---

8 And, excuse me, today how did the performance go?
9 Pretty well, thank you, fortunately.
   Would it be possible to find me a taxi in an hour and a half?
   Of course. Countess, will you also want to return this evening?

elegantly on an elbow, lecherous and alive. The Major-Domo at the door of the salotto on the *piano nobile* reminded her even more of *Ariadne* and she again tried hard to stifle the incipient giggles.

She was greeted with elaborate courtesy by her host and was still trying to compose herself by studying the dramatic mosaic ceiling when a penetrating shout of *'Ciao, Detti'* brought her down to ground level. Smiling up at her was the mischievous bronzed face of her deadly rival. Totti or less usually Maria Angela Spinelli was in theory at least Detty's main competitor. She had never discovered why her very feminine rival was nick named after a prominent footballer. Perhaps it was because she had had a childish crush on the handsome ex Roma player. Her diamond bright *soprano lirico* had caused as much of a sensation in the young artists' festival as Detty's Wally. Detty had first heard her at rehearsal when she was working at the theatre with her repetiteur. They were having a break and a coffee at the back of the stage. Suddenly their chat was stopped in its tracks by this voice, limpid and precisely sparkling as a crisp mountain waterfall, coming from the stage. It had made the difficult music of *Donizetti's Maria di Rohan* seem natural and simple and the final short but awe- inspiring cabaletta, a joy. Detty had immediately admired Totti as an accomplished colleague but, more surprisingly, they had soon become friends. She was a local girl. Her family came from Ancaiano in the hills outside Siena where her father was a prosperous and talented blacksmith achieving wonders with ferro battuto for the well-heeled, Italian, and foreign residents of the zone. Somehow that gave her common cause with the country girl from Athy, at least once Detty had explained away the Contessa bit.

'It doesn't mean much, thank God, in these egalitarian days and of course has no formal status in a republic but once you've got it you can't lose it, anyway. The German speakers are great on titles.' she had told Totti and, thinking of her crisis telephone call in during the Livonian war to Nutt Bros, the posh St James Wine Merchants, 'it does come in useful sometimes'.

Her new friend had giggled and explained that her family were life-long communists but she had absolved Detty from blame for her aristocratic connections.

'I went to school with a contessina. Her hair was always in the air and she bit her nails.'

'Mine isn't and I don't' laughed Detty.

After that, Totti had shown Detty how to find the cellars and small *trattorie* of the city where the *lampredotto* and *dolce e forte* had not been replaced by pizzas and hamburgers and where Toscanaccio was still spoken. Once Totti and her current boyfriend, a quiet young man called Alessandro who was studying architecture at the University, had entertained her to dinner. They shared a minute apartment opposite the church of San Niccolò on the Oltrarno and Alessandro had astonished Detty by producing an elegant typical meal in about ten minutes flat.

It was good to see her friend at the reception amidst so many unfamiliar faces. They spent a few minutes chatting together and started guiltily when their host came up stealthily behind them.

'*Non é possibile per le nostre bellisimme dive giovanni di parlare insieme tutta la notte*'[10] he said with a smile whirling them both off to a cascade of introductions and flowery compliments.

'You know Monsignor Jose Maria Pueblo, of course' the Cavaliere Cavalcante gestured towards the tall man in black with an El Greco face, glinting eyes and long manicured fingernails who was standing next to him.

Detty indicated that she hadn't had the pleasure and formal introductions were completed. She chatted with a number of guests straining her conversational Italian. Afterwards Cavalcante immediately returned to the matter in hand.

'Are you free in June next year, Contessa?'

The Cavaliere viewed Detty's developing bump suspiciously whilst addressing her in meticulous English. Detty was killing herself with laughter inwardly and had the greatest difficulty in stopping it bursting out. Clearly high Florentine officials were not used to dealing with pregnant sopranos but at least he had noticed, most men, she had learned, didn't.

---

10   It is not right for our two beautiful young divas to be talking together for the whole night.

'Subject to anything my agent has arranged in my absence, which is unlikely I am free. My personal commitments should be well organised by then.'

He had the grace to look embarrassed before he went on.

'Would you consider undertaking the role of *Elsa* in *Lohengrin* for five performances in the *Maggio Musicale* – in German, of course? It appears that Frau Anders who originally accepted the contract will be unable to sing due to a long-term illness and Maestro Meilin has particularly asked for you to take over the part.'

Detty at first was taken aback. She had wondered at his first enquiry if he had some small role in mind but this was of a different order. In a flash, she reflected that the immortal Renata Tebaldi had made her debut in Florence, albeit in Italian, in this very role. Once she heard that Anton Meilin was the conductor, it seemed less preposterous. He had conducted her in the Awakening at Bayreuth and she knew how much he liked her voice.

'I would be honoured subject of course to the usual conditions.'

'Perhaps you could arrange for your agent's details to be sent to me at the Teatro Communale and we will try to get the formalities out of the way as soon as possible. I believe that you know the role already?'

'Yes'

'*Allora, alla prossima, dunque, Contessa,* we will be in touch. I look forward to next year.'

As she stepped onto the drive, lightning flashed over Fiesole and the thunder cracked. She said her farewells and thanks and, ushered by the chauffeur, stepped into the black limousine, which was already drawn up in the drive. As she did so the warm, heavy drops of the first rain that they had had since the day that she had arrived some weeks before, began to fall on her outstretched bare arm. Her mind was full of the conversation with the Cavaliere with intrusions from Elsa's soliloquy on the steps of the Minster. Her enthusiasm for Florence and its people had started during the short time that they had spent there on their honeymoon but it had grown steadily during the summer. The prospect of singing this role, so near to her heart, in the centre of this city was mouth-watering indeed. She had never sung *Einsam in truben Tagen* in public although it had been so significant in her private life.

She hardly noticed that the car turned left at the Porta Romana instead of carrying on along the walls into the city. It was a dark moonless night and it was only when the bulk of the floodlit Certosa loomed above the road that she realised with a start that something was wrong. She tried to attract the attention of the driver but the interior of the limousine was soundproof and the communicator switched off. They flashed through the Telepass and onto the autostrada. She realised now that she was imprisoned in the car. Progressively the windows darkened and after a last fleeting glimpse of the high lorries on the other carriageway, all was dark and silent. She was struck by a sudden déjà vu, not of a chauffeur driven limousine on an Italian autostrada, but of a lorry loaded with dill cucumbers bumping across northern Europe. She had a tailored leather jacket on but still shivered in her Lanoure cocktail dress. The air conditioning inside the car had made her suddenly cold outside as well as in.

For some time, she was just numb then she started to think frantically. Why? She had had no clue. It might be just money, probably was, after all she was connected to an extremely wealthy family. Absentmindedly she slipped off her emerald engagement ring and put it in a concealed pocket of her underclothes. Any kidnapper worth his salt would still find it but she loved it dearly and anyway would look slightly less obviously opulent without it on. She had always left it behind during her excursions into Livonia but tonight had been a formal occasion and she had worn it. She had heard about Mafia and Sardinian kidnappings and from the publicity for *La Wally*, anybody could have known that she was in Florence. Livonia? No that was ridiculous; she must be getting paranoid after the explosion at the Conservatoire. Anyway, the reason for her abduction was not the immediate problem, so she turned to who might be responsible. Almost certainly, the driver was only an underling far down the hierarchy of the real operators. He probably didn't even know who the bosses were. Where? This was the most important question. She knew that they had gone onto the Autosole and was almost sure that they had turned south to-wards Rome rather than north into the mountains and Bologna. She looked at her watch. She had left the reception at half past midnight. It was now one twenty so they had been travelling for fifty, no, say, forty-five minutes to allow for getting going. They hadn't been going excessively fast when she had last been able to see outside and the engine note hadn't changed to suggest that they had speeded up. Say one hundred and ten kph, so they would have covered about eighty kilometres and were still going.

Almost as soon as she reached this conclusion, she felt the car slow and turn. The road surface was slightly different. They had left the autostrada. Another ten minutes and there was a distinct turn and the car started bumping and climbing. Even the presumably good suspension of the limousine was taking quite a beating. Occasionally she heard the scraping of small branches or bushes along the side of the car. The track that they were on had to be quite narrow. It must have been another thirty minutes before the car stopped. Detty could half hear some talk in a language that didn't seem to be Italian or at least not the Italian of operatic language coaches. After a few seconds silence the car door was opened from the outside and the driver said:

'*Prego, Signora*,' and stepped aside to let her get out.

Detty was momentarily put out of her stride by this apparent courtesy. She soon pulled herself together enough to protest vigorously in her newly honed Italian that she had not been taken to her hotel and would the driver please take her there at once. The driver shrugged his shoulders and said:

'*Mi spiace, Signora*' while a shadowy figure in a white baseball cap, who was standing behind two women, made a more impatient gesture with something he was holding, which Detty took to be a pistol. She was almost inclined to laugh. These were, after all, operetta villains compared with the NAS or the Gestapo. She told herself not to be stupid. She knew perfectly well that these people could probably kill or torture without any more compunction than their Nordic or Slavonic brothers in crime. She looked around her. The rain had stopped and there was a pale light from the moon. It had obviously rained heavily here too, as there were large puddles over the rough ground. These were full of water, ochre coloured in the light of the driver's torch, and streaked with the wisps of straw of the active farmyard. Her impressions were confirmed by the mournful voice of a cow from middle distant gloom. In the dark there seemed to be several buildings, mainly in disrepair, some of which appeared to be completely ruined. A large dog barked somewhere in the background, invisible. The dominating structure was a tall tower several stories higher than the surroundings. She thought about trying to make a break for it but the semi-darkness, the unfamiliar terrain and, above all, the dog decided her against it. There was also the consideration that an unsuccessful attempt to get away now would increase her captors' vigilance. She assumed that they had no means of knowing her previous reputation and, as long as she was perceived as a young society lady wearing an expensive leather jacket and a haute couture cocktail dress, she might retain some advantage from surprise for use at a future, more promising, attempt. In addition, neither her jacket nor the striking Lanoure creation was suitable for an escape across soaking wet countryside. All in all, she felt that the best line at present was to appear shocked and submissive.

The shadowy figure and the two women ushered her towards the bottom of the tower pushing her through a large wooden door. She tried to look at their faces but couldn't see any of them clearly in the darkness. The only light was provided by the man's powerful torch that he kept shining on the ground. He muttered something like *'Franca, per carita, le altre chiavi'*[11] followed by an oath which suggested that the Madonna engaged in activities which were certainly not part of Detty's convent upbringing. The younger woman, obviously Franca, scuttled off muttering further oaths, presumably in search of the missing keys, allowing Detty to try and make out as much as she could from the surrounding gloom. She could see the dim outline of large barrels around part of the walls and she nearly tripped over the protruding metal shaft of a small winepress that had been tipped over on its side. There were stacks of large plastic covered glass containers lying higgledy-piggledy against the walls, partly covered in cobwebs and rubbish. The whole had an air of abandonment and dilapidation. It didn't look as

---

11 Franca, for heaven's sake, the other keys

if wine had actually been made there for some time. At all events, the impression was very different from her father-in-law's spotless stainless steel and tiled Weingut outside Wurzburg.

After this short pause, Franca came back with the missing keys, enabling White Cap to open a door at the side of one of the large barrels. The staircase revealed was in the thickness of the wall. There was only room for single file. Franca went first, White Cap pushed Detty in next using his revolver, rather worryingly, to prod her in the ribs. She tried to take in as much detail as possible as they climbed steadily. Each flight appeared to be the length of the side of the tower. After two sides they passed another dusty door. Correct, thought Detty, this must be the first floor. After two more flights they came to a dead end with a door straight in front of them. Franca produced a key and opened the door. There was a short level platform then the stairway continued but this time instead of being walled off, they climbed, without a guard rail, round the open two sides of the square room until they emerged into the storey above through an aperture in the floor.

At this point the stairway stopped altogether, White Cap flashed his torch up to a small, locked trap door in the ceiling fully five metres above their heads. As he did so Detty saw in the torchlight the massive oak knees on the wall of the old open stairway which had continued on up but obviously had been recently and roughly removed. White Cap moved to the centre of the room looking for something. There was a grunt and he came back dragging a ladder behind him, which he proceeded to put up against the trap door sill. Grabbing the keys from Franca and motioning the rest to stay where they were, he climbed up the ladder. Detty noticed to her surprise that the ladder was made entirely of small wooden rungs let painstakingly into the rough long timber side shafts. As he climbed the primitive support curved ominously under his weight but he reached the trap door without mishap, unlocked it and flinging it back, disappeared inside. A moment later, there was a bright glow from a lamp of some sort inside the trap. After some minutes, White Cap re-appeared and climbed back leaving the door open and the light still on.

Arriving on the floor below he motioned with his pistol for Detty to climb the ladder. After a quick review of the alternative possibilities, she thought it best to obey and began to climb. She looked back once to see the frankly lecherous gaze of White Cap as he stared at the considerable expanse of her thighs and briefs displayed fleetingly under the skirt of her Lanoure model. She allowed herself a smile. This was a version of the Italian cliché of having your bottom pinched. If he really found her legs that fascinating, it might come in useful later. The ladder did bend alarmingly but reassured by the evidence that it had supported the greater weight of White Cap she continued up until she found herself climbing through the small trap door. She looked back to see White Cap beginning to climb the ladder again. Clearly, he hadn't trusted it to bear the weight of two of them at the same time.

Once inside the surroundings were startling and entirely the opposite of the dirty, dusty loft that she had expected. She found herself in a room with a carefully polished terra cotta tiled floor. On one side were a table and two chairs and on one of the others a large double bed with a baldachin and a wardrobe. The third side was screened off by an obviously recent partition to hide a respectable shower, wash basin and lavatory whilst the remaining wall was bare apart from a large pair of heavily embroidered curtains covering a securely locked window. If she was a prisoner, she was certainly a prisoner with a fair degree of comfort. She inspected the bathroom in more detail. Someone had provided a new toothbrush, face flannel, razor, shaving cream, and a clean set of towels. There was even a dispenser of Gucci gel in the shower. These items were clearly intended for male occupants. It was evidently a unisex prison. She tried the hot tap. Sure enough after running for a few moments the water was scalding and seemed plentiful.

She was roused from her bemused tour of inspection by the trap door banging shut and the noise of the lock clicking underneath. It might be comfortable, but a prison it was indeed. Nothing to be done tonight, however, she thought, and suddenly felt exhausted. She undressed and stood gratefully for some moments under the hot shower, dried herself with the thick towel and lay down on the bed. She drew the thin quilt half over her as, despite the lack of opening windows, it was gratefully cool. She wondered for a moment whether, white cap, her lecherous captor might try his luck in the watches of the night. Sufficient unto the day-or night- she thought and slipped into a deep sleep.

As the first light filtering through the chinks in the heavy curtains woke her, she was totally disorientated. She worked through various possibilities until she finally remembered where she was and the sinister, improbable events of the previous day. She got out of bed, crossed to the window, her bare feet silent on the refreshingly cool tiles and pulling the heavy curtains aside, looked down. The forest came right up to the foot of the tower on the window side. She was able to identify chestnuts, small oaks, and ash; lower down nearer the forest floor were junipers, thorn and broom. In the light of dawn, the symphony of varying greens was half-hidden under a gold sheen floating on a transparent veil of mist. Eastwards towards the hills the reflected light beneath the rising sun was of bright gold. As it moved southwards towards her over the ground, it gradually paled to a delicate rosy orange. There was no sign of humanity at all visible from that side of the tower. The forest stretched, with only the occasional patchwork clearing, as far as she could see in the direction of the gradually rising hills. The only man-made item was a distant, ugly pylon line sparkling in the morning light. The scene took her breath away with its beauty and she could not help gazing at it in wonder for some minutes suppressing the gloomy realities of her predicament. Beautiful as it was however it gave her no clue as to where she might be or how she could escape.

Her reverie was interrupted by a rumbling sound from a small insignificant cupboard that she had failed to notice previously beside the table. Investigating, she opened the door to discover a cup of cafe americano and two packets of *Mulino Bianco* breakfast biscuits and a dish of honey. Clearly, she was not to be starved into submission. She attacked the food and drink, wondering whether it was drugged but deciding that she had to accept that chance, and reviewed her situation.

There was some evidence that her kidnapping had been carefully planned, but why and by whom? She had met a number of people at the reception and it was hard to decide which if any of them might have been involved in the plot. The limousine had presumably been substituted, by some means or other, for the legitimate one. The room in which she now found herself had obviously been carefully fitted out. It was just possible that previously it had been the residence of an eccentric recluse but more probably, it had been prepared especially for the important victims of kidnapping. It could have been arranged especially for her reception but overall, she thought that this was unlikely. The razor and shaving cream for one thing was against it, although of course women did use razors, and it seemed unnecessarily elaborate for the reception of one victim. No, more likely she was in the hands of a practised gang who saw a profit in her or, alternatively, who had been employed by others on a contract. In favour of the financial option was that this pattern had a long history in Italy. It was well known that she was extremely well connected with a wealthy German family. As she was a foreigner therefore, the laws providing for the freezing of assets of kidnap victims in Italy, which had been effective in restricting the menace, would not apply.

On the other hand, the bombers responsible for the *Hansestadion* and Sovils outrages had been sent to prison for twenty years. She knew that the two men arrested with the low-grade hit men used in the attacks, were probably much more important operatives. Some sort of trade on their behalf might be intended. What more appropriate than to seize the high-profile Livonian popular heroine as a bargaining counter? She was sombrely aware that the mortality rate amongst kidnap victims was high. This meant that it was important to get out, to get away as soon as possible. It was also, though, important to get the plan right. If this were to be possible at all, it would need a certain amount of observation and planning. She carefully went round her surroundings again and was able to decide quickly that the window was not an option. It consisted of extremely thick armoured glass with massive bars beyond. Even if by some miracle she was able to get through the glass and the bars the drop to the ground of over thirty metres, couldn't be attempted. No, if she was going to get out it had to be by means of the same route by which she had entered and that did not seem at all easy.

During the next couple of days, she calculated the routine of her captors. Breakfast and lunch arrived via the lift without human escort. In the evening, however, either Franca or her mother, who Detty had discovered was called Annunziata, climbed the ladder to see that the captive was safe and sound before nightfall. Both were always armed and Franca was undoubtedly tough and completely devoted to her employers; Annunziata on the other hand had more than a touch of the all-caring Italian mother. She seemed unhappy in her role of jailer to this meek, modest young woman. Detty sensed this and immediately began to play on the old woman's sensibilities. Genuinely enough, but still begging forgiveness from the Virgin, she made sure that she was always telling an imaginary rosary when the evening visitor arrived. If it was Franca, her supplicant posture was greeted with a cynical sneer but the mother always smiled her approval of her captive's piety, once enquiring if the English girl was really or could be, a Catholic.

Detty replied winningly that she was *un' Irlandese e in Irlanda quasi tutti erano della fede Cattolica. Io propria ero stata educata in un Convento per le moniche.*[12]

True at least to some extent she would tell her confessor – if she ever got the opportunity of going to Confession again. At the same time, she cast her eyes to the ground looking as meek as possible. She thought that she was probably condemning herself to hellfire and offered up a silent prayer to St Michael, the warrior archangel, to understand and forgive her strategy.

Whether through the Archangel or not her ruse worked and she was sure that Annunziata really felt sorry for the poor captive child to the extent that her guard lowered. During a comforting embrace, it was a relatively simple matter to extract the keys from the old woman's apron. By good fortune, the lock closed automatically, snapping to as the trap shut so that Annunziata didn't need to look for the keys on the way out. This and the fact that there was a counter keyhole on the upper side of the trap, were weaknesses in the system that any trained security officer ought to have spotted immediately and rectified. Presumably the five-metre drop under the trap, the remoteness of the situation and the usual presence of armed guards and dogs, were thought to be security enough.

---

12 An Irish woman and in Ireland almost everybody belonged to the Catholic faith. She, herself, had been educated by the Nuns in a Convent

It did appear, however, that Detty had been right in thinking that her meek and bewildered demeanour might induce a false sense of security in her captors.

She allowed enough time for the old woman to get back to her *casa colonica* beyond the farmyard and then worked fast. She realised how important it was to get out before either her family or the Livonian authorities were subjected to any demand. Subconsciously she was also keen to prove, if proof was necessary, that her position as Colonel-in-Chief of the Wild Swans wasn't just an honorific post, if she survived, that is, to tell them about it. First, she prepared her rope. Two towels, a quilt and a mattress cover tied with her reef knots were, she calculated, enough to get her within two metres of the floor. She unlocked the trap without difficulty and checked that the loft below was empty. Then she made fast her makeshift rope to the ladder stay and began to climb down. She cursed that she hadn't been able to persuade Annunziata to bring her a more suitable change of clothes. She had tried and the old woman had seemed willing but had come back saying that her family were all too small to have clothes suitable for the tall *straniera*. She was left therefore with her unsuitable, and now extremely scruffy, Lanoure model and her leather jacket. As she reached the mattress cover that was the final part of the rope, it tore with loud splitting sound and she had to jump from a height considerably greater than she had planned. She uttered a silent prayer that nobody would hear and that the timbers weren't rotten on the floor below. It was OK and the timbers held as she landed as lightly as she could but still with a considerable thump. She paused on the platform below after landing and listened carefully. To her relief the late evening peace prevailed and no dogs barked.

The stairs carried her safely down to the locked door at the beginning of the covered stairway. This was a problem, as it was a sturdy lock and there was no obvious way of opening it. Puzzling for several minutes, she looked around in desperation. Fortunately, there was bright moonlight through a narrow window, which helped her to find the answer. There was a hoist through the floor on the other side of the room complete with an inviting cable that she could secure and climb down. In her relief she jumped on the rope enthusiastically and shinned down too fast leaving the inside of her thighs scraped raw and the priceless Lanoure gown rucked round her waist and in an even sadder state than previously. Otherwise, her good fortune held and there was a similar hoist leading on down. This time she used more circumspection but it still hurt her raw legs particularly round the scar of her bullet wound from the previous year. Despite some grimaces, she arrived on the welcome ground, back amongst the barrels and abandoned winemaking paraphernalia. She looked around her, searching for the door to the outside.

It was totally dark now, as there were no windows at the bottom of the tower. She stumbled around trying to remember the layout from her arrival. Eventually she located the door, which, to her disappointment, if not surprise, was firmly bolted and locked. Apart from this, the chamber seemed to have no other doors or windows. She did however find the long wine press handle, which she had noticed when they first arrived. She put it carefully to one side where she could lay her hands on it again in the darkness when she wanted it.

She looked at the door in detail noticing that it was ill-fitting and the moonlight showed through gaps at several places. She could see where the bar of the lock and the slightly thinner one of the bolt crossed the narrow strip of light. She decided that it might be possible to prise open the bolt and then perhaps jemmy the door open using the leverage of the winepress handle. She scrabbled around looking for a suitable tool amongst the abundant rubbish to insert into the door crack. Scratching her hand in the process, she eventually located a discarded food tin with the lid still attached. She bent this backwards and forwards until it came away from the main body of the tin. Inserting the lid in the crack she tried to move the bolt. The old blacksmith's iron was rough enough to give the lid some purchase in the narrow crack but try as she might it was stuck fast and wouldn't move. After some minutes of useless effort, she paused, thought, and ran her hand over the inside of the door. She found the handhold she wanted. The bolts stoutly securing the hinges had been left proud on the inside and provided her with a grip. Pulling the door in towards her as hard as she could with her left hand to release the pressure on the bolt, she again tried to move it by levering with jagged tin lid inserted in the crack with her right hand. This time to her delight it worked. She had taken the weight of the door off the bolt. Millimetre by millimetre she was able to ease the bar back moving the lid along and heaving the door towards her as she went. It was very laborious and it must have taken nearly an hour before she finally heard the long bolt clang loudly free from its housing.

The noise seemed like a pistol shot in the darkness and she held her breath. A dog near at hand barked loudly and continuously. Finally, inevitably there were voices, male and female arguing and swearing and coming closer. Detty shrank back into the wall beside the hinge end of the door holding the winepress handle that she had had no chance to use. The key rattled in the lock and someone tried to draw the bolt without noticing that it was already free, presumably reassured that the door was still locked by the key. Light from a big torch flooded inside. Detty gripped the press handle tightly thinking that she might be able to floor one of the intruders with it. The problem was, however, that there seemed to be several of them and they were presumably armed. It was best to stay hidden behind the door and hope that no one looked.

In the event, she didn't need the press handle either as a weapon or a cracksman's tool. White Cap stood in the doorway with four or five men grouped behind him. He shouted something about *controllare l'esterno* [13] followed by some more that she couldn't catch concerning *la stronza straniera*. She wasn't sure what this meant but guessed that it referred to her and that it wasn't exactly complimentary. There followed some further instructions and oaths in a strong dialect that she couldn't follow at all.

Most of the party went off to search the yard while White Cap followed by one of the men crossed to the stairway door. He rattled the door and grunted with satisfaction to find that it was still locked. Producing a duplicate bundle of keys, he unlocked the door and accompanied by the other man went inside. Detty heard their footsteps as they began to climb the stair. She slipped out of the outside door, which was still wide open and swinging gently in the night breeze. Outside was bedlam. Several dogs were barking fiercely near at hand but fortunately

---

13 Check the outside

nobody had thought to let them loose. Perhaps the men doubted their own safety when the dogs were famished and so furiously aroused. The men were scattered around the buildings shouting to each other using the high-pitched cries of the *caccia* which Detty remembered from a winter visit to Marc's cousins' castello near Lucca. It was a sort of *caccia*, she thought grimly, with herself as the *lepre*. There was very little time. However reassured White Cap had been to find the door to the stairs still locked, it would not take him long to discover the open trap door and the remains of the rope in the granary above and then the hue and cry would really start. The best shelter would be the relative obscurity of the thick wood that she had seen from her window in the tower. She might hide there and put some distance between herself and the tower without being found if, and it was a big if, they didn't lose the dogs.

She decided to go to the left round to the back of the tower. The wood seemed closer in that direction and it was away from the shouting men. She followed the wall round only to be confronted by a two-metre high close-mesh fence with concrete footings and a double strip of razor wire over the top. The fence stretched between the tower and a lower building. It seemed to be part of a compound as it enclosed a relatively narrow piece of bare land some ten metres deep with a similar fence the other side. The only access was a door from the farther building. Some sort of stockyard, she thought, but at all events, it couldn't be crossed and she had to retrace her steps and try the other side.

She had just regained the door to the tower when there was a shout from above followed by a furious stream of oaths. Her escape had been discovered. She forged on keeping close to the tower. She managed not to crash, face to face, into one of the searching men who seemed to have spread out over the entrance track. With the dogs, she had a nearer squeak, one great beast, part German shepherd, part who knows what, faced her with his slavering chops leaping high on the extent of his straining chain. There was just room to squeeze past out of range of those massive jaws alongside the wall. She prayed that the chain didn't give way. She credited herself with her fair share of courage and had done enough to show it in the past. She had to admit, however, that the idea of being torn to pieces by a starving Italian guard dog, she found unthinkably horrifying. Close enough to feel his hot breath she edged past until the dog, who finally realised that he had been deprived of his meal, allowed his front paws to return to the ground. He was still barking ferociously, fortunately in unison with several others stationed around the farm, which made the sound less conspicuous. Detty took one quick look back, saw an expression in the dog's eye which she was sure said 'You wait, I'll get you next time' and pushed her way into the, gratefully unfenced, *macchia* of the forest. She fought her way through the undergrowth determinedly for about two hundred metres and then stopped to take stock.

For the moment, she was safer from her pursuers but she realised that she had another problem, she was stuck in the deep midst of a dense mixed forest in the middle of the night. Her favourite Goethe poem, learnt as a schoolgirl in Ireland, went through her head.

Schon stand in Nebelkleid die Eiche,
Ein auf geturmter Reise, da,
Wo Finsternis aus dem Gestrauche
Mit hundert schwarzen Auge sah.[14]

She could hear the more distant voices of her captives and the diminuendo barking of the dogs. Nearer was the crackle of breaking twigs under her feet. When she stopped moving the other close sounds were an occasional indeterminate glugging noise, the sound of frogs croaking some distance in front of her and the chirping of a nightjar further in the distance. Far off to her front was a faint incongruous even roar, which sounded like traffic on a distant main road, if it was traffic it must be some number of kilometres away, she thought. How to get out of this situation and get out of it safely was a real problem. She decided that it was best to wait for daybreak and settled down amongst

---

14 The oak, a towering giant cloaked in mist
    Where darkness from the bushes peered
    With a hundred blackened eyes
    (Wilkommen und Abschied)

the cold and discomfort of the sharp twigs and thorns as best she could. It was hard to find any part of the forest floor that wasn't covered with debris of thorns and conifers. It was hard to get comfortable and during one attempt, she was brought up short by a sharp stab in the stomach. Irrationally she thought for a moment that one of her pursuers had caught her and knifed her from behind but it was only a broken branch of a tree that had snagged her, invisible in the darkness.

She drifted off to fitful sleep punctuated by nightmares mainly on the old themes from the Farm and strangely little related to her real-life situation. From one of these she woke with an intense sense of dread; her first feeling was of relief after the ghastly dream. Then she heard a sound that sent all thought of her dream out of her head. The dog was baying again and she was sure it was the same one that she had faced in her earlier encounter. Now it was much nearer and coming towards her. She was seized by desperate panic, leapt up and forced her way mindlessly through the dense scrub. The barking was gaining on her. Her resourcefulness had deserted her and she just pushed blindly forward listening to that dreadful sound getting closer. Suddenly there appeared a clearing in front of her and a strange plopping noise that she didn't stop to identify. She was suddenly up to her ankles in water before she realised that her supposed clearing was in fact a pond. She caught her foot in something and fell forward at full length into deep water. At that moment, the dog burst out of the undergrowth and stood on the bank of the pond barking with frustration. The scent that he had been following so strongly had disappeared. Detty kept very still with water up to her chin balancing on one toe that slithered in the mud below. Her unscripted fall into the pond had saved her for the moment. The dog snuffled around for some minutes before being called away by White Cap whose voice Detty identified, fortunately still some distance off.

She listened to angry, rapid conversation at the edge of the pond only a few metres away. She held her breath. At one moment, the voices were shouting, she thought that they had seen her and were wading into the pond. Then the crashing through the *macchia* resumed and the voices moved away.

The sound of the men disappeared and the occasional barking got less. She allowed what seemed an age to pass before she dared move. She stayed, dripping wet and getting cold, even on the warm late spring night, on the bank but near enough to the edge to climb back into the pond should the dog reappear. As first light broke, she was able to identify an overgrown path leading away from the tower behind her in the direction of the distant traffic hum. Not wanting to wait any longer and gratefully, thanks to the path, now able to move relatively fast and noiselessly, she set off. The glorious sun came up in front of her as she ran and soon the pond water started to steam from her dress with her exertion aided by the sun's warmth. It took her less than an hour to reach the road, a dual carriageway superhighway but not, it seemed, an autostrada. It stretched in either direction without a road sign in sight. It was relatively easy, however, for Detty to realise that the far carriageway headed north to the left of the sunrise. The road was full of the early morning heavy lorries crowding both inner lanes and with fast cars racing along the outside carriageways. She began to despair of ever being able to cross but, at last, there was half a chance and she threaded her way between two *auto-treni*, then across the front bumper of a hurtling Alfa Romeo and made the middle partition. She climbed the crash barrier inelegantly and tackled the second, slightly quieter, carriageway arriving on the northbound verge exhausted. She made for a small lay-by that she had spotted as she crossed the road, which was about five hundred metres up on the north bound side.

As Detty reached the lay-by, she realised that a large lorry had been pulled in by the *Polizia Stradale* and was having his papers and his tachograph checked. At first, she was reassured. This at least gave some measure of protection from her captors. Then she thought again that the last thing that she really wanted was a brush with the police. She instantly rehearsed the conversation:

'I am a German Contessa who has been singing as a prima donna at il Teatro della Pergola di Firenze and I have just been kidnapped and shut up in a tower by *banditti*.'

'Yes, Signorina, and I'm Benito Mussolini' or whatever Italian police say in these circumstances. No, that had to be avoided if possible but, unfortunately, it was too late. The policeman had seen her and blown his whistle. She had almost as little desire to be chased by armed police across the country as by her previous pursuers. She walked demurely towards the police car wondering what story she could think up which would get her off the hook but could think of nothing. As she looked down at herself, she realised what a terrible state she was in. Her beautiful cocktail model was damp, torn to tatters and covered in mud and bloodstains. It barely covered her decently. The jacket wasn't much better with the soft leather jagged by triangular tears.

In the event, no detailed explanation was necessary. The policemen obviously assumed from the start that she was one of the foreign prostitutes who frequented the road. One of them asked her sharply but not unkindly whether she had been attacked.

'No' she replied she was homeless and had spent the night *all'aperto tra la macchia* and had lost her way in the undergrowth. She exaggerated her difficulties in Italian in the correct hope that it might restrict further questioning. The policemen lost interest and made a vulgar remark to the lorry driver that he could have it away on his trip to Florence and drove off.

The driver who was a cheerful looking thirty-year-old assumed that she was coming with him and told her to climb up into the cab. He followed but made no attempt to drive off. Clearly, the fare was to be paid before the journey. He lost no time in unzipping and pulled her towards him. Now for it she thought, Florence and to be able to telephone quickly was desperately important but just how far would she have to go to get there?

'*Mi dispiace ma un ferito grave nelle parti intimi dello mio corpo, c'e l'ho. Era una caduta la sera scorsa e, come lo vedi, sono incinta.*' [15]She hoped it sounded right remembering strangely a similar but so different conversation that she had had with Marc after she really had been seriously hurt.

The man looked appropriately and decently concerned, beginning to assume a different role of a caring escort to his pregnant companion

---

15 I am sorry, I have a serious wound in my private parts, I fell last night and as you can see I am pregnant

rather than as a predatory male. Not totally, however. She shamefacedly felt somewhat relieved when all he demanded from her, albeit fairly firmly, was that she should do a hand job on him. She had had a horror of fellatio since her experience on behalf of Mara with the revolting Oleg. The hand wasn't too bad and she tried to masturbate him with as good a grace as possible. He seemed satisfied, remarked admiringly that she was *bellissima ma forse troppa per le strade di notte* [16] and contentedly started the engine and drove off towards Siena and Florence.

They talked with a polite lack of familiarity that struck Detty as strange after such intimate activities a few minutes before. He asked where she came from and how long she had been in Italy. She answered truthfully and was met by surprise and some disapproval that a good Catholic communitaria should be a prostitute. She just shrugged whilst reflecting inwardly that she must have a curious affinity with the oldest profession. She could face her maker with hardly a stain on her good Catholic conscience. In spite of this, however, she had during her young life been flogged as a whore and now treated as a roadside hooker. In addition, God willing, in a few weeks' time she would be in Bayreuth again singing the part of a water nymph seductress who was certainly no better than she ought to be.

Her driver now thoroughly concerned about her, and obviously keen to be shed of his responsibility, wanted to take her to the Polyclinic at Siena. She said, truthfully, that she had people who would look after her in Florence and as he was going there anyway could he take her to the hospital there. He turned the big lorry towards Careggi and dropped her with a sigh of relief at the hospital. She entered the reception with a determined air, fumbled for her wallet which was still, miraculously in her torn jacket, hid behind a pillar until the lorry was out of sight and went straight to a payphone. A quick call to Germany to the ever-available Hildegard was sufficient. She asked her to tell Marc and her parents-in-law that she was free and well and that any demands on them were false and that would they pass the same message to the Nicklaus Oblov in Livonia.

---

16 Very beautiful but perhaps too much for the night roads

That accomplished she renewed her funds from a cash point and took a bus back to the station at Santa Maria Novella. On the bus, she thought carefully about her next move. If her kidnappers were half-serious, there would be a watch on the Helvetia & Bristol where, she hoped, the rest of her luggage remained. For the moment, at least, she must avoid it, which presented her with the problem of where to go. The guest lists at the large hotels were kept for the police and easily traceable by a determined enquirer and the same regulations applied to the smaller hotels and *pensioni* which were probably only marginally safer. In any case, in her present garb she would hardly be accepted in a hotel. They would probably assume she was a drug addict and that her papers were stolen.

She got off the bus into the burning sunshine and suddenly felt good to be again amongst the marshalled Japanese tourists, German bikers and American students. Then an idea struck her. She walked the few hundred metres into the market of San Lorenzo and bought herself a generous pair of jeans and a dark green silk shirt. As an after-thought, she added a Kanga pouch and a tee shirt printed with jokes about pollution in the twenty first century in case she needed to make a quick change. A profumeria provided some much-needed cosmetics. She returned to the station and changed in the lavatories, washing off the blood, the pond weed and the mud. She extracted her engagement ring from the hidden pocket and transferred it and her purse to the Kanga pouch and with a sigh deposited many thousand Euros worth of model clothes in the station waste bin. Hoping that she looked reasonably like one of the regiment of young Northern tourists who flood Florence, she then went to have her hair done a small *parruchiere* in the via della Spada where her face, but not her identity, was known. Feeling much more herself she crossed to San Niccolò, found the old building with its plaque of fishes on the wall and rang the bell marked Spinelli MA. As she had expected there was no answer, Totti was not the sort of person to be in her flat at eleven o'clock in the morning. She suddenly felt elated and exhausted at the same time and went into the bar opposite. With Totti's instruction in mind, she ordered un caffé doppio ristretto. The barista looked surprised. Young female tourists were expected to order latte, Coca-Cola, and ice creams but Detty needed something much more fortifying. She opened La Nazione lying on a side table and began idly to read a review of *Otello* at the *Teatro Regio* of Turin. The coffee was doing good and she was beginning to feel confident and contented when a deep male voice behind her said:

'*Buon giorno, Frau Hauptmann*, I am delighted to see that you made it.'

Detty was startled and turned to see a tall gaunt man with a distinguished bearing standing behind her with a cup of coffee. He was immediately familiar to her but for the moment, she couldn't place him. She was also somewhat alarmed to be recognised at all after her elaborate precautions. After a minute, the vivid memories flooded back. Virgilio Poliziano was the man who had helped her over the wall out of the charnel yard at Königshof. She had looked for him after the end of the war but, apparently, he had acquired a new post in his native Italy. She had no idea that he was in Florence.

'*Buon giorno Lei, Professore, altretanto*, I am so glad you did too. I looked for you to thank you for your help afterwards but you had already left. It is a surprise to see you here, but a very pleasant one.

'Less of a surprise for me, as I read of an Irish nightingale in Florence, but I didn't know that you were Irish or *una prima cantante*. However, to my surprise I recognised your picture in the paper. Your face is not easily forgotten, Signora. The press made some very appreciative remarks about you. You obviously have a fine peacetime career aside from military intelligence.'

Detty felt irrationally delighted to see him. They talked of Livonia, the war, and their present lives. After a good hour he smiled and looked at his watch:

'At this time, I usually go for lunch, I would be most honoured if you would consent to join me.'

Detty looked at down at her rather ill-fitting jeans doubtfully:

'I would enjoy that very much but unfortunately I am not really dressed to go out to lunch and for various complicated reasons, I don't want to go back to my hotel just now.'

'That will be no problem at all. The trattoria that I go to is very near here and is extremely simple but I think that you will enjoy the food. There is no formality.'

Detty knew that Totti was unlikely to be back at her flat until late afternoon or evening and lunch with her agreeable old, if brief, acquaintance, was attractive:

'In that case, I will accept gratefully.'

They walked a few metres down the street past the Porta San Niccolò and went into a cool barrel-vaulted cantina. Poliziano was greeted with the warmth and deference due to an old and respected customer. They sat down at a carefully but simply laid table with the strong sunlight from the street making pools of gold on the terracotta floor. Detty had the *Riso agli Asparagi* recommended by her host followed by *Braciole di Vitello ai Carciofi*. The food, accompanied by a delicious Chianti Classico from Isole e Olena which she felt she could have in spite of her pregnancy and made her feel warm and human again. The talk ranged far and wide, starting with some aspects of their personal lives. Then they got on to Shakespeare and the Florentine wine trade and from there to the Council of Trent and its effect on polyphony in the Church. They had spent some time on the influence of the Duomo of Siena on Wagner and the composition of *Parsifal* when Poliziano suddenly stopped:

'Forgive me' he said 'but something that you said earlier has bothered me. Would I perhaps be right in thinking that your present situation is not one of ataraxia. Not as – er – uncomplicated and serene as the newspapers might have led me to believe?'

Detty was taken aback by the question and thought for a moment. She knew little of her companion but the circumstances in which they had first met together with his general mien hardly suggested that he was involved in organised crime, terrorism or indeed politics at any level. She decided to trust him, at least up to a point.

'You are correct. I was abducted from outside the house of the Marchese Coltiere, who was responsible for the initiative that brought me here, after a reception that he had given for us after the last performance.'

He looked appropriately concerned.

'Tell me how it happened.'

She did briefly, describing her kidnap, her imprisonment, and her escape. It wasn't until she reached the last that her companion's serious expression turned to a smile.

'You haven't lost your old skills then?'

'Not entirely, thank God. But I am now faced with a number of serious questions. First, was the kidnap political or mercenary? It could have been either given my circumstances. I don't know whether there have been any ransom demands that might make things clearer. I will find out but I suspect that I may have escaped too quickly. Second, I am not sure who, if any, of the people that I have met here in Florence and Siena might have been involved. Until I have some idea who I can and cannot trust, I have to be very careful who I meet and talk with, which is one reason why I was reluctant to return to my hotel, thereby publicly announcing my return.'

He nodded.

'Then there is the question of the police. Normally I would have gone to them but because of the previous reason and the difficulty of keeping a police statement confidential, I have been reluctant to do so. There is also the problem that, for several reasons, publicity might have unfortunate international consequences.'

'So, you see I am in a difficult position. I intend to go and lie low, staying with someone that I know here in Florence for a few days to see if I can learn anything. Then I must leave Tuscany but I have had an offer of a part here next year, which, under other circumstances, I would be delighted to fulfil but now I am not sure.'

He sat thoughtfully for a minute.

'I hardly like to suggest it but I do have a friend, an old *compagno di banco* –school friend, who is a Vice Questore of police here in Florence. I believe him to be trustworthy and if you wished, I could arrange for you to have a confidential interview with him-off the record- without it going through the junior and more public channels. You will know, as well as I do, that here in Italy it is sometimes difficult to be completely sure who is trustworthy but I do believe him to be an honest man.'

'It isn't only in Italy, Professore, that it is sometimes difficult to know whom to trust. I do appreciate your offer, however, and I may well take you up on it if I can but first, I must check with my family in Germany and Ireland and,' she hesitated 'other people.'

She thought he probably knew that she was talking about the Livonian Government but didn't feel that she needed to spell it out at that moment.

'Of course. Here is my card, you can contact my secretary at the University at any time or ring me at home. I live by myself and, by the way, I sometimes come back to Livonia for academic reasons, I hope to see you there.'

She raised an eyebrow very slightly as an invitation to tell her more, which she sensed he wanted.

'My wife died in Königshof. The next shot missed me, as I told you when we met before, but she was not so fortunate. They didn't like foreigners but of course I don't have to tell you, of all people, that.'

'I am very sorry.'

She wondered how many times she had said that in similar circumstances in the last two years and it always sounded hopelessly inadequate.

'I felt that I couldn't stay in Königshof. In some ways, I would have liked to and I sometimes go back at least for visits. I admired Oblov and I think that your people got near to achieving that most rare of miracles, true freedom out of darkness and a clean revolution. There were too many memories, though, too much sadness. I thought perhaps that if I went home, and was, as Dante yearned to be:

Sovra'l bel fiume d'Arno alla gran villa[17]

that it might help to heal the wound. I think it has, to a degree, but not completely, never completely.'

He broke off looking infinitely sad.

They said their goodbyes and went their separate ways, he to his little electric bus, Detty, feeling very sombre and clutching the card that he had given her to walk the few metres back to Totti's apartment.

---

17 Above the fine river of Arno in the great city
    (Dante InfernoXIII)

5
DUNGEON

Leb wohl du warmes Sonnenlicht
Schnell schwindest du uns wieder[18]!

PRISONERS CHORUS, *FIDELIO* ACT I
BEETHOVEN/ SONNLEITNER &TREITSCHKE

Vice-Questore Gatti welcomed her very courteously and produced coffee, *basso e ristrettissimo*. He congratulated her on her performance in *La Wally*, which he was *molto spiacente* to have missed. After the pleasantries, they got to business. He seemed to understand Detty's reluctance to make an official complaint, remarking that many people in Italy would feel the same, unfortunately. She explained that there could be either political or pecuniary motives for her kidnapping. She had contacted Oberdorf, Königshof and, for good measure, Ballyinch, but no ransom note or other message had been received. She was also keen to discover if anybody that she had met in the city were in any way suspicious, as this would clearly influence future contacts. He asked her

---

18 Farewell warm sunshine
fading quickly from us again

to explain in detail what had happened from leaving the Bristol until she met the Professor in the bar.

After she had finished, he sat thinking for some moments.

'You have told me quite a disturbing story, Signora,' he said at last. 'We can, however, deal with some aspects straight away. Your hosts, the Marchese and the Cavaliere are established Florentine citizens of great standing and lineage. I am as certain as I possibly can be that they are not involved in organised crime, either international or local. There are, you understand, some well-known local figures that I would be reluctant to endorse so whole-heartedly but these two would not be amongst them. On the other hand, you have met many people here, at the Accademia Chigiana, the theatres and also the various social functions that you have attended. It would be impossible to say that none of them were engaged in dubious activities or here for nefarious reasons.'

'With regard to the manner of your abduction, it doesn't follow any established pattern that is known to me. I wish I could recognise your podere with the tower but at the moment I cannot, there are many similar buildings in our countryside. The road in your description would seem to be the superstrada from Siena to Grosseto around Paglanico. That part of the highway is, you will forgive me, frequented by *ragazze extracommunitarie*. It would seem that, in your distressed condition and with your youthful bellezza, of course, you might have been mistaken for one such. We will carry out some discreet enquiries and I will let you know if we discover anything worthwhile. Can you give me a point where I may contact you confidentially?'

Detty thought.

'The best place would be Königshof'; she gave the number.

'What is the place and to whom do I speak?' he asked.

'It is the coded number of the private office of the President of Livonia. You need have no worries about confidentiality. Just say you have a message for Bernadette von Ritter and it will get to me quickly.'

The Vice Questore looked at her intently:

'You move in exalted circles.' he said, visibly impressed 'I understand even more now why you were anxious not to trigger a routine investigation. In the meanwhile, please 'phone me here if you need me, or go through Professor Poliziano. I will of course speak to you in person if you need to contact me and the line is protected. Thank you for coming here, you have certainly helped me and I hope that I may be able to help you. One final thing, have you by chance ever met Monsignor Josemaria Pueblo?

'The Spaniard with a goatee beard and a rugby forward's shoulders?'

Detty's description was out in a flash and she only reflected later that perhaps she had been inappropriate.

'Yes, I met him at the Marchese's. He seemed very interested in the current Bayreuth '*Ring*' and the *Freiheitsfest* in Königshof.'

'I do not play rugby, Signora, but I would say that you have got the right man and I am interested that he wanted to talk to you. Be careful if you meet him again. You understand that I have not said this and, *veramente*, I can be sure of nothing.' The Vice Questore spoke thoughtfully but no more was forthcoming.

They shook hands and parted.

Detty returned to the little flat in San Niccolò for an evening of music making with Totti and her delightful *fidanzato*. Early next day she would catch the train on her multistage journey back to Oberdorf and Bayreuth.

In the morning, she threw her few additional possessions together into her case, which had been discreetly recovered by Alessandro from the Bristol. She dragged herself onto the little electric D bus to Santa Maria Novella station. She was in good time for the Munich train and she went to the Edicola and bought a copy of La Repubblica keen to practise reading Italian. She glanced at the paper as she walked back to the platform. The headline involved a failed attempt to underpin the current shaky Italian government coalition. It was the article at the bottom of the front page, however, that stopped her in her tracks. *Figlia di Presidente Baltico rapita,*[19] it read. Cursing her primitive Italian, she read the article rapidly. Although she did not understand every word, the main message was devastatingly clear. Tamara Oblova, the daughter of the President of Livonia, had been kidnapped from the Berlin train

---

19 Daughter of Baltic President abducted.

on her way back to University in Munich. Her accompanying private detective had been shot dead. Mara had been right all the time, in the event poor Ilya had not been able to save her.

*

This was the year that Bayreuth should have been superb. She had the notoriety of last year. They whispered round the Festspielhaus:

'That's the girl who sang the Awakening when Anneliese Seiling hurt herself. Yes, my dear, in costume and without a rehearsal and she's only in her early twenties.'

This year she should have had the fun without the anxiety and responsibility. She only had to sing *Woglinde*, her wonderful short part, and enjoy it all. The publicity became a bit too much. But Detty had to admit that she enjoyed the festivalgoers' comments, if rather less the requests for press and broadcast interviews which got increasingly inane and far from the point. As far as the photographers were concerned, they seemed a good deal more interested in her cleavage and her thighs than her art. She was fascinated by the way that they managed to produce 'glamour' photographs, which gave no clue as to her altered shape. She realised that a modern singer was required to capitalise on all her assets, although the dear knows what the Nuns who had brought her up would have thought of it. There was she reflected with a smile, a good deal in her recent life that wouldn't have been in the philosophy of the good Sisters. She did, however, draw the line when on two days running American magazines sent her e-mails inviting her to pose nude for them for varying numbers of dollars. She refused with some force adding that anyway, thank God, she didn't need their money.

Partly because of the press and partly because there was less to do between performances, she drove home to Oberdorf quite often during the Festival. It took her under an hour and she was able to practise in peace with the help of the family Bechstein. She worked hard on Elsa and Elisabeth to try and be ready for next year. She loved the woods and the peace of the *Frankenwald*. She loved Hildegard's *Klösen* and *Forellenpastetchen* made with fresh trout from the little streams running into the Weisse Main and the Steinach. She wasn't sure that it all accorded with sensible eating in pregnancy but she felt fit and limited Max's splendid low alcohol wine to a glass a day. Marc came for a weekend and they walked hand-in-hand through the woods like a couple of love-lorn teenagers. He had been trying to trace Mara through his old unit but the search was difficult from a distance. Despite his expert knowledge, they had had become bogged down in the massive morass of east European organised crime.

The aching anxiety about Mara invaded Detty's thoughts day and night whenever she had time to think, spoiling the idyll. Guilt and her helplessness dominated every moment that wasn't busy. She wished Marc could have been there more as he was the only person she could really talk to about Mara. What had they done with her? When she had heard of her disappearance, she had wanted to rush to Livonia but Nicklaus had been firm over the 'phone:

'You would only make another target. They have tried to get you twice already. The police are so stretched. I am sorry, Detty, but I must be firm this time, please don't come. Stay safely where you are, enjoy the Festival and then go home to beautiful Ireland and rest. You need it and the baby deserves it.'

She realised that this was an order and anyway she couldn't see that she could do anything useful, so she tried to concentrate on her singing. She was boosted by the call to Christa Wagner's office in the middle of the second '*Ring*'.

'Frau O'Neill' she had said 'Maestro Dr Meilin has particularly asked that you should sing the new *Elisabeth* the year after next. Up to now we haven't been able to fix definitive casting. I am sorry it is short notice but I particularly wanted to ask you myself. I hope that you are not already booked up.'

'Of course, Frau Wagner, it would be a great honour. I will let my agent know.' Detty spluttered. One dream looked like coming true.

'These are the full dates. Are you free?'

'Subject to my commitments to this' she indicated her stomach 'I am entirely free after *Elsa* in Florence in May. They both smiled.

*

She headed home to Oberdorf from Bayreuth the morning after the last *Götterdämmerung* with thoughts racing through her head, the *Ring* just finished, *Elsa* in Florence, *Elisabeth* at Bayreuth in the future and the autumn's Freiheitsfest in Königshof. She called in at the *Festspielhaus* for her mail and to leave a couple of messages and headed for the *Kulmbacherstrasse*. The roads were quieter by late morning and the car was virtually on autopilot on the route that she knew so well. The quickest way would have been to take the autobahn but partly to avoid fiddling through the town and partly because she enjoyed it, she always took the same country route. Starting off on the *Kulmbacherstrasse*, she passed under the Bamberg Autobahn north of *Neudrossenfeld* and then she would turn down a tiny country road through the villages of *Schwingen, Weiherhaus, Neuenmarkt* and so across the *Weisser Main* and the *Steinach* at the lovely village of *Wirsberg*, then into the forest, across the *Kulmbach* to *Munchberg* road and straight home. It was a winding route and there were several possible alternatives, but she loved the flower bedecked houses, the little bridges, and the trees, most of all a beautiful beech wood, which was refreshing after the patriotic German conifers and limes.

She had just made the turn from the main Bayreuth to Kulmbach road and round the first bend onto the tree-lined, isolated stretch of the Schwingen road, when she saw it. The bicycle was black with its small front wheel twisted round; its owner was lying face downwards over the edge of the road. She was a little girl of about eight years old. She wasn't moving and there was blood on her hair and her tee shirt. Detty stopped her car, put on the hazard lights, and leapt out. She reached the child, felt her pulse and was relieved that it was strong and healthy. She concentrated on the child and heard no sound from the trees behind her. She was still feeling the child's pulse when she felt a vicious crack on her head and everything went dark.

The walls were cold and damp. Her head throbbed dreadfully, she felt physically nauseated and sick at heart. It had been so simple and after all her experience, she ought to have been more careful. But how? How could you not stop for an injured child at the roadside? Anyway, kidnaps took place in Livonia, London or Italy but not, not, in her beloved Bavaria on the edge of the *Frankenwald*. It was somehow obscene, a violation of something sacred. Once in Livonia, she had talked to a very sick girl who had been gang raped by the NAS in her own bedroom. For a long time, the girl hadn't been able to talk at all. When Detty saw her, she was a little more in touch although she still had a staring hunted look in her eyes, as if, still, all she could see was a pervasive horror. She had said that the worst thing was that she had been violated not only in her body but in her home as well. Where could she feel secure now if this nightmare could happen on her own bed? Could she ever go to bed or feel warm and comfortable again? Detty had thought that she had understood at the time but now she knew what the girl had really meant. Bavaria to her had been freedom, safety, joy and love and now all this had been abused. She dragged herself back to her predicament.

Silence was all around apart from the dripping water. She might be anywhere – there was no clue. As she tried to make out where she was, she thought she heard footsteps. Then, she was sure; they were heavy steps mixed with light, approaching down an echoing passage. Two figures came in; a small female one was in front of a much larger man. Detty couldn't believe her eyes. She didn't know whether to rejoice or weep.

'There now. You can keep each other company and give us double value. We can see what your father will agree when he watches what we intend to do with you – and rest assured we will make sure that he is able to watch it.'

The man looked very ordinary. He was somewhat overweight, wore jeans and a blue sweatshirt and stank of an unusual tobacco. He gave no clues as to his provenance apart from speaking *Hochdeutsch* with perhaps the trace of a flat northern accent but Detty couldn't be sure. He turned from Mara to Detty:

'As for you, you're a troublesome bitch but you won't get up to any tricks here this time until we are told what to do with you.'

For a long time, they just hugged each other, glad to be together again at last, however dreadful the circumstances. Mara said that she had been there for four days. She showed Detty, rather proudly, where she had made scratches on the wall indicating each day from the food deliveries. She had been taken out for exercise down the passageway when Detty had arrived.

'That's what you're supposed to do, isn't it?' she said indicating the scratches as if she was talking about the rules of some game.

A rat scuttled through the darkness of the cellar making them both start. They had no idea whether it was night or day and just huddled together in the damp cold. Then they tried hard to keep each other warm and eventually both slept. When she woke up, Detty had no idea how long she had slept. Mara, seeming to take comfort from her presence, was still asleep her head on Detty's lap. Shaking herself fully awake, she tried to take stock. It was fiendishly difficult. Neither they, nor presumably anybody outside, knew where they were. She couldn't be sure how long she had been unconscious. They could have been taken anywhere. Detty looked down at the front of her forearm. She couldn't really see in the dark but, from the sensation, she was pretty sure that she had been given an injection, so she could have been out for any length of time. It was impossible to work out how they had got there. The building was freezing and wretchedly dank but that could be from the depth of the cellar rather than the outside climate. Detty thought instinctively of Rocco's words in *Fidelio*:

'*Das ist naturlich, es ist ja so tief*'[20]

She could hear Dieter Tinsel's voice saying them as he had last summer at the triumphant performance. Come to think of it, this prison would do quite well for a set for the Act 2 scene 1 of *Fidelio*. She cursed herself for wool gathering and shook herself back to ghastly reality.

She gently moved the sleeping Mara's head off her and began to explore. There was some light that seemed to have an indeterminate source high above them. The walls were of stone but there were piles of rubble in several places and the stonework seemed fairly loose and, in part, ominously crumbly. There were several miscellaneous objects lying about amongst the rubble including plastic bottles, a piece of felt-like

---

20 That's natural, it is so deep.

material which on closer inspection had probably once been a horse blanket and the remains of a galvanised bathtub full of holes. There were no labels on the bottles and none of the other objects gave any clue as to their whereabouts.

Stumbling in the half-light, Detty tripped and half fell forward on to the only dry piece of wall in a flaking corner of the cellar. Cobwebs and mouse droppings were festooned all over it. As she supported herself on the wall to regain her balance, she felt it crack and a large section fell away. She staggered forward not knowing where she would finish up. She was terrified as she lost her footing again completely, with thoughts of dropping into a disused well or mineshaft flashing across her heightened imagination. She recovered her balance as she reached the far wall. The floor, although uneven, seemed firm enough beneath her. Very little light indeed penetrated through the opening that she had created. She appeared to be in a low cellar with a dry musty smell contrasting with the damp in the other chamber. The first thing that she made out was that the roof had partially collapsed with the rotten broken beam sagging towards the floor. The peril appeared to be from above, not, as her vivid imagination had told her, below. A noise from behind startled her. She turned round quickly but it was only Mara who had been awoken by the sound of her crash and was now putting her head anxiously through the opening.

'Are you OK?'

'Don't worry I'm fine. I seem to have found something and wonder whether it could lead to a way out. If you stand back from the opening, I might get a bit more light. Keep watch in case anyone comes.'

Mara moved away. Gradually Detty's eyes began to make out more in the gloom. At first, she thought that she was hallucinating. It was not the secret room but its contents that rooted her, stunned, to the spot. Around the walls were shadows of objects, possibly on boxes or low shelves, which she could not make out in the twilight. In the middle of the room appeared the dim outline of what appeared to be a huge refectory table. The less than half-light was enough to be able to make out the glint of gold all around, half revealing a multitude of jumbled shapes. There appeared to be precious objects on every side.

She could just make out suits of armour and jewel encrusted saddles. There were more gold objects that she could barely see but couldn't fully distinguish. She picked up something round – a coin perhaps? She thought about taking it into the light when a dim shape high up on the furthest wall distracted her attention. She could barely see it but gradually the shape became visible. It was a large cup of metal dull with age and neglect. Behind the cup was a panel, half seen, which was so dim that she couldn't make out the image.

The cup had a sheen of grey blue in the gloom but somewhere at the edge shone gold. It was impossible to see more but, somehow, oddly, she felt that something about it was distantly familiar. As she was trying to make it out better Mara, agitated, poked her head through the gap in the wall:

'Detty, I think someone is coming. There was a noise – it's still a long way off but it seems like footsteps down the long passage that leads here.'

They listened. She was right. The footsteps were getting clearer and there seemed to be more than one person. They rapidly pushed the rubble back to fill the hole as much as possible and draped the old saddlecloth, which had been lying on the floor over the part that remained. Satisfied that they had done their best to conceal their find, they crossed to the opposite side of the first cellar to try to distract attention from the fallen wall. They sat down, tried to look sleepy and waited, as the footsteps got closer.

The bars shot back and the reinforced oak door swung back against the wall with a crash and a shower of dust. There were not one but three men. The apparent leader was the same man in jeans and blue sweatshirt who had brought Mara back down the corridor. This time he spoke first to Detty:

'You've got to be moved. Apparently, it is too risky to keep you both here together.'

Higher orders again but still impersonal and no clues there, she thought. He turned to Mara:

'You will be staying here.'

'Do you want her handcuffed?' asked one of the underlings.

'No, she's a bit of an escaper, I hear. We need to avoid any games so put this on her which will make sure she really behaves. You can put it over her clothes.'

He passed over a thick belt, which the other man proceeded to put round Detty's waist over her silk shirt, which she had been wearing ever since she was taken at the roadside. At first, it was a relief that there were no injections or even handcuffs. Even her clothes had been left alone. She felt particularly vulnerable as her pregnancy would have shown if she had been stripped. At least she did not appear to be in the hands of another Oleg. Gratuitous sexual assaults, at least for the moment, did not appear to be part of the programme. She was relieved for Mara's sake as well as her own. Blue Sweatshirt was talking to her again.

'Don't fiddle with it, try to take it off or play any other tricks or else you will be in for a really big shock.'

He laughed as if he had made some sort of joke.

'Understand? OK let's go.'

She was hustled out of the door catching a last glimpse of Mara looking aghast. She obviously wanted to say something but only got as far as:

'Oh my God, Detti, tell them...'

The solid door slammed shut and Detty never heard what Mara wanted her to tell them.

The passage must have been several hundred metres long and was lined with rough hewn stone. She had not seen it before, as she had still been unconscious probably from the injection when they brought her in. Before they reached the end, they stopped and blindfolded her and she could see no more. The night air struck her face as they reached the open air and she felt herself being bundled forward with her head pushed down. She was in a car. It was no limousine but at least the upholstery was more comfortable than a pickled cucumber lorry. She felt she was becoming an expert on involuntary transport.

The journey lasted several hours and she lost count of time. There was almost no conversation; just enough to indicate that only the two underlings were in the car. Blue Sweatshirt had presumably been left behind with Mara. Detty became increasingly despondent. With every hour that passed the thread that might have linked her to Mara lengthened. Most modern cars would go more than seven hundred kilometres on a tank and that was enough to lose all trace of the starting point. To make things worse, when they did eventually stop to refuel it was not, she thought, at a service station. There was a clanking of Jerry cans from a spare fuel supply in the boot, indicating a roadside fill up. She gave up the pointless task of scanning for clues of whereabouts and started thinking of her own predicament. She assumed that she was wearing a stun belt of the sort that had wreaked such havoc with Masha and Mara and that this accounted for the guard's relaxed attitude to security. After hearing what it could do from Mara, she realised that it also reduced her options effectively to zero, as she had no wish to experience its effects. The best that she could hope for was that she would be exchanged in some sort of trade off in the future. Even this didn't seem very likely and the more she thought about it the more hopeless the outlook became. Gloomy thoughts crowded her mind and, giving up trying to combat them, as the car droned on, she suddenly felt very drowsy and dropped off to sleep.

The nightmare was one that she had had before although less often recently. She was back at the Farm, which was suddenly part of the Hansehaus. The Armourer was bending over her peering into her face. He was getting nearer and nearer and she couldn't move however hard as she tried. Later it wasn't the Armourer but Kovacs, the doctor, with his sardonic grin, telling her that it was useless to struggle. Suddenly she broke through her paralysis and felt herself shriek out and a huge searing agonising cramp pass through her body as every muscle locked tight. Confused she knew that she was awake and that it was real. She was conscious but unable to move voluntarily, twitching in distress and pain on the floor of the car.

She didn't know how the belt had been activated. Whether in her disturbed dream, she had set off the automatic mechanism that prevented the wearer removing the belt. Perhaps, rather, the anxious, inexperienced guard had been worried that in her nightmare restlessness, she was trying a trick and had activated it himself, anyway she never knew. One thing however was clear, the horrible device had been triggered and the dreadful state she was in was the result. The guards, one driving and one in the back with her, were arguing fiercely about what had happened and whose fault it was. The air was thick with expletives in a German dialect but now with so strong an accent that she didn't recognise at all and both seemed frightened by the events. Their concern didn't extend to doing anything to help her, as she lay still helpless, distressed, and blindfolded. She had slipped down over the transmission tunnel on the back floor of the car with her face and arms still twitching against the rough fabric of the guard's jeans.

After what seemed like hours but in reality, was probably only fifteen minutes, she began to get some control back over her muscles and to be able to move voluntarily. Worse however was to come; the pain in her stomach did not improve as the other cramps wore off. It was getting worse and coming in waves. Then as she felt round her nether regions, she realised that she was warm, wet and sticky. She tried to persuade herself that she must have been incontinent during the spasm but in her heart, she knew at once that that was not the explanation. She was bleeding and bleeding severely.

She began to try to tell the still arguing men in the hope that against all the odds they would do something to help her. The only reaction of the man in the back was to kick her viciously and tell her to shut up. Didn't she realise that they had enough problems already without the moaning bitch herself adding to them?

During the argument between the two men as to what they should do, the car had gathered speed and appeared to be cornering fast almost on two wheels. Detty through her troubles heard something about 'at least getting out of the city and finding a bit of space' but there was still no clue as to what city they were talking about. There was a sudden screech of brakes and the rest was blackness.

*

Occasional sounds broke through the darkness. It could be soft talk but unconnected and incomprehensible. This must really be death at last. What language was spoken in the afterlife? Heaven though was strange in other ways, now there were figures in white all right but they didn't seem to move in the right way, they flitted in and out and there were more noises. Flowers too were there in front of her, roses and some tall thin ones that she couldn't quite see. That was good she thought, she hadn't realised that heaven had flowers. Then there was Marc's voice telling her she was going to be all right. Of course, she would be all right, you always were in heaven but why was Marc there? He should be in England with the Army.

But he wasn't, he was sitting by her bedside holding her hand and whispering to her as he always whispered his love-talk. Gradually the hospital room took shape and the flitting figures became nurses and doctors. She still couldn't remember anything except that she had been in a car and something dreadful had happened. She asked where she was and was told Königshof University Hospital. She nodded at this but it made no sense.

Gradually over the next days, as the transfusion in her arm dripped its endless, varied fluids and her body creaked at every slight unguarded movement, she began to be able slowly to piece together the story from Marc. He also left the news reports for her to read as soon as she was well enough. When she was able to read the papers, after nearly a month in hospital, she learnt the full story.

The car in which she had been travelling was spotted by a police video patrol driving recklessly through the western suburbs of Königshof. The police thought that the two occupants were so-called joy riders as there had been an outbreak of teenagers taking cars and driving them away since the recent period of civil unrest.

A police patrol ordered the suspect vehicle to stop in the normal way but instead of obeying, the car, a powerful BMW, drove off at speed. After twenty or thirty kilometres of chase the police managed to sandwich the suspects between two police cars. The suspects tried to escape into a side road over the verge and had hit a bridge stanchion at speed turning their car over several times until it crashed again into a large fir tree.

The driver and male passenger were killed instantly. It was only by chance and good observation that a young police motorcyclist realised that there was a third occupant, totally unsuspected up to then, lying on the rear floor of the crushed wreckage of the vehicle in a pool of blood. The casualty doctor had managed to get a transfusion going under great difficulties inside the wreck, while the *Königshof Feuerwehr* Rescue Vehicle had worked to cut the woman free. When she was finally brought out, she was near death. As soon as it was possible to do a proper examination, it was realised that the woman, as well as having chest injuries, cuts and a broken wrist was miscarrying an advanced pregnancy. The police were also extremely puzzled to find that she was wearing an American pattern prison stun belt of a type, which is used in Court and to transport prisoners in the USA. It is categorically prohibited for use with pregnant women even in those countries where this dreadful device is authorised at all. Most civilised countries, including Livonia, prohibit its use altogether. There had been reported incidences of this equipment being employed by the NAS under the former regime both as a restraint and an instrument of coercion. This may, but only may, have been the possible source of the belt used so devastatingly in this case. Unfortunately, but not surprisingly given the circumstances, the serial number of the belt had been obliterated.

The car had been stolen, by a highly professional method, in Cottbus five days previously. There was no identification of any kind on the bodies or the woman. As soon as she was released from the wreckage, the woman, although she was in a very bad way, had been identified as Bernadette O'Neill, the possessor, after the President and his daughter, of the most photographed face in Livonia. This raised the possibility of a connection between the incident and the recent abduction of Tamara Oblova. Because of the illegal and highly improper use of the stun belt, the police were treating the case as attempted murder.

After the slow painful passage of several further weeks, Detty was well enough for Marc to take her back to Oberdorf. and after a few days to return himself, reluctantly, to England and duty. She was surprised, that this time, she found the presence of several burly Bavarian plain clothes policemen comforting, whereas previously she would have been irritated. Now she realised that she must come to terms with the fact that not only she had been brutally abused but that her resulting highly personal tragedy was now public knowledge in all its horrid intimacy. Such, she supposed, is the price of fame. She had gloried in it last year, now she must pay the price. She knew that for the moment; however, she must try and control her sense of emptiness and grief for the aching loss of her unborn child and try and do something to comfort a desolate Marc and to help to find Mara. She knew that she had a lot of information unknown to the authorities; not least, that she had seen Mara a few days ago. She had to decide who to talk to and how to go about it. The most difficult part might be that wherever Mara was, from the length of the journey before the accident, it certainly seemed a long way from Königshof. In the old days, border formalities would have given some clue but these had disappeared in so many cases and in others were easy to evade. Nothing useful could be gained from that source.

Marc had told her, at his most magisterial, that he was not going to discuss Livonia, its politics or even Mara while she was recovering. So, saying he had swept back to his misery, the dubious summer of West Wales and a new weapons guidance system. He left Hildegard to cluck over his wife as if she had been a five-year-old. A sad Sophie allowed herself an occasional amused half smile. Detty loved Hildegard and didn't entirely mind being cosseted but still she couldn't stop thinking, and the thoughts weren't good.

She sat in the orchard of the *Schloss* in an unexpectedly late Indian summer with the autumn colours in full glory around her and a detective story open on her knees. She couldn't concentrate on the book. Her thoughts revolved round two riddles. Where had Mara been and was she still there? What was it she had half seen in the darkness in the hidden room? The second question intrigued her in itself but she also realised that the contents of that secret room might give a vital clue to their place of imprisonment. What she had seen cued something deep in her past life and yet she still couldn't identify it. She went through the symbolism of her dead daughter, *Fidelio, The Ring,* of Strauss songs and operas and of the horrors of the Farm and the sewers. She had been through so much that was symbolic and dramatic. The answer still wouldn't come and she started thinking about the wider problem. One thing was now quite clear about Mara. She was being held, probably as a means of destabilising the young Livonian democracy, but certainly as a potential bargaining counter to trade off against the two arrested Belorussians who were extremely big players in the illegal drugs and arms racket.

Eventually she gave up trying to figure things out and dozed off over her book. She was woken by a breathless call from the window:

'*Frau Detti, Frau Detti, Herr Marc am apparat*'.

She dashed inside to the telephone wondering what on earth Marc was doing 'phoning her at eleven o'clock on a Tuesday morning when he had left her only the day before.

Marc was never in a hurry, even under fire, and she had to tell him how she was, that she was eating properly, that she had slept well before he came to the point.

'*Schatz*, I have had a strange 'phone call from Lawri in Lübeck saying that there was something that he thought I should know. I explained that it was very difficult for me to come because of my present commitments with the Middle East crisis, I can't say more on the telephone, but you understand. He sounded worried after that and asked if it would be at all possible for you to see him. I thought that it was odd that he had asked for you. I explained that you had just had a bad miscarriage and were resting but that I would think about it and 'phone him back. Mulling it over, I thought that, as he had asked for you, it just possibly might have something to do with this business with Mara and might be really urgent. As you can imagine I didn't like to ring you but I thought that you would never forgive me if I didn't.'

'I'll go straight up there – it won't take long and I feel OK now. Easier than asking him to come down here.'

6
LAWRIE

Hei – Wie zur Mauer sie stürmen
Die bethörten Eigenhold
Zum Schutz ihres schönen Geteufels[21]

WAGNER: PARSIFAL ACT II

The northwest wind blew, unrelentingly, the damp from the port over the Alster as she left the station in the fleeting evening sunshine. The city bustled with a self-confident hum, much thought Detty as it had done for the last millennium with the occasional unscripted interruption. *Die Welt* told her that *Der Freischütz* was being given at the Staatsoper later that evening. She knew that Lawri was not available until the following day. She checked in at the Prem on the Alster and, after hesitating, went to the theatre and booked herself a ticket. Feeling slightly chauvinistically Bavarian, she thought that she would like to see what these northerners could do. She sat over fish soup and a beer, realising sadly that she could stop worrying about alcohol now. She then returned, physically restored, to the opera house.

---

21 Heh! How they rush to the ramparts#
    To defend their beautiful witches!

The opening horn calls rolled her away from criticism into a land of memory and love to such an extent that she forgot to judge the performance at all. She was moved more than she could have imagined by hearing *Ännchen's* narrative and plea in the third act. The joyous day at Oberdorf, when she had sung it as a tribute to her lost friend came back to her forcefully. That experience had been so important to Mara that afterwards she had chosen *Ännchen* as her code name during the civil war. She came out of her dreams with a start; the Hermit was declaiming his prayer:

Doch jetzt erhebt noch eure Blicke[22]
Zu dem der Schutz der Unschuld war

She uttered a silent 'Amen' for Mara. She left the theatre and walked back solemnly along the Aussenalster. The autumn evening was warmer as the wind had calmed and there was a hint of mist over the water. She felt sharply a resolution and determination that was almost irrational. She knew that she must do something and that she now had the strength and confidence that she had not felt since losing the baby. She sensed in her bones that Mara was still alive and she was determined to get to her. She wondered whether the morrow's meeting with Lawri would take her any nearer to finding her.

She set herself up for the day with a generous Hamburg breakfast while she waited for her hired car to be brought round. Irrationally, she was relieved that it arrived intact. She threaded her way out of the city rush hour traffic and headed for Lawri's smokehouse and restaurant at the roadside out towards Lübeck. She had never been there before but, despite its unlikely appearance, she found it fairly easily from Marc's description. She went through past the scribbled blackboards and walked down between the cold cabinets stocked with every possible variety of smoked fish for off sales. As she reached the bar and the grills, the solid square figure of the owner dressed in a Harris Tweed sports

---

22 Let us lift our eyes to the one
    who has been the Protector of the innocent.

jacket came out to welcome her. She was then left to eat a gargantuan meal of local specialities, which taxed her normally healthy appetite and made her regret the Hamburg breakfast.

'You have lost a friend, Frau Gräfin?'

It was half a statement and half a question and Detty just nodded. There was a long silence. Lawri stared hard into the space in front of him as the twist of autumn grey smoke curled out of his huge trumpet shaped pipe. He seemed to be invoking inspiration from the pattern of devastation left by the head and skeleton, which was all that remained on Detty's plate of the formerly majestic grilled herrings. She waited, drawing on her *Weissbier*. The last customers were gradually departing in small groups until the smokehouse dining room, it was hardly a restaurant, was deserted. Lawri had joined her at the *Stammtisch*, reserved for regulars and special guests, near the great stove, unlit and cold in the warm autumn weather. No other table was still occupied. Eventually the pronouncement, when it came, surprised even her:

'If I were you' he said at last. 'I would look hard at the Retreat of Santa Barbara at the Abbey of Pic Noix in the Spanish Pyrenees.'

The result of his deliberations startled Detty even though she had expected something unconventional. She raised one eyebrow quizzically and waited for Lawri to explain.

'You see, Frau Gräfin, in my trade-both of them in fact' he smiled 'you get used to all sorts of people. However, when a request for plans and components for electronic detonators is traced back to a closed convent, it causes some surprise, even to me. I therefore made some discreet enquiries. It appears that life at the Convent may be – how do you say? Many facetted. You will have to forgive me, as I know that both you and the Herr Major are devout church people.

'But what could this possibly have to do with Mara's kidnap?'

'It's rather a long story but I will tell you as much as I can. For some years, members of my little association have received sporadic requests for plans or fittings for sophisticated weaponry from a group in Switzerland. As you know, although we have been known to assist in the supply of arms, in certain cases, we never do so without trying to find out something of the nature of the organisation making the request.'

He paused again drawing on his huge, flared pipe. Detty remembered only too well the speed with which, via Lawri, the Russian tanks, which had turned the Livonian Civil War in the insurgents' favour, had appeared. Marc had explained how the multinational arms traders, working under the apparently innocuous front of gourmet food merchants, took the extremely unusual step of only supplying weapons to those causes that appeared just and reasonable.

'This Swiss group was, we found, rather strange. As we peeled off the layers of the onion, we discovered that it was a front agent for a Belorussian organisation, known as Lev, even that was, we decided, probably not the controlling organisation. They exported weapons to various regimes mainly in North Africa and the Middle East. This didn't surprise us as there are many such groups operating since the fall of the USSR. The unusual part was, however, that normally these groups supply arms to other, as you might say, end-users. In a sense they are our competitors not our customers and yet here they were asking for supplies from us. I must add that at this stage we already knew enough about them to have decided that we would not be supplying them, but we were curious to know what exactly was going on.'

'Fortunately, one of our own group is a Yemeni producer of exotics such as the biblical frankincense and myrrh. By chance, Hasan also produces a particularly refined cultivar of Fenugreek in the Yemen. Some years or so ago a certain North African military dictator became convinced that this, and only this, Fenugreek, was a cure for his dyspepsia. Because of the Yemeni wars, Hasan found it very difficult to find a reliable means of delivering the herb to his customer so twice each year he would take the required amount of extract over the Red Sea and across the Nubian Desert by camel and deliver it himself. Financially the very high fee made even this extraordinary effort worthwhile.'

'In the course of these visits, he became an honoured guest of the General who grew to trust him and treat him as a friend. It was a comparatively simple matter for Hasan to raise, in general conversation, the question of arms supplies. Hasan said, casually, that that he had contacts in this field who might have access to interesting weaponry, which was of course, in a certain sense, true. As we surmised, it turned out that the General was a client of Lev, but, and now it becomes more interesting, he was becoming dissatisfied with them.'

Lawri paused again and asked the barman to bring two coffees before continuing.

'The dissatisfaction was chiefly for two reasons. The first was that their material was becoming increasingly out of date as the technology of the former USSR receded into history. He had, in fact, only recently had to issue an ultimatum to the effect that they must produce some specified state of the art items or else he would look elsewhere for all his requirements. This would, of course, explain why Lev had approached us. You see they desperately needed to find a supplier of up-to-date guidance systems to bolt onto the old Soviet stuff.'

Detty nodded.

'The other problem was unreliable delivery. Apparently, until a year or so ago Lev had used a friendly neighbouring country who had a seaport, a national airline and a dictator who did not ask questions, at least if the money was right. Most unfortunately for them, the friendly dictator had been overthrown in a civil war and the new government didn't go in for that sort of trading.'

'Livonia?' asked Detty, already knowing the answer.

'The same. Lev had told him that they were sorry that deliveries had been a bit unreliable but that they were working hard to get a more sympathetic regime restored in their neighbour by de-stabilising the present government. They didn't specify exactly how they were setting about it but I guess we both know the answer. After all, you only have to read the newspapers.'

'Or get blown up or have your baby killed or your dearest friend kidnapped' Detty blurted out flushed with anger.'

'I am sorry, Frau Gräfin, I didn't mean to be insensitive but I am afraid I was. You have been so badly hurt.'

'I should apologise, Herr Lawri, you have gone out of your way to help and all I do is to have a tantrum. I can't tell you how grateful I am for all that you have told me. It makes sense of so many things.'

'There is a little bit more but it is quite important. Perhaps we should have another coffee and schnapps before I tell you the rest?'

Detty was about to give the automatic refusal that had followed such invitations during her pregnancy, then, with a pang, realised again that it didn't matter now.

'Good idea – thank you.'

The barman had gone off duty so Lawri went to the bar himself, returning with coffee and *apfelbrand*.

'This is *hausegemacht* from our own orchard. You should see it in spring. It's a picture' he said this with the childish pride and simplicity that made him such a complex character. Then, serious, he continued:

'Hasan was concerned by what he had learnt and realised that it involved some interests of mine so he sent the gist of it to me by carrier pigeon, yes, literally, the information went to Djibouti by carrier pigeon. He hasn't caught up with secure e-mail and telephones and the post leaves something to be desired in Yemen. When I got it, I thought that I should let the Herr Major know straight away. As soon as I had spoken to him, I thought I would try and find out a bit more myself. I got in touch with our contact in Lev and told him that I might be able to get some electronic detonators, which were on their requirements list. I explained that it would be very difficult to get them to Minsk and asked whether there was a West European safe point that I could send them to. I thought that in this way I might find out more about the Swiss part of the operation. The contact said he would find out but that first I would have to provide a sample so that their technical expert could check that they were the real thing. We arranged to meet yesterday at a service area near Amsterdam. I never reveal my identity beyond a code name in these deals, except to the Herr Major, of course. I met him in rather different circumstances.'

Detty smiled. She knew that Marc had first met Lawri when he arrested him for arms trading.

'The expert was a Scandinavian, probably a Swede. He checked my sample and said it was OK. The Belorussian then agreed that the deal was on. I had decided that I must come up with some of the goods in order to keep in touch and that I must break our usual rule. We have a standard method of payment through Lichtenstein, which makes sure that the money is available when the goods are released. They agreed to use this. So that only left the question of delivery point. You may imagine that I was surprised when, instead of an address in Switzerland, they told me to deliver to the Retreat of Santa Barbara at the Abbey of Pic Noix in the Spanish Pyrenees.'

Detty who had recovered her composure with the help of the schnapps laughed:

'They chose the right Saint anyway-if she ever existed' she said

'Yes, I thought that. Patron of artillery, miners and demolition experts. However, that was not all, I was even more surprised when they told me my contact was Monsignor Josemaria Pueblo.'

'Ah, the rugby forward with the goatee beard again!'

It was Lawri's turn to look surprised.

'*Bitte?*'

Detty told him of her former meeting with this problematic pillar of the Faith.

*

The stairs at St Conleth's still creaked and still smelt of the polish spread liberally on the darkly shining old oak of the great hall and stairway. The building was a large ascendancy Georgian house, which had been taken over by the Teaching Order early in the 1900s. This had probably saved it from being burnt down during the Civil War, which had been the fate of so many similar buildings. Detty remembered the last time that she had climbed these stairs to receive the private congratulations of the Superior on her scholarship to Oxford before it was announced publicly. Time rolled back as, again, she sat outside the Superior's door on the chair reserved for visitors and pupils waiting to be called in. Mrs Walsh, the secretary, had greeted Detty warmly and had asked some hushed questions about her highly coloured career after she had left the Convent. She had now, rather reluctantly, returned to her word processor. Apart from the soft thud of the keyboard, the only sound to be heard was the ticking of the handsome long-case clock, which stood opposite the imposing inner door.

As she sat waiting, Detty thought over her tactics for the thousandth time. Rather more than her last honoured visit, it reminded her of the many times that as a talented but free-thinking student she had had to pay visits to the Superior after some minor offence or irregularity. The problem this time, however, was very different. She needed to get Mother Immaculata's recommendation for a visit to the Abbey of Pic Noix and the Retreat of Santa Barbara. Ironically, she knew that she could have got the necessary introduction from The Sacred Heart at Ziatow or indeed any other Convent in Livonia but any reference to Livonia would immediately alert the enemy. It was safer, therefore, if more difficult, to go back to her Irish roots. She was very reluctant to lie to the Superior but, equally, to tell the whole truth about the reason for her going was impractical and might be counterproductive. She had decided on a partial truth and hoped that she could make it sound plausibly convincing whilst at the same time not lead her into deep sin. Her Jesuit confessor at Oxford she knew would have approved of her practical attempt to reach a greater good and absolved her but she was not so sure about Mother Immaculata.

At that moment the door opened and the Superior with her handsome smiling face, came out into the Anteroom.

'Bernadette, how very good to see you' she said in an Oxford English modified only by a slight native softness.

'Come in and please sit down. Will you have a coffee?'

Mrs Walsh was asked if she would be so kind as to get the coffee and the Superior closed the door.

'Thank you for all your letters. I was so terribly sorry to hear about the baby. How are you feeling now?'

'Still very empty but I am keeping busy with my course at Manchester and some singing engagements.'

'And high politics in Livonia? Are the troubles serious?' the Superior smiled. Detty knew of old that she was very well informed about the world stage:

'It's an unstable area, so some unrest is to be expected but of course the most serious thing at present is the kidnapping of Frau Tamara, the President's daughter.'

'And a close friend of yours?'

'Very close indeed, Reverend Mother.'

This wasn't the way that Detty had wanted the conversation to go but she realised that it would be a mistake to change the subject abruptly. Fortunately, at that moment, the Superior did it for her.

'How about the Royal Northern College of Music? Is it all practical singing or do you do any theoretical work. I remember your compositions while you were here, do you still compose?'

Detty smiled:

'It is very largely practical singing at performer's level without much opportunity for composition. I am, however, doing a musical historical dissertation and I wondered if I might ask you a favour in connection with it?'

'Please ask.'

'I am studying the music of the pilgrimages to Santiago di Compostella. There is an immense amount of material available. Some, however, of great interest, which is not well known, is, I think, still in Monasteries along the routes but particularly in the Pyrenees. It would help my work to visit their libraries and I wonder if it would be at all possible to provide me with an introduction to these Houses so that I can visit them.'

'Which Houses mainly interest you?'

'There are three in particular. The Convent of the Incarnation at Alderita, the Abbey of Pic Noix and perhaps the Convent of St Theresa at Lasquete.'

'The Incarnation is a sister House of ours so there would be no difficulty in your visiting that and, indeed, staying there. It is in a wonderful position. I visited it for an Educational Conference about ten years ago. Pic Noix is very near at hand at the head of the next valley. I don't know anyone there personally. The Abbess of St Theresa I met in Rome so I can certainly introduce you there. When do you want to go?'

'Straight away if I can. The dissertation needs to be finished by the end of the year.'

'May I ask you in turn one favour before we part?'

Detty, startled by this sudden reversal of roles stammered.

'Yes, of course'

'Would you come and sing for us at the open day before Christmas? It would be such a great event to have our famous pupil back.'

'Of course, I will. What sort of programme?'

'I have thought of that. If you agree perhaps a small operatic excerpt, one or two songs – Irish or foreign as you wish, and possibly a couple of Christmas pieces with the Choir to finish. Is that too much?'

'Certainly not. Would it be all right if my husband came to accompany me? He loves Ireland and I would like to show him, and show him off, at my old school.'

The Superior smiled. She remembered that Bernadette O'Neill had never been one for beating about the bush.

'Of course not, he would be most welcome.'

'I'll let you know nearer the time the pieces that I have chosen in case you want to change anything.'

'Certainly, but I am sure that I won't.'

*

The train had been the way to travel. She preferred it and anyway it was less ostentatious, more anonymous than driving or flying, besides it was very quick through France and got her closer to her destination. She changed at Bayonne from the TGV onto the slower train that would take her through to Saint Jean Pied de Port. She had talked to the Superior at the Incarnation who seemed anxious to welcome her and had offered a car. The car was waiting at the station for her, the driver a cheerful sun-beaten Basque, carried her rucksack with due ceremony into the boot of the car. She wound down the window of the car in the fading heat of the late summer day as they climbed into the cool of the mountains. The panorama of cork oaks, mixed with the scent of the wild thyme and the sound of the cicadas took her back to Italy, and yet it was different. Somehow it sounded sparser and wilder even than her tower of incarceration in Tuscany. Her room in the strangers' house had a low-beamed ceiling. It was sparsely furnished but somehow very comfortingly reminiscent of her early convent life. Despite her anxiety to hurry, she spent the first two days in the library, partly seeking her avowed material on the pilgrim music, partly to establish her bona fides. On the third day, she got up early as usual for Matins and then clutching her introduction from the Mother Superior of The Incarnation, she began her walk back towards the Camino di Santiago and Pic Noix. The Superior had been kindness itself and had tried to telephone through to Pic Noix to arrange for Detty's visit. She had come back from making the call looking puzzled.

'I think it will be all right' she had said 'I got through to one of the brothers who seemed reluctant to pass me on to the Prior or anyone more senior. At first, he said that they didn't have visitors, which seems very strange particularly as they have a Retreat for both men and women attached to their House. When I explained that you were not an ordinary visitor but a music scholar from Ireland, he relented a little and said rather grudgingly that he supposed you had better come. To tell you the truth we don't have a lot of contact with them, as we are very busy teaching and they have very different activities, manuscript calligraphy and training associated with Opus Dei and that kind of thing, I believe, but of course we all serve the Lord in our different ways.'

It was this doubtful beginning that had decided Detty to make the journey on foot. If she appeared as a pilgrim scholar in the time-honoured way, she thought it might be more acceptable. She stopped for lunch at the only village she passed. The meal consisted of *Ardi-gasna* cheese from the black faced ewes that had watched her, suspiciously, as she walked, washed down with a generous glass of the full bodied, gutsy Navarra wine which stood up well to the fierce challenge of the cheese. Her father-in-law would, she was sure, have approved. She was in some doubt however as to how to make her approach and whether it would be obvious where women were allowed to go. Also, she realised that if the Retreat really was the centre of clandestine activities, strangers wandering aimlessly around would immediately be suspect. She mulled this over while sitting in the bar over her food. Deciding that it was probably pointless making plans in advance, she gave up and took in her surroundings. There was only one other person in the bar. He was a fair-haired man in his late twenties with a high forehead. He was eating a meal similar to hers. As she looked round, he smiled and said:

'Are you going to Compostella?' The voice had a soft drawl from south of the Mason-Dixon Line.

Detty smiled back and nodded.

'Eventually, but I've got some other things to do on the way.'

As they talked, she learnt that Craig, her companion, was a postgraduate student of medieval European history from Duke University. He was touring Europe collecting material for a PhD on the treatment of the poor by the military religious orders. They talked for some time about their research interests until suddenly he said:

'It's quite extraordinary, you know, earlier this year I was in the Baltic and was invited by the Professor that I was visiting, to attend an investiture of the Livonian Order of St Nicklaus in a place called Königshof. I wanted to find out if the work of the medieval knights was in any way reflected in present day activities. Well, this was an impressive ceremony but the strange thing was that one of the high functionaries of the Order, a Commander, was a striking young woman and do you know – she looked really like you.'

'How queer but, as I have told you, I'm from Ireland' said Detty relying on the truth, if not the whole truth, exaggerating slightly her accent and trying to look much more relaxed than she felt. She thanked heaven that he had previously only heard her speak Latin and German. The last thing that she needed at this juncture was to have her cover blown in such an unexpected fashion.

He was a pleasant guy but she was relieved when they said their goodbyes and went their separate ways. He continued along the main path whilst she took a steeper track leading through the *maleza* towards the still-hidden Abbey, which, she thought, from the map should be high over the next ridge. She looked back to the main track stretching white into the distance below for a moment. She tried to find Craig who should have been on it but he was nowhere to be seen. She thought that that was a bit strange but there could have been many reasons. She went back to thinking about her own route and after a short while she was relieved to see the rounded, grey slated towers arising out of the densely wooded slope opposite. Her track wound between the trees, crossing the now-dry bed of a winter stream at the bottom of the valley. Not long after the first glimpse, she lost sight of her objective again as the track began to climb underneath the Abbey. She trudged on now climbing steeply round wild cork oaks and rocky outcrops invading the track. It was hard going and brought home to her that she was still weak and unfit after her miscarriage and accident. The afternoon sun was hot and she was glad that she had remembered to bring two bottles of water and also of her wide-brimmed hiker's hat. However, the trees provided shade and the altitude, some freshness.

The Abbey had disappeared for so long that she began to think that she had indeed lost her way. Then the track turned sharply in front of her under a massive overhanging rock and emerged onto a wide gravelled forecourt. The Abbey re-appeared and soared above her. On either side were the twin towers that she had seen across the valley, between there was a shallow arch guarding the heavy timber main doors, which were firmly barred. Above the first arch was another smaller one over a parapet and above that rose, massively, the central cloche with its latticework drum surmounted by the hexagonal tower. On her right, stretching downward into the valley was a long lower building with three stories of small windows. She imagined that this might be the Retreat. On the remaining side, to her left were a number of small buildings of simpler construction in timber and plaster, which could have been storehouses. In the middle of these stood a gatehouse enclosing a wide wrought iron portcullis, which apparently opened onto the main drive up to the Abbey from the Pamplona Road.

There was not a soul about. The sun, now trapped into the treeless courtyard, beat down even more fiercely as she inspected the great door for signs of a bell. There were none. To the side, however, recessed under the left-hand tower was a small door with an old-fashioned iron bell pull. She pulled the bell and the door opened quickly revealing an aesthetically austere young monk. He peered enquiringly and disapprovingly at her. The image of *Leonora* flooded into her mind. It was not her idol, the triumphant *Retterin* of *Fidelio*, rather that other *Leonora*, the wretched *Leonora di Vargas*, throwing herself on the mercy of the Father Superior under the moonlight at the gate of the Convent of the Madonna degli Angeli in Verdi's *La Forza del Destino*.

Infelice, delusa, rejetta
Dalla terra e del ciel maladetta,[23]

'*Mi liamo Bernadette O'Neill*' she stammered hoping that here in the Pyrenees her name, at least, would help her gain acceptance.

'And what do you want?' asked the young man with unbending severity 'it is the hour of the Mass.'

Detty, thoroughly wrong-footed, stammered again conscious that she stood condemned for blasphemy in the young monk's eyes.

'*Lo siento mucho,*' she said acutely conscious of the banality of the words:

'I have an introduction from the Mother Superior at the Convent of the Incarnation to the Father Superior here to study in the library.'

She proffered her letter, which the young man took distastefully.

'Follow me. I will take you to the Strangers House at the Retreat. You can wait there until a proper time.'

She followed his wafer-thin erect figure across the courtyard to the entrance of the lower building that she had noticed earlier. Without looking at her again he showed her through the shadowy hall into a waiting room furnished with dark furniture and smelling of beeswax polish and, more faintly, of incense. Without a word, he then turned on his heel and departed, turning the key in the lock as he went. The house was eerily silent. She assumed that the residents, if any, were at Mass. She sat down to think.

From her Convent schooldays onwards, she had visited many religious establishments and, although it was true some were more solemn than others, the sacred law of hospitality was always obeyed. This seemed to be the exception. Not only had she been greeted with cold disdain but also, she had been locked in. Why?

The obvious explanation was that there really was something sinister to hide in this Pyrenean fastness. Lawri was no fool and certainly wouldn't have sent her on a fool's errand. On the other hand, there might be several perfectly innocent explanations. It might be just a measure of the severity of the Rule or it might be the fact that she was

---

23 Unhappy, downcast, rejected,
Accursed in earth and heaven.

a woman invading a male abbey. The last seemed less likely as she knew that it was not an exclusively male preserve. A nunnery was attached to the Abbey and the Retreat was said to cater for both men and women, although so far, she had seen no evidence of either. She settled to read an ageing dog-eared copy in Italian of *La Famiglia Cristiana*, which was the only reading matter available. After about half an hour, her young monk returned, he now looked slightly less severe, and beckoned to her to follow. He led her back through the small door with the bell and immediately into the gate tower and up a spiral staircase. The stairway led to a small landing on the first floor. The monk knocked at the only door. Detty panicked. She had been jocular about Jose Maria Pueblo to Lawri in the safety of Lübeck, but supposing she found herself face-to-face with him now, which seemed more than likely? He had been introduced to her in Florence and she knew that she was not easily forgotten, even by a man of the cloth.

She heaved a sigh of relief. An imposing man, much taller than Pueblo, had opened the door, revealing a bare room furnished with prayer desk and, rather incongruously, computer and fax machine with their accessories. The tall, dignified man was smiling warmly at Detty:

'I am Father Ferdinand, the Abbot here' he said in English 'Thank you for your visit to our community. I am sorry that you have been kept waiting but, you understand, the Office must come first.'

'Of course, Father'

'But for all that, you are most welcome. You are studying the music of the *Camino Frances*? Well, you are in the right place. We have a wealth of Archives here relating to the Way of St James.'

*

The Library, the Conservation Studio and the Scriptorium formed a large complex on the first floor of the Abbey over the chapel. Behind lay the refectory and the dormitories, which were forbidden to outsiders and most of all to women. Even the nuns in the sister house just a few hundred metres down the valley were allowed in only during the closed monks' Mass to clean. The layout however meant that Detty could be allowed a desk in the semi-public atrium between the library and the Scriptorium. This wide space housed several desks for the use of scholars visiting the Abbey and a massive oak refectory table with information leaflets about the Abbey and its work arranged on it. From her desk, she was able to see through the wrought iron gates that lead to the library at the back overlooking the cloister and to the Scriptorium at the front overlooking the courtyard in front of the chapel. On the far side of the Scriptorium through another door was the Restoration Studio devoted to the repair and welfare of the magnificent collection of manuscripts and incunabulae, which the Abbey housed. These Detty could see in the library through the gate on her left. Serried ranks of cream coloured vellum-bound treasures stretched back on their stacks as far as the eye could see into the deep recesses of the library.

One of the Librarian brothers had been placed at Detty's disposal to fetch the texts that she needed from the stacks. He had told her that, until the Civil War, the Library had been completely open to visitors. The spate of post-war thefts had forced the order to close the library and observe the most rigorous security measures.

It was, however, the Scriptorium that was the Abbey's real pride. One of the last remaining in the world, it followed the great ancient tradition of monk-calligraphers who had copied out the literary heritage of the world until the advent of printing in the fifteenth century. The manuscripts of Pic Noix, she learnt, had become world famous and, although modern, were scarce, collectible and fetched increasingly astronomic prices. Only the previous year an illuminated copy of the lyric poems of the Nobel Laureate, Miguel Maria Jimenez, had been put up for auction by the poet's estate. It had fetched a figure at a Sotheby's sale in New York, which rivalled the sort of amount to be expected from a fine medieval Book of Hours. The Abbey produced perhaps twenty or thirty large books a year with varying degrees of decoration and illumination. Many, she had learnt, were used as presentation volumes by the Spanish state and other prestige public bodies. Recently however they had also developed a series of handwritten pamphlets, mainly biblical texts from the Latin vulgate, which, whilst still much prized, were clearly more widely commercial.

Detty looked across through the inner open gate at the two monks each with small piles of these exquisitely written pamphlets in front of him. She then turned her attention back to King Theobaldo of Navarre and the songs of the Troubadours on the Way of St James. She had learnt a bit about deciphering the script and the words were beautiful. It was however difficult to decide exactly how the music had been played and sung. Many of the modern performing versions contained a good deal of guesswork. One thing that she had been told was certainly true. Here at Pic Noix, there was indeed a wealth of material on this music. Normally her fascination in the work would have been all-absorbing but, at this time, she was acutely aware that her first task was to trace Mara. There had been nothing during her first day spent at the Abbey to arouse her suspicions and she was beginning to fear that it was all a wild goose chase.

She cleared her table, piling the texts to one side and gathering up her notes. She had to wait some minutes before her monk appeared and she could return the texts to his custody. She looked at her watch. Time for supper and Complin. She went down to the Chapel where the two communities, men and women, had gathered. To her relief there was still no sign of Jose Maria Pueblo. Far away with anxiety and frustration, she listened to the gloomy verses of the ninetieth psalm. She didn't know the Spanish words but from their similarity and from her ecumenical Oxford days, she recognised many of the lines in the King James Version:

> 'Thou turnest man to destruction; and
> sayest, Return, ye children of men.'
> *Again later:*
> Make us glad according to the days,
> wherein thou hast afflicted us, and the
> years wherein we have seen evil.

The mood was congruent with her despair and helplessness. The Office over she wandered out into the warm evening sunshine and down through the gate onto the road up from the valley. Deep in gloom and unconscious of the need to find her return route, she left the track and plunged deeper into the *maleza* amidst the cicadas and the pervasive scent of the wild thyme. She realised that she had gone further than she had intended and started to try and retrace her steps. She had no real fear of being permanently lost because she knew that by following the contour of the hill she should, eventually come back to the track. The light was beginning to go, as the sun came down to the mountains. She did not want to seem impolite and draw attention to herself by being late back at the hostel. She realised she was not going back the way that she had come and was beginning to get slightly anxious as the scrub was quite thick.

Suddenly, to her relief she saw a flattened passage in front of her going in the right direction. It looked like a rough path and something or someone had passed along it not long before. It wasn't very wide and she stumbled over the shoe before she saw it. It was a plain trainer bearing a well-known maker's ticket stitched to the side. Gripped by a sudden chill in the warm evening, Detty realised that the shoe was still on a foot. Horrified she parted the scrub, revealing first a bare leg, then a pair of shorts, blood-stained tee shirt, rucksack open with its contents spilled out and finally the white still face. It was Craig, the young American that she had lunched with the day before. She covered the body up again quickly and stumbled back to the track trying to think. There was one fact. Craig had been shot, murdered. There was no way that his body could have been there, in that state from natural causes. Although she had not turned the body over and seen the actual wound, from the blood it must have been in the front or the far side of his chest. He could not have injured himself that severely from a fall and somebody had rifled his rucksack. Natural causes were impossible.

This conclusion however raised more problems than it solved. First why? Was it a casual bandit killing for theft? Possible, but unlikely. A professional bandit would realise that a walking pilgrim was unlikely to be the bearer of riches. Was there a maniac operating in the area? Imponderable. Was there some unknown personal reason for his death, for example a *crime passionnel*? Again imponderable. Her last thought was the most worrying. Was Craig's declared motive for being there, like her own, a cover for other activities? If so, he had been discovered and brutally stopped. She had fled from the body with a definite sense that she herself might be in even more danger and now this feeling became even stronger. As she reached the track, she had an impulse to turn right and leave Pic Noix forever. She realised however that to run now without explanation might arouse suspicions and lead the murderers, if they were connected with the Abbey, to her tracks round the body. The other, and the true reason, that she decided to go back was the realisation that she might actually be nearer to discovering Mara's whereabouts.

She reached the strangers' house, which was to her relief still unlocked. Exhausted she slipped into bed, relieved to be on the first floor, away from possible intruders, at least from the outside. She did not get to sleep for several hours, tossing and turning until youth and exhaustion took over. Suddenly the sun was streaming through the narrow window, the birds were singing and it was times for Matins and the day.

The library was exactly as before and she tried to get on with her work and put the image of Craig's body out of her mind. She envied Brother Placido as, a few metres away he calmly and carefully, wrote out his beautiful texts. Today he was by himself in the Scriptorium. His companion presumably had duties elsewhere. After Matins they walked back together to the Library, he told her he had been a mining engineer for some years in Australia before entering the Order and, rather incongruously, spoke good English with the heavy accent of the Australian outback.

'May I look at one of your texts?' asked Detty.

'Of course, I'll show you one.' he replied.

The text was from St Paul to the Ephesians, on the duty of obedience, in the Latin of the Vulgate. The Chancellery script was perfect and beautiful. The capital letter of each passage was left blank.

'Brother Luis, the illuminator, fills that it when he decorates the margins.' Placido explained.

'Are they all illuminated?' She asked fascinated.

'No some are plain text and there are different degrees of illumination. Obviously if a lot of gold leaf is used it costs more.'

'Who buys most of them?'

'Mostly churches, mainly in America but also recently South America and Eastern Europe.'

'They must be expensive. Can people in Eastern Europe really afford them?'

'Some people seem to have the money, however that is really nothing to do with me. I am just the calligrapher. Brother Luis and his department handle all the business side as well as the illumination. Here he is now.'

A tall monk with deep-set eyes and a heavy beard shadow appeared from the stairs carrying a dozen small cardboard document tubes. He looked disapprovingly at Detty and with a muttered word in Spanish. Detty, feeling guilty, scuttled back to her own work. Brother Luis collected the pile of finished texts and added them to the document tubes. He had large hands but still had some difficulty in holding everything. Suddenly the bell rang for Tierce and the two monks hurriedly left. Visitors were not expected at this Office so she stayed at her desk but found it hard to concentrate. Idly she noticed that the contents of one of Brother Luis's tubes had slipped out and fallen on the stone floor. She got up to retrieve the roll intending to put it safely on Brother Placido's desk. She rattled the wrought iron gate but it had clanged shut as the brothers left so, unable to get into the scriptorium proper, she put it carefully on the side of her own desk to give it back when he returned after the service.

The *Camino Frances* demanded her attention again. She had found a previously unknown text of Pilgrim songs, which she was trying to decipher. Although she was excited by her find, it was difficult to concentrate and she struggled too with the strange notation and its irregular marks, which she usually found an absorbing challenge from the past. Perhaps it was the horror of the day before but her concentration was wandering. The marks didn't make sense and the message from long ago didn't emerge clearly. Out of the corner of her eye, she saw the decoration on the edge of the roll, which had dropped out of Brother Luis's tube. She assumed that it was the finished, illuminated, version of the text, which she hadn't yet been shown. Her curiosity overcame her and she unrolled the parchment. She was thunderstruck. Before her eyes was a riot of gold leaf, fabulous beasts, branches, florets, and stars in the initial capital and round the margin, all executed with minute meticulous beauty and skill. She looked at it in wonder gazing at the multicoloured flowers and animals intertwined in apparent disorder but, in fact, composing an elegant and harmonious whole. It was amazing to think that such things could still be produced today. She compared it to the musical score she had just being studying but she had to admit it was far more beautiful although, of course, it had no underlying meaning to be unravelled.

Sighing she put the text down and replaced the letter on top in order to re-roll them together. She glanced at the letter. It was mundane, modern, and, to her surprise, in English. The address was the Church of Santa Barbara, Novoborosina, Ukraina. It said that the text was enclosed as ordered, to the purchaser's specific requirements and that it was hoped that it would be to their entire satisfaction. Payment had been arranged in US Dollars to a certain account in a bank in Kiev and would they check to see that the details of their account were accurate. Detty quickly rolled the two gently together and was idly wondering what the cost of a thing of such beauty would be. When Placido returned from Tierce, she gave him the text commenting on its remarkable beauty. He smiled:

'It won't be sent for a few days. I'll leave it with you until to-morrow so you can really admire the miniatures but don't take it out of the building and you must let me have it back first thing to-morrow.' He put it carefully back on her desk.

'Brother Luis is a genius and a many sided one. He was an academician as an engineer in Russia before he joined the order. He learnt to illuminate in a monastery in – in' he hesitated, trying to remember 'one of those little countries that are always being fought over and changing their name – Moldavia – no that wasn't it but like that.'

'Moltravia?' prompted Detty.

'Yes, that's the one. I think it's called something else now. Monsignor Pueblo introduced him to us.'

Detty held back her urge to tell him exactly what it was called now but did ask innocently.

'Is Monsignor Pueblo a member of the Order here?'

'It is his Mother House but he is seldom here! He is a travelling Legate, attached to Opus Dei, I think. He arranges for charitable goods for the third world to be collected here and then dispatched to their destinations. He travels all over the world but it is strange that you should ask as he is due here to-morrow in connection with some goods from a charitable foundation in north Germany, I think. He sometimes dispatches a few scripts as gifts and tokens of gratitude to those who have helped him overseas but Brother Luis arranges that with him.'

Detty, anxious to have some time to digest all this information, went back to her desk. She pondered over the beautiful scroll for some minutes then her thoughts drifted. Almost certainly, the letter addressed to the Ukraine near the Belarus border was one of Monsignor Jose Maria's little 'thank yous' but she wondered what further significance it might have. Undoubtedly her presence at Pic Noix would be much more hazardous once Monsignor Pueblo arrived. On the other hand, she desperately wanted to know more before she tried to leave.

The Way of St James was now even more inaccessible as she tried to make sense of the strangely disquieting information she had gleaned. A text addressed to a small town in the Ukraine and a man who had learnt to illuminate like an angel in Livonia, introduced by a high cleric who seemed to bode nothing but evil. She finished work, supped frugally in the Strangers' House. She went straight to bed without her usual walk in the cool of the mountain evening. She felt now that it would lead only to danger or even death. She tried to study her part as *Tatiana* in *Onegin* but her mind still kept circling round the events of the day, finding no answers although she was sure that she had uncovered at least some parts of the jigsaw but there must be more that was escaping her.

Frustrated, she went to bed and tossed and turned. She thought of Marc and Bayreuth but somehow her mind always turned back to Mara, Craig, Brother Luis, and the increasingly sinister Monsignor. She was obsessed with the feeling that the vital clue was under her nose and she was failing, in not seeing it.

About four she finally slept. Of a sudden, she was wide-awake. It was six o'clock, the birds were singing in the glorious Pyrenean dawn chorus and she knew what it was that had troubled her. Why was Brother Luis informing his clients that payment would be made to a bank in Kiev? First, although it was possible that the Order had a bank account in Kiev it seemed unlikely and, second, the wording, which at first, she had taken as a request for payment in slightly quaint foreign English, was in fact a notification of payment in entirely correct business English. A further factor, which like the others was that payment was to be made in US dollars and had to be checked. This was the job of the recipient not the sender. Another thing, a payment to a Spanish Monastery would surely have been in Euros, the established international currency of Europe, whilst on the other hand a payment to an Eastern European agency, particularly a somewhat dubious one, might well be required in US dollars. The conclusion was that the notification related to payment for something other than the beautiful text accompanying the letter.

She got up and walked in the orchard listening to the singing birds in the morning freshness. It might not be safe but she was in no mood to care. If the payment was the other way round and not for the text, why send the text? Such objects were extremely valuable and she knew that these modern illuminated documents already fetched huge sums in the auction rooms of the world. Surely, they would not be given away wantonly? The whole riddle was like walking up a mountain in that no sooner was one crest scaled than another appears beyond.

The answer had to lie in the text and probably, she felt, related to something more valuable, possibly many times more valuable, than the beautiful scroll. She knew what she had to do. She needed copies of the scrolls, at least one, if possible, more. She needed a cipher expert. Something niggled at the back of her mind about cipher experts. She could send it to Marc in Norway but that would be complicated and would take too long. First, get the copies anyway.

She spent the day on tenterhooks. There was no question of concentrating on the pilgrim songs but she tried to look as normal as possible. It reminded her of the night exploit at the Farm. Eventually it was time to leave for the Office. She allowed a sheet of notes to fall onto the floor under her desk. It wasn't much but it might just give her a needed excuse if she was caught returning later. She kept in the shadows at the back of the Abbey. Monsignor Pueblo had indeed come.

She recognised him sitting next to the Abbot. She slipped out of the church promptly at the end of the service.

At midnight, she put on a bum bag with her passport, money and credit card and took her darkened back-packers torch, hiding everything beneath a chunky sweater. Fortunately, even in summer there was a nip in the night air at this altitude so she thought the sweater wouldn't seem completely absurd. She crept back towards her desk with the excuse ready that she needed the notes that she had left there. The outer gate to the library was firmly locked. Tantalisingly she could see the scroll was still there on her desk but she couldn't reach it. Disappointed, she abandoned the attempt and climbed the stairs towards the upper offices. Luck was with her. Father Luis's studio was open and the scrolls for dispatch were lying on his desk in their tubes. She seized three or four at random. The Abbot's room was up another short flight of stairs and she needed the copier that she had seen there with the computer. The door was locked. All was in vain.

She searched about helplessly. Put the scrolls back and abandon the attempt, she thought. She would have just one more try; she frenziedly shook the door in frustration. It didn't give. Suddenly an alarm shrilled through the building. She knew that evil was around her and that they had killed already, possibly in error, but killed they had. In blind panic, still clutching the original scrolls, she ran down the stairs, missed the ground floor and found herself in the basement.

It probably saved her life. She could hear the search going on above her accompanied by some very un-Christian oaths. There in the gloom was a window. She dared not shine her torch. She fumbled towards it. It was locked but only on the inside and easy to undo. She climbed through the window into the grateful cool night air. The undergrowth was thick but she knew, roughly, where the path down to the road should be from her previous walks. Force forward through the scrub – she said to herself – it must be soon. Suddenly the *maleza* cleared and to her right was a field with several horses grazing in the moonlight. This everyday sight began to restore her confidence.

Then she heard the dogs. As once before in Italy, she froze, dogs terrified her and this time there was no pond to shelter her. She looked about desperately, stuffed the scrolls into her tee shirt and, in her panic, performed an entirely automatic, apparently senseless action. She flung herself at the nearest mare throwing her leg over her back and digging her heels into her side. She clung on desperately waiting for the horse to bolt with fright. To her relief and surprise, the mare was not spooked by the assault but started to canter down the field. As they gathered speed, the girl from Kildare bent low over her neck and muttered encouragement into her mount's ear in English and Irish, as naturally as she had done since she climbed onto her first pony as a tiny child. The Spanish mare recognised the firm, assured touch of a natural horsewoman and broke into a gallop towards the grim darkness of the wood, as Detty clung on. The black wall of forest hurtled towards them and Detty saw herself being torn by the ragged branches. Her mount knew the land better than she did, however, and the next moment they had jumped a gate and were rushing together down a previously hidden woodland path. She clung on bareback still whispering endlessly the endearments that girls have been sharing with horses since the special relationship between the two first began.

Of her own accord, the mare dropped to a canter as they left the woods and there below the rider saw the few night-time lights of a village. They continued down the mountain more slowly. There was now no apparent sign of pursuit.

She dared not disturb anyone in the village and took her mount into an empty, juicy, lowland field just outside the last houses to wait for dawn. She lay down and dozed fitfully with the mare cropping noisily but tranquilly beside her. Twice a car passed with headlights full on and once she heard the sound of shouting from the village below.

As dawn broke, she realised that she had been riding a young Haflinger filly, who now stood unconcernedly cropping the grass. Wet and wet-eyed, she kissed the horse and muttered her thanks and goodbyes before turning to walk to the bus stop in the village street. There were two or three shops. The small grocer and baker showed some signs of life. She felt hungry but didn't want to declare her presence to the shopkeepers who might be interrogated later. The third shop was a sort of general farmers' store, which was still in darkness. She lingered in the doorway trying to make herself as inconspicuous as possible. A pleasant voice behind her startled her. She didn't hear or understand what the woman had said but thought probably that she had asked if she needed something. She shook her head smiling and, fortunately, at that moment a bus arrived.

She climbed on board muttering:

La ciudad, por favor[24]

A heavily accented stream of Spanish greeted her. She only caught:

'...*los billettes*...'

She assumed that he was saying that she should have had a ticket before getting on the bus and muttered:

'*Perdoneme!*' smiling at him as winsomely as possible.

It must have worked because he shrugged his shoulders, smiled back and motioned her into the body of the bus. Nevertheless, she must have stuck out like a sore thumb on this morning Navarraise workers' bus full of locals. For the moment, there was nothing she could do and sat silently thinking out her next move. The bus crawled further down the mountain stopping frequently to pick up school children and women probably going to do their shopping. The rush hour to work was already past. While they waited at one stop, a jeep rushed past full of men. It was going too fast for anybody inside to be recognisable but she was almost certain that it was the one that she had seen parked at the monastery. She hoped that her pursuers, who had must have realised that she had taken the scrolls, hadn't already found her mare,

After an age, they arrived in the main square of a medium sized town. All the passengers started to get out and Detty joined the middle of the crush to the exit. As she reached the exit, she stared in horror across the square. She stumbled and missed her footing, just recovering herself. The jeep, which had passed them on the mountain, was parked outside a bar across the square. The occupants had finished their morning coffee and were trooping out of the door. They wore jeans and gilets, which bulged ominously at the pockets. Worse still, two of them Detty realised that she had last seen in monks' habits singing the Office across the

---

24 The town, please

Monastery chapel. There was nowhere to go. If she walked on with the crowd, she had to pass within a few metres of the jeep and she would be bound to be recognised. If she ran off by herself, she would be even more conspicuous. Frozen with fear, she hesitated, waiting amongst the small group who were still at the bus stop. Most of the men had got back in the jeep but seemed in no hurry to move off. After what seemed like hours but was probably no more than seconds, the group began to stir and a second bus, larger and smarter than the other, swept round the corner into the square. Keeping her head down, Detty climbed onboard with the others. The woman in front of her asked for St Jean and, automatically, she did the same. Apparently, this time it was OK to pay on the bus. She shoe-horned herself into a seat and checked that the scrolls were still in place under her sweater. She looked back at the jeep as they pulled out of the square. To her relief, the men were still reading their papers and it made no attempt to follow and presumably they would not think to search the regular morning village bus.

7
RUNES

Verträger Runen
Schnitt Wotan
In des Speeres Schaft[25]

WAGNER: *GÖTTERDÄMMERUNG* PROLOGUE

Detty wondered anxiously where they were going. She thought that St Jean was familiar. But there were many St Jeans in France and she hoped that it was the right one – St Jean Pied a Porte. The signs said that they were heading towards the village of St Etienne and she was reassured. She must have seen it written up somewhere on her travels and she knew it was in the right direction. It was not until they reached the unguarded French frontier at the bottom of the pass that she knew definitely, with relief, that they were back in France. A short time later they crossed the river into the wide Place Charles de Gaulle of St Jean.

She got out and immediately made for the small station on the outskirts. There was one more train to Bayonne that day but she had to wait three hours. She walked back to the centre and as the tourists and

---

25 Wotan carved contracts into the spear's shaft

pilgrims began to mass, exhausted she flung herself into the Bar des Pelerins and ordered a pastis, quickly followed by *un croque monsieur, une coupe rouge* and finally a coffee. Feeling more relaxed she walked up the riverside path out of the town, sat down by the stream and tried to work things out. Instead, lulled by fatigue and the alcohol, she fell fast asleep and awoke with only ten minutes to go to catch the train. She just made it, and once on the train to Bayonne, it all seemed clearer. She needed a cipher expert who could at a stroke confirm or deny her suspicions about the manuscript. She thought again of asking Marc who she should go to. He was, however, in Norway or England, she wasn't sure which at that moment, and, anyway, possibly not in immediate touch with his Stuttgart colleagues. Much as he cared about Mara, Detty felt that it would be unfair to go straight to him and she should at least try her own contacts first. That meant Liese Zahnsdorf. It was very late when she got to Bayonne and she felt it was better not to try and 'phone Livonia that night. She found a small unpretentious hotel in a side street, which didn't seem too concerned at her lack of luggage and foreign accent. She showered and flung herself into bed.

By six o'clock, she was up and walked down to the river. The morning was fresh with the sun still behind the Pyrenees to the east. For reasons of security, she had not brought a cell phone but she found a public 'phone box and dialled the Hansehaus on her scrambled number. Fortunately, Falk was on duty again and her spirits increased as she heard his friendly '*Ja, natürlich, Frau Hauptmann*' as she asked for the private number of military intelligence. She smiled to herself thinking that whatever titles she acquired, she would always be Frau Hauptmann to him.

She rang the number and asked for Frau Hauptmann Zahnsdorf after giving her identification.

'Frau Major Zahnsdorf' came the stiff correction,

'Oh *Entschuldigung*, I did not know.'

'She was promoted two months ago.'

'She's not coming into Headquarters today as she is lecturing at the College but you will probably get her there before she starts.'

Detty rang the Military College and was told, yes, Major Zahnsdorf would be there but hadn't arrived yet. Could the Frau Komturin try her mobile phone?

Detty feared the lack of security at both ends but felt that there was no alternative. She got through to Liese who was in her car stuck in Königshof morning traffic.

'Detty, why hello! Where on earth are you? I bet you are sunning yourself on the beach somewhere.'

'Lost in France-well no- not exactly. I need to talk to you about international trade on a more secure line. How long will it take you to get to the College and do you have a private phone?'

'Twenty minutes and yes.' came the crisp reply.

Detty wrote the number on her wrist.

'You can't very well 'phone me. I will call you back in exactly twenty-five minutes and by the way congratulations on your promotion.'

'Thanks, I was pleased – for the Unit as much as for myself. I took the boys and girls to a disco in town and we had a rave up to celebrate. It was a great night, like the old days in Bratislava. OK then back to business, I won't start the lecture until I hear from you.'

Detty thought what an unlikely sort of Major her friend was. To celebrate her promotion, she had gone out to a disco. In addition, Detty, who knew her well, was prepared to bet, that Liese, all girl, had danced unselfconsciously to the rock music that she loved with the men who she commanded and who worshipped her. Liese could do that and yet demand total respect and discipline the following day when her unit might have to face all manner of unknown dangers.

She put the 'phone down, went to a neighbouring news stand and bought a copy of *Le Monde* and sat in café leafing through the pages, as she drank a coffee and munched a *pain au chocolat* to try and quell her impatience. After twenty minutes, she went back to the phone. It was occupied by a young woman engaged in a giggling conversation, which showed no signs of finishing. Detty waited a moment, wondering why the girl hadn't got a mobile and then tapped her on the shoulders:

'*Excusez-moi, mademoiselle, mais, a ce moment, ma Grand-Mère a souffert une crise cardiaque.*'

She thought that the grammar was execrable and begged forgiveness from the Virgin for the lie but felt that it was more believable than the truth, 'my best friend has been kidnapped by gun runners.' At all events, it had the desired effect. The girl put the 'phone down muttered apologies and fled. Detty dialled the Königshof number and to her relief Liese answered immediately. She explained that she needed help deciphering something.

'Ancient or modern?' asked Liese

'Both'

'Intriguing'

'It's very important.'

'Yes, I thought so. I think we can help but can you get the material to us?'

'Difficult, I had probably better bring it myself.'

'OK I'll have the right people ready. How long do you think?'

'If all goes well, I should be there on the Berlin plane tomorrow evening.'

'I'll meet it.'

'I'll try and buy a mobile here and let you know if I'm delayed.'

Next Marc. She got straight through to London and learnt that he was back there at his NATO office. He would ring her back immediately. There was something immensely reassuring about his voice speaking in quiet soft German. It was the voice that had first stirred her on the Farm run seemingly centuries ago.

'What on earth have you been doing, *Schatzi*? Are you OK?'

She told him briefly, keeping it confidential over the dubious security of a public 'phone box.

'I had guessed some of it from Lawri – I spoke to him. What happens now?'

'I am taking the stuff to Königshof to get it read.'

Professional dubiousness came over the line in the silence before he spoke.

'Are you sure that they can cope? You should have asked me and I would have got it done at Stuttgart.'

'I think that they are good enough, or so I have been told. It's a Livonian problem and it seemed right to let them tackle it. Your people have been compromised enough by us already.'

Marc smiled to himself at the 'us'. To have a wife belonging to three nations all of which she cared for passionately was fascinating, if complicated.

'OK but let me know at once if there are any difficulties and' he paused 'can I come over? I've got some leave due.'

She could hardly believe her ears. The joy of being with him again was almost more than that the relief to have his support. He was the one person that she felt that she could rely upon completely; with him, she could finally share her burden. She realised now how tired she felt. The weeks of effort chasing after seemingly hopeless clues about Mara, so soon after her miscarriage, had left her drained physically and psychologically. She also had another anxiety. At every possible opportunity, she had done vocal exercises and practised her new parts.

She was becoming increasingly aware that her voice was also tired. It worried her that the one-time stream of seemingly effortless sound, that, as she now realised, she had arrogantly taken for granted, no longer came as it should. She needed a rest and a voice teacher, Eileen, or Haydn, badly and felt that she must get both soon if she was not to suffer permanent damage. Marc's presence would ease the stress of the next critical phase.

She got the cellular phone and a few charged refill cards and paid her bill at the hotel ready for the morning. For a short time, she sat by the river over a café-cognac and then, dizzy with tiredness, she went to bed and slept at once.

She shuddered awake to the call at five in the morning, showered and went down to the hotel porch, praying that the taxi company would take seriously the call at this hour to a side street hotel. A cheerful North African face appeared at the desk and they went out into the misty dawn carrying just a hint of autumn. The French internal flight was primitive, as always, but mercifully on time. She had two hours to get to Charles de Gaulle, round Paris, but took no chances with the morning traffic and leapt into a taxi immediately. The driver was lecherous but mercifully fast as a driver, as well. She told him brusquely, that she wasn't a tourist, didn't want to see the sights, his or the more conventional ones, and as far as she was concerned, Paris was just an interchange. She then felt guilty at lying about a city that she loved and admired, particularly when it looked so welcoming in the warm autumn weather. When they arrived at CDG, she over-tipped the driver in penance for her guilt.

To her surprise, the autumn weather was still fine when she blinked out of the plane at Königshof. Liese, looking very un-Major-like in jeans and a sweater, was waiting for her at the airport inside the exit. They kissed warmly but both knew it was a serious meeting. Detty knew and appreciated that Liese knew the urgency of the situation. The latter then flashed her military intelligence pass liberally and whisked Detty out of the Terminal into a waiting staff car. The driver, yet another FWL veteran, allowed himself a brief:

'Welcome home, Frau Komturin,' to Detty before heading them out into the usual misty Baltic morning.

As they drove along, Detty explained the problem in a little more detail, but decided to wait until they arrived to get the texts out of her hastily purchased grip.

'I have the right person for you back at the office' said Liese 'or at least I will have, if they have mended the lift.'

Detty raised a questioning eyebrow.

'You know her. Remember the Young Swans Passing Out Parade?'

'Tanya Lobokova?'

'The same. She's brilliant. We think that she's probably the best young cryptanalyst in Europe, possibly in the world. You can see now why we wanted her in the Corps so much, wheelchair and all.'

'Is she really that good?'

'I think so and hope so because I know how important it might be. Of course, we are assuming that you are right and there is some sort of cipher hidden in the texts.'

'God help us all if I'm wrong.'

Tanya smiled a greeting from her wheeled chair. Beside her was a gaunt tall man who Detty immediately recognised with astonishment as Virgilio Poliziano.

'*Professore*, what on earth are you doing here? I thought that you were still in Florence.'

'I have come back to Königshof for a Summer School, *Contessa*.

They told me this morning that Leutnant Lobokova had been enquiring at my old department whether anybody there was a palaeographic expert. I have some slight knowledge of medieval scripts so I came straight round. Can we see the material?'

Detty spread the Texts on a low table in front of Tanya. The young girl craned forward, with Poliziano looking over her shoulder. For a quarter of an hour, only the insistent ticking of the wall clock could be heard. Detty began to feel uncomfortable, perhaps she had made a dreadful fool of herself and the calligraphy would reveal nothing.

'There is something strange in one of these, *Contessa*' said the Professor 'and I think you might be on to something.'

Detty's heart leapt with a glimmer of relief,

'But I need to thrash it out with the Frau Leutnant here as I know nothing about codes. There is a strange order in the positioning of the *puncti elevati* in one document, which is out of line with normal practice and the other texts. I am not sure what, if anything, it means and that is where I need the Frau Leutnant's help. Can you give us a couple of hours together and then we will let you know if we are getting anywhere?'

'Almost certainly I will need the full set of computers if we are to make progress. I think, therefore, that we had better go down to my room,' said Tanya 'before we go down though, you may be interested to hear that over the last year we have been picking up odd electronic mail, from Belarus and the Ukraine and, occasionally, from inside Livonia itself. This hasn't yet made any sense so far. Liese knows that I have been working hard on it and there might be, just might be mind, some connection.'

Liese nodded.

'I will take Detty out to a meal and we will leave you in peace. Let me know. on my mobile when you are ready for us.'

At Detty's request they went to the Golabki in Königshof, an old Polish restaurant said to date from the days of Jan Sobieski. It had a timeless, tranquil atmosphere, which had survived the turmoil it had seen pass by its doors. The curious *Zur* or white borsch still intrigued Detty and the venison with cream and juniper, which was the chief dish of the house, was as good as ever. Her eyes though strayed often towards Liese's mobile 'phone wondering when, and if, they would get any news.

As they were getting to the end of their meal, they had to fight off the advances of an English businessman, somewhat the worse for beer and vodka, who assumed that two attractive young women dining by themselves must be ravenous for male company. He listened attentively but uncomprehendingly to their conversation in *platdeutsch* and then suggested in loud English that he should join them at their table. He was taken aback when Detty changed to her unquestionably native English, albeit with the soft refinement of Kildare, to tell him that they really were rather busy talking business and wished to remain alone. Rather mischievously, they then continued their conversation in Russian. The visitor's jaw drooped lower and lower until he could restrain himself no longer and broke in again to ask Detty how an English girl came to be so fluent in these strange languages. She pointed out that he obviously hadn't spotted her accent and that the Irish were blessed with greater fluency in foreign languages than their English neighbours.

It was now past midnight and the entertainment was wearing thin. The Englishman opened his mouth to ask a further question but just at that moment, mercifully, Liese's phone rang at last. She answered it quickly:

'*Ja, Major Zahnsdorf am apparat*' then after a pause '*Ja, Augenblicklich*'
They got up, paid rapidly, and went out to Liese's car with the Englishman behind them muttering to himself in his cups:

'Funny country if they have Majors who look like that in their army.'

Back at the office Tanya and Virgilio, looked tired but satisfied.

'*Vai, Signora Tenente, sei il capo*'

Tanya nodded in acceptance and started:

'The Professor spotted that these strange palaeographic punctuation marks called *puncti elevati* were conventional in some texts but strangely spaced in the one designed for the Ukraine, which was with the letter. There were relatively few *puncti elevati* in the whole of the document. We counted sixteen, which is too few for a simple alphabet, and which confirmed my first impression that we were looking for a key, not a cipher in itself. It appeared that we were dealing with something quite old fashioned, as nowadays we wrestle with quantum cryptography, which makes all of this seem refreshingly antiquated. I will cut a long story short, fascinating as it is, and come to the main findings. The text gives a numerical key, which is discovered by the relationship to the number of letters in the adjacent words. There is a pattern of triple encryption, which means that the significant number is found in different relationships to the *puncti elevati* each time. A few trials on the computer sorted this out and fairly quickly we had the numerical key, which had to be the only one possible for the data.'

'There were now two questions. Why had our opposing organisation not used the existing technology and transmitted the key using an asymmetrical technique of public key cryptography and where did we go to find the main encrypted text?'

By the time Tanya reached this point Detty was feeling completely out of her depth. She felt however that it was safe to leave it to the others who appeared to understand what was being said.

'The first one was the most important, if our findings were to have any practical use.' Tanya continued 'Fortunately, we already had our hands on the answer. The key was needed to decipher the text that was being transmitted to and from the Belarus/Ukraine and sometimes from inside Livonia. As you know, we had already been working on this problem. What we had discovered was, effectively, a one-time pad for these electronic signals and we have been able this evening to get the computers to decipher a lot of the content. Before we talk about this, however I would like briefly to go back to the second question. Why did they use this charmingly old-fashioned method?'

Tanya's description, to Detty, conjured up an image of a sepia print or a nineteenth century sampler. She wouldn't have thought of using 'charmingly old fashioned' to describe a highly technical code – but each to his or her trade. She tried to concentrate again.

'We can't of course be sure of the answer but there seem to be three possibilities. The authors may have felt that the recipients didn't have the know-how to deal with an asymmetric key. This is unlikely as you can buy the technology off the shelf easily. On the other hand, the authors may have been so intrigued with the idea of using a mock thirteenth century text to transport a twenty first century key that they did it almost as a show-off, a bit of fun. This is attractive but unlikely. They seem to be a very nasty and highly professional crowd.'

She looked at up Poliziano seeking confirmation and he nodded quickly.

'And neither of us thinks that they would have adopted this method as a piece of attractive erudition, it's just doesn't fit in with the information we already have about them. The third and, we believe, the most likely explanation, is that they were worried by our activities in this Unit. For obvious reasons, I do not want to go into too much detail but, in common with most cryptanalytic units, we have been working on quantum computer development for cryptanalysis. Now it is a feature of this type of work that nobody goes public about his achievements. Supposing, just supposing, that we had developed a quantum computer which could decipher their asymmetric key they may have thought that it was safer to use a heavily disguised one-time pad that could be transported to its destination without crossing the Livonian border. Again, I stress we cannot know but it is thought provoking that without Detty's unusual range of clandestine activities they could well have been correct.'

Tanya paused and looked round the gathering to check general understanding. Detty's head was whirling with the jargon but she felt that she had got the main message.

'Just before I return to the text that we have deciphered; I must give you two words of caution. The first is that we have only discovered one key from the one-time pad. The essence of the pad is that after a certain length of time, usually pre-arranged, the page is literally or metaphorically torn off and the next key comes into use. Presumably, in this case, a new text and key would be sent from the Pyrenees into the Ukraine. When this happens, we will, of course, have lost our key and know only the general outline of the method that they are using. It may well be, however, that in this instance, as soon as they realised that Detty had escaped with the compromising text, they stopped using the key immediately. It would be a considerable risk to trust to luck that their, rather kindergarten, method of hiding the key in the text, would prove sufficient. They would, of course, face the difficulty in that if they stop using this key, they may not have a readily accessible replacement. They don't seem to send out keys in advance and, even, fortunately for us, transmitted a good deal of encrypted text using this key before it could have been delivered to the Ukraine. This might be because it is a safety second copy of the key already in use, which would be unprofessional as it would double the risk of discovery. More probably, it is just to allow the material transmitted to be held for deciphering some days later when the key arrives.'

'Now we come at last to the deciphered material. Thank you for your patience.'

She passed a printout round the table.

'As you will see much of it consists of intended movements of old Soviet weaponry to various murky parts of the world some quite remote from here. But how about this "Transhipment Vkzif3sw149?"'

She looked up expectantly.

'Three kilometres south–west?' said Liese.

'That was what we thought.'

There was silence for a minute or so.

'*Vierkirche zum Interfluss*?' said Detty hesitantly at last.

'Problem solved by the Colonel-in-Chief.' said Tanya, a touch cheekily.

'I think it must be that and the rest is just the date. They don't mention a time but that may be standard i.e., the same at each venue. Anyway, from our point of view, we can watch it fairly easily for twenty-four hours on the 14th of September. It took us some time studying the map to arrive at Vierkirche as so many places in Livonia begin with a V.'

There was a mighty sense of relief, which was almost palpable. At last, they seemed to be getting somewhere.

'How did you get *Vierkirche* so quickly, Detty, and you're not even Livonian.'

'I shall challenge you to a dual with my ceremonial *Komturschwert* if you accuse me of not being a Livonian but having seen the way you handle that wheelchair of yours you would probably outmanoeuvre me hopelessly. Anyway, I'll tell you. I was stuck in the mud – literally-just outside *Vierkirche* for several hours before we crossed the *Fojn*. I had to wait for the FWL engineers to pull my jeep out; it was most embarrassing. There was the village sign with one pole shot through. Anyway, I kept looking at this drunken sign and wondering how there could be four churches in such a tiny hamlet when I couldn't see even one. Somehow, it stuck in my mind. I must find out, one day, how it got the name.'

Liese laughed and glanced out of the window.

'Good God, it is dawn already.' she said, 'Time for coffee.'

*

Mara had lost count of time. The brief period with Detty seemed unreal, like a dream. She wondered whether her disturbed mind had imagined it. But no, the aching worry of the effect of that terrible belt on her pregnant friend was real enough. She had tried to yell after Detty to tell them she was pregnant but was drearily sure that no one had heard. It would probably have been useless anyway. These men were thugs of the lowest order, brought up in misery and taught to despise the loving and the precious. How would they care about a strange girl and her unborn baby? It had been hopeless from the start. She feared the worst.

Shortly after Detty left, the routine changed. She learnt more about her surroundings. The chamber that imprisoned her was damp and windowless but did have a solitary low powered electric light bulb on a cable run through a small hole high on the crumbling wall and a primitive camp bed with blankets that had not seen a wash in years. A second entrance was opened and the original door locked. The new exit led through a small lobby, which contained an old washstand and bowl and a modern portable lavatory. On the outside of this was a heavy barred metal door obviously of recent construction and between the two rooms was a folding shutter that could only be operated from the far side of the main door. Twice a day the shutter was closed off and an invisible person left food and water, both for drinking and washing, and changed the container on the lavatory. Some trouble had obviously been taken to see that the prisoner saw nobody but the two warders, who came into her room once a day and were her only human contact.

One always brandished a pistol while the other fixed a stun belt, which by this time she recognised immediately, round her waist muttering in bad Russian:

'Don't try anything or you will pay for it.'

Mara knew this anyway only too well from her previous experience. Thus equipped she was led through the two doors onto a small landing with a spiral staircase leading off it. The warders motioned to her to climb the staircase and followed behind her. After seventy-eight steps she emerged into the light which nearly blinded her, particularly when it was sunny. She saw the sky clearly but the high stone parapets hid everything else from view. There had been slits in the wall presumably for defence but these had been crudely blocked up presumably to stop prisoners seeing out. The space was a square measuring about four metres on each side that she was allowed to walk round for about half an hour until the warders signalled her to return down the staircase.

All the time she was exercising one warder casually brandished his pistol and the other the control unit of the stun belt. She felt in perpetual danger but, she could face the idea of being shot rather better than a repeat of her experience with the stun belt that she had undergone at the Farm. The always-present memory of this was so sickeningly horrifying that it completely removed any satisfaction that she might have had from being in the daylight and the fresh air. She did not trust the guards and of the two, the one with the stun belt control, who was an overweight, slobbering brute, was the most unpleasant. She wouldn't have been surprised if he had activated the belt accidentally or even for sadistic fun. He was always eyeing her up and down with undisguised lechery and muttering obscene remarks to her in a peculiar Russian with an accent that she couldn't recognise. Once in an unguarded moment, his companion called him 'Pepe' and, from this, she thought that he might be Spanish or South American.

For several weeks this routine continued. It was beginning to be cold as well as boring and frightening. One morning without warning the two guards were accompanied by a tall coldly manicured-looking man. He talked to them in a language, which she thought was Spanish, but which she didn't understand. To her, he addressed not a word giving her only a steely, appraising glance from the sharp eyes high in his narrow face.

*

There were four days to wait but then there was Marc. Suddenly as she saw his smiling confident face on the runway for the first time, she realised that everything might be OK. They had lunch together, talking little, just content to look at each other after so long. Then there was briefing at the Unit. Marc kept silent, taking it all in. He nodded once or twice in agreement. He only spoke at the end of the meeting. He turned to Tanya and congratulated her on her cipher analysis. She thanked him quietly but was clearly delighted to be praised by the man who had led the tanks across the *Fojn*. After the meeting, Detty led Marc back to the Hanse Hotel for supper in their room – soup, cold ham, salad, and beer followed by a long-awaited bed. Detty woke in the night feeling guilty that they had had such pleasure while the fate of her friend was unknown.

The morning brought a scrambled phone call from the President enquiring quietly after them both. Detty didn't know what to say. She stammered that they were fine. Afterwards they went to the planning meeting at the Unit. Action was better than waiting. They went through the details of what should be done at the interception of the transhipment. Liese outlined the general plan. They should wait at the tentative liaison place. If they were correct, they could try to intercept and tag the trucks and anyone else who turned up there. It probably would not be difficult to identify the arms dealers' trucks as, even on the main road east from the Interfluss to the Ukraine there were unlikely to be too many legitimate travellers stopping in a lay-by for a meeting. Tanya and Liese together with a young Lieutenant in the unit called Irina Malinowska had gone down in the evening of the day before to examine the area. They had found a lay-by in exactly the position indicated by the message. They felt as certain as they could be that this was the place designated for the exchange.

*

Plastic bottles, old newspapers and worse were strewn about the desolate lay-by. The tarmac was stained with oily patches witnessing the passage of many an ageing, maintenance-free lorry. Thirty metres from one end, a disconsolate looking prostitute in her white thigh boots, black vinyl miniskirt and cheap artificial leather coat walked up and down.

The nights had turned cold during the past week and the Indian summer was clearly passing. It was past midnight and there was a chill in the air, which suggested that the northern winter was not far distant. A second girl appeared from the shadows dressed in the same way. She nodded briefly to her companion. They exchanged places. The first girl came towards the shadows and climbed gratefully into the concealed jeep.

'You are both far too sexy for safety' said Detty.

Liese only grinned and struggled to slip a pair of padded tracksuit trousers over her bare legs and short skirt.

'I don't know about being sexy.' she said. 'All I know is that I'm frozen.'

'Seriously' said Detty 'You might have made yourselves up to look a bit more raddled. If our quarries' lust overcomes their sense of duty, we shall all be in trouble.'

'I don't think that is very likely. If I have assessed this organisation correctly, the drivers will know that to go off with a tart on the job rather than doing their work, would get them a bullet in the back of the neck and that's not worth any one-night stand.'

'I just hope that you're right.'

At that moment, the rumble of a big diesel was heard approaching down the road and a large, aged articulated lorry squeaked and groaned into the lay-by. The young prostitute hitched her negligible skirt even higher over her thighs and, with an exaggerated waggle of her hips tottered on her impractical high heels through the mud and oil towards the cab. She opened her leather coat to reveal her cleavage with one hand while she quickly thrust the other under the wheel arch.

'Do you teach all your junior officers to solicit so convincingly?' murmured Detty.

'Better not tell her father that – he's principal of a Lutheran seminary in Königshof.'

They held their breath for a moment waiting for the driver's response. He looked tempted but eventually, as Liese had forecast, the prospect of a bullet in the back of the neck overcame his sex drive and he motioned her away.

A large, covered van had joined them silently and Irina went up to the other driver as he climbed down from the cab. She quickly recovered the second bug from her briefs whilst voluptuously tempting the new arrival. He also hesitated but, again, fear or a sense of duty decided the issue but fortunately not before Irina's hand was able to secure the second bug under the wheel arch of the van.

'So far so good!' Liese whispered watching the two drivers carefully. They were now having a furious conversation. One of them produced a revolver and was waving it in the direction of Irina. Detty held her breath hoping that the Wild Swan marksmen who had been detailed to deal with this eventuality had the two drivers securely in their telescopic sights. Fortunately, the second, older man seemed to have won the argument by asserting that killing the young prostitute would be an unnecessary and messy complication. He walked over to her apparently unarmed, gave her some money, and told her loudly and firmly that she should go down the road to the village, which was about two kilometres away and not re-appear for at least three hours. Irina apparently satisfied walked off and the transfer of goods between the two trucks began. There was sweating and swearing as the crates were moved by means of a mobile forklift which was produced from the back of the larger truck.

After about an hour, the drivers sat down together for a cigarette and then drove onto the highway and disappeared. The van turned west, the lorry east, both going back in the direction that they had come from. As soon as the vehicles had disappeared, men and women appeared from the scrublands on every side. Marc who had been camouflaged with the sharpshooter congratulated Irina on her courage. The young officer thanked him with a smile on her face:

'I thought you were going to compliment me on my performance' she said impishly.

'I wouldn't dare do that in front of my wife.'

Liese had got the bugs ticking satisfactorily on her monitor.

'Nothing to do now except watch and wait.'

'And breakfast' added Marc with a Bavarian enthusiasm for the inner man, as he jumped into the jeep, newly arrived from its hiding place.

'Interesting!' exclaimed Liese 'He's turned off into the country to the old pontoon relief bridge. It sounds as if he is trying to avoid the main bridges over the *Fojn* so he's gone the roundabout route.'

She continued watching the blip on the screen intently as they turned south at the junction towards Bialovsk and started to overtake the early morning trucks carrying concrete and ballast towards the great new bridge. This huge structure was thrusting across the river to the *Interfluss* and Poland. It would soon replace the tattered remains of the much-repaired original, which Detty remembered so well from her arrival in the war zone. They were all silent gazing through the windows at the misty icy sunrise over the marshes and the smoky city of Bialovsk. Winter was on its way in earnest.

The hotel had been an attractive eighteenth-century coaching inn remarkably undamaged by the artillery and bombing of the war. Detty remembered it as a remarkable haven of peace when she had had dinner there a couple of times during the campaign. The prosperity of peace and the re-building contracts had exacted their price. The foyer was crowded and sounded like the Tower of Babel. There were Dutchmen, Italians, Germans, and other nationalities not immediately identifiable. Typically, the visitors had one hand on their breakfast coffees and the other on a mobile 'phone or a briefcase full of papers. The military party had reserved a screened off part of the restaurant when they had arrived the night before and they were glad of the relative quiet and privacy now.

Liese gave a quiet sigh of satisfaction as her bleeper landed north of the airfield at Lovets and remained stationary. She attacked her breakfast of smoked fish, sausage, and boiled egg with gusto. Marc looked on in admiration.

'After breakfast we get up an assault group from the Swans and have a look.'

'*Jawohl, Frau Major*' said Marc with only a touch of irony and a lot of admiration.

'You'd better keep out of the way; you'd only make them nervous.'

'Can I come if I promise to behave myself?'

'I think that that might be arranged. In fact, I have a job for you, Herr General, -you can act as the personal bodyguard of Leutnant Lobokova and make sure that you look after her. She's very important.'

'That will be an honour' said Marc – this time without any twinge of irony. It reminded Detty, with she had to admit a touch of jealousy, of the old-world courtesy that had won her heart back at the Farm.

Liese spent half an hour on the telephone, bludgeoning, cajoling, seducing, and using every other method that she could lay her hands on to get the relevant personnel, information and permits to go to the site. At the end of a seeming age, she turned to the assembled company and reported:

'I need to explain to you where our van has stopped and why I think we may be near to unravelling this dreadful business and possibly, hopefully, finding Mara into the bargain. Behind the airfield at Lovets is a large industrial complex and it appears that our van, loaded with whatever they transferred in the lay-by is heading there by means of isolated back roads making sure that they evade any possible inspection. *Nieder Lovets* was a German forced labour camp, which was then used for political prisoners under the Soviets. The first democratic Moltravian government had far too much to cope with to bother about this deserted waste land.

When the Fascists took over, they used the complex briefly as a concrete moulding works where 'undesirables' and 'inferior aliens' were made to work as slave labour at the production of concrete slabs of various, especially bespoke, dimensions. Then suddenly production stopped and the entire huge complex of nearly ten square kilometres was abandoned. We never knew why and when we came back to the site, we tried to find out. The area is; however, a massive tangle of distorted reinforced concrete and it is difficult even to enter many parts of it. In addition, there are a number of booby traps left by the various occupying powers, which make casual wandering extremely dangerous.

It seems that our van has penetrated to the heart of this monument of twentieth century civilisation and that we must try and follow. It won't be particularly easy or safe but I guess none of us have been too familiar with safety recently.'

She looked around and noted the silence of assent. The mood of good-humoured badinage had changed. She was now deadly serious.

'We have two assault platoons of the Swans, a bomb disposal squad and two back-up intelligence units. They should be here in half an hour. I have arranged to have the gymnasium to brief them. We can wait no longer.'

Liese had assumed a natural stature that everybody accepted-nay-admired. The Units arrived in subdued order barely disturbing the morning coffee of the visiting engineers and the travelling reps, as they filtered down the back stairs to the gymnasium.

Liese asked quietly for the doors to be locked once everybody was inside. She briefed the young men and women with just a touch of the native platdeutsch of her schooldays. Finally, she asked for questions. There were none.

'We leave in an hour. Good luck everybody and thank you all.'

They filed out. Detty, looking like any other twenty-five-year-old in padded trousers and a fleece, against the cold, stood inconspicuously hiding beside Marc near the door. It was useless, however. In turn they faced their former Commander in Chief as they left the hall and saluted smartly. Detty realising that concealment was useless, and discourteous, stepped forward and returned the salute with a smile, murmuring *'Viel Gluck!'*

Liese beckoned Marc and Detty into her jeep and signalled to the driver to move off. They were in the middle of the small convoy. Liese was thinking aloud:

'The problem is that we need desperately to reconnoitre carefully and yet we mustn't give the alarm.'

'Refuse trucks, perhaps' said Detty with half an eye on Marc.

Marc shook his head.

'Sorry for the bad joke but they would smell a rat – even if it didn't squeal in a well-trained soprano.'

He thought for a moment.

'You might have a point though, Detty.'

He turned to Liese.

'Why don't you get your father to crash a plane?'

Liese looked startled and Marc went on:

'No, I'm serious. If an ace pilot could point his plane at the ground between the airfield at Lovets and the industrial site, and then bail out, it would provide a splendid diversion and a reason for having lots of people around. Surely, your father has some superannuated fighters. What about the ancient Moltravian MiGs of happy memory?'

'I almost don't like to ask. The pilot would take a considerable risk but there is a lot at stake.'

She suddenly smiled.

'Daddy, will you crash a fighter for me? It's a bit like *Salome*, isn't it? Still, I suppose it's a bit different from the usual daughter question 'Daddy, can I have a new dress for the party. I'll try.'

She dialled a number.

'Can I speak to Apollo, please?'

The old wartime code names were still often used, almost for sentimental reasons. She was connected and explained to her father, rather breathlessly, what she wanted. Clearly, he protested and there was a long expostulation inaudible over the line. She did her best to persuade him but was clearly failing. At last, she said:

'Actually, it wasn't my idea. Marc von Ritter suggested it.'

Suddenly, and disgracefully, it all seemed different. Ulrich Zahnsdorf demanded to be put on to Marc who was congratulated for his inventiveness. All would be arranged at 10:30 hours tomorrow.

Liese was resigned:

'What it is to be a child – nothing changes. I'm still the baby girl to him. A daughter is not without honour, except in her own family. Anyway, thank you, Marc. We will go to *Lovets* to bivouac for the night and be ready for the morning.'

8
THE BUNKERS

Pandemonium, the high capital
Of Satan and his peers

MILTON *PARADISE LOST* BK1 LINE 756

Crashing a plane needs care. Liese and Irina, back in role as itinerant prostitutes, did a careful reconnaissance of the perimeter of the vast old industrial site. They found the whole area completely derelict and redolent of the horrors of the past. Twisted metal of hastily constructed plant, abandoned shells of rusting vehicles and, most moving of all, primitive huts where the luckless humans had lived, suffered and usually died. The only possible current access to the ruins was by way of a broken road that had had little use and no maintenance since Nazi slave labour built it more than half a century before. The road led through the woodlands until it was blocked by abandoned excavators and some other huge machines across the path. These, Liese informed them later, were face shovels formerly used in the open cast mines which left Detty, not for the first time, wondering how Liese had got her inexhaustible general knowledge. To superficial inspection, apparently, the road was impassable, but on closer examination, Liese thought that the machines could probably be moved enough to allow vehicles to pass along the road. At all events, there was no other entry port.

They met up back at the 'Woman in Armour' at Bialovsk. General Zahnsdorf was waiting chatting with Tatiana Lobokova. With them was a younger, sandy-haired man wearing a FLL uniform and pilot's wings. The General was very formal:

'May I introduce Hauptmann Miecek who is our ejector seat instructor and has volunteered for your mission. Hauptmann, I would like you to meet Komturin O'Neill, General von Ritter and ....' He hesitated looking at Irina 'I'm sorry but I don't think we've met before.'

Liese supplied the name.

'My apologies, Leutnant Malinowska,' he smiled and went on 'and I think you know Major Zahnsdorf.'

Miecek smiled and shook hands. Detty noted that the introductions followed strict protocol and Marc's honorary Livonian rank was used. There were no concessions to gender and no mention of the relationship between General and Major Zahnsdorf.

'Perhaps one of you would be kind enough to explain exactly what you need from Hauptmann Miecek.'

Liese got a map from her briefcase.

'Thank you very much for coming to us, Hauptmann. You will be familiar with the territory around the old armaments factory and camp. We believe that somewhere inside the site is a base depot for an international drugs and gun running operation. It is also possible that it is used for other purposes and even that an extremely important Livonian kidnap victim is being kept there.'

Detty was pretty sure that the bright young captain would know the identity of the kidnap victim but, clearly, Liese had thought it unnecessary to spell it out.

'We do not want the occupants alarmed or they might flee or destroy vital evidence.'

Detty flinched. That 'vital evidence' might include Mara herself, she thought gloomily.

'Ideally, we would like a crash with a considerable explosion over the road and as near as possible to the perimeter of the complex without damaging anything inside. Is that remotely feasible?'

She raised one eyebrow quizzically.

'I'll do my best, Frau Major, but you must understand that it's a bit of a tall order. Even with computer flight management, which is somewhat uncertain in these antique planes, which are all that we can spare, I cannot guarantee pinpoint impact. That is if I am to eject safely some time before.'

'That's fine, Hauptmann, do what you can and we will take it from there and, of course, your safety is paramount. No kamikaze acts please, just miss the airbase and the industrial complex.'

They shook hands again with good luck wishes all round and Jan Miecek and Ulrich Zahnsdorf left together. As they reached the door, the General allowed just a hint of domesticity to creep in, whispering discreetly to Liese:

'When all this is over, do come and see us. Your mother was complaining last week that she has forgotten what you look like.'

'Of course, *Vati*, but as you know I have been a bit busy.'

She turned back to Detty, Irina and Marc:

'Right, let's have a drink and I'll give you all a bit of background after dinner. You eat well here and I find serious conversation makes the food get cold, I'd rather leave that for coffee if it's OK by you.'

Marc nodded whole-hearted appreciative agreement. A colleague after his own heart, he thought, and then with more than a touch of male chauvinism, that she would make somebody a wonderful wife. He knew that it wasn't for lack of opportunity. Liese with her ash-blond hair, beautiful figure and great sense of fun had had a kaleidoscope of transient affairs, including her present one with the FC Königshof midfield tactician, David Sensky, but her job in intelligence had sometimes restricted intimacy. The FWL had always remained her first love.

They had beer and vodka in front of the log fire in the bar. Most of the places in this part of Livonia burnt coal from the remaining open cast pits. The coal was very cheap but the quality awful. Detty remembered vividly one place outside Bialovsk where she had been unable to see across the bar for the fumes. Afterwards the sulphurous stench had pervaded her long hair for days in spite of several washings. This hotel was run by Kurt Steuermann, an ex FWL quartermaster who knew the problems of local coal. He insisted on the much-dearer logs. He had rather quirkily christened the place '*Die Dame in Rüstung*' 'The Woman in Armour', when most of his competitors had stuck to Hotel Post, Hotel Königshof or similarly unimaginative titles. As he served their drinks, Liese who knew him well of old, asked him the reason for the odd name:

'When I escaped from the fascists, I went to England and took a job as a barman in a pub in London called 'The Goat and Compasses' then I had another job in the country in Dorset at a pub called 'The Silent Woman'. Then of course I joined the FWL but I remembered those English inns. I rather liked these daft names and I thought that if things changed and the country was ever free, I would open a place in Moltravia with a similar strange name. I want to go to England as soon as I have time to get one of those proper swinging inn signs which I have ordered but I haven't been able to go yet – too much work.'

'But why '*Die Dame in Rüstung*' – 'The Woman in Armour'?' asked Irina.

Kurt looked from Detty to Liese with some embarrassment.

'I thought it would be a tribute to ... to our struggle.'

He finished lamely and turned quickly to serve other customers.

They finished their venison and red cabbage with gusto. Kurt appeared asking if the venison had been satisfactory and whether they would like the *Kirschtorte* that was the speciality of the house. Not the Schwarzwalder variety, they were to understand, but the paler, lighter local one. As they agreed that that would be delicious, Liese asked whether it would it be possible to have coffee, cake and slivovitz in a quiet side room as they had some business to discuss.

'*Ja, naturlich, Frau Major.*' came the reply and Detty thought that for a moment he was going to salute. Liese asked politely and kindly:

'Kurt, a bit less of the 'Frau Major', if you could. This place is teeming with strangers and I'd rather our military status wasn't spread abroad.'

'*Jawohl, Frau........meine Frau*' as he showed them into a private room, also with a log fire burning in the grate, and left unobtrusively to return with the coffee, schnapps, and cake.

Liese giggled:

'Old habits die hard. I don't think we will ever alter him and that is half his charm. It's his sort who won the war. He loves it when we come here; it reminds him of what he calls the great days. I'm not sure they were so great with the whole of Bialovsk peppered with enemy shells and a mass of mud and craters. Now to business.'

She looked round before continuing.

'In former times the great forest of the *Ostwaldmark* stretched from *Königshof* to the *Fojn* and eastwards past *Zablovsk* beyond the present Russian frontier. It was heavily wooded and was populated only by migrant hunting tribes and some great commanderies of the Teutonic Knights and Knights of the Sword. They were a pretty rough lot. It wasn't until later that the Hanseatic Law of *Königshof* and the more humanitarian presence of our own Order of St Nicklaus reached into it. The timber from the forest had always been useful for charcoal burners and smelters making iron and steel tools and weapons. Later, in the seventeenth and eighteenth centuries, land-owning aristocrats built hunting lodges. They found the old commanderies, which were now largely derelict anyway, far too draughty, and uncomfortable. So it remained a poor and backward area until the beginnings of industrialisation. Superficial coal was then found under the forest. This led to smelting with coke and a nucleus of heavy industry round Lovets, which grew into an industrial town of some eighty thousand people at its largest. They produced a wide range of metal products but chiefly agricultural tools, domestic equipment, and component castings. It was quite advanced technology for its day. The industry declined because of instability – war, revolution, and competition – during the earlier part of the twentieth century.'

'When the Germans overran the area, the plentiful supply of resources, raw materials, and workers in the form of slave labour made it an ideal site for a munitions plant. They built several massive factories, an enormous camp for slave labourers and a special railway branch from the Bialovsk to Kiev main line. This served the complex with people and supplies and, of course, carried away the finished munitions. Because of high security in the area and the appalling atmosphere, Lovets itself became a ghost town but there were large numbers of people in the camp, the barracks, and the airfield.'

'In 1945 in the face of the advancing Russians, the Germans evacuated the complex and dynamited it systematically and only wreckage remained. The Russians crudely restored the airbase and the communists re-opened the munitions factory, which was, I believe, also run by slave labour. Much of the countryside was submerged under industrial waste and pollutants. As you know the first democratic government here only lasted a few years and had more pressing problems than the re-instatement of the wastelands behind Lovets which was left abandoned.'

'We come now to something that has always puzzled me. When Travsky and the Fascists seized power nothing very significant, as far as we could tell, happened at Lovets. Increasingly, however, it was made a high security area, although it was still apparently completely derelict. This might have been for humanitarian reasons and it is true that the whole zone is unpredictably dangerous but, as you all know, that hardly checks with the usual Travsky approach. Even my father, who commanded the Lovets air base at the time of the Fascist take-over, never knew the reason for the secrecy. He was, of course, removed from Lovets soon after. There were theories that the secrecy had something to do with armaments or atrocities but no one was sure. Because of the risks the present Government decided to leave the area out of bounds until it was possible to clear the ground properly and make it safe.'

*

Even though she knew that it was going to happen, the crash shattered Detty's consciousness with a vivid flash back to the car explosion at *Schloss Krenek*. She crossed herself and muttered a prayer for the safety of the pilot. Miecek had done his work well and the plane, loaded with bombs, had exploded straddling the road about eight hundred metres from the entrance to the site.

The airfield sirens screamed and the rescue vehicles and ambulances streamed out of the base. The response was entirely genuine as only the station commander and the pilot knew that the crash had been planned. To avoid having to skirt the fire in the dense undergrowth, helicopters dropped the intelligence party and an assault force from the Wild Swans on the far side of the fire. Several other rescue helicopters were already circling the blaze, which made them less conspicuous to any watchers inside the site. The use of choppers in this situation would seem entirely natural. With the assault force concealed behind them, Liese, Irina, Detty and Marc cautiously entered the site. There wore tin hats and overalls labelled Emergency Rescue Service over their protection suits.

Not even during the war had Detty seen such dereliction. On every side were collapsed sheds and warehouses, torn up concrete and broken glass. Belfast confetti everywhere, she thought, remembering her childhood newsreels of the troubles in Northern Ireland.

'Look at those' whispered Marc suddenly as he pointed to a wheel track recently made across the weeds penetrating the split concrete. Soon there were more and more of these over oil slicks and where the ground was soft enough to show them. Vehicles had used the road recently and in numbers.

They crept forward again under the shadow of the wreckage at the side of the road until they were about five hundred metres inside the complex. There was a sudden crash of metal on metal to their left amidst the debris. They froze. There was another crash as a piece of metal fell near the position of the first noise. Then nothing more.

'Might have been an animal' said Liese and started to move forward very carefully again alongside the piled jagged wreckage.

'Radiation hotspot' she looked intently at her counter 'I wonder whether it's just local or will go on increasing. No, it's falling off quickly probably depleted uranium shell heads somewhere.'

They turned the corner round a huge mass of twisted girders and edged cautiously towards the door of a large hangar, which seemed almost intact but roofless. A burst of machine gun fire from a wing of the building on their left shattered the silence. They pressed back to relative safety between the steel debris.

Liese spoke rapidly pinpointing by radio, the origin of the fire to the commando force behind.

'Can't do anything until they've sorted our friends out.'

Two mortar shells zoomed purposefully overhead exploding close to the site of the machine gun burst. Silence once more. They waited. More fire from behind and to the left. More mortars. More silence. Then shouting:

'*Nos redimos, nos redimos*' followed by, in terrible English 'Surrender. Don't shoot. Surrender, surrender'

Half a dozen ragamuffin figures with machine pistols harnessed over their heads appeared from the wreckage.

'Stay where you are. Throw down your arms. Hands up and don't move.'

Liese gave her instructions in slow carefully articulated English. They hesitated at the sound of a female voice, then realising that it meant business, they seemed to understand and obeyed shivering with fear.

The back-up Swans took charge of the prisoners while they continued to creep forward again towards the hangar. All quiet. Liese peered round the hangar door, which was half open after the last mortar explosion. She gasped:

'Just have a look at this!'

Detty and Marc looked inside. Lined up were row after row of missiles and launchers, armoured personnel carriers, and mortars. To Detty they looked well maintained. Marc muttered:

'A bit out of date but brand new and in very good shape. I think that we have just discovered why Travsky didn't want intruders here. Our advance must have trapped this gear in here. They can't have got this lot in since the war.'

'Or out for that matter' said Detty thoughtfully as they crept through the hangar edging carefully from weapon to weapon.

'No, presumably Travsky connived in a profitable arms trade and they used this place to hold stock and the airfield at Lovets to move it in and out.'

'Wouldn't your father have had to know about it, though, Liese?'

'No, he was moved out of here soon after the Fascists seized power. It was completely under NAS control and so was the airbase, at least until we established the FWL in the *Interfluss*, then as you know they had to re-start proper air force operations here.'

'Sadly, this must have been what they were anxious about and not Mara. We have been chasing a wild goose.'

They reached the end of the hangar. A small back door was open; rather disconsolately, they walked up to it and carefully looked outside.

'This place really is full of surprises!' exclaimed Marc as they looked out onto a patch of rough grass, which led to more ruins with a difference. Stone, not steel; old, not modern. A lone lichen clad tower rose high out of the tumbled masonry. Behind the tower was another flat stretch, then, after this time-warp oasis, industrial wasteland started again.

'That must be the old Waldhof commanderie.' said Liese 'I knew that there were still supposed to be some ruins of it somewhere in here but, of course, we never had the chance to look before.'

'Do you want to look now?' asked Marc deferring to Liese as Commander.

'It seems a bit of a waste of time. I should think it's quite interesting but this doesn't seem the right moment for an archaeological dig. They don't seem to have used it recently and it wouldn't be suitable for their sort of activities. I can't even see how you get in. Might be better to go back and see what we can get out of that fine force of fighting men that we've just taken prisoner. We will come back later when the Swans have checked it for booby traps.'

'I was kept with Mara in some sort of old ruin before they moved me.' murmured Detty thoughtfully 'It's a thousand to one shot but there is something familiar about the stones. Could we have a look?'

'Of course, if it rings some sort of bell. If you think it might be of any help we'll go in now.'

They looked for signs of movement on the grass. There were some but of dubious significance. They could easily have been caused by the men from the hangar. There were no obvious wheels. Most of the doors to the tower were either covered with collapsed masonry or had been crudely blocked with recent cement and mortar.

'Must have used it for something for them to bother to do that' murmured Liese 'Perhaps you are right to suggest we have a look.'

They searched for an entrance in vain.

'It wouldn't take much to unblock one of these arches' suggested Marc.

Liese nodded.

'I'll get the guys up with a bar.'

In a few minutes, two engineers appeared in a jeep.

Before long, they were inside a dark, damp, gloomy chamber at the bottom of the tower. An iron door was locked on the far side. The sappers checked for booby traps and broke the door open with a cutter. They found themselves on a spiral staircase. At once, they sniffed. To the non–smoker stale cigarette smoke is detectable in tiny amounts. There was no doubt that someone had been smoking on that staircase in the quite recent past.

'Marc and Irina, could you go up and look at the top with Keppel? Vierchow come down with the Komturin and me and we will try to see what's underneath.'

Detty kept trying to suppress her conviction that she had once been near to this place. She kept telling herself that it was her anxiety over Mara that was playing her false. They climbed down the spiral staircase. There was no door at the bottom but only an arch leading down two more steps into a room directly under the one where they had entered. There was another arch on the far side leading to more blackness. The floor of the room and the passage opposite was covered in stinking, freezing water. Liese tested it for depth. It came over her service boot.

'About thirty centimetres' she said grimacing 'Here goes. I hope the floor is solid.'

She set off across the water. Detty, feeling glad that she had accepted the army fatigues and boots, followed, with the sapper bringing up the rear. About ten metres into the passage, they came to a tee junction reached by some steps, which mercifully took them above the water.

'Left or right?' asked Liese answering herself by turning right. A short straight passage led to a stone staircase and up to a door. It wasn't locked. They were back in ground floor chamber through a door that was hidden behind some false masonry painted thickly over the rough wood.

Liese produced some military plat Deutsch vernacular.

'Not easy to see with only a torch' said Detty trying to be soothing as they trudged back down the stairs to try the other way at the junction.

This seemed more promising. The passage was long and straight. They walked for some minutes. Detty wondered where they were going as she calculated that they must be well past the ruins by this time but she couldn't be sure of the direction. She still felt that she knew the place but had seen nothing that she truly recognised. She was desperately keen not to make a fool of herself and lead them all on a worse wild goose chase.

'There's another one!' exclaimed Liese pointing to another door disguised by false masonry like the other. They broke it down easily. A short passage led to another reinforced door with recently oiled hinges. After a short ministration from Vierchow, it swung open. This time Detty knew that she had been right:

'I've been here before!' she said to Liese and the incredulous young soldier.

'They kept me here with Mara. They didn't come from the tower. They came the other way. I can remember hearing the footsteps along the long corridor. They must have moved Mara. She scratched the wall. There are her day marks. She was proud of them. She felt that it showed that she knew the proper prisoner routine. I can work it out.'

She counted the scratches.

'Fifty-six. Then there are some irregular ones at the end.'

She exchanged desperate glances with Liese. Each wondered if the irregular scratches were signs of their friend's weakness or distress. Liese examined the scratches carefully for some while:

'I don't think its distress.'

She voiced their unspoken fears,

'I think that she was trying to write something. It might be writing 'et' or 'ed'.'

Detty examined the scratching again.

'There is no clear P but the ep, ed or te might be from Pedro or Pepe or Pete. I think one of the guards was Pepe or Pedro, it might mean him. They only moved her recently, I think, I would need a bit of time to work it out exactly, what with my time in hospital but it can't be more than about a week.'

'They seem a bit faint. Are you sure that she made them?'

'She certainly made the first ones. She was doing it before we were here together. If you don't believe me, I'll show you something else.'

She guided herself across the chamber with her torch and found the saddle cloth still where she had draped it hurriedly over the hole in the wall. She dragged it to one side and pulled Liese to the gap with the young soldier following. They shone their flashlights inside and gasped. The chamber, half seen by Detty before in the gloom, scintillated with gold and silver as they swung the powerful army torches about. One object high and dark on a back shelf arrested their lights in a searchlight cross beam from the torches.

For an age the three of them stood struck dumb gazing at the plain dark shape in awe then Detty put her torch down, crossed herself and knelt in the rubble to pray. She thanked God for their discovery and prayed for Mara and Livonia. Both at that moment seemed close, vulnerable, and very dear. To her surprise, she felt the other two kneel down beside her. At last, Liese got to her feet and said briskly to Vierchow:

'Go and find Leutnant Malinowska and the General and bring them down here. Oh – and get a photographer from the Unit to come as quickly as possible. This moment must be recorded.'

Acknowledging the order in a hoarse whisper he disappeared, leaving Liese and Detty still looking, silent and unbelievingly, at the scene in front of them. Liese dragged her 'phone out of her pocket and punched a number.

'*Herr General Zahnsdorf bitte*' then '*Vati*, we – Detti and I – have found *Der Kelch von Zablovsk* – yes – the Chalice itself. I only know it from pictures of course but I think it must be genuine. Nobody in their right minds would have hidden a forgery like that. Yes, at Lovets with a great treasure of artworks – pictures, sculptures, jewellery, armour, and silver. No unfortunately not Mara although she was here. I thought that this was so important that I ought to ask you before moving anything as the base is under FLL jurisdiction.'

Detty, hearing only one end of the conversation, was amused at the way normal military etiquette had lapsed. Liese, senior officer though she was, was so stunned at the magnitude and huge importance of finding the sacred national symbol that she was asking advice from her father like a small daughter. They were talking again and gradually it became more military.

'Yes, photographs first, armed guard on the store and the Chalice to General HQ in Königshof under escort. Yes, we will need backup. We have a good bit more to go on about Tamara and, stupendous as this is, I don't want to take any of our selected people off the search at present. OK I'll tell the people at Lovets to expect them and find quarters. Thanks, *Vati*. Yes, of course I will report to General Malinov. I don't want my career to come to a full stop.'

She clicked the End button and turned to Detty grinning:

'Fussy fathers are always fussy fathers, aren't they?'

'I don't know' said Detti 'I usually keep mine well out of the way.'

'I think he finds it hard to believe that I'm a Major in the FWL.'

'But you did ring him for advice.

'Sure, but that didn't include a lecture on basic command communications.'

Detty gave up but still thought that, for once, Liese was being rather hard on her father.

She couldn't sleep. Champagne had been uncorked by Kurt and drunk in quantity and too quickly. Meanwhile the stupendous news had been broadcast on the late-night television as the news hounds thundered at the door of 'Die Dame' for interviews.

Marc slept his usual silent tranquil sleep while she tossed and turned her mouth dry and heart and brain racing. She almost hated him for it. Then she hated herself, she shouldn't have been celebrating while Mara was still missing. The certainty that finding The Chalice was a sign that they would also find Mara was ebbing away. Guilt was taking its place. Why should Mara want to draw attention to Pepe or Pedro? They were small pawns in the game. What could be their vital significance? Had something dreadful been done to her after those last distorted scratches? Where was the centre of an organisation that could attempt to destabilise a complete country in order to further their gun running? These were big time players. Who did control the whole operation? Certainly not the pathetic hoodlums that they had captured today. The pseudo monks in the Pyrenees or Monsignor Josemaria Pueblo? The latter seemed much more probable, however appalling, but then who ran the Ukrainian end?

If the material at Lovets was effectively sealed off and couldn't be moved after the FWL victory the year before then why were lorries still coming there from Kiev? If heavy weapons couldn't be moved via Lovets, how was it being done or had they given up? She knew that huge quantities of weapons and war materials were still leaving the Ukraine. She must find out more. Suddenly there was a flash of lightning and the thunder rolled. Rain rattled against the windows. That at least should put the paparazzi off, poor folk! Exhausted she slipped off to sleep.

She was woken by the dawn chorus, a foul head, and a worse mouth. Marc slept on untroubled. She pulled on a tracksuit, evaded the reporters by traversing the cellar and slipping out through an old drayman's door which Kurt had thoughtfully showed her the previous night. The morning air made her feel fresher at once. She passed briskly along two side streets until she thought it safe to return to the riverbank. She ran fast for about three miles out of the town before stopping in a copse to do her voice practice. It sounded dreadful to her but given the circumstances she wasn't entirely surprised. Resigned she turned for home and ran back angrily and even faster. A voice behind her stopped her short as she approached the hotel.

'*Contessa! Che piacere*! How are you?'

'Evil, thank you. *Professore*'

'I can't believe that! But why? You have found this nation's symbol, the sacred Chalice.'

At that moment they were set upon by photographers, a phalanx of microphones demanding sound bites and Kurt's Borzoi bitch who clearly felt that somebody needed her help but in the melee wasn't at all certain who she was supposed to attack or defend. Fortunately, Kurt had pressed into service two of the larger of his former colleagues who now stood guard at the entrance to 'The Woman in Armour'. Behind these two formidable ex Commandos, they reached the relative security of the bar and struggled to regain their breath.

'*Viva la democrazia*!' said Poliziano 'now tell me why the most beautiful lady in Livonia is feeling evil.'

'Because I-we-haven't found Tamara Oblova.'

'But I thought you had new clues.'

'We have but we are still a long way off. At best time is precious; at worst something dreadful could have happened to her already.'

'What exactly have you found?'

'The chamber where we were both kept prisoner. The secret vault that contained The Chalice led off it. It was walled up. I broke the wall down by accident by falling against it when we were both shut in there. I couldn't see much at the time, as it was so dark, so I just covered up the hole. I am sure that none of our captors knew it was there. Yesterday we discovered the whole Nazi hoard exactly as it had been sealed up sixty years ago.'

'Amazing, but how precisely does that give you more information about Signorina Oblova?'

'There were some scratches on the wall. They measured the days that she was kept there and according to my calculations, she was there until a week ago. Who knows what happened then?'

The most dreadful thoughts rushed through Detty's mind just as they had done in the night. Poliziano however asked calmly:

'Was there anything else?'

'Only some irregular scratches. She might have been trying to write something.'

'Have you any idea what they meant?'

'It might have been a name Pedro or Pepe but there is no clear P. The guards were Spanish speaking and there was a Pepe but it doesn't add up to much.'

She trailed off despondently as Liese came into the bar with Marc. Coffee arrived.

'Would it be possible to see the vault?' asked Poliziano, coming out of a reverie.

'Of course, you can. We are going down again now. Join us if you want to.'

*

Poliziano studied the scratches intently for some time. He then turned round abruptly and asked Liese:

'Has Leutnant Lopokova seen these?'

'No' admitted Liese.

'Then I would like her to do so. If we agree, we may be on to something important.'

It was late in the afternoon after Tanya had got down to the ruin and they finished studying the scratches together. This time Poliziano spoke with a question:

'Can Signorina Oblova use Cyrillic?'

Liese looked at Detty who shook her head:

'I don't know either way.'

Liese went on:

'As you know we usually use Latin script even for Russian here to avoid administrative chaos but almost all educated Livonians can write in Cyrillic and, although we can't be certain, we can assume that that includes Tamara.'

'Well, it looks as if Signorina Oblova or whoever scratched these was writing in Cyrillic and that the absence of a P is accounted for by the last two vertical scratches which together could make a Cyrillic 'P'. The next scratches are not very clear but they could be Cyrillic 'ete'. That would make Pete so you may be right that she was trying to say something about the guard Pepe or Pedro or some version of Peter and never got the chance to finish but Leutnant Lobokova thinks that it might not be so simple.'

He looked at Tanya who continued

'We can be fairly certain that the message was never finished but I'm puzzled by two things. Why write in Cyrillic in the first place as it certainly wasn't her normal script and why suddenly start calling Pepe or Pedro, Peter or Pete using the German or English name. I think that there is a strong possibility that she knew she might not have time to finish and was in a hurry. It is also possible that she was trying to disguise what she wrote from the guards who almost certainly could not read Cyrillic.'

'Even in *stampatello* – block capitals I mean.'

'Exactly, so what might it mean?'

There was silence in the chamber, broken only by a pervasive distant drip of water, while Tanya looked round at each in turn waiting for a suggestion but none came so she continued:

'I have a theory and it is only a theory. Suppose she intended to indicate something Russian by using the script, wanted to obscure it from prying eyes and was interrupted halfway through the word. The Russian word that she was writing could have been '*Pyeterboorg*' not her guard's name but her intended destination.'

'St Petersburg, of course' Liese looked rather abashed 'Might well be so. We have suspected that that may be their heavy weapons outlet now Lovets airfield is effectively closed to them so they could have transferred her there but how do we find out where? It's a big city. Like looking for a needle in a haystack.'

'Do you fancy a weekend in Lübeck, Detty?' Marc asked his startled wife quietly in English.

'You think we might be getting some idea of yer man's whereabouts?' asked Detty in return in her best Ulster imitation.

Marc quickly reverted to German and explained that he thought Lawri might be able to help them. There was general agreement that this, however far-fetched, was the only hopeful course.

A rapid coded phone call to Lawri explained that they wanted to know if their Spanish religious establishment had a branch in St Petersburg. Lawri said that he thought that there might be a daughter house there but he would try and find out while they were travelling.

The plane connections were hopeless and the only solution was to throw their bags into Detty's Z4. She drove furiously for the frontier relieved to have something to do. At first, they were silent, both deep in thought. After doing a slalom between a horse and cart and a huge pothole she laughed:

'It seems like last time, although I suppose it's a bit different.'

'We seem to be making a habit of it, don't we? When we left them all just now, it felt like *Wotan* and *Loge* going down to *Nibelheim* to get The *Ring*. They looked that depressed.'

'Which way round?'

'Oh, you're *Loge* – he's half-female anyway. I am just *Wotan* pompously and ponderously trudging along in your wake.'

'Bullshit – but it would be fun to sing *Loge*. How about it – the first soprano *Loge*?'

'There's the little matter of the range.'

'We could sort that out. A bit of transposition would do the trick and after all women have played Hamlet.'

The frontier had been sealed at the time of the Lovets operation to guard against any attempted escape. It had been opened again but the FWL guards had obviously been told to be hyper-vigilant. The autumn evening had been dark for some time and the FWL guard peremptorily demanded their papers and shone his torch into the little sports car with its German number plate. He seemed unimpressed by the German and Irish passports and, without reading them, muttered something about foreigners and asked them to wait. As the guard turned away to consult his superiors, Marc called out:

'*Ein moment bitte!* and got his FWL identity card out of his wallet passed it to the impatient returning guard. Detty, realising what Marc had done got fished her card out of her bag on the car floor and thrust it through the window. Collapse of guard.

'*Entschuldigung, Herr General und .. und Frau General, Frau Hauptmann, Frau Gräfin, Frau Komturin…….*'

The gate had swung up and they were driving past the solitary German guard who gave them a bored wave through.

'And they make jokes about us using too many titles' said Marc as Detty nearly drove into the ditch in paroxysms of laughter.

'You, *mein Schatz*, are definitely suffering from the serious disease of *honoritis Livoniensis multiplex* – are there English words for it?'

'Well, they certainly aren't any Irish ones but the English are much keener on titles than we are' she answered, still convulsed. The more cheerful mood lasted until they were having a very early breakfast in their suite in the Kaiserhof Hotel in Lübeck.

*

Lawri drew on his huge pipe.

'It might be difficult. I have heard that they were a bit disturbed by a wild foreign woman – Irish – my informant thought who infiltrated the Monastery and then rode off through the night like a banshee with important documents – extraordinary behaviour you must agree.'

'Absolutely' said Detty, the corners of her mouth twitching.

'Did they ever find the miscreant?'

'Surprisingly, they didn't which has made them even more suspicious. They have become extremely nervous and have covered their tracks very well this year. The monastery is at Kovel in the Ukraine but that is several hundred kilometres away. They used to use a tractor warehouse at Gregorsk about fifteen kilometres outside the city but they changed it this year and we don't know the new depot. I suspect that they are changing them every few consignments but, for what it's worth, we think that one is near the centre, possibly in the Petersburg docklands but beyond that, for the moment, I can't help you.'

Detty looked at Marc.

'Do we go?'

'No other choice.'

Lawri poured all of them another *Weissbier*.

'If you will forgive me making a suggestion, Herr Major, the airport at Petersburg is under constant surveillance by several organisations and I would not like to guarantee the safety of yourself and the Frau Major if you use it. One of our agents was assassinated within a few kilometres of the airport last week. Motorcycle drew level with the taxi, burst of machine pistol fire and kaput. Very sad he was a good man – hard to replace.'

'Do you have a better route?'

'It so happens that I might have. I have a shipment of, shall we say, engineering materials from Rostock to Tallinn by a Bahamian registered coastal trader. It's only an hour's ride from Tallinn to St Petersburg. I think that they might have a double cabin to spare if I asked them.'

'Tell them we are a shy honeymoon couple.'

'Of course, Frau Major, and I will order Champagne for your cabin.'

'Herr Lawri, you are a miracle.'

He was as good as his word. They left the car in Lawri's care and he took them to the *Lübeck Hauptbahnhof*. In two hours, they reached

Rostock and shortly after were slipping out between the old Hansestadt's *molen* and sipping champagne. They were enjoying living up to the expectations of their assumed role. They made the most of their three-day journey which included a visit to Visby to unload. Normally Detty would have been ashore trying to trace the Hanseatic connections of Gotland but their second honeymoon occupied them fully and they were leaving the harbour before either of them realised that they had docked.

As they entered Tallinn, Marc received a scrambled message on his phone.

'Try warehouse near the Maryinsky with canal front and backing onto *Ulitsa Reisen*'. They both, not for the first time, mentally, toasted Lawri, who had worked hard and well. Tallinn fascinated, as they landed in the early morning, not least because of the comparison with Königshof. They had thought that there was a direct train to St Petersburg but its schedule, if any, seemed obscure. They decided to make the best of a bad job and take the roundabout but certain service via Pskov arriving at the Warsaw Station in St Petersburg much later than they had expected.

Exhausted by the several connections on what should have been an easy journey, they made their way by taxi to the St Petersburg Hotel booking in as Professor and Dr Retten, academics from Stuttgart studying Orthodox Church Music. The identities had been hurriedly arranged by Colonel Kramm with the co-operation of Stuttgart University. They didn't imagine that their new identities would fool any serious operator in St Petersburg but it seemed slovenly not to make some attempt at cover. It might also gain them valuable time while their real identities were investigated.

The St Petersburg Hotel had been Marc's choice. Musical academics would be more likely to use the large anonymous hotel east of the Neva than the much more luxurious and closely monitored Grand Hotel Europe on Nevsky. Detty regretted the gorgeous suites of the St Petersburg stories and the immediacy of the great Prospects. However, she saw the sense of the choice and was cheered by the view of the cold morning sun on the Winter Palace and a gargantuan Russian breakfast that was the more welcome after the fast of the day before.

9
DEAD SOULS

*But if you don't mind my asking,
how do you wish to buy these peasants?*

GOGOL: *DEAD SOULS*

The canals and Neva made the journey difficult. It was not really complicated but would make it a bit of a problem to go back and forth frequently, if they needed to comb the target area. They poured over the city map, regretting now their decision to base themselves so far from the centre of things. The metro station was a fair walk away and they would have to change. Taxis were out as they were easy to trace and follow. They were about to leave the breakfast bar and set off when Detty, with sudden irrelevance, asked Marc whether he would like to go to the theatre.

'OK, I give up,' said her long-suffering husband.

Mark was now fully accustomed to his wife's flights of fancy.

'I'm supposed to be doing *Tatiana* at the *Maryinsky* next year if the authorities will give a foreigner a work permit. I thought it might be useful to try and visit the theatre. It's very near to *Ulitsa Reisen* as Lawri said. I'll have to call myself O'Neill of course but that shouldn't matter.

After all I'm not the first singer to travel incognito and, as far as Lev is concerned, two identities might be helpful in confusing them.'

She made a telephone call and disappeared across the road to the river to negotiate with a boatman. He seemed on the point of giving up for the winter although the river wasn't due to freeze for several weeks. In a few minutes, they were crossing the Neva. Detty wished that they had brought thermal underwear as the cold north wind made short work of her leather trouser suit. The *Fontanka* was more sheltered but only slightly warmer. The grandeur of the waterside palaces made up for the cold. Like good tourists, they craned their necks as they passed under the Nevsky Bridge but were too low to get a good view of the fabled Prospekt. Once past Nevsky, they began to search for likely warehouse areas. Until they reached the theatre, the buildings remained disappointingly residential with strong echoes of former grandeur.

The visit to the theatre was cordial and courteous. There was the usual rehearsal schedule in progress but they were able to visit the stage, dressing rooms and the pit. Detty even got a chance to try the acoustics. They took coffee but declined lunch, correctly claiming another engagement. North of the theatre, they began to find canal side warehouses. There was an eerie silence about the district. No one seemed to be about although it was just half past one. A huddled figure, surrounded by anonymous bottles, was lying immobile in a deserted repository doorway, the only human presence. There were many such in St Petersburg now.

They turned a corner and came upon another warehouse, again apparently abandoned, which stood between the *Ulitsa Reisen* and the canal. No other fitted Lawri's description. Detty squeezed Marc's hand. Silently they both looked for an entrance. On the road front of the building, there were firmly locked and barred transport gates but a passage led round to the side along the canal. Nobody appeared as they slipped into it. The railings stretched out over the canal but they were able to climb round over the carelessly arranged barbed wire. Marc flattened himself on the wire trying rather unsuccessfully to minimise the damage to Detty's Lanoure leather trouser suit, which she had deemed necessary for their Maryinsky visit.

'I always seem to be writing off Lanoure models' she whispered.

'If this visit works, I'll buy you the entire Winter Collection.'

They were on an open wharf occupied by piles of empty wooden pallets and rusting cranes, which were abandoned and sticking up into the pale blue autumn sky at crazy angles. Detty shivered then started to read the names burnt onto some of the pallets.

'Mainly Russian, a few Scandinavian, Estonia, and one each from Portugal and Livonia – pretty normal sort of mix for here I should think.'

Marc nodded and moved away from the water to examine the small door into the ground floor, which seemed to be, or to have been, offices with the main storage space on the floors above them. Marc looked round to make sure nobody was about on the wharf over the canal then slipped on gloves and jemmied the door muttering.

'I've always wanted to try a Russian prison.'

'You speak for yourself – you weren't in The Farm – officially at least.'

'I'm not here officially. You can just see the headlines "German intelligence officer caught spying in Russia"'.

'"With his wife – the well- known IRA female serial assassin"'

'You didn't assassinate anybody for the IRA.'

'The papers won't let that worry them. They're usually far further away from the truth.'

'*Wie steht dann ' Dramatischsopranistin Einbrecherin,*'[26] in *Das Bild*?'

For a moment, it had been hysterical but now the door had given way and they were back to basics in the grubby interior. The ground floor was remarkable only for its disappointingly empty spaces. There was a goods lift but, predictably, it was switched off, or, more probably, had long since ceased to work at all. A small stairway led to the floor above. This was more promising. Crates of varying sizes, some very large, were marked in Russian 'Agricultural Machinery – Origin Russian Federation'. There were several forklift trucks, which presumably had taken the place of the superannuated goods lift.

'Odd sort of export' mused Marc 'but it could be genuine. We can't

---

26 How about then 'Dramatic soprano turns burglar?

open these cases they are far too large and firmly sealed; it would take us days even with my knife. Better to try and find some documentation, an office or something.'

This seemed a forlorn hope. However, after much searching, they came upon another set of stairs, tucked away behind a huge crate, leading to a small gallery on the third floor. A short corridor with a couple of small internal windows overlooked the main goods floor. Detty looked out nervously. Neither of them was armed and there could be no escape if they were discovered. A highly scented lavatory separated two unmarked doors.

'Somebody has been here recently.' Detty wrinkled her nose. The first door broke open easily. There was a shelf of reasonably neat cyrillic files and a very old Soviet computer.

'Let's look at the other one and then come back.'

A dark stain seeped under the second door. For a moment, Detty felt that her worst fears were about to be realised. Marc tried the handle, pushed, and almost fell inside when the expected resistance didn't come. A bare tidy desk was in the centre of the room. Around it lay four bodies still oozing blood from their wounds. Each had been shot several times. A quick look reassured Detty that they were all male and, incongruously, she heaved an enormous sigh of relief. They looked round. The room was bare. There were no papers and no sign of Mara. The only things left in the room were the corpses. She looked at the first body and with a start knew that she recognised him. For a moment, she couldn't think where she had seen him before then realised that he was the man who had brought Mara to her in their dungeon at Lovets. He was dressed differently but he still had the same peculiar stench of tobacco as before. The next corpse was entirely unknown to her, as was the third. The fourth man was lying on his front. They turned him over and she recognised him instantly. Albeit without his soutane, he still had the severe features of Monsignor Jose Maria Pueblo's chaplain who had followed his chief round Florence and Pic Noix.

'No doubt about the connection then— at least we have proved that.' commented Marc, as she told him that she recognised the chaplain from Pic Noix.'

'But no Mara. Let's have a look at the other room.'

It was difficult to do a thorough search but all the records appeared old and irrelevant dealing with entirely innocent timber and manufactured goods. Some of them dated back to Soviet times.

'Let's get out while we can and have a think.'

They slipped back over the wire not a moment too soon. A dilapidated Lada containing four men entered the narrow lane and stopped some distance in front of them. Detty smoothing the remains of her elegant leather suit strode purposely forward towards the car.

The shoulder holsters and machine pistols across their laps were obvious as she looked into the car. She smiled charmingly.

'I wonder whether you can help us. We have come from the Maryinsky Theatre and lost our way. We are foreigners as you can see. Can you direct me back to Nevsky?'

'What are you doing here?' scowled the man beside the driver who seemed to be the leader, fingering the machine pistol.

'As I said we are lost' she smiled again.

'Why do you come from theatre? Nobody is there at this time. It is closed.'

His manner betrayed a familiarity with interrogation. Probably ex KGB thought Detty.

'I am a singer and my husband and I had an appointment with the Director.'

'You lie and I will check. What is your name?'

'Bernadetta'

She added the 'a' in deference to Russian inflection and was relieved that second names are not used in Russia. She saw no reason to reveal more of her identity than necessary.

He pulled out his mobile phone, punched a number and asked peremptorily to be connected to the Director of the Maryinsky. Impressively quickly it was done. The speaker asked his questions politely but not obsequiously. He cancelled the call after confirming the truth of Detty's claim. There was no apology but his manner was much less aggressive.

'OK. Turn *naleyeva* then *ftaroy naprava*'

'*Spaseeba* for your help.'

'*Nyehza-shto*!'

Detty reflected, not for the first time, the strangeness of the criminal classes still using the customary polite forms of the country. The Mafia said 'Permesso?' when they entered the house to shoot you and American hoods still said, 'You're welcome!' In this respect, Russia was no different.

'That was a near one! Thank God for your foresight in making that appointment.'

They walked away studiously slowly; hands held.

'If it hadn't been for that we should have been two more in the charnel house.'

'It still hasn't brought us much closer to Mara. Do you think that they will realise that we found the bodies?'

'Difficult to know for sure. It depends whether that lot actually did the killing. Even if there are two groups involved and it wasn't just an internal job, there is no real doubt that they are connected with one lot or the other – the killers or the killed.'

They turned the corner. The huddled figure in the doorway stirred and peered at them in the darkening afternoon through the blood-rimmed eyes of skid row. Unexpectedly he spoke:

'You are looking for the *dyevooshka*.' it was more a statement than a question 'jumped and then gone in the barge.'

At this moment shouting started from the corner they had just left followed by car doors banging and engine revving.

'They have found something. This is where we get out' said Marc urgently pulling Detty away into a run. They crossed the street in the opposite direction to Nevsky, disappeared down two alleys, hid in another doorway and waited. They heard more shouting as the car shot off in the direction of Nevsky then silence. After some minutes, they cautiously emerged and headed back to the doorway. The old man had gone. They looked around but there was no sign of him.

*

The warehouse was cold and Mara was hungry. Her captors seemed too busy with other matters to think of feeding her. The windows were barred but she could see through the bars to the canal below. Where was she? Obviously, a northern port but was it in fact St Petersburg? After she heard them mention St Petersburg, she had overheard more talk about lots of other places including several ports – Antwerp, Hamburg and Rotterdam and others. She began to think that her impetuous Cyrillic scribble had been a terrible mistake. It was long odds that anybody would find it and even longer that they would recognise it. To add to her misery, she now realised that if they did by chance find and interpret the writing it might put them off the scent. She turned back to the present scene. There were no further clues. Only the cold, grey sky and various warehouses including the one that was her prison. A coaster was moored to the quay below. The stern was out of her view and she could not see any evidence of a name or port of registry elsewhere on the hull. She then tried to analyse the journey but without success. She had been shut in a van for the first part, then bundled into a small aircraft for several hours then a shorter journey in another van. She had been made to wear one of the dreadful belts for the whole journey and every time they changed vehicles, a foul-smelling black hood had been put over her head. At least now, she was free from both hood and belt, which they had removed before locking her into the room. This made her think that wherever she was she had arrived, at least temporarily, at her destination. They didn't even seem to think that there was any harm in her seeing out of the window. At first, she had thought that she might be able to attract the attention of somebody in the warehouse opposite or the ship below but there was no one. The place seemed completely deserted.

There was a noise on the stairs. Footsteps on the creaking wood and conversation. This time it was Russian – a dialect but native Russian. She couldn't catch exactly what was being said but it was angry:

'Nothing but no-good con men' several expletives 'learn not to double cross ……. mother fuckers' then several more expletives.

The voices were louder and clearer.

'They should still be here. The van's outside.'

The door was unlocked roughly. The key must have been left on the outside. Three very angry strange men looked in. Mara caught a glimpse of the machine pistol that the third carried. When they saw that the only occupant was a girl, they uttered more oaths and slammed the door shut. Mara listened for the sound of the key turning in the lock. It didn't come.

The newcomers had apparently gone on past the foul lavatory to the third door without bothering to lock the first room. Suddenly voices rose to screaming pitch in anger. Mara sensed her chance but her hand was no sooner turning the knob on the unlocked door when the stutter of machine gun fire froze her momentarily. Then she realised in a flash that, whatever was happening two doors down, it was now or never. She opened the door and fled across the gallery down the stairs to the landing below. Desperately she searched for a way down. There was a crashing on the gallery above followed by boots coming down towards her. She was about to give up and hide as best she could, when, suddenly, she saw the small stairway to the ground quay. Ever more loudly the footsteps thumped behind her as she scrambled down the tight curving stairway. As she reached the quay, she reckoned they must be only just round the corner behind her. To cross the open quay for about fifty metres without being caught and probably gunned down was impossible. On an impulse, she jumped onto the moored coaster, crawling through the rail, and tearing her tattered jeans that she had worn continuously since her kidnap. Hidden behind a capstan she stopped for breath. There was still shouting on the quay. An open hatch was a short distance across the deck. She crawled to it, slithering down a steel companion ladder onto an oil-stained bunk, reeking of the pungent tobacco that Russians reserve for their *papirosi*, long-tubed, cheap, cigarettes. She had met these foul-smelling contrivances before and was now sure where she was. It was certainly Russia and in a major port. Her first guess had been right. It had to be St Petersburg. Not that it helped much until she could safely get off the coaster and out of the warehouse area. The chances of getting any help from her friends were effectively zero. They wouldn't read the message, if they did, they wouldn't understand it, if they did they wouldn't come to St Petersburg or be able to find her and it certainly wouldn't be now. No, she must get off the coaster and get out of here rapidly. But how? There was still shouting on the dock from the men who had crashed past her upstairs. No chance of moving – better to lie low until they had gone.

Rather than getting less, the noise increased and was now on board the ship itself. There were strange rumblings then the engines started and the shouts and rumblings increased. Somebody threw a kit bag through the hatch and it landed on Mara's stomach winding her. Fortunately, the owner did not look down after it but went off about his business.

In other respects, the situation was much less reassuring. Daughter of the Hanse and sailor as she was, this was a new situation. Apart from sailing across the Baltic in a reconstructed medieval cob, a fair bit of experience in a racing dinghy but with Andrea usually navigating and a few trips to the old docks at Königshof, her experience of commercial ships was almost nil. She had crossed the English Channel and the Irish Sea and had once launched a ferry for the new Königshof to Stockholm service. Neither this ceremonial exercise nor her racing experience qualified her as a navigator. She was, however, sure that the ship was leaving the quay and that she was trapped on board. There was nothing she could do except to hope that by some miracle she could avoid observation until they arrived in some friendly port where she could escape. She knew that she was in the hands of apparent enemies of her former captors and perhaps her enemies' enemies could be her friends. However equally she had been a witness to the violent events at the warehouse. It would be difficult to explain her situation convincingly and this lot appeared to be extremely trigger-happy.

She tried to arrive at a convincing strategy to use when she was discovered. She had decided on the plan that would give her the best chance and looked out of the starboard porthole almost fatalistically. In front of her astonished gaze, instead of the docks or the widening estuary was the most splendid, majestic building that she had ever seen. Remembering pictures from the past, she knew that she was looking at the Winter Palace of the Czars. More important, for the moment, she realised that they must be heading inland and not out to sea. Whilst she stood trying to figure out the significance of these developments, she heard a noise behind her, a muttered expletive, and a hand iron-clamped on her shoulder:

'Who the hell are you?'

She recognised him from the party in the warehouse but he wasn't one of the leaders.

'Anna Nickolaevna' said Mara looking simple and adding a strong coarse Livonian accent to her Russian.

'Oh, are you? What the fuck are you doing here?'

It was native Russian but with a heavy Ukrainian accent.

'Well, you see...'

He didn't wait for her answer grabbed her arm roughly and started dragging her after him up to the deck and aft to the wheelhouse.

A bearded man in a woollen cap was standing by the helmsman. He seemed to be the boss although was simply addressed as Mikhail Ivanov. Mara's captor explained how he had found her.

'What are you doing here then?' Mikhail repeated the question more gently and without expletives but then silkily he added:

'I think you're a police agent. You were sent here to spy on us. Osip, tie her hands and shove her overboard – quietly. Its dark nobody will see. She won't last long in the river at this time of year. We can't take a chance on what she's seen already.'

'No, Sir, please, Sir, I mean no harm. I'm not a spy. It isn't what you think.'

Mara was using the Livonian peasant Russian that she had cruelly mimicked with her girlfriends at school. He paused and looked at her long and hard.

'Tell me who you are and how you got here then' he snapped, looking unconvinced. Mara knew that her life hung by a thread and she had to be convincing.

She launched into her prepared story. She did it rather well. At the same time, she silently thanked her valiant stoical rural compatriots whom she had mocked with her posh Convent schoolmates.

'Anna Nickolaevna, Sir' she said 'men came to the village, Stirsk, near Litovsk in Livonia where I was born. Dad works on a farm. They wanted me to go to St Petersburg, Sir, said it was where the emperor used to live and was very grand. I could have a good job as a dancer with money, nice clothes, a car and a flat of my own perhaps even jewels.

But it wasn't like that at all when I got there. Sent me to a big house all right but I was treated like a slave from the start. There was no pay, they locked me in most of the time and they made me work all day. I had no papers and they said that if I didn't behave, they would tell the police who would rape me and put me in prison. The mistress beat me from the start and the Master – well the Master –you know, Sir, you know what they do. Then the mistress found out that the Master had had me and she went into a terrible temper. She called me a dirty little tart, but it wasn't my fault was it, Sir, I didn't want to and he was rough. She beat me every day, really bad, then burnt me with a poker. Got her son to help. I couldn't take it no more. I managed to get out of the house and ran away but they followed me through several streets then I ran down the passage by the quay. There was no way out and then I heard a car coming I thought it was them or the police. I leapt onto the ship to hide and that's why I am here.'

'I don't believe a word of it. It's all lies. You're a spy. Throw her overboard.'

Osip made to grab her.

'It's the truth, Sir, Here look at my back where I was beaten and burnt.'

She threw off her sweater and fleece and tore her shirt up showing the terrible scars still on her back from the torture she had endured at the hands of the NAS the year two years before. It saved her life. There could be no doubt about the reality or severity of her punishment or it's aftereffects. In the flickering shadows of the wheelhouse light against the Neva darkness, neither the plastic surgery nor the age of the damage were evident. Paradoxically Mikhail winced at the sight of the injuries to the girl that he had been quite prepared to drown a moment before. He was shaken. A third man had arrived from the engine room and was standing back in the half-light during the exchange, quietly he said:

'I think she's telling the truth. Why don't you send her with the others. She's older than most of them but still young and has a good figure. She's tasty enough if you don't see her back.'

Osip added coarsely 'The punters won't see that if she's lying on it. It might make us a bit extra.'

The men laughed lewdly but Mikhail nodded and Mara knew that, temporarily at least, she had won a reprieve. She was locked below in a crudely converted cargo hold. There were wooden bunks all round and an antique smelly oil heater but it was still cold. She was brought soup and dark bread. Then she wrapped herself in a soiled blanket from a pile in the corner and lay down on the hard bunk. The irony of being saved by her Farm torture filled her mind for some minutes then exhausted and careless for the future she slept.

She was woken sometime later by torchlight, shuffling and the sound of low voices almost drowned by the noise of the engines running slowly. The sound of water against the hull had stopped. The hatch opened and several figures entered the hold. They took no notice of her. One of the men pointed out the blankets and bunks then climbed out through the hatch, locking it behind him again, as the engine speed increased and the waves once more slapped against the hull. Mara knew that there were now other people with her but was too tired to be curious and slept again. This sequence happened twice more during the night.

She woke once more as Osip arrived with a bowl of barley coffee and another of buckwheat pasha. It was morning but not dawn in those wintry northern latitudes. Mara looked round at her companions as they warmed themselves with the basic food. There were now seven of them in all. The others were all girls some in their early teens, the oldest about Mara's own age. It appeared that four of them were pairs of sisters. Gradually they told their stories. Two of them had lived in an old Soviet collective farm now run by a gang boss. He had told their parents that their daughters could earn big money in America as waitresses and he could arrange for them to go there. The girls, only fifteen and sixteen, were desperately sad at leaving their families but they were country girls with little experience of the world and they still believed they were on the way to a good life.

The other stories were very similar. One time it was travelling recruiting agents who had come to the town or village offering glittering prospects to the girls as dancers and much needed money to the parents. Other arrangements had been made via the local Mafia bosses and the girls had been given no choice but they had always been told they had an excellent future. Sometimes it was as waitresses, sometimes dancers, sometimes shop assistants or office workers; all good respectable jobs which allayed parents' fears. Mara listened to their stories but kept quiet. No purpose would be served by panicking the girls by telling them of her certainty of the nature of the future that was in store.

The feeble Russian dawn of early winter came at last and they were allowed on deck for air. They were in a wide waterway amidst flat countryside. It could have been anywhere in Russia or elsewhere. On the horizon were a few ugly modern farm buildings otherwise there were wide fields with no obvious crop. After about an hour the ship approached a run-down quay and Mara could see a group of people standing waiting. They were all locked below before the ship reached the quay and, sure enough, four more girls were ushered in to join them after the stop. After dark, they saw the lights of a large town followed by a wide lake. There were more stops that night and the following day the number in the hold reached twenty. After that the stops became fewer as the river passed through endless tundra punctuated by occasional forests and fields. Slowly the total of 'passengers' reached about thirty and that seemed to be the final number. On the fourth morning, the river was much narrower and light ice was forming on the water causing some consternation amongst the crew. The year was getting late. They nosed towards another quay this time adjacent to a large village. On the other side of the river was an airfield with a few quite modern light planes at one end and some old Soviet military wrecks at the other. Once more, the girls were locked below before they reached land but not before Mara had noticed that the party on this quay were all male.

There was talking and the clink of glasses above but no sign of moving on. After they had been moored for about fifteen minutes, Osip appeared down the hatchway.

'All of you take your clothes off and sit on the edge of the bunks.'

Even Mara, who had more than an inkling of what was in store for them, was taken by surprise by the staccato command. The other girls looked non-plussed and remained motionless staring at Osip thinking that they had misunderstood him.

'I said take all your clothes off and sit on the edge of the bunks.

Quickly now.'

Osip, who had been through this procedure before, slapped the nearest girl hard round the face. Tears streaming down her bruised cheek she started fiddling with her anorak.

'I said get on with it all of you' he shouted dragging a pistol from under his jacket.

Having seen something of the determined brutality of the crew when she first came aboard, Mara realised that there was no alternative and started to undress quickly. The other girls followed her example, one by one, urged on by Osip waving his gun. When they had stripped to their underclothes, they looked round dubiously at each other until Osip left them in no doubt that these also should be removed. They were told to put their clothes on the upper bunks and sit in a semicircle on the lower ones. When they had been fully dressed, the hold had been far from warm but naked they were frozen. They shivered with their teeth chattering violently as they edged close to each other for some warmth. The cold almost made them forget the embarrassment and humiliation.

Osip produced a bunch of numbered wristbands and clipped them on each girl's left wrist. Mara looked at hers. It was number 23 – a number she never forgot. As soon as he had numbered the last wrist, he shouted '*Gatova*' through the hatch. Five men clambered down the ladder. Two were definitely Arabs wearing western fur overcoats but with aga banded kaffiyehs, the remaining three appeared to be southern European but as they all spoke a version of English, interspersed with a smattering of Russian, their exact origin was uncertain. It appeared to be a sort of auction sale. Each girl was stood up in turn, made to turn round slowly. When the examination was finished, the agents took it in turn to start the bidding. The final price was in American dollars mostly between $300 and $1500. The various factors influencing the price of each girl were coldly discussed. When the sale was settled the dealer put a marked tag indicating his ownership on the girl's right wrist and she was allowed to dress. Each sale was conditional upon medical examination. With vivid memories of the farm, Mara wondered when this would take place and what further indignities it would involve. She was now really too cold to care. The sale worked through in numerical order of wrist tags so girls in the twenties had to freeze for much longer than those with lower numbers.

Her own sale was quite fast. She was bought by one of the Arabs who had previously grumbled vigorously at the poor quality of the merchandise and the waste of time coming all this way. He had previously only bought a pair of blond eighteen-year-old twins and was now looking for an intelligent older girl to fulfil an unspecified special order. He seemed fascinated by blondes and, as he stroked Mara's hair, his forbidding face broke into a gentle smile. Unlike the Europeans, he seemed not to care about the state of her back although suggesting that it would mean a lower price and eventually offered $800, which in the absence of competition, was accepted.

Mara dressed, grateful at last for the warmth of her clothes. Her purchaser took a quick look at the remaining girls, decided that none was of interest and announced that he needed to leave that afternoon. He would pay the deposit and take the girls that he had bought to a house in the town where they would be medically examined by his own doctor. If his doctor was satisfied, his deputy would make the second payment and the third would follow via the agent in Minsk once the pathological tests were cleared. Mikhail agreed that, as he was a regular customer, that would be satisfactory. As she was led off the boat, Mara's mind was in turmoil. The experience that she had just suffered, the modern version of a slave market, had been horrible in the extreme. In one sense, she was relieved that the Arab had bought her. He seemed a more cultured and dignified man and less likely to rape his charges immediately than the knife happy European hoodlums. On the other hand, dangerous and terrible as life on the streets of Europe might be, escape would be much easier there than in some closed Arab establishment in a remote country.

They were put in an old army jeep and driven down a hideously pot-holed road to a group of disused Collective Farm buildings just beyond the village. The Arab and his retinue of two men and a woman, all wearing western dress, were camped out in one of them. There was a brief conversation in Arabic and the three girls were locked in the second story attic behind two locked and barred doors. They had obviously used these premises before. For the first time Mara was able to talk to the twins, her two companions; her first surprise was the discovery that they came from Western Karelia and regarded themselves as Finnish not Russian. Their parents had even adopted the dangerous step of giving them Finnish names, Helli and Ruta. The Karelian patriotism of their parents had inevitably paid its price. In the days of unrest following the fall of the USSR, their parents had made powerful enemies who sent them to Siberia without trial. There was doubt whether they ever got there alive and, certainly, they had never been seen again. The twins were toddlers when their parents disappeared. They were fostered by a 'suitable' Russian couple, who allowed them to retain their initials but had renamed them with safely Russian names Helenka and Ranya. Both had done well at school and were heading for University, Helli to study medicine and Ruta physics. In due course, curiosity about their roots made them delve, unwisely as they now realised, into local archives and ask around. They discovered a good deal about their parents and their real names but also uncovered some considerable skeletons in the local power cupboards. None of this passed unnoticed and one dark autumn evening as they got off the bus to go to their foster home, they were bundled into the back of a van and by stages to Mikhail's operation. As tall attractive eighteen-year-old blondes, they had fetched the highest price at the auction thus providing profit, as well as security, to their hometown local Mafia.

Mara took all this in and realised that she might have found resourceful potential allies. In return, she told them something about her Livonian origins and that she was studying at university in Munich. She stuck, however, to her alias, Anna Nikolaevna, and said nothing about her VIP status. She just said, truthfully, that she had been kidnapped while on holiday. They seemed to accept that this was an enduring risk of being young and female in Eastern Europe.

They were provided with a meal and then called one by one for medical examination. To Mara's relief, the woman who carried it out proved kindly and quite sensitive. There were the usual blood tests and swabs but even the intrusive part was gently done. Very different from her similar experience at The Farm, she thought. They were locked into their attic and later that night they heard a helicopter land and take off again. The chief Arab was not seen again. They presumed that he had taken the helicopter and moved on to other business.

For two days after the examinations, the girls were shut in the attic and Mara took the opportunity to look around. The window was unbarred and quite large enough to climb out but underneath was a sheer drop of over ten metres to the ground. Presumably, that was why the Arabs had not seen fit to lock and bar it. She was surprised; however, that they had not considered the possibility that one of them might attempt suicide rather than go abroad into slavery. They did, after all, between them represent a sizeable investment. In this situation, Mara kept thinking of Detty and her resourcefulness 'What would she do if she were here?'she asked herself. Mara didn't know exactly where they were. But whether it was Russia or Belarus, escape here must be, if possible, an easier option now than later. After all, she spoke the language and knew the culture and she had the law, such as it was, on her side. A later attempt to get out of an Arab country, on the other hand, where she would be a piece of legitimately owned personal property, would be even more fraught with difficulty. She would be strikingly foreign, in speech and appearance, and a woman to boot, with all that implied in a Muslim culture. Somebody would own her, wherever she finished up and he might reasonably be expected to have widespread contacts and influence. But how to escape from here? The window seemed the only way and her thoughts turned to the blankets that had thoughtfully been plentifully supplied to keep out the accelerating cold. She knew it was possible to make sheet ropes but blankets? She also wondered how far to involve the twins. They were bright but inexperienced. Having heard their story, she would like to have helped them but realised that three women were much harder to conceal than one, although there were also advantages to being together. She reasoned that she really had no choice, as they would know what she was doing anyway.

By the second evening, she had almost decided on her plan when something happened which forced her to act quickly. Late, after their soup and lamb stew supper, the woman doctor unlocked the door and came inside accompanied by her usual armed bodyguard. Instead of her normal coat shirt and baggy trousers, she was covered from head to foot in the veiled black chador, the traditional veil of Muslim women. She carried three similar garments.

'We leave to-morrow for your new home' she said kindly and softly 'these are what we wear there. They are not difficult but you had better try them on to make sure you wear them correctly, as we will leave early in the morning. You can put them on over your sweaters and jeans. There is no need to get cold,'

The girls each took one of the long, loose garments and slipped it over their heads covering their bodies completely. Each then adjusted the gauze part so that she could see through.

'That's quite all right. Sleep well and be ready early to-morrow.'

Locking the door securely, they departed. As soon as the footsteps had retreated, Mara summoned the others.

'Are you game to try and get out?'

'Yes, if we can, but how?'

'We knot the blankets together. We move that bed frame across the window and tie the blanket rope to it. We then climb down one by one and jump at the end if the rope doesn't reach the ground. If the bed moves, it will jamb in the window frame. We then get out of town as quickly as possible and try to get to somewhere with a telephone. After that, I may be able to help a bit. I have some contacts.'

They both nodded. The six blankets were piled in between them and the started knotting the blankets diagonally frenetically. It didn't go well. As Mara had feared the blankets were much harder to knot securely than sheets and the two knots used up a lot of length. When they had finished, they had about six metres of rope and some of that had to be used reaching and tying on to the bed frame. They tied it on and opened the window. The end of the rope dangled forlornly about six metres above the concrete surface outside. It was far too high to jump onto a hard surface without the near certainty of serious injury. They looked forlornly at each other. It was Ruta who spotted the chadors hanging behind the door after they had tried them on. They were long and strong. They pulled the rope in and feverishly lengthened it using the garments. Each added over a metre to the rope and when they tried again the end was a respectable two and a half metres above the concrete – plenty safe enough once they had allowed for their body lengths below the end of the rope.

'Which one of you two is the youngest?'

'I am' said Ruta adding 'by half an hour,'

'You go first then Helli and I go last.'

'Why?'

'Children first, Captain last to leave the ship,' her Hanseatic upbringing had after all rubbed off. They laughed but it was high pitched with tension. At once Ruta threw her leg over the sill and gently let the rope take her weight.

They held their breath. The rope creaked on the sill but held.

'Difficult to do this in a chador' was her parting shot and she was gone rhythmically hand over hand down the oddly made rope. A light jump at the bottom landed her gently on the concrete. With just a nod from Mara, Helli followed Ruta down. The rope creaked a bit more insistently but Helli arrived safely beside her sister. Mara, smaller and shorter than the others had more trouble climbing over the sill. The rope jerked as it took her weight. She started to climb down. She had only descended just over a metre and an ugly ripping sound broke the silence. The rope was tearing and there was not chance of going back. Fully seven metres above the ground Mara crashed down. The twins as if by instinct joined hands under her. From that height, small as she was, Mara struck the girls' linked hands with force. The three of them finished up in a heap. They picked themselves up and rubbed various bruises and inspected grazes but there was no serious damage. The twins' quick thinking had saved the day. Fortunately, the icy east wind from the Steppes was blowing noisily through the bushes and the Arabs' rooms were on the far side of the ground floor. The noise had passed unnoticed. That was one gain. They quickly untied the knots in the blankets and wrapped them over their heads and round themselves against the bitter wind.

At a quick trot, the oddly dressed group headed off from the old farm buildings towards the main road and the village. At first, fortunately, there was no sign of life. Then they became conscious of a buzzing sound getting louder as they approached the first building. It was a low single-story building with a corrugated iron roof. The doors were open and down each side was a line of cows. A wide red flexible pipe was attached to the bottom of a tank and lead to a small tanker labelled *Malako* and the name of a firm, which was parked outside. Clearly, milk was being loaded. The engine of the tanker was running and the buzzing came from a pump behind the cab on the tanker. Engine running must mean keys in ignition thought Mara although there was no driver in sight. Probably, he or she was in the farmhouse having tea while the tank filled.

'Come on' she said to the others and pushed them into the cab. She paused to close the tap on the end of the pipe, twist it free and lower it soundlessly onto the concrete yard. She jumped into the cab, found the clutch, crashed the gears as she struggled to master the unfamiliar controls and moved off with a series of jerks through the gate. The twins watched anxiously as they moved erratically up to the road junction. Fortunately, it was still dark, the wind was getting even stronger and it had started to snow. Nobody appeared to have spotted them. Maybe the shutters in the primitive farmhouse were still closed to preserve the last bit of heat. Once on the main road, Mara changed up with less difficulty and accelerated as rapidly as the clapped-out vehicle could manage. The road stretched featureless in front of them. The twins kept looking behind them but couldn't see anything because of the milk tank. Meanwhile Mara glanced repeatedly in the wing mirrors. They had been travelling for about half an hour when they saw lights in front off the road. Either they were coming to an industrial complex or a small town. Whatever it was, the lights appeared to lie to the right of the road. The three of them were looking so intently for a junction, that the lights of the car behind were quite close when Mara spotted them through the driving snow in the rising gale. She yelled at the twins to get down on the floor and flung one of the blankets over them. Next, she grabbed the workman's peaked cap and pulled it down over her matted fair hair and stuck a *papirosa* from a packet lying on the dashboard in her mouth. If the lights belonged to the pursuing driver or his farmer client, it wouldn't help. If it was anybody else it might. She recognised the car and its two occupants as it drew level with the tanker and waved her down. The man on the passenger side nearest to her was brandishing a revolver at her through the open window. She had to stop.

What followed would have been comedy if the stakes hadn't been so high. The Arabs who had no Russian got out of the jeep and started gesticulating and pointing. Mara keeping her head in the shadows of the cab waved her papirosa out of the cab and adopting a most dysphonic growling basso let out a stream of Russian obscenities that her father certainly didn't know she had learnt at the Sacred Heart Convent. She didn't really care if they thought she was female or male as long as she was convincing as a foul-mouthed yokel. As she was in full voice, a second car arrived, this time it was indeed the legitimate tanker driver and the farm manager both armed with AK 47s, which quickly induced the Arabs to throw down their rather inadequate pistols.

The balance of power was now radically altered. Thinking quickly Mara changed roles as well. She quietly took off the cap, threw down her still unlighted cigarette, wrapped the blanket round her shoulders and burst into floods of tears. Helli and Ruta had now emerged from under the blanket and climbed out of the tanker also feigning tears. Mara explained, falteringly, how these dreadful foreign ogres had kidnapped the three girls (that part at least, almost true) and were taking them off into unimaginable alien slavery (that part completely true) by means of stealing the tanker (completely untrue). In the heat of the moment, the loopholes in the story didn't seem obvious to the two countrymen who immediately saw themselves as heroes protecting Russian womanhood from foreign tyrants. One proceeded to telephone the Militia and the other to threaten to emasculate one of the Arabs with a well-placed shot from his AK47. Mara did not think that this was the moment to explain that she wasn't Russian and her two companions would prefer not to be. No defence was possible from the tongue-tied Arabs and the only remaining anxiety was the incorruptibility or otherwise of the local police.

She needn't have worried. The two young Militiamen who arrived commendably promptly in a police car knew at once that this bizarre scenario required someone more senior. They handcuffed the two Arabs and bundled them at pistol point into the car. They then politely suggested that the *dyevooshki*[27] might like to remain until a second police car arrived which would give them a more comfortable ride into town.

The Captain of Militia at Novojardov was in his early thirties and undeniably handsome. Mara explained that she was not a Russian national and asked that he might interview her alone. He looked doubtful and explained that another officer must be present and the interview taped. Mara could see no way round these apparently reasonable regulations and agreed.

The captain called in his senior woman colleague. Mara began a simplified version of her story. She described herself as Anna Nikolaevna, the daughter of a Livonian official. She told them that she had been kidnapped for political reasons but, as a result of a turf war in St Petersburg, she had found herself in the hands of an entirely different Mafia gang, who had sold her to the Arabs. Before she said more she said that she would like the Livonian Embassy informed of her whereabouts. To her immense relief he agreed readily but said that there was a snag. Unfortunately, the fixed 'phone line had come down in the gale and the cellular signal was very poor in that remote area. One of his young officers had managed to make a call that morning from the top of the neighbouring grain silo. He would ask him to do his steeplejack act again and notify the Livonian Embassy that Anna Nikolaevna, one of their citizens, required assistance.

---

27 Young ladies

10
THE FLAME OF TORCHES

Dispense the wine,
Let the forest trunk crack and blaze,

AESCHYLUS: *THE EUMENIDES*

They had searched for as long as they could but it had seemed hopeless. Marc only had three days left of his leave, as he was obliged to return to London to be briefed for a NATO meeting in Washington. Military discipline had to prevail over his shadowy attachment to a small foreign country, its citizens, and his personal considerations. In addition, Detty started to feel extremely unwell. Marc was familiar with the dubious reputation of St Petersburg water in particular and public health in general. Detty thought privately that there might be a more positive reason for her problems but she was not even overdue yet and it was far too early to hint at possible alternative cause.

The search was, anyway, like looking for a needle in a haystack. The St Petersburg district and the upper Baltic coast were riddled with waterways and islands, each with its share of coasters, motor barges and small ports. Winter was closing in and access was becoming difficult in many places. They looked desperately for the vagrant old man who had first given them the strange message about the girl on the boat but he had vanished. Anyway, it was quite possible that he had been mistaken or even that he had made it all up. Detty, aware that she was under stress at a critical time in her career, tried to keep up study and vocal practice but the conditions made it far from easy.

They kept the Hansehaus informed about their lack of progress. Nicklaus was kind and stoical – he had been through so much. The scent was growing cold and they had no choice but to quit. There was no point in going back to Livonia to report their failure in person. Detty felt a coward and almost a traitor as they booked themselves on a direct flight from St Petersburg to London Gatwick and sat waiting in miserable silence. Neither of them was used to failure. It was a depressing and chastening experience.

They spent the night at Henley. The little house, normally so welcoming, was damp and cold. Detty made a desultory attempt to make the supermarket titbits, which they had bought on their way from the airport look appetising. Marc offered her a Jameson, which she refused. Raising one eyebrow at her, he poured himself a large one. Nothing that they did improved their mood or altered the harsh facts. If she was still alive, Mara was somewhere stuck in the on-coming Russian winter; they had searched for her and failed.

In the morning, Marc took the early train to Twyford and Paddington. As they kissed goodbye, Detty clung to him refusing to let him go and felt more and more wretched. She knew that the Washington trip might last at least a month and she felt completely desolate at losing him now. She was struck by the irony of the superwoman of Livonian independence clinging to her man like a lovelorn maiden in a nineteenth century novel.

After the train departed, she pulled herself together and 'phoned Eileen Vaughan in Manchester to find out if, as a wayward pupil, she was still persona grata. She was told, with a laugh, that she was. Her old digs however were full so in desperation she telephoned The Salutation and was warmed by a welcoming reply from her fellow countryman that they had indeed got a room. Packing a bag, she embarked on the stop-start journey to Manchester via Reading. She tried to work on her scores but concentration lapsed and gloom overcame her. She got out the neglected notes on the music and songs of the *Via Frances* but it all seemed a pointless muddle. She had the permitted half of Guinness in the bar when she arrived at The Salutation and feeling dog-tired went to bed.

She awoke feeling nauseated but more cheerful and crossed the road to Eileen's room at ten thirty for her appointment. The practice went badly and even Eileen seemed a bit alarmed that her star pupil's voice was so lacklustre and shapeless.

'Never mind. You clearly haven't been able to do as much proper practice as usual' she said trying to be encouraging.

'We will take it slowly at first and I'm sure it will come right. The Cassidy won't be too demanding and there is plenty of time before the *Tatiana* and the *Elsa*.'

Detty valued her support but knew in her heart of hearts that the real problem lay deeper. She went for a private practice but still wasn't getting anywhere near her normal standard. Disgusted she put on her Barbour jacket and started to wander aimlessly towards the middle of town through the chilly late November Mancunian drizzle. City were playing United in the Cup that evening in front of the television cameras and there was a buzz in the air. Although ignorant of the niceties of the game, she enjoyed the excitement of a good football match and like many of the Irish, she had a soft spot for Manchester United. Normally she would have relished the atmosphere, watched the match in a pub or even tried to scrounge one of the unobtainable tickets. Not today, however. She didn't even know where she was going. More and more depressing thoughts about Mara flitted across her mind. The more desperate and hopeless the situation seemed, the more Detty realised how much she loved and missed her. Next to Marc, Mara and Liese Zahnsdorf were the most important people in the world to her; more important she realised guiltily than her own family, although she loved them dearly too.

At first, the ringing seemed to be coming from another pocket in the crowd. She couldn't stand mobile phone jingles and had the plainest, most common ring tone. The noise went on and she realised it was hers. Her 'phone was deep in the Barbour jacket. It must be Marc she thought with a sudden thrill of pleasure as she frantically dug in her pocket trying to free the snagged phone before it stopped ringing. Eventually she was able to punch the green button and give a panting,

'Hello'.

'Frau Komturin'

'Ja' she replied surprised and breathless.

'I have the President for you' said the very formal German voice of one of Nicklaus Oblov's Personal Private Secretaries.

'Detti, are you all right? Ivan looked a bit worried when you answered.'

'Yes, I am fine. I am in the rain in a street in Manchester and couldn't get my phone out of my pocket. I thought it must be Marc.'

'Sorry to disappoint you but listen. I thought that you might be at Oberdorf. I wondered if you could do us yet another favour, but if you're in England, I'm sure that it isn't possible.'

His voice was serious and puzzled. Detty sensed that something very important was going on and he was trying to sound calm.

'Don't worry about my being in England. Go on.'

'Well, David Pfister, our Ambassador in Moscow, has had a strange call from a policeman in a Russian country town near Torzhok. The signal was awful and it was very hard to understand the message. They said that that they have in their charge a female who has said that she was a Livonian citizen, called Anna Nikolaevna, who requires assistance. At first, I wondered whether it could be a hoax or even another kidnap trap. Liese has checked it out with the organised crime set up in Moscow. They have sent people to investigate and say that they are sure it's a genuine call. The weather has been atrocious there in the last few days. They know something about the problems that we have had and are surprisingly sympathetic. They themselves are having major tussles with terrorism, which may be the reason. They want a representative of ours to go down there informally and they said that, just to be sure, they would arrange an armed escort for whoever we send. Apparently, there are two other people with the woman, which is a bit strange. It's probably a wild goose chase but with that name, I did wonder………'

There was a pause on the line,

'The problem is that David himself has a meeting with the President of Russia and their top brass which will last all this week, ironically, about control of cross border crime. Of course, he can't miss these and there are only juniors left. Our Embassy there is very small, as you know. You know what you mean to Mara and if it could be her. Seeing you might be……. I can't imagine what state she might be in…… after all this time…...'

His voice trailed off.

'Tell Liese to meet me at Moscow Airport, if she can, with the Embassy Official and the armed guard. I'll get there as soon as I can and let you know ETA as soon as I've got it worked out.'

'But Detti………'

'No arguments. Oh, and by the way express me a visa to British Airways at Heathrow. I should get to Moscow sometime to-morrow. Please find out if Liese can come and get there by then.'

'Yes, I should think so but Detti……….'

'No arguments, please. I'm on my way.'

Only afterwards in the taxi on the way to Manchester Airport did she realise that she had been barking orders down the telephone at the hugely revered President of Livonia.

She scrambled on to the six o'clock Manchester to Heathrow shuttle, thought that she had forgotten her passport only to discover to her great relief that it was still in her Barbour pocket from the St Petersburg trip. She had only the clothes that she stood up in, but that was a problem that the Heathrow shops could probably solve. She found that there was no plane to Moscow until 09:45 in the morning. She collected her visa, miraculously already arrived via a courier using British Airways which made her, for once, feel grateful to the Saxons. She bought some clothes and essentials, booked into a hotel and 'phoned Eileen Vaughan to make her peace after her sudden departure from Manchester. To her relief, Eileen seemed amused rather than angry. Detty was grateful to have a broad-minded woman of the world as a voice teacher. She supposed that having one of your students whisked away on an errand of high-level diplomacy was, at least, a bit different from the usual hassles. She then 'phoned Marc but got his voice mail so she left a message in their personal code. After that she threw her usual caution to the winds and went down to the hotel restaurant and ordered a mixed grill and large glass of claret. She enjoyed them as she had enjoyed no food or drink for months. Somehow, this time she felt, it had to be all right.

Detty's confidence had begun to evaporate as they prepared to land in Moscow. It was already far into the afternoon.

'Mrs von Ritter?'

The British Airways Cabin Director woke her out of her reverie. She nodded startled.

'One of our staff will take you to the VIP lounge. You are expected there.'

Surprised, she murmured her thanks.

Liese was waiting in the lounge resplendent in her Major's formal uniform wearing the distinctive white and green cockade of the FWL. She was talking to two men, one was wearing a civilian suit and the other, the uniform of the Russian militia. Detty, entering unnoticed, paused to take in the scene. As she watched she realised how much it meant to Liese to be standing, proud in Moscow, the capital of their former oppressors, the Soviet empire, wearing the smartly distinctive uniform of her independent homeland.

'May I introduce Colonel Andrei Sobakov of the Russian Organised Crime Bureau'?

'Colonel, this is Komturin O'Neill who has come as a Special Envoy to assist us. Detti, I am not sure if you know Dietrich Herbstmann who is one of our Counsellors here in Moscow?'

They all shook hands and Sobakhov suggested that they went straight to the car as they could talk on the journey. It would take them two hours, he explained, and, unfortunately, due to the three-hour time shift from London they would not arrive until after seven in the evening.

The Russians had been as good as their word. A large Mercedes limousine had been laid on together with a body of armed outriders who both secured their safety and cut a path through the evening Moscow traffic. As they travelled Sobakhov explained that during the last few weeks co-operation between Russia, Poland and the Baltic States had made inroads into the huge regional organised crime structure and that they had been able to make a number of arrests. They had acted quickly in this latest affair and already had detained the main Arab trader and two of his henchmen together with a senior Russian Mafia operator. They were sure that there were others even higher up the chain. They had hopes of more progress and the high-level talks in Moscow were important. Detty took the opportunity to enquire nonchalantly:

'Do these people have any connections in Italy or Spain?'

'That's a strange question and it's the second time that I've been asked it in the last few days. Apparently, your ambassador asked my boss at one of their meetings. I think that the answer may be that they do but its early days. We have some sorting out to do.'

The weather was getting worse and worse. About halfway to their destination, they changed into a police car with four-wheel drive and snow tyres. After an exhausting four hours on a journey that should have taken two, they finally reached the town late in the evening. In a few minutes, they would triumph or be plunged into hopelessness yet again.

*

The captain, apologising, had asked Mara and the others to stay in the Barracks for security reasons. Apparently, he had had orders from higher up. The Militia barracks were not exactly comfortable but the men rushed around doing their best. The girls had been put in the staff common room where a wood-burning stove struggled manfully against the giant force of the encroaching winter. They were given warm blankets and camp beds for the night. The following morning, they were served a massive Russian breakfast, which had denuded the store cupboard of the Mess as well as those of the wives of the married officers. Mara stood by the Common Room window looking out on the snow, which lashed against the wind-torn, grey winter scene. In the wood opposite, the firs sprang and arched in the icy gale. Despite the raw ruthlessness of the scene, she was enjoying hugely her first morning of freedom after sordid captivity and the constant fear of death. Not for the first time in her young life, Mara felt profoundly grateful to a group of men whose main task was to be rough and tough but who somehow had been able to produce simple human kindness to strangers that they barely knew. She was also quietly pleased with the resourcefulness that she had used to master-mind their escape. Detti, she thought, would have been proud of her.

The captain came in early and enquired anxiously how they had slept. The girls reassured him, thanked him, and said how grateful they were to the rest of the staff for the trouble that they had taken.

'There are some big wigs coming from Moscow today to sort things out – an officer of ours and some of your Embassy people. I'm not sure how many and who they are, but the Livonians seem to believe your story and be very concerned about you.'

He looked kindly but rather sceptically at the ragamuffin girl with her newly washed fair hair in rats' tails, who was still wearing filthy jeans and a torn sweater. She was pretty and lively to be sure, but anywhere in his part of Russia such girls, cleaner and more tidily turned out, could be found in plenty. He couldn't for the life of him see what all the fuss was about.

'They will have to come by road in this weather – no helicopter could land- so God knows when they will get here.'

The captain met the 'big wigs' at the entrance gate and was surprised but not disappointed to discover that, with the Colonel of his own force and the Livonian Counsellor, were two were two extremely personable young women. With a start, he realised that one of them, in uniform, outranked him and changed a slightly risky joke to a more formal greeting. It had been dark for hours and the freak storm had brought the power cables down. Only a stuttering oil lamp lit the barracks common room. Detty and Mara stared at each other for some moments across the unreal, distorting shadows in near disbelief. Convinced at last that they were both really there, they fell into each other's arms, oblivious to the presence of the others. It was Mara who finally remembered her diplomatic manners. She turned to the captain and the twins:

'Detti, permit me to introduce Helli and Ruta from Karelia, who were captives with me, and this is Captain Berinsky who is in command of this station. Helli, Ruta and Captain please meet Komturin Bernadette O'Neill, Gräfin von Ritter, my dearest friend, and Major Liese Zahnsdorf of the Livonian Intelligence Corps.'

'Wow, Anna, you do move in high circles' said Ruta smiling at the formality of the introduction, which she guessed correctly had been done mainly for the benefit of the Russian officials.

Detty turned to the Colonel and the Counsellor with smiles and laughter:

'Mara, I would like to present Colonel Sobakhov of the Russian Organised Crime Bureau. Frau Major Zahnsdorf and Herr Herbstmann from the Livonian Embassy, I think that you already know. Colonel, may I introduce you to Frau Tamara Nickolaevna Oblova, daughter of the President, and First Lady of the Hanseatic Republic of Livonia. Perhaps, Captain Ferensky, you would also like to meet Frau Oblova in her true colours.'

'Wow' said Helli and Ruta in chorus again even more loudly as the Colonel and Captain shook hands with Mara.

'I am delighted that we have been of service to you, Frau Oblova, particularly at this time of increasing co-operation between our countries, I am sure that our President too will be very pleased to hear that you are safe. We had heard about your kidnapping, of course, but never dreamt that you would escape under such strange circumstances.'

*

Livonia did not go in for official planes. That sort of extravagance was not for a country pulling itself up by its economic bootlaces. Exceptional situations, however, demand exceptional measures. After hearing the news of Tamara's escape, General Zahnsdorf, had telephoned the President and, stressing that this was a special case, had offered the services of an air force plane. Predictably, Nicklaus had refused, unwilling to allow his family to appear to be privileged in any way. For once Zahnsdorf had insisted and told him, with his tongue in his cheek, that it was nothing to do with the Presidential privilege; it was for security. He added with a laugh that he was unwilling to trust his own daughter to Aeroflot again.

Nicklaus chuckled and said that he thought that Liese Zahnsdorf had demonstrated that she was quite capable of looking after herself.

'That may be so but it's a question of engineering' said the FLL chief 'Anyway, the real point was that Liese wants to be back to see her boy friend play in the Champions League match against Glasgow Celtic tomorrow.'

The city was, as he would know, consumed by football fever. The tie was the reward for an extraordinary victory in Rome. The normally tight and polished Lazio defence had suffered an uncharacteristic momentary lapse of concentration. David Sensky, for Königshof, had passed between the forest of legs for Klaus Willens to punch low the vital away goal that had reduced Rome's Stadio Olimpico to eerie silence. The dizzy heights of the quarterfinals of the Champions League had resulted. It was the perfect way to open the new *Hansestadion* and the perfect dress rehearsal for the national World Cup qualifying match against Germany the following week.

Nicklaus replied slightly acidly to his friend that the Air Force chief didn't normally telephone him to discuss football. Ulrich Zahnsdorf, unabashed, continued that it would not be possible for Liese to see this great game if they had to come on a scheduled service via Berlin.

In the end, Nicklaus had capitulated with grateful good grace at this obvious subterfuge:

'I thought that I was the President here but I seem to be being ordered around by everybody these days. I had an earful from a certain Frau von Ritter two days ago.'

'We have all had that from time to time, Sir.'

'All right then. Have it your own way but don't blame me if we both get roasted by the opposition press.'

'This time, I don't think that even they would dare.'

So, it was settled and a smart FLL HS 125 landed at Moscow late in the afternoon to collect three young women from the VIP lounge. The two Karelian girls had already said a tearful farewell and had promised to visit Livonia. They had then left for St Petersburg where, because of their part in this sensational affair, they had both been promised jobs and a flat. The Russians had been lavish with their hospitality. They had provided a scrambled telephone line for Mara to make a long call to her father and copious food and drink. Liese wondered, a little cynically, if this largesse was because of the recent high point in Russian-Livonian relations or whether it was because they rather enjoyed having three attractive young females as VIPs. It might be a welcome change from the usual aging corpulent dignitaries. The provision of an FLL jet was, though, a surprise to them all.

'However, it's quite true, I do want to be there for this match in the new Stadium' Liese admitted after she had heard details over the radio of the high-level discussion between the President and her father before they took off.

She went on to tell the others the rest of the news. There had been Europe wide arrests largely because of some good co-operative international intelligence work. The brains and leading people in the organisation were, however, still at large.

'They haven't got everybody then?' Detty yearned for some real peace and quiet and was disappointed.

'By no means but there has been an enormous operation involving almost every European nation. In Russia, apparently, there have been terrible inter-gang turf wars. The Russian mafia gangs saw that an international group were using their territory in Belarus and St Petersburg and were not amused. One result you saw in the warehouse at St Petersburg. In the end, the feuding was quite helpful to us as it resulted in a good many breaches in their security. Anyway, we have Mara back, which is a great start and, for the moment, we can concentrate on winning against Celtic this afternoon and Germany next week.

'Any chance of a ticket for to-day's match? I've always been a bit of a Celtic fan' asked Detty.

'You're trying to wind me up' Liese kicked out at her friend's shins playfully 'but I suppose we can arrange it. The President would never forgive us if we didn't let you in and he is coming too. I am not sure whether the box is full. Do you want me to get the Hansehaus again and find out?'

Liese spoke to the pilot. There followed a conversation over the radio punctuated by laughs. She came back into the cabin smiling.

'Of course, there's a ticket for you, Detti, but the President wants to speak to you after the match.'

'It sounds a bit like an interview with the headmaster.'

*

The Scots were well-organised and tight in defence. Although Königshof pressed for the first half, nothing resulted. They nearly went one down after the interval when a spectacular Scottish break out of defence put the ball in the net only to be judged dubiously offside to the relief of the crowded stadium. At the final whistle, it was a goalless draw – still, the return in Glasgow couldn't be worse than Rome when it came to searching for miracles.

In the excitement of the match, Detty had nearly forgotten the President's summons. He hadn't however and cornered her at the end of the match as she stood on one side waiting for him to leave the box.

'Detti, I wanted to ask you. Can you sing for us?'

Detty, genuinely puzzled, replied:

'Well, I thought that I had already – a bit.'

'No, Detti, you misunderstand me. I mean for the match next week'.

'What on earth?' Now she was really surprised.

Liese, in the background, was grinning from ear to ear.

The President continued:

'Can you manage to prepare fot it in a week?

'They don't want me to play, do they? I'm not sure that I know the rules. Now if it was hurling or Camogie that would be different.'

Liese, behind them in the back of the President's box, now dissolved into uncontrollable laughter.

'Detti, I am not explaining myself very well' said the President sounding unusually embarrassed and diffident.

'But if you were prepared to sing the National Anthems at the Stadium for the match with Germany, we would all be very grateful.'

'What – both of them?' Detty was, for once, taken aback.

'Yes, of course, the German Ambassador was very pleased at the idea.'

She pulled herself together.

'It would be a great privilege but you must admit that I am a little short of rehearsal time.'

'You can go to the Stadium and practice with the new amplification.'

Nicklaus was almost pleading – and with the ignorance of the uninitiated,

'Of course, I will – never fear' she showed a confidence that she did not feel.

She spent most of the next week practising repeatedly in the new Stadium to the frustration of the technicians. Normally, she hated amplification outside and had never sung at an important occasion in the open air. To-day, she was ashamed of herself, playing the traditional prima donna in front of the patient sound crew, but she had to get it right. After two sessions of three hours, she was reasonably satisfied that together with the long-suffering technical team, they would produce the right sort of sound. She thanked them all and went off to the German embassy where she had been invited to have lunch with Marc.

The players stood attentively in line. David Sensky, Liese's boy friend massive and reassuring as the mid-field general in the Livonian ranks.

Detty didn't notice, she just focussed on the task in hand.

In spite of her prejudice against amplification and the background noise of the huge new stadium, somehow, she began to feel more confident. She was almost beginning to enjoy it as the Wild Swans Band stuck up the German anthem. She could not hear the sound of her voice and yet she knew that:

Einigkeit und Recht und Freiheit fur das deutsche Vaterland
Danach lasst uns alle streben bruderlich mit Herz und Hand!
Einigkeit und Recht und Freiheit sind des Gluckes Unterpfand
Bluh im Glanze dieses Gluckes bluhe deutsches Vaterland!

It sounded right as it went sailing out over the Stadium, as it had done once before over Neubrandenburg riverbank. The home crowd were unusually respectful, possibly more as a tribute to the singer than the hymn. The German team and their supporters applauded as the two teams had stood to attention. The excited crowd realised that this was an important moment and was suddenly silent.

After a moment's pause, a quiet rumble the drum roll swelled onwards and onwards, louder, and louder creating suspense. At last, it burst into the grand melody that had seen them through so much. The *Freiheitsleid* was thundered out from nearly sixty thousand throats with shattering force. The engineers said afterwards that, even after careful preparation, they needed to keep turning up the spot microphone to allow Detty to be heard through the crowd. The German press said that the noise of sixty thousand voices roaring the Livonian hymn was worth a two-goal lead before they started.

Then to business, the home team started well. Passes were strung together from the midfield masterminded by David Sensky. Willens, the striker hit the crossbar and then had another shot brilliantly saved by the German goalkeeper. At half time, it was nil-nil and the partisan members of the Presidential party all agreed that Livonia should have been ahead. The second half started with a fierce German onslaught, doubtless inspired by a managerial tirade in the dressing room. Desperate defending and fine goal keeping saw the home team through and they even began to counterattack effectively. In the last quarter, they had the best of the game seldom out of their opponent's half. That didn't prevent the Germans scoring on the break in the eighty-eighth minute. The Presidential party left the box silently. Somebody unwisely muttered that it was 'only a game'.

'That's all you know' retorted Liese turning fiercely on the offender and at the same time realising that any chance that she had had of Christmas domestic bliss had disappeared in the back of the Livonian net.

Detty had to hurry away from the match getting through the subdued capacity crowd as best she could. She arrived at the Hoftheatre slightly late on foot, changed into her chorus uniform of cream blouse with black skirt and was just in time to go into the hall with the others. She slipped as unobtrusively as possible into her pre-arranged seat the end of the soprano section of the chorus and opened her score. There was a slight stir amongst her neighbours which quickly quietened. Almeida Tulla escorted by Helge came onto the platform to warm applause, which was more than a routine welcome. Almeida's presence was deeply appreciated and highly significant to the local audience.

Detty settled to the job in hand, delighted to be there. Bernard Meisl had faithfully arrived again to direct the *Festspielchor*. She had had to plead with him to be allowed to join the chorus:

'Certainly not, Detti, I don't want my chorus upset by undisciplined *Dramatischsopranisten* ruining our elegant balance. Anyway, you would scare the others.'

She sensed a twinkle in his eye although he was more than half-serious.

'Please, O please!' she had said wringing her hands and using her begging gambit complete with pleading wide green eyes 'I do so want to sing with them.'

'You'll have to get yourself a proper outfit, attend rehearsals and mind that you don't make too much noise.'

'*Jawohl, Herr Meister*'

She knew that she had won and had thoroughly enjoyed the final rehearsals.

The warm applause for Helge von Grunstrand hushed and the woodwind sighed the lament of Russia under Mogul power. The dark subdued beauty of the first statement of Nevsky's song contrasted with the martial trombones of the crusade to Pskov. The exhortation for the people of Russia to arise passed from the women to the men. The Teutonic army darkly approached, followed by their heroic antagonists and the military thunder of the battle itself. As she relished the Russian text of the soprano line, she felt a traitor and fingered the clasp of the Falcon of St Nicklaus pinned to her blouse.

For this evening and its message, the disloyalty was worth it. She knew that the German knights closely related to her Hanseatic heroes, would be defeated in the Battle on the Ice in the inevitable order of things. After all, this evening, the Russian mother lamenting her loss was being portrayed by a black South African; it was a world stage now. Almeida chilled the hall with the unfathomable riches of her contralto. The searching song of the Russian woman looking for her man grew eerily out of the ether of eternity. This, more than all the other contributions, gave the evening a special momentum. The black African heroine brought her life, her country, and her continent to join the Russian widow's grief. Her lament seemed so real that it left the audience and chorus emotionally drained. It was all they could do to pull themselves together to celebrate *Nevsky's* triumphal entrance into Pskov. Helge paused for a moment to honour the lament then wound the Philharmonica up for the great finale. Detty enjoyed being able to watch him without the distractions of the stage, which had prevented her seeing much of the orchestra in *Fidelio*. His pride in the ensemble that he had created and nurtured was plain to see. Casting a guilty sidelong glance at the impassive face of the *Chorleitung* in the wings she let one small reef out of her voice as she rose with the other sopranos in the high paean of triumph.

Detty listened to the applause for others shaking the foundations of the old theatre, as it had once thundered for her. She was well satisfied the country was again united and the nation, her adolescent godchild, was ready to march on again. Next week she could return to Oberdorf for the Bavarian Christmas she so loved.

Back at the Hansehof Hotel, she had time to think about the concert over a glass from the *bocksbeutel* of her father-in-law's special low alcohol wine. This was now listed at the hotel, largely she guessed because of her own liking for it and, possibly, also because of the generous discount offered by the producer. Marc had been able to come just for the concert. He had left his glass unfinished on the table when he had gone to telephone the military attaché in London in the vain hope of postponing his return. She dived into her briefcase and opened the score of The Children of Lir although she knew it well enough. Suddenly, she was aware of two men, smartly but anonymously dressed in lounge suits and ties, standing in front of her. She was instantly afraid. Her own assassination attempt and kidnapping together with Mara's experiences had made her sensitive and suspicious about anything or anyone unusual.

They smiled and the taller of the two spoke to her in English with the harsh accent of the Bronx:

'Ms O'Neill?'

'Who wants to know?' she was still anxious and unsure.

'Dave Walsh and this is Jeff Klovsky. We had better come straight to the point.'

Both men produced identity cards with photographs purporting to have been issued by the CIA.

'We wonder whether you can help us.'

'Why should I be able to?'

Detty was now getting anxious. She had no idea what a genuine CIA identity card looked like. She thought from the movies that they usually showed shields. Anyway, the recent malefactors in her life were quite capable of getting forgeries quite good enough to deceive her. In addition, even if these men were genuinely from the CIA, then what did they want with her?

'We have information about an organisation trading in arms and narcotics and believe that you may have had some contact with them.'

'What on earth makes you think that? It sounds to me as if you have been misinformed. Possibly, you would like to discuss the matter with Major Zahnsdorf of the Livonian Intelligence Service who is due here any minute. I am preparing for a concert and waiting for the Major and my husband who is just making a phone call.'

She tried to surround herself with as many invisible allies as possible and deliberately looked towards the Hotel entrance in the hope of spotting Liese, who was indeed due to join them for a drink.

'No, you've got it wrong. We are sure that you are the right person and we don't need to involve the so-called intelligence service of this kind of banana republic.'

Detty controlled her fury and replied haughtily.

'Whether you are really from the CIA or not, you clearly have no idea how to behave as guests in a foreign country. Livonia has an increasing export trade but to my certain knowledge it does not yet include bananas.'

With that, she got up and shaking inwardly, walked slowly over to the Reception Counter.

'Frau Komturin?' enquired the former FWL commando on duty as receptionist.

'Please see that these gentlemen leave the building. They have accosted me unannounced and are annoying me.'

'But hang on a minute...'

The visitors took one look at the face of the receptionist and, deciding that it was too late to send for the Cavalry or the Marines, scuttled, discomforted, out of the building.

*

The winter dawn was still some time away but the hotel window was just beginning to turn from black to a hint of grey. Marc answered the 'phone thinking that it must be London again. He turned to his sleep-drugged wife and said:

'It's for you – Liese' he whispered 'she obviously hasn't fallen on her sword yet after yesterday's match but I wish she would choose a more civilised hour to 'phone for a girly chat. I've got to get up early tomorrow.'

Detty was too sleepy to resort to the violent physical response that she usually adopted when her husband teased her with sexist remarks. Anyway, she was sad that he was leaving again in the morning. She always seemed to be saying goodbye to him but that, she supposed, was the fate of a soldier's wife and she conceded to herself that she was luckier than most. She took the 'phone in her right hand and rubbed her eyes with her left.

Liese was always an early riser and sounded disgustingly efficient.

'I gather two gentlemen from the CIA upset you last night.'

'They really were from the CIA then. I thought that they were a couple of hoods.'

'The two aren't entirely incompatible... but yes, they are from the CIA and want you to go to Spain with them to find your Monsignor Pueblo. They rang me after your interview at the hotel. I think that they were somewhat chastened.'

'I'm glad to hear that but they still can't see me today, I have a solo to sing in the Festival tonight. Anyway, I doubt if we will find Pueblo at Pic Noix, he only goes there occasionally.'

Liese recognised the icy cutting edge in her friend's voice and tried to analyse why she was so uncharacteristically waspish. With a sigh, she rang off and tried to placate the CIA men who couldn't understand that a two-bit concert should take precedence over a threat to the Union.

*

As a tribute to her native land, she wore an orange sash completing the Irish tricolour. The green and white of her dress was as always, the green and white of Livonia. This time it was not a hastily cobbled together dress scavenged from rag chests for an army concert. There had however been some anxiety as she had waited for it to be delivered from the Rue Castiglione. The gorgeous Lanoure model showed in front a white dart with the emerald green shot silk gathered around. The skirt was ruched up above her left knee and then fell in cascades to finish in thick folds round her right ankle. She knew that it might be called exhibitionist, if not tarty, but she didn't care. This was a special occasion and deserved a special frock. From the reception that they got when Helge led the soloists on stage, the audience agreed. The chorus and other soloists, both vocal and instrumental, had come from Dublin but the orchestra was the Königshofer Philharmonica under von Grunstrand, who had rehearsed the relatively simple score exhaustively, in a search for a special perfection. Detty half believed that she was still in a fantasy world as the chorus behind them and the audience facing them shuffled to their feet as the orchestra launched themselves into The Soldier's Song. To hear *Amhran Na Bhfiann* in Königshof, the city once of torture, death, and the morning arrest, was the fulfilment of another dream- a real dream which she had had many times in the Farm and the Winterburg in her frustration, fear, and misery. She found herself silently mouthing the Gaelic words as watched Kevin doing wonders on the Uillean pipes. Her close-up picture, looking, as she said, half-witted, was on Livonian television and every newspaper the following morning with headlines like *Unsere Heldin ehrt seine Mutterland* which nauseated Detty in the cold light of dawn. At the end, Helge indicated Kevin who was applauded warmly. The *Freiheitsleid* followed. Detty thought that she got a broad wink from Kevin as they settled down for the *Children of Lir*. She was facing the audience and nearly burst herself trying not to laugh or wink back.

By the time, they took off for Paris the atmosphere with the Americans was better. Detty had agreed to meet the CIA men after the concert. When they came into her dressing room, she was still feeling that almost manic sense of euphoria that always came after a good performance. They were accompanied by an apprehensive Liese who seemed unreasonably relieved when Detty greeted them with a smile. Dave Walsh, the younger American, had an engaging smile, which Detty had been too furious to notice at their first interview. He seemed to have done a full social skills course since the night before. To Detty's surprise both Americans treated the two women with exaggerated courtesy and respect.

'I'm sorry, Countess. We sure owe you an apology for last night but we want to thank you for allowing us to come to your concert. It was a real privilege.'

Liese, in her role as diplomat, had got them into the performance thinking that it might smooth troubled waters. The stratagem had succeeded beyond her dreams.

'It was wonderful to hear Irish sung. You see' he continued looking bashful 'my family originally came from Wicklow but, of course, I know that most all Americans claim Irish ancestors. It must bore you real Irish stiff.'

'Not at all, I believe you, with a name like that. Wicklow is full of Walshs. Now first we go for supper at the Golabki as I'm famished and then I want to know how I can help you.'

The old Polish restaurant was its timeless self. Andrei the proprietor who sported long white moustaches and professorial glasses beamed his pleasure at their arrival and kissed the women's hands before bringing iced Sobieski vodka all round. They gave their orders, *Zur, pierozki*, venison and hare in various styles and with different garnishes. The visitors went up a step in Detty's estimation. Previously she had believed that all Americans lived on Coca-Cola and Big Macs.

They got down to business.

'You see we have reason to believe that the organisation that you came across in the Pyrenees is implicated in planning terrorist attacks in several places in the world including the United States. A tanker was sunk in the Gulf of Mexico last year and our investigations led to the sort of technology associated with Lev. We have rounded up a good many of the operatives ourselves and, clearly you have done more, but…'

'Monsignor Pueblo?'

'Sure, he seems to be one, possibly the chief, organising genius behind Lev and that's a large part of the problem. Because the Church is involved, we must tread very carefully. To offend the American Catholic population by a false move would be politically embarrassing, particularly with the mid-term elections pending. We need therefore to get our hands on Monsignor Pueblo. We need to try and find out as much as we can about his connections with certain Middle Eastern and Asiatic rogue states. We need to do it with a good deal of caution to avoid a media outcry that we are persecuting an innocent Catholic cleric. We have a common interest here with the Russians and yourselves in Livonia in crushing this extremely powerful and dangerous Lev network. May I add that despite our tactless remarks last night, we are conscious of how much you have done already and we sure appreciate it.'

Detty smiled at this. Liese maintained a poker face, but clearly, she had not wasted time in setting the record straight about the progress already achieved, without CIA help or, apparently, prior knowledge.

'But where do I come in?' asked Detty.

'You have been in Pic Noix. You know your way about and the faces. That will help considerably in gaining access. We want to return there under cover and, if possible, quietly get Monsignor Pueblo to come to Washington to answer a few questions. We have got hold of one of his contacts in the US mafia who has given us enough information to get him to want to come with us to the States. We would also be keen that this mission was undertaken under Livonian auspices so that the United States was not seen to be involved.'

'I see' interjected Detty, with a park of her old animosity 'You are quite happy for the media to crucify us for persecuting the Catholic Church as long as your President is not involved.'

'Something like that' said Dave producing that smile again.

'At least, you are honest about it' Liese said, coming to his aid:

'I don't understand why Pueblo wasn't arrested when the others were rounded up?' asked Detty thinking that it would not be the moment to ask why Dave seemed so certain that they would be successful this time.

'Two perhaps three reasons, first we lost touch with him. The US agent who was trailing him disappeared. He has not been heard of since then. We are assuming the worst and, if he is dead, we don't know how much he revealed, possibly under torture, first.

'This agent, what did he look like?' Detty asked urgently.

Dave described him. It was Craig, her erstwhile companion in the Pyrenees to a tee.

'I am afraid he is dead' she said and described how she had found his body on the path below the Abbey, half covered in the undergrowth.

'However, it's not much comfort but I'm pretty sure he wasn't tortured, He had been dead some hours when I found him and they wouldn't really have had the opportunity.'

'We thought that he must be dead.'

'I met him before at lunch at an inn. I liked him. He told me that he was studying for a doctorate in medieval history. He seemed well informed.'

'That was quite genuine' said Jeff very quietly 'It was his passion as well as his cover. I knew him very well. You see he was engaged to be married to my sister. Caused quite a problem in the family – you see my father can't stand southerners, but he was gradually coming round. I shall have to break it to Gail. I think that she has always known really, but you still hope.'

During the silence that followed Detty felt a rush of respect and sympathy for this man that she had hated and despised only the night before.

'What was the other reason for not catching Pueblo with the others?'

'There were two really. We had information that he had left Pic Noix for Columbia and when we got our people in Bogotá to investigate it, he had already moved on from there and we didn't know where he was. He really is a slippery customer.'

'Sounds as if they needed one of your bugs up his soutane, Liese'.

Detty wondered to herself what Mother Immaculata would think of this highly improper suggestion from one of her star pupils.

'Good idea but you would have to catch him first and, as you saw down on the *Fojn*, planting bugs isn't always that easy.' Liese laughed. 'Was there another problem?'

'Yes, in the CIA we really didn't have enough to nail him. It is a tricky situation. He is after all, as we have said, a genuine senior Catholic priest and abducting him from an Abbey in another sovereign territory is a tricky undertaking. We could have put that right if we had come to you or the Russians first but, mea culpa, we didn't.'

'I'm not sure that I would be much help to you. I did after all make a rather high-profile exit from Pic Noix last time. Besides, I'm not exactly inconspicuous amongst a Spanish crowd. I'm not sure that your expedition would be helped by having me arrested for horse stealing or worse.'

Dave and Jeff spent a moment gazing at this remarkable Irish woman. They had to agree about the last point. Their companion, they had noticed outside was six foot tall with a magnificently athletic figure. To this was added below shoulder length red gold hair glinting in the restaurant candlelight. She would not melt into any crowd, let alone a Spanish one.

'We may have to keep you under wraps some of the time, but your guidance and knowledge would still be invaluable to us.'

'OK, then I'll come. Liese will tell you that I'm always ready for a scrap. It's the Irish blood, I suppose.'

'Thank you. We sure appreciate it.'

*

There was fog in the morning and the plane to Paris was delayed. Eventually, they boarded but there was still no sign of it taking off, apparently due to some difference of opinion between air traffic control and the Air France pilot, who gave them his version of the situation over the intercom in Maurice Chevalier English.

'What else do you expect in a banana republic?' Detty remarked wickedly.

Jeff had the grace to blush.

They were three hours late when they eventually got to Paris and there was no flight to Biarritz until morning. A faceless airport hotel for the night was the only solution.

11
THE PRISONERS

O Himmel! Rettung! Welch ein Gluck!
O Freiheit! Kehrst du zuruck?[28]

PRISONERS CHORUS *FIDELIO* ACT 1
BEETHOVEN/SONNLEITNER & TREITSCHKE

In the morning the fog, which intermittently seemed to be blanketing the whole of northern Europe, covered Charles de Gaulle. In the white mist, the airport spread like an etiolated amoeba with its limbs disappearing in swirling vortices. There were no flights. They sat and waited and waited and waited. Not for the first time, Detty wondered how such a glorious city could have such a terrible airport. Perhaps this was unfair. Schiphol, Peretola, Fiumcino and even Tegel didn't really do any favours to the cities that they represented. And Heathrow? Surely the most infamous concourse of the airborne damned, Dante's *perduta gente* of business travel and plastic food.

They had nothing to do but drink flavourless coffee and chew plastic

---

28 Oh heavens! Deliverance! What a blessing
Oh freedom! Will you return.

wrapped long-life polystyrene American muffins, which had supplanted the croque monsieur of yesteryear. It was, surprisingly, Jeff who expressed what they were all thinking:

'I guess that they had better food than this at the freeway cafés in this country a few years ago. We have a lot to answer for – Home of the Brave, Coca-Cola, and the burger bar.'

'And the stun belt' added Detty with a venom and impetuousness that she instantly regretted. She admired Jeff for voicing critical thoughts about his compromised homeland that to too many would have been unthinkable. She had no need to turn the knife in the wound to relieve her still daily hurt. Jeff looked at her quizzically for several minutes saying nothing but wondering what lay behind the outburst.

It was late morning before the fog cleared and they were able to take off. After the ninety-minute flight, Biarritz hove in sight bordered by the green blue sea sparkling in the winter sunshine. From the aircraft, it seemed refreshingly peaceful and bright. Dave had got the message that their VIP guide wasn't over enthusiastic about airport hotels and had booked them in at the sumptuous Hotel du Palais muttering to Jeff that if the office grumbled, they would just have to get lost. Jeff indeed wondered how the Finance would regard the check for four of them at one of the most expensive hotels in France, particularly as it included two young women, albeit in separate rooms, which however would add to the expense even if it demonstrated professional discretion and chastity.

Detty on the other hand felt guilty and that she had behaved badly and was embarrassed that her whinges about the airport hotel in Paris had had such a dramatic effect. As they sank into the carpets on the way to the Villa Eugenie, she whispered to Liese that she wasn't really expecting Napoleon the Third's love nest, only something where there was a human presence, a comfortable bed and waiters who didn't spill the soup. Liese just smiled and noticed that her friend's embarrassment didn't prevent her tucking into *Filets du Bar Poelé* followed by *Ris de Veau Regence* washed down by the mouth grabbing *Jurancon Sec*, albeit, in Detty's case, in sadly small quantities.

The eastern dawn was fleeting over the misty north face of the mountains as they set off the following morning. Jeff drove the hire car, an anonymous four-wheel drive jeep, towards St Jean Pied de Porte and the route of Detty's bus journey. The Pyrenees were a relief to her after the hassles of air travel. They stood bare, green, and noble, unchanging, much as they had been when Cathar shepherds, centuries before, had used them as a refuge for their bodies and a sanctuary for their faith. She felt a moment's nostalgia for her own lushly different Wicklow mountains. She jerked herself back to the present, throwing aside sentimentality and wondering what human darkness these mountains held now. They would soon know.

They had no option but to take the risk of driving right up to the Abbey, as any other approach would have taken too long and might have been disrupted by the weather. After they reached the junction with the road from Pamplona to the Abbey, they kept their fingers crossed that nobody would stop them and start asking awkward questions. Their cover, flimsy as it was, was that they were American travel agents coming to prepare for a tour along the Way of St James, which they were planning for the next year. Their lack of Spanish might be a problem in substantiating their cover but otherwise it could be an advantage in evading intrusive enquiries.

In the event, they met no one and needed to produce no explanations. They passed the nunnery below the Abbey, which seemed deserted. Detty thought that that might not be strange as the female community had always been small, no more than twenty or so nuns she thought, so they could all have been out for the day. There was nobody about as they drove on ready to produce the 'Oh Gees' of the dumb tourists. They parked unmolested behind the strangers' house, leaving the jeep out of sight and walked up to the main Abbey buildings. Their footsteps crunched on the gravel accentuating the silence. The great gatehouse of the Abbey was eerily deserted and the doors uncharacteristically were locked open. On one was a notice *'Prohibibido el Paso – acesorestringido!'* but no further explanation or indication of who was responsible for the order.

'I guess that doesn't mean us' said Dave dryly walking through the gate.

Still nobody. They edged warily forward with Dave and Jeff fingering their shoulder holsters. Still nothing to be heard. The birdsong that had flooded the summer mornings was stilled by the cold of winter. Off the courtyard, a wide arched porch contained the chapel door on one side and the door to the long staircase leading up to the library complex at the back. Dave cautiously tried the great ring handle of the Chapel door. It opened. Inside was deserted and dusty. The usual smell of fresh incense was absent but nothing had apparently been disturbed. After looking round, they returned to the porch. The door at the back leading to the staircase to the library and scriptorium was also unlocked. Warily they climbed the polished wooden steps, which creaked loudly in the silence reminding Detty of St Conleth's. The atrium at the top was just as she remembered it with, amongst others, her desk, where she had worked on her study of the music of the *Camino Frances* and the massive oak refectory table still with its incongruous information leaflets. The openwork wrought iron gates were locked as they always had been but she could see the Scriptorium and the Library through them. They looked as usual, except that there were gaps in the stacks and a thin layer of unaccustomed dust covering the open surfaces.

They glanced at each other non-plussed.

'Seems the heck of a way to come to find that the bird, correction, all the birds, have flown' said Dave adding 'We had better go down to Pamplona and make some discreet enquiries about what the hell is going on here. It's a bit awkward as we have no official status in Spain and Uncle Sam isn't always popular poking his nose in. As you know, we baited the hook to persuade Monsignor Pueblo to come with us of his own free will. We didn't reckon on having to involve the Spanish authorities but that might have to change now.'

As he finished, speaking Detty was half conscious of a very faint distant rumble breaking the surrounding silence. To hear better, she moved to the top of the stairs above the open door below and listened. Sure enough, there was a low-pitched noise and it was getting slowly nearer with intermittent changes of rhythm and pitch. It was now loud enough for them all to hear. A large diesel-powered vehicle must be coming towards the Abbey and she knew that there were no side turnings for many kilometres. They were getting company at last.

They held their breath as the rumbling grew nearer and nearer punctuated by the brief growls as the driver changed down yet again up the steep slope. The tension was almost unbearable as the lorry echoed under the gatehouse. Suddenly it came in view. The tension vanished in gales of relieved laughter. Down the side of the lorry was the familiar red logo of Coca-Cola.

'Globalisation has even reached here!' said Dave still laughing 'I'll just go down and see what they're up to.'

He headed down the long staircase, Jeff followed, leaving the women watching the scene from the atrium window.

The lorry was manoeuvring in the courtyard and trying unsuccessfully to back into the covered porch below them. After a lot of twisting and turning, a man got down from the passenger side of the lorry and yelled to the driver in Spanish they couldn't understand.

Liese had stopped laughing well before the others and as the Americans disappeared down the stairs, she whispered hoarsely:

'This isn't right; something strange is going on. Why do they want Coca-Cola in a deserted Abbey and even if they do why is it being delivered to the Chapel and the Library?'

Before Detty could reply, events took over. A white Volvo saloon swept through the gatehouse and stopped in the courtyard. A man got out. Even without his clerical dress or goatee beard, Detty recognised the features and broad shoulders of Josemaria Pueblo instantly. Worse still, he looked up at the atrium window and had obviously seen her. Without pausing or a flicker of recognition, he strode into the porch and they heard the key turning in the heavy lock. When the men reached the bottom of the staircase a few moments later they could only hammer from inside the massive door shouting for it to be opened. It didn't budge, upstairs and down they were all prisoners.

Pueblo spoke to the men and although, behind the window, they couldn't hear what he said, it was clear that he had told the truck driver and his mate to give up trying to get the vehicle inside the porch and leave it in front. They all got into the car and drove off through the gatehouse. Detty turned towards the stairs to go down and tell the others what had happened. Suddenly Liese yelled:

'Down! Under the table! Now!'

Detty dived under the thick oak as the explosion roared, followed by, rumbling of falling masonry, suffocating dust and the sensation of the floor moving. Then blackness. She wasn't sure how long she was out.

As she came round, she looked for the familiar surroundings of *Schloss Krenek*. Gradually, she realised that it wasn't *Schloss Krenek* but still could not remember where she was or how she had got there. The explosion had played a trick on her mind and she thought that she was back at the music school when the car bomb had exploded. Gradually she took in her true surroundings. A man in uniform was standing over her pointing a machine pistol at her as another man in a surgical gown pushed her onto a stretcher. Her ears were ringing, her eyes burning and every part of her body throbbed. Worst of all she had a pounding headache. Her body belt with her personal documents was being examined by another man in the same uniform. They were talking Spanish and slowly she realised that they must be guardia. They bundled her into an ambulance. She hurt terribly as the ambulance swished from corner to corner down the mountain road. After a seeming age, she was rolled onto a trolley, out of the ambulance, through a doorway and onto a bed in a bare room. A man in civilian clothes came in, spoke to her in Spanish, shrugged his shoulders when she didn't understand. He made a cursory physical examination, said something to the policemen and left. She assumed that she was in some sort of hospital but her only constant companions were a policeman and policewoman sitting at the end of her bed with machine pistols across their laps.

After some hours the monotony was broken by the arrival of another trolley, which wheeled her through to another part of the hospital where they X rayed her skull and various limbs. The manipulation required for the X rays made her complaining body even more wretched. She tried to ask for something for the pain but didn't make herself understood. All she got was a scowl. Kindness to patients didn't seem part of the programme and it began to dawn on her confused mind that she was being treated as a suspect and a pretty unpopular one at that.

She tried to get her thoughts straight throughout a sleepless night. On the few occasions when she did manage to drop off in spite of the pain, the police woke her by starting a loud conversation. She wondered whether she was being paranoid or whether they really were doing it deliberately.

Morning produced some bread, a cup of coffee and a change of police. As the winter light began to filter through the high window, a man in a suit arrived. He made no attempt to introduce himself but sat down at her bedside. To her surprise, he spoke perfect English and started immediately to question her:

'What is your name?'

'Bernadette von Ritter,

'But your passport says you are called O'Neill. Why do you use an alias?'

'I don't. O'Neill is my birth name, von Ritter my married name.'

'You are Irish?'

'Yes'

'You were trained as a terrorist in Ireland?'

'No, I am not a terrorist.'

'If you are not a terrorist, why did you explode a bomb at Pic Noix.'

'I didn't'

'Either you did or other members of your party did. You will not help yourself by being obtuse. How much did they pay you?'

'I don't understand what you mean.'

'How much did they pay you to blow up Pic Noix?'

'I don't understand. Nobody paid me anything and I didn't blow up Pic Noix.'

'I suppose the explosion was due to an earthquake then' his sarcasm was cutting.

'If you didn't blow it up, what were you doing there?'

Detty thought as fast as her muddled brain could work. She could tell the whole truth but she didn't know who this man was and, in any case, the truth wasn't very credible. In addition, she presumed that the others were being interrogated separately and she didn't know if they would try to stick to the agreed cover story. She thought that she had better try.

'I was with a party of travel agents working for an American company. We lost our way and found ourselves at the Abbey.'

'Where you went through 'No entry' notices and let off a bomb. Really, Ms O'Neill you will have to try harder than that.'

'We wanted directions. There was nobody around so we went inside looking for someone to ask. Then this van arrived and a car and suddenly there was an explosion.'

'You mean your bomb went off before you could get clear. I don't think that is up to the usual ETA standard. They won't hire you again. Mind you, they won't really be able to. You are not helping yourself by not telling me about your contacts but you will have plenty of time to think better of it. I will leave it there for now.'

He turned to go to the door.

'Please tell me how my companions are.'

He looked hard at her for a moment, said nothing and opened the door and left. The police fingered their machine pistols, smirked at each other and laughed unpleasantly.

Previously Detty had been too preoccupied with her own troubles to think much about the others. Now she was acutely anxious. Either something dreadful had happened to them or her captors were using innuendo and uncertainty as a weapon against her to help them in their interrogation.

The interrogation was repeated daily sometimes with hints about the dreadful fate or confession of her companions. She always answered as truthfully as she could without revealing the whole story. After three days the monotony was broken when she was transferred into what she assumed was a women's prison. She was treated with a rough callousness and intermittent indignities, which were, however, mild compared to her experiences under the NAS but the frustration of confinement with no apparent end in sight began to get to her. She was denied consular access on the grounds of her terrorist status. She repeatedly asked to be allowed to send a message to her husband and eventually this was granted. She wrote to him at Oberdorf not mentioning his rank and simply saying that she was detained in Spain suspected of terrorist activities. She was not at all sure that the message would be sent although she had tried to avoid anything that might alarm the inevitable censors.

When she was left alone, she sat on her bare bunk and reviewed her predicament. On the positive count on this occasion, she had not been flogged, put in a chain gang, or threatened with mutilation so she had to think of Spanish imprisonment as being greatly superior to her treatment previously by the NAS. On the other hand, she had been imprisoned without having committed any crime and there was currently no sign of either discharge or a trial. She tried to think things out. After repeated interrogations, it was clear that the Spanish authorities still regarded the explosion as a Basque separatist outrage and assumed that Detty was part of an ETA link-up with the IRA. She wondered why they had not checked her security status with London or Dublin or whether they had done so and simply didn't believe the answers.

She wondered yet again what had become of the others. She had hoped that after her transfer to prison she might be in contact with Liese, if the latter was still alive, but there had been no sign or mention of her. Whenever Detty had asked about her friend, her enquiries had been greeted with a silent shrug. Detty tried to persuade herself that this wasn't significant as Liese would certainly have been sent to a different prison and, if her own treatment was anything to go by, she too would have been kept in strict solitary confinement.

She wondered what the Livonian authorities had done. Of course, if Liese was dead they might well have done nothing. The rule was that as a live undercover agent you were on your own. Once dead, no Government was going to embarrass themselves by claiming a corpse after an unauthorised mission to a foreign country. Detty shuddered miserably. She knew that Liese's passport described her non-commitally as *Schreiberin*, clerk, and gave no clue to her military rank. Despite the latter's influential family that was the way it had to be in the intelligence service and that was the way it would stay. Aside from the tour operator cover, Liese officially was only one of the many East European tourists who flooded to Spain whenever they could find the means. She knew the rules and she would expect to be treated no differently from any other agent.

Detty reflected that she herself was, however, in a different situation. Her personal fame, or as she preferred to think of it, notoriety would undoubtedly have attracted popular media attention, if her fate had been known. This had apparently not happened and she could only assume that the Spanish authorities had succeeded in keeping the whole Pic Noix incident secret. The circumstances of the affair were indeed strange. Her mind teemed with questions. Why was the Abbey deserted when they reached it? Was it a co-incidence that Pueblo arrived the moment that they were on the scene? If so, it was a very strange one. Why did he want to blow the Abbey up, as he most assuredly did, in the first place? The plan must have been made in advance. Nobody could hi-jack a lorry and stuff it full of gelignite on the spur of the moment, but the timing might have been altered to coincide with their visit. If so, how was their presence in the area known? It was true that they had taken no particular precautions to conceal themselves and indeed their cover story precluded this. Why were the Spanish authorities so convinced that this was an ETA outrage? Surely ETA did not normally blow-up religious institutions, she knew that they generally concentrated on politicians, police and tourist centres, and the Spanish knew this well and yet still seemed convinced of the ETA connection.

All these questions went round and round in her head and yet still failed to pass the dragging time. Her best hope was Marc. He knew the true story of the events, which had led up to their mission, and was resourceful and expert in intelligence matters. Over two weeks however had passed since she had written and there was still nothing. She began to feel more and more certain that he had never got the message or, alternatively, that he had been unable to contact her.

The Christmas that she had expected to spend amongst the friendship of Oberdorf passed in a solitary cell and still nothing happened. She couldn't understand why there was not more reaction, more fuss, good or bad. In between trying to work out her predicament she practised her scales daily and worked on the parts that she was learning from memory. She was increasingly uncertain if she would ever get a chance to perform them. At first, she coughed a lot, her voice was thick and croaky from the dust that she had inhaled during the explosion but gradually her voice began to come back. The staff were initially amused and christened her *la canarina*, but later the joke wore thin and she knew that her daily vocal exercises began to irritate them.

Then, one morning, apparently no different from any other, a female warder appeared and stood aside deferentially allowing a different man also in a suit to enter. This time the visitor introduced himself as Carlos Morales but gave no indication of his provenance or status. He also spoke to her in good English but much more gently and respectfully than his colleague. He enquired how she was being treated. She replied well enough although she was not amused at being detained without cause and without trial. Like his predecessor, he asked about her reasons for being at Pic Noix on the fateful afternoon. She stuck to her previous story. After a pause, he came to the point in a rather roundabout way:

'*Senora*, we have come by information now makes us think that we may have been mistaken in believing you and your companions were employed by a Basque terrorist group. I am sorry that this has taken so long but it has been an extremely complicated case and there were several false leads. An officer from the intelligence service of one of our European partners is coming to see me this afternoon and is extremely anxious to meet you. Are you prepared to see him?'

'I wouldn't have thought that I had much choice' she replied angrily.

'Perhaps not but it seemed courteous to ask.'

'That certainly makes a change. Perhaps you could extend your courtesy further' she added with heavy sarcasm 'and let me know what has happened to my companions.'

'Do you not know?' he seemed genuinely shocked 'I will tell you. Unfortunately, the explosion killed Mr Walsh instantly. Mr Klovsky was taken to hospital alive but died soon afterwards. The doctors tried hard but could not save him.'

Detty stared into space at this grim news not daring to go on to the question that was at the forefront of her mind. She knew that she must ask eventually:

'And the woman, Liese Zahnsdorf...?'

'Is alive and well – although she was hit rather hard on the head by the leg of the table that undoubtedly saved both your lives. Like you, she was concussed and claims to have no recall of the events leading up to the explosion. Because we thought was there was a risk of a terrorist break out attempt, she has been kept in another prison but I will arrange for you to see her as soon as I can. The foreign officer also wants to see her but he seemed more interested in you.'

Detty wondered who this strange man was who was interested in seeing her. He had, until now, only been referred to as 'a foreign officer'. She faced the routine prison lunch with more than usual relish. Morales, she thought, had really explained very little in detail but Liese was alive and apparently virtually unhurt. The tone of the morning's conversation had been completely different from the previous interviews. She was very sad at the deaths of the Americans but in other respects, the world and the future suddenly seemed altogether brighter.

Shortly after three in the afternoon, the female warder returned followed again by Morales. They stood aside and Morales said:

'*Senora*, I would like you to meet…'

He never finished as the steel doorway was filled by the broad-shouldered figure of Colonel Kramm smiling at Detty and holding out his hand:

'*Guten Tag, Frau Leutnant! Wie geht es Ihnen?*[29] I am sorry that I have been so long finding you.'

The soft Wurttemberg accent immediately reminded her of the language of Schiller and the music of Schubert. She realised in a flash how lonely she had been and how comforted she felt by this quietly authoritative presence.

'*Guten Tag, Herr Oberst, jetz sehr gut, danke*[30]. It is very good to see you again.'

Detty realised that Kramm had used her former temporary rank deliberately and it certainly had the desired effect.

'But we didn't realise that you knew the Senora and that……….'

'I am sorry. It was very rude of me. I should have explained that this lady is a long-standing friend and a former distinguished military

---

29 Good day, Lieutenant, how are you?
30 Good day, Colonel, now I'm fine –thank you.

intelligence colleague. As I explained to the Minister in Madrid this morning, she has been helping NATO and Interpol to try to round up the Lev organisation but that, because of the highly secret nature of their mission and because Lev has a number of agents in high places, she came to Spain with her colleagues secretly. Unfortunately, despite these precautions, their mission apparently still became known to Lev with the disastrous outcome that you witnessed at Pic Noix.'

'At least the leak could not have been from a Spanish agent, as we were kept in the dark'.

Morales was mildly reproachful:

'No, our contacts in Washington think that they may have traced the mole there'.

'As you have identified and vouched for the *Senora*. She will, of course, be released with her colleague, who I understand is also an allied intelligence officer as soon as the formalities are complete.'

Liese arrived in the afternoon and clasped Detty in a very unmilitary embrace. She appeared a lot thinner than before but was as cheerful as usual and apparently unharmed by her experience. They flew to Madrid for dinner and the night as guests of the German embassy.

'We need to pool our information' said Kramm as they sat together over coffee and Kaiserstuhler Marc which regretfully Detty had to leave untouched.

'Not tonight, you understand, but soon. I must go to London to see Marc who is coming back from Washington. I am sure that you, Frau Detty, will wish to see him as soon as possible and he, I know, has been very anxious. Perhaps you and the Frau Major could both join me for a few days in England? Major Zahnsdorf, would you be able to come and to delay your return to Königshof? You can, of course, use the secure facilities here to contact anybody that you need to.'

*

Rashly Detty had issued an invitation for them all to join her for the debriefing meeting at their house in Henley. The *Oberst* had the spare bedroom but Liese had to make do with a sofa bed in the study cum music room at the top of the house. When Detty apologised her friend burst out laughing.

'You seem to have forgotten some of the places we have slept in, together and separately, *meine allerliebste Freundin.*'

'Yes, but we are not in The Farm or a Spanish prison now.' Detty protested.

A prolonged breakfast enabled Liese and Detty to give the *Oberst* their account of the events leading up to the Spanish catastrophe. They then drove to Heathrow to meet Marc, whose joy and relief was written all over his face. Marc insisted that they went for lunch at his favourite pub outside Henley. On arrival Kramm, wearing a Harris Tweed jacket, flannels, and brogues, stretched his legs out under the battered oak table and contemplated the froth tracing its patterns down the side of the half empty pint of cask-conditioned bitter. Sitting in an English pub, like many anglophilic Germans, he appeared more English than the English. Liese, her neck and chest still sore and on her first visit to England, looked at the large jug of barely chilled tawny fluid in front of her with some suspicion. Not that she minded beer. She could down the *peeva* of her native land with the best. As a soldier and the partner of a footballer, she knew her way around the beer-drinking scene but this was a new experience.

Marc was digesting the great news that his wife was pregnant again and, moreover, appeared none the worse for a spell in a Spanish prison. He was enjoying himself. Sitting in a pleasant Oxfordshire pub with his adored Detty, his boss and Liese was definitely an improvement on endless Pentagon protocols and NATO paperwork. In addition, he enjoyed good bitter with the relish of a Bavarian who had absorbed the highways and byways of brewing, albeit in a different style, with his mother's milk. He had acquired in his turn a distinct whiff of anglophilia and was keen to show off the local beer to his connoisseur chief. Detty alone felt uncomfortable. She was struggling to appear the perfect hostess under circumstances that were, to a degree, artificial. She had needed all her resolve fighting down morning sickness to dress four brace of woodcock, which had been presented to her by a local farmer friend with a ceremony, which would have befitted the crown jewels.

'It rare enough to hit one let alone four brace' he had said 'but we had a pretty good day last week – three hundred birds with eight guns mainly pheasant but some partridge and these little beauties. We would have loved to have them ourselves but we're off to Norfolk to my son this weekend and the daughter in law doesn't do game. I know you'll do them justice what with Marc's colleague being over and all. Germans have a fine palate for game, I know, I've met them on the shoots in Scotland.'

All of this was true but for all the royal rarity of the birds, dressing them whilst fighting down morning sickness was a challenge, even though, due to her Irish country upbringing, she had handled game for as long as she could remember. The job was now done and she was beginning to feel somewhat better as she listened to Colonel Kramm:

'Jeff and Dave had, as perhaps you already know, laid their trap for Pueblo by impersonating members of a Columbian gang who the Americans already had – how do you say it in English – banged up. This might well have worked if their security had been watertight. Unfortunately, there was a leak, somewhere in the CIA, and Pueblo got to know that his contacts could not be who they claimed to be. Almost at the same time, Pueblo decided that he could no longer operate from Pic Noix. The abbey is, was, a genuine monastery and only a relatively small number of the brothers worked with Lev. This was both its strength and its weakness. It was strong because it was an ideal cover, weak because it was necessary, to some extent, to conceal the criminal activities. Pueblo had two advantages, however. He is extremely eminent in the Church hierarchy, a personal friend of the late Pope and was a director of the Vatican bank. He was offered a Cardinal hat but refused it on the somewhat ironic grounds that it might hinder his work in under-developed countries.'

The listening group looked incredulous and laughed.

'Yes, I know, but it is amazing what you can manage if you have enough domineering insolence. Just take your hero, Richard Wagner, for instance, Frau Bernadette. Anyway, Pueblo managed to turn this façade to a further advantage. Under pretence of arranging famine relief, he stored substantial quantities of material at Pic Noix and other ecclesiastical centres. We also believe that he kept extensive computer and paper records at Pic Noix, under the pretence that they were associated with his trade in illuminated manuscripts and with his charitable work. For a long time, nobody dared to pry into his activities, he was simply too important and anyway there was really no reason for those around him to be suspicious. Gradually, however, questions began to be asked further afield. The attempt to destabilise Livonia backfired and failed to restore the useful rogue state that Lev needed. Rather, it stirred up a hornets' nest and put some highly competent investigators on the trail of the criminals. Prominent amongst these was Frau Leutnant Tanya Lobokova and even more important yourself, Frau Major. We all owe a considerable debt to your organisation. It was quality intelligence work performed to the highest standards – congratulations.'

Liese nodded her thanks for the compliment but said nothing.

'The international trap was beginning to close and Pueblo knew it. He had to evacuate Pic Noix before he was caught in flagrante but first he had to get rid of the stocks of arms and all the computer records and paperwork. This was going to be difficult, as he could not make the genuine community suspicious. He hit on an evil but brilliant idea.

I should explain that trade in materials for biological warfare is one of his sidelines and his contacts in this field, probably the North Africans, were to prove useful. We think that he decided to create an epidemic at Pic Noix that would require its evacuation. His expert friends must have recommended the *Legionella Pneumopilia* bacteria. We think that he obtained a sizeable supply and put them, probably unaided, in the Pic Noix water supply. The plan worked excellently. Several of the older brothers developed symptoms of the disease and one died before it was possible to make the diagnosis. The health authorities demanded the complete evacuation of the monastery and surrounding buildings pending a full public health investigation. Monsignor Pueblo, on behalf of the Church, said that no investigation of the closed part of the Abbey could take place until permission was obtained from the Father General in Rome. In the meantime, he would personally supervise the securing of the Abbey's library and other treasures which were too valuable to be exposed to risk from water engineers and health officials. At a stroke, he had evacuated the Abbey and provided himself with cover to move trucks in and out of the premises – all of course driven by Lev henchmen.

Predictably, the permission from the Father General proved difficult to obtain, as there were administrative problems and delays. Your visit with Herr Walsh and Herr Klovsky might have proved inconvenient to Pueblo if he had not had an agent in a senior position in the CIA. This agent had already provided information about the previous operator sent to Pic Noix, which had resulted in his murder, as I think you know. Well, he or she had equally accurate information about your visit and forewarned Pueblo. Fortunately, Frau Bernadette, your first visit to the Abbey in search of Frau Tamara who was, by the way, never actually held at Pic Noix, escaped their attention. It was known only to the Security Service of the FWL, which seems more leak-proof than the CIA. Congratulations again, Frau Major.'

'A question of small being beautiful – or at any rate, easier to make watertight, Herr Oberst.'

This time Liese had allowed herself a smile.

'Very true, as we have known to our cost, in the past. Anyway, fortunately Frau Bernadette's cover held, at least until she departed from the Abbey riding bareback in the best style of the Wild West.'

Detty smiled ruefully as the others laughed.

'I think Herr Marc needs another pint of bitter and I will join him. What about you, *meine Damen*?'

Fortunately, Liese was still struggling with her first pint so it was not so obvious that Detty's was still full. They both declined. Kramm went to the bar waving Marc, who had half risen, back into his seat and returned with two more pints.

'As it was however, the second time round, Pueblo and Lev knew every movement of your quartet as soon as you left Königshof. At first Pueblo seems to have been concerned as to how to deal with you, clearly you had to be killed but it might be messy and awkward questions might be asked. Then he hit on a neater solution and it almost worked. First, he organised some reports of suspicious sightings of unusual, possibly foreign, terrorists associated with ETA in the area. He assumed that you would head for the Abbey and did nothing that might impede you. He kept his agents watching you closely and waited until you had entered the Abbey unmolested and then arranged for a disguised truck bomb to blow up as close as he could get it to the library, the offices and yourselves. The explosion would be massive and he hoped that it would render unrecognisable any remaining evidence of his activities. In any case, in the confusion he would be able to remove or destroy any remaining Lev records and materials. He assumed that you would all be killed and the authorities would imagine that you had been blown up whilst planting the explosives – a classic terrorist *Selbsttor*-own goal, I think that you call it in English. In the very unlikely event of any of you surviving, you would still be suspected of terrorism and be detained for long enough for him to complete his clean up and disappear. Sad to relate, it has, in all essentials, worked out as he planned. Monsignor is an extremely shrewd and careful operator. There were two things that saved you. The driver couldn't get the truck right under the arch below the atrium thereby slightly lessening the force of the massive explosion and Frau Major Zahnsdorf's presence of mind pulling you both under the oak refectory table.'

'Does your department have any idea where Pueblo is now, Herr Oberst?' asked Liese.

'Unfortunately, we don't. Obviously, he may be holed up in Russia or the Ukraine but given the careful planning that he has adopted before, he may well not have done the obvious and anyway the hinterland of Russia, Belarus and the Ukraine are difficult enough areas to search even for their own authorities, let alone outsiders. He is probably not working alone and even he may have possible superiors. We aren't sure. We still must tread warily in order not to upset our newfound friends there.'

*

Ever since the Farm days, she had been an early riser. Just after six, she slipped the embrace of her still unconscious husband and rustled into her favourite salmon silk negligée as silently as possible. The mist was swirling off a damply cold February Thames with its forlornly beached rowing boats as mementos of a distant summer. It eddied round their dormer bedroom window. She crept down the two flights of stairs to the kitchen. The scene of devastation left over from the night before provoked the first wave of nausea, which she fought off with iron determination whilst she surveyed the ghastly array of congealed plates, wine-stained glasses, and half consumed rolls. The second wave of sickness caught her unawares. She nearly failed in her dash to make the downstairs cloakroom where she rolled herself into a foetal ball on the floor, turned her head sideways over the lavatory pan and vomited intermittently for a miserable quarter of an hour.

After a seeming age, she felt able to emerge and, with the courage worthy of a Commander of the Order of St Nicklaus, ran the hot water and started on the glasses. She cursed herself for not getting Grace, the delightful fellow Irish girl that she had met at Mass to come in and help. Grace now did the small amount of housework required by their infrequent visits a couple of times a week. Detty was sure that she would have been only too pleased to come and tidy up the wreckage of the dinner. Everything had been arranged so quickly that the aftermath hadn't crossed her mind. She had felt rather proud of herself. At Madrid Airport she had slipped off to telephone Neal's Yard for some Irish cheeses and then made another call to Ben Charles at Nutt Bros for some dinner wine worthy of her husband's connoisseur boss. After discussing the matter with Ben, she had ordered a six case of Krug, two bottles of Taylor 82 (pre-decanted) and a case of mixed Grand Cru Cotes de Nuits together with two bottles of Corton Charlemagne. Marc who had been thinking in terms of the local wine merchant, which was sadly no longer the force that it had once been, was delighted. The washing up had not entered her mind and she could hardly 'phone Grace for help at six thirty on a Sunday morning. 'Get on with it, girl,' she said to herself, 'you are not the first woman in the world to suffer from morning sickness.'

The array of clean glasses gradually increased without making any apparent impression on the clutter. Still the meal had been a success. The Krug had produced a gentle look of reverent enchantment in Kramm's eyes and, she had to admit to herself that the scallop mousse, created from the best available ingredients from the local supermarket, had tasted very good with the Corton Charlemagne '99. Then, of course, there was the woodcock, which rewarded Detty's efforts of the previous morning and was subtle and delicious with the '87 Clos de Tart, which Marc had selected from the available burgundies. The Gubeen and Milleens completed the feast before the port. This was accompanied by walnuts and cobnuts, which had been sent unmarked with the wine order. Marc, not unnaturally after recent events, suspicious of unmarked packages opened it extremely carefully but found nothing inside except nuts and a note from Ben saying:

To my Diva, with homage, these are from last year from my garden in Kent. They should go well with the Taylor. Your slave as always, Ben'

'Idiot' said Detty 'but it was sweet of him.'

Marc, who was by this time used to a variety of males being in love with his wife, just laughed and agreed.

12
THE TRIUMPH

The race is not to the swift.
Nor the battle to the strong

BIBLE PROVERBS 84 23

Ralph O'Sullivan was an old college and medical school friend of her father's. He was now a popular, successful, and very senior gynaecologist in Dublin and kept consulting rooms off Parnell Street within a longish stone's throw of the Rotunda Hospital. He was always cheerful, rubicund, and smiling. He had kept up his friendship with the O'Neills and had known Detty since she was a baby. He was a frequent visitor to the old stone house in Ballyinch for a day's shooting, a round of golf or a meeting with Brian at one or other of the Kildare racecourses. In spite of his familiarity and relaxed character, Detty felt nervous. She knew that Ralph had a couple of horses in training with Christy Lorne and wondered whether his first enquiry would be about her or Firebrand.

Of course, her fantasies were groundless; he was extremely professional and concentrated on her and her pregnancy. An expression of genuine agony contorted his face as she described the fate of the last one. With a concerned efficiency, he did the necessary examinations and carried out a scan showing the baby, which thrilled her but made her achingly sorry that Marc could not have been with her to see it. He arranged blood tests and details of the booking for confinement. She was able to assure him that the morning sickness was at long last improving. She discussed her professional bookings and confirmed what she had already worked out. May in St Petersburg and Florence would be fine but Bayreuth in July should be cancelled. Detty really knew this already but dreaded ringing Christa Wagner to tell her. She had been so kind that it seemed the last straw to tell her that she must find another *Woglinde* at this stage. It was however inevitable. Apart from the vocal side the athleticism and skimpy costume of a *Rheintöchter*, albeit not as revealing in this production as in some others, was hardly suited to a singer approaching the final trimester of pregnancy.

'Do you have any problems you haven't told me about?'

'Only one, my right leg has started aching abominably below the scar ever since I've been pregnant – it did a bit last time as well. That and the morning sickness, first told me that I was pregnant.'

'I saw the scar – was it a riding accident?'

'No' she said and hesitated and he looked at her enquiringly.

Somehow, it seemed wrong to talk about the Livonian war here in the peace of Dublin 'it was a sniper's bullet.'

'I think that this is the first time that I have met a combat wound as a complication of pregnancy but I daresay there were others around here in '16. It is natural enough though that it should be sore, pregnancy dilates the veins and below a wound like that, the leg would become congested. Support tights will help, I will arrange for you to get the right sort and keep the leg up as much as you can when you are sitting down. Otherwise, as far as I can tell now, you are fine and, as you have seen, the baby looks grand on the scan. We will do another one later which shows more detail. Can you come back in a month?'

She nodded and was about to add 'I shall be in England for Cheltenham' when Ralph produced the broadest of smiles and pre-empted her by asking at last:

'Now tell me, how is she?'

They both knew who 'she' was without further explanation.

'She's fine. Looks grand, taking hurdles like she can't get enough and Christy's very happy.'

'You'll be winning it, then?'

'I don't know about that. You know the Triumph, there are a lot of decent four-year-olds around and you know the race record of good horses isn't that great, but she has some sort of a chance. We'll see. Are yer going over?'

'I'll not miss it. I was about to tell you not to get too over excited but I suppose that's a waste of time.'

'Completely. I'm scared stiff already so the Lord knows what I shall be like on the day.'

'Anyway, we will all keep our fingers crossed.'

'Thanks a million.'

*

She drove straight to Kilmartin to take a last look at her filly before going back to England. It was wet but not cold and, as she drove past, the grasslands of the Curragh seemed to stretch to infinity shimmering in the breeze and the misty rain. She had her own key to the yard. She said hello to Sam, the girl who 'did' Firebrand and three others and was quickly in her box with that fine head and arrogant look of eagles. Detty whispered to her that she could conquer the world then thought that she knows that already. Suddenly a voice behind said softly:

'She looks grand, doesn't she? She went well this morning. It is ideal for her now – she likes a bit of cut. I hope it lasts over there until the Festival.'

'She's grown' Detty staring expertly with undisguised admiration at the filly's shining chestnut quarters.'

'Sure, she's furnishing beautifully.'

Detty followed Christy across the Yard and into the house for tea. She was full of mixed emotions. Of course, it was hugely exciting but frightening too. Firebrand was theirs, very precious and personal for so many reasons. On that Thursday at Cheltenham, she would belong to the world. Of course, she had run before in public, but smaller races at Irish courses were nothing like the Triumph Hurdle, the opener on Gold Cup Day at the jumping Mecca with half Ireland there, rooting for her as they always did.

Aunt Deidre was used to anxious love-lorn owners and realized her tough guerrilla of a niece had really got it bad. She produced tea and the famous Barmbrack 'should only be at Hallowe'en really but know how you love it'. They talked of breeding and tactics and the Gold Cup where a new English wonder-horse was said to be a near certainty to beat the reigning Irish champion.

'It takes a good one to win it back-to-back. There haven't been many and this Gulf and Bust looked a really good horse in the King George, never came off the bit, but Jim didn't take his and Cheltenham is different. Californian Piper likes the Course and Jim has saved him for the big one. He's got a big heart for the Hill and you never know at Cheltenham.'

'You don't, surely' Detty forced a grin but felt a deep void in the pit of her stomach. She wasn't thinking about the Gold Cup. She lingered and realized that she didn't want to leave. There was comfort in sitting with the people who knew and understood her idol. The next time she would see her would be in public. With resolution, she got up, kissed goodbye, and drove the few miles home.

Her mother was excited about the antenatal visit and wondered why this strange daughter of hers seemed oddly detached about it. She had never shared the family passion for horses and didn't reach the diagnosis that her sister-in-law had instantly recognized. Detty was still spiritually in the stall at Kilmartin; in time she would be thinking of nothing but babies, but, reassured that all was well with hers, not before Cheltenham, emphatically not before Cheltenham.

*

Marc put the phone down, reassured that NATO and Catterick could wait one more day before extracting their pound of flesh for his absence. He crossed the old wood floor of the Cotswold inn to where Detty was re-reading the assessment for the Triumph Hurdle for the third time. Convinced at last that however many times she read it, it would still say:

'Time Out Tim is a worthy favourite, in this graveyard race for favourites, and is clearly the one to beat after two easy successes against good company at Newbury and here. Delta Dumper also ran on well to win at Sandown in January and there were excuses last time out for his failure at Chepstow. We may not yet have seen the best of him and he is an obvious threat. The best of the rest amongst the home team seems to be Standard Pint and Holefernes. Of the Irish challengers, Worthy Altar has the credentials after wins at Leopardstown and Newbury and is an obvious danger. Firebrand seems to have taken to hurdles well after her third when still green at the Leopardstown Christmas meeting followed by a very useful race when second to Worthy Altar at Punchestown with Sissy Sibilant fourth. Although this Festival may have come too early for her, she is a useful filly and sure to win races.'

She threw The Racing Post aside with a sigh as Marc sat down and grinned across the remains of the boiled eggs and half demolished toast.

'Bayreuth was nothing to this, you know.'

'*Im Stall liegt eine Stutchen:-*
die hat sie Furchten gelehrt?'[31]

'Don't tease me, its unkind today' she kicked his foot under the table, laughing at his misquotation from *Siegfried* about what it takes to learn fear.

'I can't wait to see her again – make sure that she's OK.'

'Do you think Christy would be running her if she wasn't? Anyway, he rang last night to tell you she had travelled well and eaten up.'

'I know but.......ye know…'

*

The sun, weak and watery after the morning's cloudburst, broke through the slate and white clouds striking the Cotswold grey roofs of the

---

31 In a stall stands a filly
    From her I have learnt fear

houses. It gradually moved up Cleeve Hill; a very small patch dancing over the light and dark green of the hedges and fields spotlighting this filigree patchwork until, triumphantly, the little spot of sunlight arrived at the summit. That is why it is called The Triumph Hurdle thought Detty inconsequentially making a mental note to ask Christy at a more appropriate moment how the race had got its name.

Somehow, lunch, elegantly served, had no appeal for her and she thought guiltily of the hunger, which was still a daily menace in the country that had honoured her and which she loved. She felt her stomach turn over with tension and cursed herself for the stupidity of being so nervous. After all, she had hardly felt like this when facing torture and death itself. She looked over at Marc who seemed outwardly unconcerned but she noticed that he kept glancing over the green polyhedron of Prestbury Park to make sure it was still there.

Able to control herself no longer, Detty picked up her green and gold race card and flicked through it pausing from page to page and hoping to give the impression to the others round the lunch table that she was studying form for the Gold Cup and the County Hurdle. Then thumbing nonchalantly to the front of the booklet, she checked the entry once more:

The JCB Triumph Hurdle Race (Class A) for four-year-olds Estimated Total Prize Fund £200,000, (Grade 1)
Detty turned onto the third page of the massive entry list and there she was:
26 Firebrand (Ire) (25) 10 9
Ch f Illumined – Fair Fighter

Owner	Countess B. von Ritter
Trainer	C. Lorne, Ireland
Breeder	C.Lorne, Ireland
Jockey	J.P. O'Donoghue

Colours Green with white stars, orange armlets Blue and white quartered cap

Form -32
Made a good start over hurdles with good third in the Christmas meeting

at Leopardstown followed by a fine half length second to Worthy Altar at Punchestown running on. Acts on any going including soft. Smart filly to be considered. Rating 137

It makes it sound easy, thought Detty, but for one thing. This is the Triumph Hurdle with the best four-year-old juveniles in the game entered from three countries. Still there had been rain overnight and the going was good. It would suit her well.

Christy looked at her quizzically between the leather furrows, which narrowed his blue eyes almost to a slit. She knew so many of these weather-beaten faces, acquired after many years squinting critically over the gallops. Through wind, rain and occasionally even sun, the trainer could not afford to miss a thing if he or she wanted to make a success of this tough, fragile profession. He knew and shared what she was going through; only he did it for a living. He picked up his hat and binoculars and said quietly:

'I think I'll be going down now to her. I'll see you in the Paddock.'

She was caught by the TV and its racing guru on her way to the Paddock. She managed a few words but could not remember afterwards what she had said – something about it being far more terrifying than the Livonian Civil War. Would Firebrand win? She made the standard answer that she had some sort of a chance, if she got the luck, but it was always a terribly open race. He let her go.

*

It was a good break. Jess had her covered up on the rail in mid division. It looked OK but Detty wondered whether she should have been tracking the leaders, Delta Dumper and Holofernes, a bit more closely. Just my anxiety she thought; she's going beautifully. She reminded herself that Jess was one of the world's top jump jockeys and that this wasn't the Ladies Race in the Kildare Point-to-Point. They got to the far side at the highest point on the course and the race began to unravel. Jess moved Firebrand up a notch and she passed three or four horses taking closer order on the approach to four out. She simply flew over the hurdle passing another three horses, including Worthy Altar, her one-time conqueror, in the air. She was sixth but closing all the time on the leaders including the favourite who was still on the bridle. Jess also sat as still as a rock just letting the filly do her work as she approached the third out- closing, closing, closing as if nothing could stop her. Suddenly it all changed. Holofernes who was dropping out of the lead slipped and punched through the hurdle, horse, and rider somersaulting. The two behind had no chance and crashed into the flailing Holofernes. Jess who was close up and accelerating to challenge the leaders had no chance either. He and Firebrand joined the heap of human and horseflesh writhing over the stricken Holofernes. Detty was just aware of her head swimming. She looked down from their box to try and steady herself. Through her swirling vision, a face momentarily appeared in the crowd below, sinister but familiar. She looked up again with Cleeve Hill gyrating round and round as Marc caught her. The next thing she knew she was in the First Aid Room lying down with Marc holding her hand. He was saying quietly:

'It's alles OK – the doctor has seen you and says you just fainted, it happens in pregnancy, something to do with the circulation but you are all right and so is the baby.'

Detty was first relieved but then felt an unreasonable irritation:

'Sure, I'm OK and the baby but how about her and Jess.'

'She's all right too and so is Jess. He's fit to ride Californian Piper in the Gold Cup. Firebrand really is fine – looks better than you do at this moment. She's back in her box in the stable and ready to do it all again.'

Detty kissed him. He did know what was important in critical moments – he always had done.

In spite of the nurse's disapproval, she insisted on going back to her box for the Gold Cup. She apologized to Christy and her family and in-laws for behaving, as she put it, like the pregnant heroine of a Victorian novel. The Gold Cup parade was already under way and soon the hush descended, the big screen and the binoculars tense as they came under orders. The first circuit was fast but tactical with the two big names watching each other closely. Both jumped fluently but Gulf and Bust, the English hot favourite, simply flew the fences, standing off and drawing gasps from the crowd. Detty was sitting, reluctantly, at the front of the box. Christy, a close friend of Jim Keegan, Californian Piper's trainer, was standing just behind her chair. She heard him mutter to himself as Gulf and Bust flew over the last in the first circuit, to prolonged applause, 'Maybe a bit too artsy.' Nobody else heard him. The Irish holder, Californian Piper, had been given virtually no chance in the morning papers of repeating his victory which had been seen as a bit of a fluke anyway in a sub-standard Gold Cup, but he was staying in touch and going well, but less flamboyantly. He moved up steadily and just led at the last but was soon joined by Gulf and Bust who seemed certain to go on and win easily. But Jess, riding the race of his life, called for something hidden in the Irish horse, he came again and they tussled all the way up the hill. At the line, the gasping spectators couldn't split them.

'Photograph, photograph' said the dispassionate voice of the announcer and the whole racecourse waited in silent tension apart from a few bookies shouting odds on the photo. Detty couldn't hear which one they favoured but even the photo odds seemed close. After what seemed like an age, the same calm voice announced:

'First, number ni....'

The rest was drowned in the Irish roar, with a bit of German help that could have been heard in Bristol. Californian Piper had joined the small Olympian band of immortals who had defended the Cheltenham Gold Cup and Jess O'Donoghue, despite his multiple bruises had given the efficient, but uncharismatic, English Champion Jockey a lesson in how to ride a finish which would long be remembered and talked of in the bars of Kildare and Kilkenny.

When the excitement began to die down, Detty begged Christy to take her down to see Firebrand who was enjoying the attentions of the faithful Joe, Christy's travelling head lad and Sam, her own stable girl.

'Sure, she's fine' Joe said reassuringly.

'All the same' said Christy 'we will get the vet to look her over before taking her back. If we're not sure we might take her out of the Punchestown Festival but we'll see.'

As they left the stables, an English trainer walked past. He was obviously a friend of Christy's but Detty didn't recognize him or him, her.

'Bad luck today, Christy. She looked splendid. Make sure you look after her.' he added with a smile.

'Of course, we will. This is her owner who thinks the world of her and she'll roast me on a pike if I don't.'

'And at least one other thinks the world of her apparently,' laughed the Englishman. Christy and Detty looked puzzled as he shook hands with Detty.

'Surely, you've heard. Hills have made her eight to one for next year's Champion Hurdle after a huge ante post bet – not by the connections then, I assume. It was very bad luck today but somebody else thinks she's a winner.'

'Is she entered?' said Detty incredulously to Christy.

'The heck she will be.' said the astonished trainer.

'But surely Triumph horses, juveniles, don't make Champion Hurdlers the following year.'

'They don't often but this one is special.'

'I think I shall faint for the second time. Is this common – I mean to have a huge bet the year before the race?'

'I should think it's a record if they have cut the odds that far on a four-year-old who wasn't in the frame to-day but you'd have to ask the bookies to be sure.'

*

Manchester drizzled mistily and unendingly, truncating the increasing daylight of the late March days so that it was uncertain where day started and ended. Not that Detty minded, she was there to work and after the excitement of the Festival, she needed time to gather her wits. She worked tirelessly with Eileen on the two demanding roles that had to come before her pregnancy halted her career for the time being. The coaching was going well. Her voice was now back in good shape and her interpretation of *Tatiana* was developing well. She worried about the next few months. She had been assured that she could manage both roles but it was still a responsibility. She was a very young singer and to appear as *Tatiana* in Tchaikovsky's home city was daunting to any foreigner. Her strong Russian was to her advantage but even so, she spent some time with the College Russian language coach. He expressed himself delighted and surprised to find a young English-speaking singer who really understood the language. He occasionally looked a bit puzzled and did enquire where she had acquired her slight Livonian accent. Obviously, he didn't read the newspapers and Detty simply said that she had spent some time in Livonia.

'A holiday?' he had enquired.

'Working, really' she replied truthfully but uninformatively.

'Oh, a holiday job, I imagine' He clearly thought that as she was a performer diploma student of unusual talent, she had worked in Europe for money and language experience. This was common enough.

She had no desire to give him her life story and anonymity was rather a relief as they started work again. He professed himself entirely happy with her Russian and added, rather regretfully, that no more sessions would be necessary. Detty felt rather ashamed to be relieved that she had been able to go to him unrecognised after her near notoriety in the rest of the College. She was glad to avoid further probing and was relieved to get back to intensive musical coaching with Eileen. Each weekend, she took the first train that she could get on a Friday to Reading and, usually, was met by Marc from London.

One Friday however Mark was going to be kept late at a meeting and she had to compete for the limited number of taxis at Reading station. She missed out on the first batch but was assured by several drivers that they only had short trips and would be back for her 'in a trice'. The trice proved a long one. She was just beginning to wish that she had tried to get back to Twyford in time to catch the branch line connection on the single track to Henley when a voice by her side said:

'Looking for a mini cab, madam?'

She jumped, looked round at the owner of the voice, and fled back into the station in blind panic, cannoning into a large constable of the transport police.

'In a hurry, Miss?'

The remark was more jocular than critical and Detty trying to hide her Irish accent, said rather obviously that she was late for a train. Like many Irish children, she had been brought up to believe that the British police were only a short remove from the Gestapo. However, they had never really proved a problem to her and on this occasion, she was distinctly comforted by his bulky presence.

'Which one was that then, Miss?'

'The one to Twyford' She blurted out the first place that came into her head.

'Don't worry, there's another in ten minutes' he reassured her.

She had no alternative but to cross the bridge to the appropriate platform and wait for the train indicated by the policeman. At least she didn't have to face the station forecourt and its mini-cab driver with the strangely familiar long face. On the short journey to Twyford, she tried to order her thoughts. Had she really seen Pueblo or was it her disordered imagination heightened by the tension of work and pregnancy? She had dismissed the face in the crowd at Cheltenham as a figment of her imagination, as she fainted, but this time the face and the voice fitted. He was wearing dark glasses, odd in itself, on a cloudy late March Day in England, but it did mean that she could not see his astonishing eyes, which would have clinched the matter. Anyway, what was a dignitary of the Church, albeit a criminal one, doing driving a mini cab in Reading? Were there mini cabs in Reading? Had he just made the whole thing up hoping to get her into his car for a purpose that she couldn't guess? It seemed more likely he was just trying to scare her. It was not the obvious reason she was sure. She had been at the receiving end of more than her fair share of perverted sexual lust but she was sure that Pueblo was immune from this vice at least. Her acute female antennae put him down as asexual or perhaps a latent, disciplined gay. Her reverie was interrupted by the train slowing for Twyford and the simultaneous appearance of a ticket collector. She had no ticket, tried to explain, sounded lame, and was made to feel that she was a criminal lucky to get away with paying an exorbitant penalty fare. Fortunately, there was a train to Henley waiting in the branch line platform. It was well after ten when she got home exhausted physically and mentally.

She had intended to wait up for Marc but instead slumped into bed and was deeply asleep when he arrived well after midnight. She stirred, kissed him but the story could wait for the morning. She told him over breakfast what had happened. Marc was definite.

'It must be Pueblo. You are not the hallucinating sort and you couldn't possibly have expected to see him in that unlikely situation. But why? What does he want?'

'I have got quite used to people wanting bits of me for their own particularly nasty purposes but that is not his style.'

'No, I don't think its sexual and he's not a maniac-just a very ruthless and capable criminal who is trying to recover from a serious setback and thinks you can be forced to help him – but how? I'll chew it over, both the motive and how to protect you, over a hot stove.'

He started work on bacon and eggs with British enthusiasm and Teutonic thoroughness.

She buried herself with her piano in the mercifully insulated little top room at Henley while he happily experimented with Anglo-German cooking in the little kitchen two floors below. Detty claimed now that his cooking was improving more than her singing. They laughed about it together. The late-night suppers after she had finished work were accompanied by *trockenwein*. It had been selected by her father-in-law to be especially low in alcohol and came from the family estate in the Steigerwald. Detty had brought it back stuffed into in her overloaded Z4.

'We will have to bring the Mercedes next time.' Marc said, as they wistfully consumed the last bottle.

'I should stop anyway, most of the antenatal class here are scandalised that I still drink wine in pregnancy, although Ralph said it was OK with low alcohol within reason and even the midwife said that she didn't think a glass or so would do any harm.'

*

St Petersburg was at its beautiful worst. The grey clouds scudded in westward from the Gulf of Finland – not yet a thaw to crack the ice cap on the Neva but enough to make the snow in the streets soft, filthy, and beginning to smell with that peculiar putrid odour of old metropolitan slush. Detty had met it before in Königshof where she realised with envy the worst would be over by now and the streets beginning to dry. The extra kilometres south made a big difference in the spring. The Livonian summer wasn't long but it was warmer and more persistent than St Petersburg's.

She was staying at the Grand Hotel Europe on Nevsky. There was no reason for anonymity or disguise, which would have been impossible anyway, this time. Although outrageously expensive, she could afford it and the Kirov hierarchy approved of their imported young diva staying at one of the City's best hotels. It was comfortable enough but even from the beautifully temperature-controlled rooms, every sight of the cloud covered sky and streets covered in a murky grey granita made her feel depressed.

That, however, was not the only problem. As she sat at breakfast in the Mezzanine Café of the hotel toying morosely with a delicious sort of brioche and letting her coffee get cold, she felt uncomfortable for two reasons. The first was worrying but straightforward. She was sure that she had seen Pueblo again as she went through the formalities at the airport before the long taxi ride into town. He, if it was he, was wearing a hat and was muffled in a scarf and she had only glimpsed him before he disappeared into the men's cloakroom. She felt certain but a small voice kept telling her that she was paranoid and was seeing this man everywhere. It was a no-win situation, she reflected, as if it wasn't him, she was going off her trolley and if it was, there was certainly danger, particularly as she still didn't understand what he could possibly want with her. This dilemma made her edgy but she could do nothing about it.

The second problem was more of an immediate worry. The Kirov did not normally employ foreign guest artists. This was partly because of economic reasons and partly because talented Russian singers were being employed in opera houses all over the world. In a nutshell, if you had plenty of your own why purchase outsiders? Superficially, the same argument might apply to the USA but the Metropolitan was obsessed with having all the best of everything and was in a much stronger economic position. In the rest of Europe, give and take with the large, best-funded houses competing for the big names was the order of the day.

All of this Detty knew. It didn't take a lot of inside knowledge as any opera magazine assumed that its knowledgeable readership knew the situation. Her own case was an exception. She knew that Gregor Metzhedrin, the internationally famous music director of the Kirov, had, by sheer chance, heard her *Brünnhilde* in *Siegfried* at Bayreuth the year before. He was immensely excited by her voice, had made some enquiries, discovered her Livonian connection and that she was, inter alia, a fluent Russian speaker. He immediately visualised her as his ideal *Tatiana* and, as he put it, at their first face to face meeting, eyeing her closely for a reaction, she was 'young, beautiful and with a voice from the angels'. Detty had learnt not to blush and was getting used to flattery but she certainly was not going to pass up this opportunity.

The economic difficulties were overcome partly because she accepted a modest fee and the Russian Government proved co-operative, as they were keen to placate Livonia as part of their attempt to get organised crime under control. What better opportunity than to give a boost to the career of Livonia's favourite daughter? Unfortunately, their enthusiasm did not reach down the ranks of the Kirov hierarchy and she was encountering, in the theatre, an atmosphere that ranged from the frosty to the downright hostile. It wasn't her singing. Her voice was in great shape and at least at present she felt that her pregnancy had given her voice a richness and steadiness that she had not had previously.

No, the fact that the rehearsals were going well and the fact that Metzhedrin was delighted made matters worse. The rank-and-file staff, from the choristers through the orchestral musicians to the dressers and stagehands definitely regarded her as an interloper who was doing a talented local singer out of a top role, which might have made her career.

All that she could do was to brazen it out but it was not the most welcoming situation for a young artist who felt that she was playing away from home for the first time. She did get some support from the young Russian baritone singing *Onegin*, who made up for the insensitivity of his stage persona, by being kind and supportive in real life. Detty appreciated this, the more as she realised that such kindness from a young man to his pregnant colleague, who did nothing to hide her love for her husband, must be entirely altruistic. Even from Stefan Archenko however, she tried to hide the fact that her husband was a German army officer, which, she feared, might make her already uncomfortable position even worse. Over sixty years is a long time and in no way could Marc be held responsible for the horrors of the siege, but she knew that there were those around her who would use any opportunity to stoke the growing hatred. Her respect for Stefan grew even more when he revealed just before she finished their engagement that he had been born near the Livonian border and had studied the Livonian war closely. He knew of her escapades and Marc's involvement almost as well as she did. Never however did he gossip about it at the theatre.

She was glad when the General Probe arrived and was almost looking forward to it. Singing and acting her splendid role wasn't a problem. She even felt that the presence of the photographers and invited audience might let some fresh air into the unpleasantly claustrophobic atmosphere that she had to endure. Her dresser, who Detty assumed was straight out of the ex-KGB, to her great surprise, even wished her well She sailed through the huge letter scene feeling good and was gratified by a warm outburst of applause from the rehearsal audience. At that moment, the theatre was plunged into darkness and fire alarms wailed everywhere. Eventually the emergency lights flickered on, enabling the cast and audience to leave the theatre and await events. Detty's costume for the bedroom letter scene was, of course, a nightgown and negligee. It was pretty enough, in fact, she loved its femininity and bump hiding qualities. It was however entirely unsuitable for a St Petersburg street in April with a north-east wind hurtling down from the artic and slush running over her satin slippers. Again, the gallant Stefan came to the rescue and insisted that she wore the overcoat, which he had already put on for scene three, over her shoulders.

A furious Gregor Metzhedrin strode about, bent and tense, looking, thought Detty, like Eisenstein's *Ivan the Terrible*, beard, and all, and threatening to get the entire staff of the theatre sacked. He was only slightly mollified when he learnt that there was no fire and the failure was nothing to do with the theatre but was city and region wide. The antiquated grid had chosen this precise moment to demonstrate its resentment over years of lack of maintenance. Detty dared mutter to the irate Maestro, that at least it wasn't the opening night. Even she was greeted by an icy stare before a smile cracked:

'Of course, you're quite right, my dear.'

Mollified at last, he got down to reorganising the shattered dress rehearsal, which was eventually completed. It was not exactly reassuring but Detty felt that she had acquitted herself reasonably under the circumstances.

After the trials and tribulations of the General Probe, she approached the opening night with a feeling almost of anticlimax but, at least now, the theatre staff had something else to takes their minds off the foreign interloper. At last, it all came right, she knew that her heart and soul were inside the tragic *Tatiana* and that her performance was convincing. At the first night, the critical audience gave her an appreciative but guarded reception but with each succeeding performance, the warmth increased until the last night when the applause and cheering, if not quite Königshof, was very gratifying. She was able to go to the airport the following morning to catch the Berlin plane with a good feeling of mission accomplished, made better by the fact that no unwanted faces appeared in the crowd. She was also looking forward to her three days at Oberdorf for Easter before going to Florence for *Lohengrin*. It was only late morning as she gazed out of the taxi window at the darkening wintry sky thundering in from the east as it whisked her from Schonefeld Airport to the *Bahnhof*. The driver said lugubriously that it would snow before evening adding that it would be worse in the south. His expression suggested that those mad enough to leave civilisation and go to Bavaria, deserved all that was coming to them in the way of bad weather.

He was right about the weather. Winter may have been jerking to a slushy close, with an unusually early spring, in St Petersburg, but that year, it came late and with force to Franconia. She had hardly had time to embrace Max who met her wreathed in smiles at the station when the snow started to fall. By the time, they crossed the bridge over the Saale it was snowing so hard that she couldn't make out the notice proudly announcing *Freistaat Bayern*. She thought of the first time that she had crossed the bridge with Mara and how Marc had jumped out of the car to welcome them to his beloved homeland. How she had grown to love it herself since then. They turned off the Autobahn and began the drive through the forest with the snow lying ever thicker on the road making the four-wheel drive with its snow tyres earn its keep. The light flickered through the trees onto the snow lying in ridges between the lines of conifers alternating with birches and ash. The snow was coming in sudden bursts. One moment grey and white gloom surrounded the car, making it hard to see the road, but seconds later the sun pierced and sparkled on the white and green world. The national colours of Livonia and a bit like our racing colours, mused Detty. Somehow, it always came back to green and white. They turn off onto the road to Oberdorf, through the village and past the *Schwarze Adler*. Round the corner they turned left past the gatehouse and there was the *Schloss* with the steely winter sunshine catching the old donjon – home at last. Hildegard and Sophie were at the door chorusing that they must warm up, as if they had done a traditional *Winterreise* in true Schubert style rather than an admittedly difficult drive in a well heated *Vierradantrieb*. The traditional *Glühwein*, cautiously sipped, was welcome all the same.

'Is Marc here yet?' Detty asked between sips, trying not to look too anxious and lovelorn.

'No, but he got off all right- no Americans this time – but apparently the flight was delayed by the weather. He said he would ring again when he knew more.

'I hope you don't mind but you're in his old room under the tower in the *Jungflugel* as Hildegard still calls it. We tried to get the Lodge done in time but the central heating has been a disaster – we had four *Installateuren* here on Friday, each with a different opinion, as to what was wrong. Anyway, you can't go there without heat so you will have to wait to use your new home.'

'It will be all the better…'she was about to add when the baby comes but superstition stopped her 'anyway it's wonderful that you have been to so such trouble to give us a home here.'

'We have to find some way of seeing our *Schwiegertochter* and, of course, our son occasionally' laughed Max. Detty nearly added '*und eurer Enkel*' but a sudden image of herself struggling, bloody and in pain, in the well of a car stopped her. No chickens were going to be counted prematurely this time. She had bought nothing for the baby and outside the family told only those who, for professional reasons, had to know. Christa Wagner had been charming, offered her congratulations and said that there was no problem as it was in good time and this year's *Woglinde* could be taken by a young Finnish soprano who was promising and they were grooming.

'Not too promising I hope' said Detty with her tongue in her cheek 'It's not like you, Frau O'Neill, to sound jealous. Anyway, she's not as young as you are. All you have to do is be ready for *Elisabeth* next year or Maestro Meilin will never forgive either of us.'

Detty had been dreading the call to Bayreuth and felt hugely relieved that it had gone so well.

It was nearly nine and they were more than halfway through *Abendessen* when the 'phone rang. Detty jumped with excitement, blushed, and told herself to behave like a mature married woman, not a teenager awaiting a call from her boyfriend. But she did want to see him. Max passed the phone to her. After anxious enquiries as to how she was, he reported his progress. He had eventually got to Franz-Joseph-Strauss two hours late and had tried to hire a *Vierradentreib* to be greeted by supercilious smiles —what did the Herr expect in this weather – of course, none were available. His military *Ausweis* had produced a little more action and, they thought that a four-wheel drive would be back and available around midnight. Marc had therefore booked himself into a hotel to get some much-needed sleep and would be up in time for breakfast assuming the car materialised.

'I shall come and get you,' said Detty decisively.

'You will not! First, that car of yours will behave like a motorised toboggan in the snow. Second, it will take you at least three hours to get here in this weather. Third, I am told that there has been a bad accident south of Pegnitz and the road will be blocked for some time. And fourth, although it may have escaped your notice, you have an advanced pregnancy and' he added pausing for breath 'before he starts, my father is not coming either and although the first and last reasons don't apply to him, the middle two are enough. I will be there early tomorrow.'

Detty was used to getting her own way but she knew when she was beaten.

'*Jawohl, Herr Major.*' She didn't think her heel click was audible over the telephone but it made Max, who was listening in, smile. 'So that is that' said her father-in-law still laughing.

'Yes, I rather think it is. I do love masterful men or at least that one.'

He was as good as his word. She had just had time for a bath when he was in the room, kissing her and giving a proprietorial pat to her bump. After breakfast, they dressed up and walked in the garden. They started throwing snowballs at each other and laughing like a couple of kids, coming in eventually drenched and pink from their exertions. After coffee and dry clothes, Detty set to work with Marc at the beloved Bechstein. They went through Detty's Act Two scene starting with the beautiful '*Euch Lüften, die mein Klagen*'. Marc, like number of baritones had at one time tried to develop a countertenor and enjoyed marking *Ortrud's* part for his wife. It was good music making and useful. Detty was beginning to look forward to Florence. She knew that it wouldn't be easy. The Florentine public had mixed feelings about foreign operas and foreign singers but she felt confident that she could do herself justice.

As the afternoon closed in it was time for more warm clothes for the short walk to Father Dieter's *Karfreitag Mass*. The young priest joined them for the traditional Good Friday dinner of pike quenelles and local trout. The talk was of music. Before going to his seminary, Father Dieter had sung in the *Regensburger Domspatzen*, the oldest boys' choir in the world, so he took a professional, if rather awestruck, interest in Detty's career. He happened to mention that his old choir had an Easter concert the following afternoon in their home cathedral. Detty said wistfully that she had never heard the choir live.

'Well, we can go, if we can get in that is.' Max looked mischievously at his son expecting an outburst.

Marc revolved his glass of *Steinwalder Bürgerhäuser, trocken,* staring into it thoughtfully.

'I think that you are bad for Detti, Papa, you get up to tricks when you are together.'

'We are bad for each other to be sure' she said it in English with her stage Irish accent, which always made them laugh.

This time Marc ignored his wife's interjection and went on 'however the weather is much better to-day, I think that the *Autobahnen* are clear and if we go via Nürnberg and avoid the *Fichtel* we should be all right to-morrow. Can we really get in, Father Dieter, do you think?'

'I will telephone. The weather may have put some people off and they usually reserve some space for VIPs but, if I may I will telephone now, because time may be important.'

'Of course, Father, use the study. Will you be joining us?'

'I would like to very much but at Easter it's not possible. I have preparation for Sunday and many country visits. I am looking forward to the Cantata on Easter Day. The choir will be augmented from the other villages and should have a really good four-part structure. Another time, I would like to sing an alto part myself if you have no one else in mind. There isn't an alt solo tomorrow of course so it doesn't apply. I sang countertenor in Regensburg when I was older and continued at my seminary. Pastoral work here hasn't left much time but I have tried to get voice back recently and, if I may say so, a family performance like tomorrow would be excellent practice. It wouldn't be professional or anything like that of course and I would be frightened of singing with you, Frau Gräfin.'

He smiled nervously at Detty.

'We would love you to do it and it would complete the soloists from the home team which would be wonderful. I am sorry that we didn't know before or we could have chosen a Cantata with an alto part. Sadly, it is a bit late to change now.'

'No, no of course not'

She was thinking to herself also that she would bet that he would be good despite his modesty about lack of practice. Once a *Domspatz* ...

'In the meanwhile, I will 'phone ADAC and see if the roads are

OK for tomorrow before coffee' said Marc retiring to the hall with his *Handy*. Both answers were positive. The ADAC said the roads were now OK and no more snow was expected. Even the Fichtelgebirge Road was in a good state with the usual added warning 'if you take a little extra care and don't speed'.

Father Dieter's contact at the Dom had said that they would be honoured to see the Herr Graf von Ritter and his family. Detty said, in an aside to Marc, that obviously having an ancestor who was the lover of an Austrian Empress still gave them some clout.

'You may joke, Detty, but Bavaria is an old country and these things still run deep.'

She usually knew his responses but this time Detty was left wondering whether Marc was being serious or not.

The concert was worth every kilometre of the hundred or so they had driven. They arrived in time for lunch and for Marc to photograph the family and, in particular, Detty, against the full grey Danube, with the snow covered *Steinerne Brücke* in the background. The picture of his anorak clad wife with her long chestnut hair blown behind her in the bitter east wind was always one of his favourites. Secretly, it reminded him of that other occasion when she had stood in the platz at Königshof with the burning wreck of the Winterburg behind her. He would never forget her expression, triumph at mission impossible achieved, but also sadness, humility and grateful thanks to the Almighty. There had been no time for photos then although he treasured a newspaper one of the burning fortress, which showed her only as a dot in the distance.

The programme at the Dom centred round Pergolesi's *Stabat Mater* with added pieces by the more local composers, Hassler's *O sacrum convivium* and the *Credo, Sanctus*, and *Benedictus* from Lasso's magnificent but strangely named *Missa Bell'Amfitrit'altera*. It was, however, the atmosphere of the wonderful Gothic church with its central but divided Annunciation, which made the experience mystic. At the end, they walked out into the *Domplatz* to be greeted by a scene more of Christmas than Easter. The sixteenth century *Benedictus* stayed in Detty's inner ear for the whole silent journey back through the snow to Oberdorf.

On Sunday Bill arrived, attracted, thought his sister-in-law bitchily, more by the food and wine than by the religious significance of the festival. Whilst lowering a huge breakfast, he muttered that he hadn't seen enough of the lovely Tamara recently:

'Good thing too' muttered Detty grinning

'We are sour this morning. Where is the Easter *gute Absicht* then?'

'It doesn't extend to seducing my best friend.'

'Seduction is reserved for elder brothers, is it?'

'I would point out, Herr Graf, that we are a respectable married couple and anyway' she continued laughing and complacently patting her stomach 'he did it to good effect.'

'So I hear, *ich gratuliere dich, Frau Gräfin*'

'*Vielen dank*'

There the silliness stopped for the moment. Bill returned to his breakfast and Detty to mugging up her score for the morning's performance of the Annunciation Cantata, *Wie schön leuchtet der Morgenstern BWV1,* this had been Detty's choice for no better reason than the fact that she loved it and, she had to admit that it contained a great soprano solo. Such was her influence in Oberdorf that, although strictly not seasonal, it had been adopted without question. Theoretically, it was to be a 'come and make music' effort without much preparation just to mark the Easter Festival with music in a way which had become a tradition. Detty knew very well that the choir would have rehearsed thoroughly. She had a reputation to keep up. She loved singing Bach as a discipline and a pleasure after romantic music but it was not something ever to be taken lightly and she had practised the lovely *Erfüllet, ihr himmlischen göttlichen Flammen* most assiduously.

The performance took place, after Mass later that morning. To her surprise, it was obvious that Bill, also, had taken it seriously. After all his banter, he produced an accurate crystal tenor *Unser Mond* und *Ton der Saiten.* She found herself wondering, not for the first time, why, with that voice and a musical family background, he hadn't joined the none- too -crowded ranks of professional tenors. Marc had, as usual, sung a musical, unfussy rendering of the bass Rezitativ *Ein iridischer Glanz.* Max, with the excellent support of Trudi Meyer at the organ, had conducted the musicians and handled his small ensemble of varying abilities with skill and tact. If they didn't sound like the Stuttgart Bach Collegium, which could hardly be expected, at least they gave a sound platform for the chorus and soloists. It was very enjoyable music making and they all adjourned to Easter lunch glowing with cold from the unheated church but also with a sense of achievement.

13
EIN RITTER NAHTE DA

*'In lichter Waffen Scheine ein Ritter nahte da,
So tugendlicher Reine ich keinen noch ersah;*[32]

RICHARD WAGNER: *LOHENGRIN* ACT I

The Easter idyll was over and, all too soon, they were both in Marc's hired *Vierradentreib* on the road back to Franz-Josef-Strauss airport. Marc had to get back to London and Detty to Florence, to start the rehearsals for *Lohengrin* opening that year's *Maggio Musicale Fiorentino*.

Detty had almost decided to drive to Florence. She loved her Z4, her little silver bullet, even if Marc had been rude and likened it to a toboggan. It had been sitting at Oberdorf waiting for her and she hadn't had a chance to use it. Marc and reason however prevailed this time. What was the point of driving across the Brenner in very unstable weather only to leave her car in an expensive Florentine garage for three weeks? After all, Detti, he had said, you will be busy and you know Florence. You need a car in that city like ice-skates in the Sahara. This

---

32 In shining armour, a knight appeared before me.
  I had never seen such splendour,

phrase was part of his colloquial English, Detty didn't know where he had got it from and she had never heard anybody else use it.

They were both quiet on the cold early journey. They felt miserable to be leaving each other again but savouring the wonderful four days that they had just had together. Marc continuing a dialogue, which they both understood but had been completely unspoken, said:

'But I shall be there for your last night and we can go to your Totti's prima together.'

It all seemed rather a long way off. There was the challenge of four other performances of *Elsa* to sing first and her confidence that she had felt when she left St Petersburg was diminishing. They parted at the airport and went through security. Mark's flight to Heathrow left at ten whereas Detty's to Florence was not until eleven, so she sat down for a long wait. She was mightily relieved that there had now been some time without any fleeting appearances of the El Greco face. She dared to hope that she had left that particular nightmare in St Petersburg. She realised, though, with something of a start, that it was in Florence that she first met Monsignor Jose Maria Pueblo and learnt of his sinister reputation. She wondered how he had come to be ordained and, as a highly committed Roman Catholic, she found it difficult to understand. Giving up the conundrum, she turned to the more immediate challenge of *Elsa*.

She knew that she could sing the part and, barring accidents, sing it very well but it was the psychological aspects of the character that were troubling her. She had known and sung the first and last act for her own pleasure for several years and she thought that she knew the role well. She had never paid so much attention to the second act and yet she had come to realise, as many had done before, that Act 2 is possibly the most crucial. It contained Wagner's most advanced thinking and music to that date. It is here that *Elsa* must convince that her other worldly behaviour is due to mysticism not just stupidity. In front of a modern audience, brought up on cynicism and feminism and without much time for the mystical, this is far from easy. She hoped that she had got some ideas over Easter both from the run through with Marc and the concert at Regensburg. She had had a very real mystical experience in that Cathedral on Easter Saturday. If she could only take that with her into her interpretation and convey it to the audience, she would achieve her goal. It was a tall order and she was unsure of the reactions of an Italian audience. She had had a considerable success as *La Wally* the year before. That however was an Italian favourite, one of their own, as they were inclined to say, and it was really a student performance to boot. She still had her Irish origin on her side, which seemed to help with the Italians, but for the rest it was Wagner, always a love-hate composer for them. He was respected, yes, but, despite his many associations with the country, hardly loved. Some PR work, she decided must be done. Too many northern singers, and that included Anglo-Americans, nowadays descended on Italy with inflated ideas of their technical superiority and didn't give the cradle of western music the respect that its inhabitants thought, rightly, that it deserved.

She had hopes of the production. It was a joint effort with Covent Garden, as was becoming increasingly common in these cash strapped days. The producer and designer, who were a long-standing English team, were original but not of the uncompromising avant-garde. She had been to London to see the production and liked it. It had a timeless quality stressing the enduring rigidity of public mores and private treachery. *Elsa* was dressed simply but very attractively initially in simple shifts, which stressed her sexual allure, and later in classic splendour. Her presentation made *Lohengrin*'s devotion appear slightly less altruistic than it had sometimes seemed elsewhere. At the London version of the same production, her colleague as *Elsa* was an attractive American with a good voice who, however, produced emotionless music and had a bovine stage presence. She never rose above the dumb college kid next door, and never got near to getting into role. Detty had been appalled and thundered out her condemnation to Marc over the washing up at Henley. Marc was a little shocked, as he had never seen her so critical of a fellow artist. She even mentioned it to Hank Schliessen who she had had to telephone in the States on their Livonian music college business. He commented laconically that it was a difficult role and, in his time, he had sung *Lohengrin* opposite all sorts of sopranos. At that point, Detty had broken in saying:

'Don't tell me that sopranos always cause problems or I'll never speak to you again. And, another thing, you don't have to tell me that *Elsa* is a difficult role. May I remind you that I just happen to be opening the Florence Festival with it next month.'

'I've never sung it with you, honey, perhaps we should put that right?'

'I wish you were. I have a Russian who I've never met. I seem to be surrounded by Russians these days, not that that is usually a problem.'

'At least you can be grateful it's not a bovine American. Anyway, toi toi for the Communale. It's a strange theatre but OK when you get used to it. I know you will be dead gorgeous; you can't help it. I am in Berlin for *Tristan* and by the way, Anneliese sends her love and best wishes.'

Anneliese Seiling, Hank's *Isolde* in Berlin, was the leading dramatic soprano of the age. Detty had replaced her for the *Siegfried Brunnhilde* in Bayreuth when she had fallen and broken two ribs. Detty admired her hugely as an artist and a person.

'Please thank, Frau Seiling, and give her my very best regards. I hope her poor ribs are now completely healed. You can also tell her how grateful I am to her for breaking them.'

Hank laughed.

'I will but I think she knows that. I'm going to try and get down to hear you if the dates are OK. *a presto, Contessa*!'

They both laughed. Detty found Hank's undisguised chat-ups always refreshing. She did wish he were the *Lohengrin*. She felt hugely confident when she sang with him. She must get used, however, to not having him always around.

She awoke from her reverie with the announcement to board. Like an automaton, she followed the crocodile down the passage and onto the aircraft. Not for the first time, as she squashed into a cramped seat, she wondered why she hadn't booked cabin class. She could easily have afforded it, now even from her own earnings, but somehow it seemed an outrageous waste on such a short flight and the old habits of the penurious undergraduate died-hard.

Once she had fought with the overhead locker and struggled to do up her seat belt, wondering idly if lap belts were good for developing bumps, she got back to the puzzle of *Lohengrin*.

Elsa is seen as being stupid because she fails to realise that loving an unknown is impossible. She has however lived on her dream as the only light in her life of unremitting enmity, sorrow, and loneliness. When her mystic faith turns the dream into a reality, she really could not, emotionally or for that matter practically, reject any condition attached to the salvation which offers her the only chance of living again and avoiding a shameful and terrifying death. Only later, with the 'help' of *Ortrud* does she realise that you cannot love, in the fullest sense, a man that you do not know. She is true to her emotional make up in that only true love will do. '*dir geb'ich alles was ich bin*' is no form of words, for her it is as real as *Lohengrin's* condition but the two are incompatible which neither realises until later. For Detty, this was particularly poignant, as she had sung this very passage, after her own liberation from horrors, at her romantically contrived Easter engagement to Marc at Oberdorf. At the time, they had joked about her already knowing his name, but if he had really been unknown, and had to remain unknown, the intimacy, which sustains real love, would have been missing. This is *Elsa's* plea and she does not have to be portrayed as weak, vacillating and neurotic to make this dilemma real. Both protagonists have problems, which resonate with life in the twenty-first century. *Elsa* faces the same dilemma as anybody who discovers a partner's past has been kept secret from him or her. Examples, she thought, could be having a criminal record, a problematic family history or being involved in secret activities of any kind, even legitimate ones. *Lohengrin*, on the other hand, faces the situation of any prominent person whose relationships will be affected, often destructively, by their star status, too much money or demanding job.

Almost as soon as they were airborne, they seemed to be descending to Peretola with the Appenines clearly visible below them. The plane had been small but even so, it seemed to take an age for the luggage to come through. Her case was almost last. Just my luck she thought with a touch of paranoia, now the taxis will have all gone. She realised that she should have done the prima donna bit and asked the theatre to send a car to meet her but she still wasn't used to her new status and hadn't thought of it. She dragged the heavy case onto a trolley and out into the arrivals area.

'*Ciao, Ciao, Detti, bentornata a Firenze.*'

There was Totti bouncing up and down and shouting her greeting in such a manner that no one present could have guessed they were listening to one of Italy's most promising young singers. Detty had no idea how she had got to know the flight number or the time of arrival but she had. With an unstoppable flow of news and talk, they manipulated the trolley out to Totti's new *macchinina*. To the relief of both of them, Detty's large suitcase and dress case fitted inside but took up most of the back. Totti threw the little car into the Florentine traffic with native aplomb, missed the way twice round the endless junctions, but finally finished up outside the Helvetia and Bristol. On the way, she had had to convince two policemen, fortunately male, that she was conveying an Irish VIP to the Hotel and should be allowed to enter the ZTL, the limited traffic area. Both policemen had looked at the two youngsters in jeans and sweaters with considerable incredulity, thinking that neither looked like a VIP or for that matter a potential guest at the Helvetia and Bristol. Totti's minute green Fiat was poles apart from the big blue Lancias, which were the accepted conveyances for VIPs. In both cases, they eventually decided that the girls were attractive enough to be given the benefit of the doubt and let Totti drive through.

Detty was just allowed to go to her room, see that her luggage was delivered and tip the porter. After that Totti whirled her off to a late lunch across the river, ignoring her pleas that she ought to ring the theatre.

'Don't be silly, they will all be at lunch, ring at four.'

Detty having forgotten about Mediterranean habits realised that this was probably sound advice. She then tucked in to *riso nero* and a massive *Fiorentina*, which she shared with Totti. She decided that one reason amongst many that she was looking forward to having her baby was that she wouldn't have to feel guilty every time that she had a glass of wine. She noted ruefully that the wine here was very different from her father in law's specifically prepared low alcohol sort.

She was eventually allowed to ring the theatre. She was greeted with warm elaborate courtesy and asked if she could go round straight away to meet the production team and go through the rehearsal schedule.

Over the next few days, she worked hard and began to accumulate a score of pluses and minuses. The producer, Keith Ayling, was, to her great relief, completely in sympathy with her interpretation of her role and indeed made some very useful technical suggestions as to how she could get the mystical nature of *Elsa* and her impossible dilemma across to an audience.

'You are a strong woman, with a vibrant expressive voice, and it would be entirely wrong for you to play *Elsa* as a neurotic wilting violet. She plays for high stakes and eventually loses, inevitably, in a showdown that is, in its way as cosmic as *Götterdämmerung*.'

Detty herself probably wouldn't have gone as far as that but at least it gave her a free hand with her interpretation. Her repetiteur, new to the post, was a young man called Marco Valentini. She found him a brilliant musician but too much in awe of her. He was invaluable, however, when it came to help with the balance with the acoustic and the orchestra.

Anton Meilin, the conductor, was, of course, her main reason for being there in the first place. Although they had only worked briefly together, they had a profound mutual admiration that made things go very smoothly. The orchestra played brilliantly for him. She came to the rather heretical view that a fine Italian orchestra could put a degree of emotion into a score like *Lohengrin,* which some of their more northern counterparts would have difficulty in equalling. Privately she tried to tackle the Maestro about this. Even without witnesses, he wouldn't commit himself in such a sensitive area, which made her think that perhaps, to some degree, he agreed.

When it came to the cast, the *Heerrrufe* was a German bass who had sung *Fasolt* with Detty in *Das Rheingold* at Bayreuth. *König Heinrich* was jolly, laughing Pole who brought light relief to rehearsals between bouts of producing the most gloriously rich bass voice. Max Hieren, the young Bavarian base baritone, who had earned Detty's eternal gratitude by coming at short notice and a shorter fee to sing *Don Pizarro* at Königshof, was the *Telramund*. So far so good, but the remaining cast members made Detty more wary. The *Ortrud* was an Italian from Bolzano who was bilingual in German and Italian. She fitted her role well. She was hostile, jealous, and defied all Detty's attempts to at least achieve a passable professional accord. Now Ortrud is a part with great music and in a way, rather like *Waltraute* in *Götterdämmerung*. To put it bluntly, she has the opportunity to put her soprano colleague in the shade. Furthermore, Detty realised as soon as she heard Claudia Höchner sing, that she was very, very good. She seemed keen to take on the young Irish unknown with the odd past history, who she clearly regarded as a dilettante and a professional lightweight. That, Detty supposed philosophically, is, however, what *Lohengrin* is all about. She did, however, make a resolution that she should play her own interpretation and sing her own part and not be tempted to overstretch herself in an attempt to outdo *la Claudia*. This left her tenor opposite number, the name part. Mikhail Valentin came from Tula south of Moscow and had sung with success at the Bolshoi and elsewhere in Russia. He had little experience abroad. He spoke no Italian and only rudimentary German. He was however good looking and had a bright steady voice with a real heldentenor timbre. There was only the slightest suggestion of the over-pitching which can be a problem for Slavs singing in a German opera. He had learnt somewhere that Detty spoke Russian and attempted to have a continuous conversation with her in his native tongue, in the process cutting everybody else out of the dialogue. This had no appeal at all to Detty, who was trying hard to be diplomatic, both to her hosts and the rest of the cast. To cap it all, Valentin was conceited and obsessed with his person and persona to the point of narcissism. Detty had just to try and avoid getting into a situation in which he could monopolise her.

His behaviour was at times very strange and there were moments that seemed quite dangerous. In the year two thousand, a special production of Verdi's *Macbeth* had been mounted in Florence to celebrate the one hundred and fiftieth anniversary of its first production there, at the Teatro della Pergola. An American Verdi society had wanted to mark the occasion. After consultation, they had ordered a sword from the last true swordsmith working in the ancient cutlery town of Scarperia in the *Mugello* above Florence. The sword had been presented to the city at a ceremony and used in the Macbeth production. It had subsequently been added to the Teatro Communale armoury for safekeeping, occasional display in the public areas of the theatre and for use in subsequent productions, should it be appropriate. Nothing could be more appropriate than a new *Lohengrin* production and the fine sword duly burnished was added to the props. It was this weapon, albeit with some safety taping, that Mikhail Valentin was keen on brandishing round the stage like a demented Cossack. Eventually, it was pointed out that, unlike some stage swords, this was a real weapon, which, despite the safety measures, was capable of inflicting severe injuries. After being thus restrained, Valentin contented himself by standing endlessly in front of a mirror, admiring his image, resting on the weapon in true *Lohengrin* style. Detty genuinely feared for Max Hieren's safety and to a lesser extent her own when it came to the dress rehearsal and the performances.

Her dresser was a lovely young woman called Ilaria for whom nothing was too much trouble and who seemed to have a marvellous way of always getting things done. After the dragon of Bayreuth and the hostility of St Petersburg, Ilaria was a jewel beyond price. She said it was marvellous to have some vibrant young artists around 'and you, Signora Contessa and *la Totti* have made this year very exciting'. Detty noticed that she was Signora Contessa but Totti was Totti or *la Totti*, not only to Ilaria but also to everyone who knew her. In fact, Detty would have taken a long time to discover her real name if she had not seen her as Maria Angela Spinelli on programmes and official posters. Detty voiced her fears about safety in view of Valentin's gung-ho habits to Ilaria as the *prova generale* approached. Ilaria assured her that the management were aware of the problem and had taken steps to control it. What these steps could be Detty couldn't imagine, but soon the other demands of the moment put the problem out of her mind.

The showdown with Claudia Höchner came three days before the *prova generale,* with their rehearsal of the second act. Anton Meilin had arranged to for Detty and Claudia to spend the morning with him sorting out the problems of the complex and difficult Act two second scene and part of the third. Claudia was at her most hostile, casting snide asides at Detty's professionalism and trying to frighten her with remarks about Florentine hostility to foreign artists. Detty just smiled, got quickly into role when required and poured out a stream of flawless soprano voice as required. Halfway through the session, Claudia realising that she was getting nowhere, gave up obstructing. Possibly fearing she might compromise her own performance if she continued to be difficult, she decided to co-operate. By lunchtime, they had achieved a convincing collaboration and were both congratulated warmly by Anton. Detty left feeling that, even though *la Höchner* would never be a bosom friend, at least she could work with her. One hurdle was behind her.

The tenor problem was at the same time more enduring but less serious. When on stage at least Valentin was so concerned with presenting his own persona that he left her alone. As *Lohengrin* remarks at the beginning of the third act, they have, until then, spent no time alone. In this respect, the third act duet is central and, despite the character problems of her opposite number, they sang excellently together and the scene went well. Several rehearsals of the final fight were needed before it was felt Max Hieren was in no real danger. Max was a relaxed young man and joked about getting body armour.

'All the same we could do without real '*Unheil in dies Haus*" quoted Detty when they were having a coffee together.

The outside world seemed almost to cease to exist but every fine evening she tried to walk to the Arno or if she had more time through the Cascine for a breath of fresh air. She loved watching the amazing sunsets and the strong changing light over Fiesole and Monte Morello. The walk became a bit of a routine, interrupted normally only by the heavy April downpours or by trips upriver to San Niccolò to have coffee or dinner with Totti and Alessandro.

One evening, however she had changed in her room and was about to go out for her constitutional when reception rang to ask her if she would accept a telephone call. The caller spoke good English but with a marked accent probably, but not definitely, Italian. He asked if he was speaking to the Contessa von Ritter. Detty said he was, so he introduced himself as Professor Santini, *responsabile* at the *Museo Mori* at Siena. His museum, he explained, specialised in armour, mainly medieval, but some classical. He understood that the Contessa was in Florence and recently been associated with some particularly interesting finds in Livonia. He wondered whether he could come and see her so that he could arrange a visit to Livonia, perhaps with her guidance. There would, of course, be a consultant's honorarium for her. Detty thought that this was all very odd and asked him who had given him this information. He explained rather vaguely that it had come through 'the academic museum network' but didn't elaborate. She explained politely that she was not an expert on armour and was here to sing in Florence. She suggested that he contacted the Livonian embassy in Rome, who would probably be able to help him. The following day she knew that Totti would be at the theatre and they met for coffee.

'You are virtually Sienese, Totti. Can you help me with a bit of information?'

'Drop the 'virtually', *cara, sono Senesi DOP tutta e propria, e, come tutti noi altri, molto orgogliosa.*[33] My village is in the hills just to the west of the city. When all this is over' she gestured broadly around her towards the theatre, 'we will blow the smog of Florence out of our hair, you will bring Marc and come and meet my family. Babbo makes really lovely things and he would adore showing them to you both. But what information do you want?'

'That would be wonderful. I loved Siena when I was at the Chigiana and would like to see more of the countryside but tell me, what do you know of the *Museo Mori*?'

Unusually for her, Totti looked blank.

'In Siena?' she asked,

'Apparently.'

'I have never heard of it. Mind you, that doesn't necessarily mean much. I am not in the tourist trade and small museums and picture galleries do come and go according to private whims. Siena is a small city, *communque*, and if it was of any importance I would expect, at least, to have heard of it at some time or another.'

'OK try another one. What about Professor Santini?'

'Sure, I was taught Greek by him at the Liceo.' Totti grinned.

That's true but I doubt if it's the one you're looking for. There are lots of Santinis around Siena, it's a bit like your Smith.'

---

33 I am completely Sienese and like all of us extremely proud of it

'Or O'Neill where I come from.'

Detty explained about her strange telephone call.

'I should ring the *Assessorato alla Cultura* at Siena. They are in charge of cultural affairs and if they have no record of this chap or his museum, then it doesn't exist. In fact, I'll do it for you now.'

She got the number by dialing 0577 on her *cellulare* and rang the number. This time Detty noticed with amusement she announced herself as *Dottoressa Spinelli* confirming Detty's own belief that handles do sometimes come in useful. A short wait and rather longer conversation confirmed that the *Assessorato alla Cultura* had no knowledge of the Professor or his museum.

Detty pondered. She still had a little time left before her appointment with Keith to go through some blocking for the last scene of Act Three.

'No time like the present' she said half to herself as she clicked a number on her mobile 'This is Komturin O'Neill, can you put me through to Major Zahnsdorf?'

There was a short pause. 'Liese, can you ring me back on a scrambled line? Where am I? I'm in a bar outside the Teatro Communale in Florence.'

There was another rather longer pause then Detty's mobile rang.

'Liese, there's something I think you should know. I have no idea what it means but I have been telephoned by a spurious museum official here in Italy asking about Livonian armour. I think that he is probably referring to the Chalice find but how he knows about it and what he wants with it, I have no idea.'

'You know he's spurious?'

'Yes, my expert guide here, who is Senese, enquired from the city authorities in Siena, where he claimed his museum was sited. There isn't one.'

'What exactly did he ask you to do?'

'He wanted me, for a fee, to take him to Livonia to look at armour.'

'OK We'll do some checks. I'll get Tanya onto it. Are you OK?'

'Yes, I'm fine. It's very exciting. I'm singing a major part here.'

'And the baby?'

'Seems fine too. This is my last engagement, then it's feet up as the expectant mum.'

'I'll believe that when it happens. All the best.'

Detty felt relieved to have contacted Liese. Totti was grinning.

'You do have a number of aliases. That was a side of you I haven't seen before. I won't ask who you were 'phoning. It sounded top security.'

'It was and, anyway, I haven't heard you refer to yourself as *Dottoressa*.

'I do have a laurea, I am entitled to call myself Dottoressa but it's not often helpful in our trade.'

'Neither normally is calling yourself Commander unless, of course, you want to get murdered in Don Giovanni but there are times ……'

They both laughed and had another coffee.

*

The *prova generale* went very well. The *Maggio Musicale* chorus was in fantastic form. When the curtain went down on the photographers, Friends, and usual dress rehearsal audience, Detty and Max Hieren turned round and applauded the chorus. The other principals joined in, with the predictable exception of Valentin and Höchner who had other preoccupations. This gesture went down very well and the smiles and the *buon giornos* became even warmer.

After the *prova generale*, Detty's public relations campaign hit a stroke of luck. The Tuscan paper, *La Nazione*, had asked for an interview, which she gladly granted at the Bristol after the dress rehearsal. Much to her disappointment, Totti had had a piano rehearsal at the same time as the *prova generale* for *Lohengrin*. She couldn't attend but they had agreed to meet afterwards, go back to the Bristol for a coffee and a chat. They were then going to have dinner out in the Chianti together with Totti's boyfriend, Alessandro, who was to pick the two girls up from the hotel. Although she had put the appointment in her diary, in the excitement of the dress rehearsal, she had momentarily forgotten the reporter from *La Nazione*. When they got to the Hotel, Detty's old friend the Concierge greeted her:

'*Signora Contessa*, there are two gentlemen from *La Nazione* waiting for you – one a photographer. As I know them, I have taken the liberty of saying they could take their equipment and go up to the lobby on the third floor and wait for you there. I hope that is in order?'

'Of course, that's fine. I'm sorry, Totti, I had completely forgotten about this interview, I am really sorry.'

'I'll go and do some shopping and come back later.'

'No, wait. Come with me. It will give them a different angle. Two sopranos for the price of one, that sort of thing. You can help me out when my Italian gets stuck.'

'Are you sure you don't mind?'

'Of course not. It will be fun if you don't mind that is.'

The young reporter from the *Cultura e Spettacoli* section was waiting with his photographer. He took one look at Totti and was taken aback.

'I am sure you know, Signora Spinelli, *la mia amica del cuore*'. Detty waved a hand towards Totti and resisted calling her *Dottoressa*.

'She has agreed to join us –if you don't mind that is.'

'*Signora Contessa*, everybody connected with Florentine music knows *Signora Spinelli* and in a fortnight's time, I think everyone in the whole world will know her.'

'I entirely agree with you' smiled Detty.

From that point, the interview took off. How had they met? How they had been rivals in last year's competition but had become close friends? The coincidence of two *affascinanti giovani cantanti* starring in the first and second productions in this year's *Maggio Musicale Fiorentino* was very exciting. The differences between their repertory and voices were discussed in detail. Then they got onto their partners and personal ambitions. Detty talked of her genuine and increasing love of the Italian repertory and how one of her ambitions was to sing *Desdemona* and *Leonora* in *La Forza del Destino*. The reporter went on to the details of Detty's life and career. They dealt with the Livonian war, her unexpected performance at Bayreuth and her marriage and pregnancy and finally her views on *Lohengrin* and its meaning for today. Then there were the photographs Detty and Totti together, talking, embracing, arm in arm and at the end there were a few of Detty alone looking relaxed.

The following morning the front page of *La Nazione* carried a large photograph of the two of them arm in arm with the caption *"Una Toscana d'adozione e una Toscana di nascita: Le due amiche fanno la risplendente constellazione gemella del nuovo Maggio*"[34]. There was also a more detailed article on the *Lohengrin* in the *Cultura e Spettacoli* page inside with stage photographs and comments on the production, conductor, and other artists. The only mention of Claudia Höchner was that she had sung mostly in Austria and Germany and that her father was active in the *Sud Tirol* separatist party. This was not going to help in Florence and Detty began to feel almost sorry for her. She told herself sternly that the woman was a bitch and that she, Detty, should not behave like *Elsa*, the innocent.

Shortly after breakfast, there was a telephone call asking if Detty and Totti could repeat the same interview for the benefit of *RAI Telegiornale Regionale –Toscana* that very evening. She said she would be pleased to but they must ask Signora Spinelli.

'Oh, *la Totti*'s already agreed' came the reply.

Detty's PR campaign had succeeded beyond her wildest expectations.

Buoyed up by the happy turn of events she gave the performance of her life in the prima. She was gratified by a respectable number of 'Bravas' from around the house. It was a warm reception for them all for a very good performance, probably as good a reception as a largely foreign cast in a German work would ever get in Florence with its highly critical audience. The principals again applauded the chorus and orchestra, which was well received in the house.

The first person into her camerino was Totti with Alessandro in tow.

'*Detty, favoloso, proprio favoloso*. I confess that I have never really understood Wagner before. Now I see what it means; you made it so moving. *Bellissima davvero*. I was so *commossa* that I was in tears at the end.

'*Anch'io*' added the quiet Alessandro.

After that tribute there followed others in various forms. She was able to return to the Bristol feeling elated.

Two days later the reviews were exceptionally good and very complimentary about her acting and musicianship. She particularly

---

34 A Tuscan by adoption and a Tuscan by birth the two friends make the resplendent twin constellation of the new Maggio

liked *La Repubblica*, 'Bernadette O'Neill was beautiful and movingly convincing in the part of *Elsa*. Vocally she has the rare quality of a fine *bel canto legato* combined with a warm dramatic voice, beautifully controlled in its thrilling high notes and flawless *passaggi*. This is star quality.' You can't get much better than that, she thought.

*

The final performance was over and it was getting late. Marc had had to leave almost as soon as the curtain was down to change for the mayor's reception at the Palazzo Vecchio. Detty knew she would be short of time and she saw no point in adding another change to the several that she had already had to do in the performance. She had therefore brought her Lanoure cocktail dress, newly sent, late, but just in time, from Paris with her to the theatre. The wonderful Ilaria, her *vestiarista,* had pronounced it *una veste bellissima* and clearly relished the idea of helping Detty change into it to pick up Marc at the hotel and go the short distance to the Palazzo Vecchio for the Sindaco's reception for the cast.

The line of visitors and well-wishers had been gratifyingly long. By the time the last left, she knew that the theatre was due to close and she had little time to get to the Palazzo Vecchio. Ilaria had helped her into her dress and was busy hanging up her court costume from the last act. The telephone started ringing and at the same moment, there was a tap at the door followed by a polite male voice calling '*Permesso?*' Not more, thought Detty, ignoring the telephone, thinking that she was in a madhouse not a Prima Donna's *camerino*. After checking she was decent, she called, crossly '*Avanti*'. The door swung open to admit not one but two young men, neatly dressed in dark suits and ties, as befitted operagoers from stalls. Behind them, fleetingly, Detty thought she caught sight of a third, more sinisterly familiar figure who rapidly disappeared. The other discordant notes were that their visitors both produced machine pistols from under their unbuttoned, well-cut overcoats and pointed them at the two women.

Detty shouted in anger, German with a strong Livonian accent, coming automatically.

'*Was in Himmel macht das?*'

Ilaria screamed loudly.

At that moment, the telephone stopped unanswered. After assuring themselves, that the two astonished women were not going to offer serious resistance, the shorter of the two men let his machine pistol go swinging on its shoulder strap. He then gestured to Detty that she should put her wrists together. She shouted:

'*Non lo faccio io nulla*' and yelled '*Ladri*-robbers' at the top of her voice, echoing down the deserted corridor. The taller man slammed the door with his foot, let go of his pistol in turn, which also swung free from its strap and grabbed Detty, pinioning her shoulders, whilst the other completed the task of handcuffing her with electric cable ties. She kicked the man behind her hard so for good measure, they put another tie round her ankles. As soon as Detty was immobilised, they turned to the still screaming Ilaria and handcuffed her. To stop her screaming, they stuffed *Elsa*'s girdle into her mouth as a gag fixing it with yet another tie so tightly that Detty worried that the woman would suffocate.

'Tie her legs too' and then by way of explanation to Detty 'we will untie your legs to walk out but you will have the pistol at your kidneys and any monkey business you both, and anyone else in the way, are dead meat, *capite?*'

The Italian they spoke was vulgar, probably foreign, but Detty's own knowledge, though improving rapidly, was not sufficient to detect any regional nuances. They started to look round the dressing room with their backs to the door apparently searching for something. There was a grunt of satisfaction as one of them found Detty's handbag. He looked through it not, at first, interested in the several hundred euros it contained but as an afterthought, he took them and stuffed them into his pocket. Dissatisfied he let the handbag fall to the floor and joined his partner searching the makeup on the tables opposite the door into the corridor.

A moment later, that door crashed open. A huge figure rushed through it, brandishing a gleaming sword. The gunmen turned at the noise. With lightning slashes, the newcomer struck first one and then the other interloper across the forearms, as they were reaching for their guns, opening bloody gashes on all four forearms. The gunmen yelled in pain and surprise. The newcomer grabbed the machine pistols one after another, slashing through the leather straps holding them. As they hit the floor, he kicked them out of the way behind him. He then stood with the heavy sword pointed threateningly towards the cringing bleeding gunmen and, in a rich American drawl, addressed them in a mixture of Spanish, English and Italian.

'You. *Hombre, slega Senora O'Neill's* feet and hands with mano piu OK altrementi io tronco tua testa!'

The man with the least injured of the four forearms got the message and gingerly and painfully taking hold of the scissors from the dressing table snipped the ties from Detty's feet and ankles dropping blood copiously down the pale silk of her Lanoure model as he did so.

'OK, vamoose back where you came from, hombre.'

'Have we got any more of those ties, Detty? '

Henry Schliessen was warming to his task, still pointing the murderous sword at the two cringing figures.

'I think he's got a pocket full. I'll look'

Detty fished around in the wounded man's pocket. She took back her money and then produced a bunch of the innocent looking but highly effective ties. This manoeuvre smeared more blood down her dress. She bound the wrists and feet of the two men together, released Ilaria from her gag and handcuffs and then set about using various pieces of costume to staunch the men's bleeding. It's a good thing that we have had the last night, she thought to herself. Hank interjected:

'I suppose we ought to get an ambulance and let the cops know. They have so many different sorts here, I never know which lot are the right ones.'

'*Cento tredici per lo Soccorso pubblico di emergeza compresa la polizia e anche l'ambulanza. Posso farlo?*'

'*Lo faccia pure, Ilaria,*'[35]

---

35 113 for emergency public assistance which includes police and ambulance, Shall I do it?
Please Ilaria

Detty passed her the telephone and she proceeded expertly to inform the authorities that police and ambulance would be needed for a serious mishap at the Teatro Communale. She also had the common sense to inform the *portiere di notte* dozing at the front desk. From somewhere she produced the direct number of the mayor's office at the Palazzo Vecchio and said that unfortunately the Signora O'Neill had been unavoidably delayed by an accident at the theatre.

There was a moment's pause, Detty, who was no nurse, tried anxiously checking the captives' pulses. They seemed satisfactory as far as she could tell. She smiled at Hank:

'Where was the Swan then?'

'You said that you wanted to do it with me so I thought I would put it on for real. But this is a swell sword. They don't usually give us swords that really work, just as well that one did. It's a beauty.'

'You used it pretty well.'

'I used to do a bit of fencing and, in my sort of parts, you always have weapon's instructors chasing you.'

He grinned and pointing the sword fiercely at the two terrified men sitting on the floor and sang in full tenor voice:

'*Durch Gottes Sieg ist jetzt dein Leben mein*
Ich schenk'es dir, mögst du der Reu'es weihn[36]

The noise of a Heldentenor renowned for his great voice, singing out in a small room added to their terror. They didn't understand a thing and their panic increased as the young woman in the bloody dress, in a powerful true soprano, took it up:

> '*Oh fand'ich Jubelweisen*
> *deinem Ruhm gleich*
> *dich würdig zu preisen*
> *zum höchsten Lobe reich.*
> *In dir muss ich vergehen*
> *vor dir schwind'ich dahin*

---

36 Through God's victory now your life is mine
I will spare it. May you devote it to repentance.

> *soll ich mich selig sehen*
> *nimm'alles was ich bin.*[37]

'I wish' said Hank laughing 'but I think young Marc would have something to say about that. We did it well though, didn't we? Pity about the chorus.'

'The Chorus would have been fine but the tenor was better than tonight, although, praise be, they liked it well enough. And here, I think, right on cue comes our chorus.'

There was a tramping of feet in the corridor and in trooped a miscellany of young men from *le forze d'ordine* (both Carabinieri and Polizia), ambulance men, doctors, representatives of the theatre, representatives of the mayor, representatives of the press, all talking at once. Almost last came the senior police, who were, much to Detty's satisfaction, headed by *Vice Questore Gatti*. Detty was mightily relieved to see a familiar face in the crowd. He made straight for her, concerned at her blood-stained dress.

'Are you all right, *Contessa*?'

'I'm fine, *Vice Questore*, and glad to see you. We were interrupted by two ruffians carrying machine pistols as I changed after the performance. We were saved by the prompt intervention of Mr Henry Schliessen, my colleague, the famous American *tenore*. He is a strong man and did some damage defending Signora Ilaria Berti, my *vestiarista*, and me.'

'So, it appears, *Contessa*,' the *Vice Questore* looked round the bloodstained room 'how did he manage to do that?'

'With *Lohengrin's* sword, *Vice Questore*'

'With what?' he said incredulously then 'But he wasn't singing was he?'

---

37 Would that I could find a song of jubilation.
equal to your glory
worthy to laud you.
rich in the highest praise
In you I must melt away
Before you I fade into nothing
That I may see bliss
Take all that I am

'No, only fighting, I am not sure how he managed to get hold of the sword either but I am extremely glad he did. It is, as you may know, a genuine one made by an old skilled swordsmith in Scarperia.'

'I did read about it. It certainly seems to do some very genuine damage.'

'I shall introduce you' she pushed through the crush to where the two metres high American tenor was towering over the crowd:

'Hank, please meet *Vice Questore Gatti*, who will be in charge of the investigation here. He has been very helpful to me in the past. He will, I think, want to ask you some questions.'

'I should be very surprised if he didn't. I am very glad to meet you, *Vice Questore*.'

'The questions can wait until to-morrow, Signor Schliessen, you appear to have had a very tiring time. I imagine that you are staying in Florence.'

'Yes, at the Excelsior but I do have to be back in Berlin on Friday – for the final *Tristan*.'

'Wonderful'

Detty wasn't sure whether he was talking about Hank's *Tristan* or his stay in Florence. 'I am sure that will give us enough time and we can always contact you again later. Your agent will know where you are. And you, Contessa, are at the Helvetia and Bristol as usual.'

'Yes, my husband and I are staying on to hear my friend, Signora Spinelli, in her *prima* as *Lucia* next week.'

'That will be an exciting evening but, Contessa, forgive me, I have not had a chance to congratulate you on your brilliant *Elsa*. I had the pleasure of being at your *prima* and treated myself to the luxury of a second performance. It is rather unpatriotic as a Florentine but I love Wagner above all composers and, *senza complimenti*, you gave us the most brilliant and convincing *Elsa* that I have ever heard.'

'*Grazie, grazie infinito, Vice Questore*, that makes all the effort worthwhile.'

A breathless Marc rushed up to them, not registering the ambulance men and poliziotti who were escorting the two wounded gunmen down the corridor. He took one look at his bloodstained wife:

'For God's sake, Detty. Are you hurt? What's all this blood?'

Images of her miscarriage haunted him 'I have only just heard. I was waiting at the Hotel for you to go to the reception. Then they rang and told me from here.'

'Marc, I'm fine. It's not my blood. It belongs to the two ruffians who invaded my *camerino* with machine pistols. But' she looked down at her ruined dress 'I don't have much luck with Lanoure models in Tuscany, do I? Excuse me, may I present my husband Marc von Ritter- Vice Questore Gatti.'

After the usual hand shaking and greetings, Marc turned to Hank.

'The taxi driver told me something about you doing a real life *Lohengrin* and saving Detty and her dresser from kidnap or worse, by rushing in with a drawn sword. I obviously must thank you but there must be more to it than that.'

'I'm sure that there is more to tell but yes, that is exactly what he did' interrupted Detty.

'Forgive me for a moment, but I need to make some telephone calls. Would you like me to let *il Sindaco* know of your problems at the same time?'

'Thank you very much, *Vice Questore*, that will save us from a lot of embarrassment at not appearing.'

After a few minutes Gatti returned:

'*Il Sindaco* sends his compliments. He has heard about the terrible happenings at the theatre. He says he is very sorry about what has happened and feels that it is a slur on Florence. However, if you are able, he would still be honoured if you came to The Palazzo Vecchio and in order to make that possible, he has asked the House of Alberti to send round a selection of gowns so that you may possibly find one that you could accept, with the compliments of city of course. A car will be at your immediate disposal. And of course, Signor Schliessen must come also.'

Detty felt that she was past receptions but, with this degree of courtesy, excuses were difficult. The rapid appearance of a young woman who said she was from the House of Alberti and the selection was ready for the Signora in an adjacent dressing room, decided the issue. Acting decisively, she chose a dramatic dress in a very original silk whose colours changed from purple to burgundy with the fall of the fabric and the angle of the light. The neckline was low opening out in violet fronds over the corsage supporting the off the shoulder loose, petal like violet sleeves. Lower the folds gently smoothed out with the colour modulating to rose-purple at the waist. The colour gradually deepened to burgundy as the gentle folds of the ankle length skirt were reached. The young woman kept apologising that the model could not be fitted properly, as would have been usual. In fact, it hung miraculously well as it was. It even made her look slender despite her pregnancy, which Detty realised, was becoming more prominent, at least to her. The effect was stunning but she had to admit certainly different from Lanoure and different from her usual style. She liked it because it was daring and the obvious iris theme was a delicate tribute to the insignia of the city of the Giglio that had been kind to her. She also had to admit a more practical, less aesthetic advantage, over the other models. Her shoes and accessories, which she couldn't possibly change, went perfectly with the new dress.

Her change was accomplished at speed, with the help of Ilaria, and the young woman from the fashion house. Very rapidly, they were speeding in the official car through the almost deserted streets of midnight Florence to the salone at the Palazzo Vecchio. Obviously, the whole reception had been put on hold for them but everybody was still there. Marc and Hank, who had accepted his last-minute invitation, stood back, and allowed Detty to make her entrance to warm and prolonged applause. Marc was as bewitched as ever by her beauty. Mesmerised, he watched her glide across the floor with her chestnut hair and shimmering silk glinting in the candlelight. The mayor, younger than she expected, received her warmly with a flawless English greeting.

'Thank you for bringing so much pleasure to Florence. I am so sorry there have been problems to-night.'

'It has all been my pleasure. The immortal Renata Tebaldi first appeared in the *Maggio Musicale* as *Elsa*. It has been daunting but a great privilege to follow her. I think the production has been a great success but that has been due to a very fine tenor' she flashed a smile at Valentin.

He, typically, was talking endlessly about himself to a group of women who probably didn't understand a word and didn't notice Detty's acknowledgment. She continued:

'And, more than anything, to the superb chorus and orchestra of il Maggio Musicale Fiorentino.'

Anton Meilin, who was standing within earshot, nodded at this, justified, tribute to the two fine ensembles.

'I must also thank Maestro Meilin and my other fine colleagues.'

Meilin joined them and bowed saying:

'I think that this is the moment to point out that a certain famous but very demanding London music critic came out to Florence just to hear Signora O'Neill. Having heard her, he wrote in his newspaper that she has now achieved technical mastery rare in one so young, added to natural vocal beauty. Moreover, she was the first singer he had heard since Anja Silja, forty years ago, who had been able to make *Elsa* both dignified and believable.'

This was news to Detty but she found out later that it was true. Sir Henry Knight had admitted in The Times that he had gone to Florence just to hear Detty's performance. He had added the comments that Meilin had just quoted.

14
THE PATRIOT GAME

Fenian Song: The Patriot Game *Dominic Behan*

'Now at last we can ask you, Hank, tell us how on earth did you appear here, as a *deus ex macchina*, yesterday?'

The three of them, Hank, Detty and Marc, all looking a little the worse for wear after a short night, were sitting in the *Giardino d'Inverno* of the Hotel Helvetia e Bristol with cups of coffee of varying sizes in front of them and a basket of rapidly diminishing *pasticceria* in the middle of the low table.

'That's easy. It was, initially, very frustrating but I suppose it sure as hell worked out pretty well. I was determined to get down here to hear your last night, Detty, and then go back to Berlin for our final *Tristan* on Friday. I was going to get to Tegel for the morning flight to Frankfurt and change on to the two thirty-five to Florence. I had arranged a ticket for the show here, although I am delighted to tell you it was quite difficult. The lady in the ticket booth said it was all due to the brilliant, young Irish singer who had taken the city by storm.'

'Pull the other leg and it will play *Einsam in trüben Tagen*' said Detty making a rude face at him.

'Anyway, it all seemed fixed and Anneliese insisted on getting up and taking me to Tegel. We were at the same hotel. She really is a good girl. I could easily have got a taxi. She must have been dog tired particularly after four performances and we had been hard at it just the night before.'

Detty was fascinated and slightly shocked to hear her heroine, the great diva, Frau Seiling, referred to as a 'good girl' but she knew Hank Schliessen had the habit of winding women, even famous ones, round his little finger. She assumed 'being hard at it the night before' referred to singing *Tristan und Isolde* together. With Hank, however, you could never. be entirely sure. He liked girls – good or otherwise – and they liked him.

'Anyway, there was a burst water pipe on the road. Anneliese, who is a *Berlinerin* born, although she lives in the Rhineland now, thought she knew a short cut. It worked out kind of like short cuts do and we were over an hour late. I missed the flight and therefore missed the 14:35 from Frankfort to Florence. The next one was 18:40, which gets in at 20:25. OK, I thought I'll miss the prelude but I can whistle *Nun sei bedankt, mein liebe Schwan!* in the taxi, after all I do know the tunes. Wrong – we then waited nearly three hours on the runway because some hoodlum, with distorted views on social justice, had put a bomb under one of the fuel tenders. They found it and defused it, thank God, as a result of a tip off, but nobody was allowed to get off the plane and the police had to check everything and everyone. It was half past nine before we took off and after eleven before we got to Florence. I wasn't happy but thought, as I'd come all this way, I might still be in time to pay my respects to a beautiful lady even if I was too late to hear her sing. I had forgotten how far it is from Peretola to the theatre and by the time that the taxi got me there; they were obviously keen to shut up shop. I asked the guy at the stage door, who fortunately remembered my doing *Florestan* here, if you, Detty, were still in your *camerino*. He said you were and that he would telephone you. He added that two gentlemen had already gone to visit you. They were very late and were still down there, he said looking fiercely at me. He was clearly disapproving but I wasn't too darn sure whether we were dealing with a moral or trade union issue. I didn't wait to find out or for the result of the phone call. I said I knew my way and hurried down to see you.'

'I passed my old dressing room on the way and noticed the sword with the horn and some other bits and pieces that, for some reason, had not been collected by props, were still lying about inside. Your *Lohengrin's* dresser had presumably left them there for collection later. I thought it was a bit casual and that swords, particularly valuable ones, which usually go straight back to the Armourer, shouldn't be in an unlocked dressing room. However, it was none of my business and for the time being, I thought no more about it. As I approached your room, I heard a muffled scream and then you shouting angrily first in German, and later in Italian. Then a male voice I didn't recognize said something about tying somebody up and shooting them. You didn't need to be a Sherlock Holmes to know that something bad was going on. I wondered whether to phone the cops but thought it would be too late by the time they got here. Then I remembered the sword, decided to intervene with a bit of help from surprise, and the rest you know.'

He looked at his watch.

'I suppose that I had better go off now and repeat all this to your friend Gatti at the *Questura*. See you for dinner tonight. I can't wait to meet your Totti.'

'I bet you can't but look and don't touch. She's got a very nice *compagno*.'

'Would I do anything else?'

He looked at his watch again and disappeared towards the front hall. It was only just after ten but Detty and Marc felt exhausted already by the dynamic tenor.

'What does it all mean, Marc?'

'Let's go back a bit. We have three strands. First, we must assume that Pueblo is stalking you but why? Neither of us thinks it's sexual and he can't want to assassinate you because he really has no reason. Anyway, he has had opportunities already, so there must be another reason for it.'

'Your reasoning is chilling, but I agree.'

'OK, then second, a false professor rings you up from a museum that doesn't exist and wants you to show him Livonian armour. This may mean that he has some sort of interest in the Lovets discovery. Not the Chalice but something else to do with armour. It's hard to see why medieval armour is important to modern gunrunners, if and it's a big if, there is a connection.'

Third, two gunmen break into your dressing room and try to take you and your dresser captive. Presumably they were, once more, trying to kidnap you but what were they going to do with you having got you?'

'I shudder to think after my other adventures.'

'It might not be quite as dramatic as those were, it could be that you were needed as a counter to trade off for whatever it is they wanted.'

'But what?'

'Armour, armour, armour.....

'I rang Liese about the pseudo-Professor after I discovered he didn't exist and neither did his museum.'

'I am glad that you did. Somebody needs to take a very careful look at the armour discovered at Lovets and I assume that is exactly what Liese or her gang are doing.'

'I hoped that she would get back to me before this but obviously my mobile has been turned off a lot of the time. She wouldn't leave a message for security reasons.'

'Interesting thought. *Elsa*'s *Handy* going off on stage. It's bad enough when it happens in the audience.'

'Doesn't bear thinking about.'

Dinner was not posh but *tipica* in one of Florence's barrel-vaulted cellars where the beef came from the Val di Chiana and the Chianti went down your throat forever. Hank predictably was enjoying himself, flirting with Totti who responded with the age-old talent of the Italiana, *affascinante ma intoccabile*.[38] Detty observing this, realised that she knew some Irish girls with the same skill but it was rare in northern climes. Alessandro was quite philosophical and talked happily with Detty and Marc. Hank announced that he wished more than ever, now that he had met her that he could stay for Totti's *prima* on Friday but *Tristan* and Berlin called.

'Perhaps I can do a swap, I'll sing *Edgardo* and your fella can do the *Tristan*. Who is he by the way?'

---

38 Fascinating but untouchable

'Fellow countryman of yours, Walt Jonah. *Finche non mi domandi di cantare Isotta, tutto bene*[39] Totti pulled an expressive face.'

'I'll coach you and we'll do the second act of *Tristan* together next time I'm here.

'Where do I come in?' exclaimed Detty '*Quella* is good enough already without poaching my *fach*' she said mixing her languages cheerfully and pointing accusingly at a grinning Totti.

'I've never heard Jonah but I believe he's excellent. The best lyric tenor to come out of the south, they say.'

'I think he's *bravissimo* and very easy to work with.'

Suddenly Detty's mobile did ring. She answered and looked instantly serious:

'Detty, it's Liese. The line is scrambled. Listen, you were right. There are nearly two hundred kilos of near weapons quality enriched uranium 235 in two false suits of armour. They were stored in a second chamber behind the main treasure room and accessible from the other side. That is why they probably never found the treasure. We only found the other chamber after we made another detailed search. We had moved the Chalice, of course, and some of the small things but the rest we left under FLL security guard until we could find a safe place for them. And another thing, the cases, the outside of the armour, we think are made in a totally radiation proof amalgam which was produced by German scientists in the Soviet Union before the wall came down. Tanya, who else, knew something about it already and mugged up the rest. There isn't even a flicker on the most sophisticated counter, until you get inside the case. They must have been Pueblo's insurance policy against a rainy day, which has certainly arrived for him now. In the wrong hands, it would get him a very substantial pension. We are to blame in that we should have noticed it earlier. We will set a trap and may need your help. I will be in touch again. How was the show?'

'Fabulous, thanks; people have been saying very nice things about me. The head's swelling.'

'I thought that you had had so much of that sort of thing that you were immune.'

---

39 As long as you don't ask me to sing Isolde, OK

'You're never immune. Thanks, Liese, for letting me know. Keep in touch,'

'*Schwarze treffen* – bulls' eye?' enquired Marc, one eyebrow up quizzically

'*Genau* – but better not say more here. It's a bit public. I am sure very soon we will be able to tell you all everything.'

Realising that something dangerous and tense was going on, the others, tactfully, didn't ask about the call and they got back to food, wine, and music.

*

At last, they were able to get to their seats in the *platea*. Detty had her hand shaken and had been embraced repeatedly in the foyer. There had been a bit more hype in that day's *La Nazione*. It was only a short piece: '*Il gran tenore americano*, Henry Schliessen, who had been visiting the city, had expressed great regrets that he has not be able to stay to hear Maria Angela Spinelli's prima in *Lucia di Lammermoor* tonight. Unfortunately, he has a singing engagement in Berlin himself tonight. He hopes to return to Florence very soon to sing in a production. Bernadette O'Neill, on the other hand, the young Irish soprano who had scored such a tremendous success as *Elsa* in the opening *Lohengrin*, and her husband *il conte von Ritter* have stayed on specially for the *Lucia di Lammermoor*. She is eagerly looking forward to her great friend's performance'. Detty thought, a touch smugly, that she was getting quite good at Italian sound bites. She was glad that at least here, nobody interrupted you or asked awkward questions.

Being in the front of the house as a member of an audience felt strange. She was tense and anxious for Totti. This meant so much to her. It was the opportunity of a lifetime. The lights dimmed. The conductor was duly applauded. The first three scenes of intrigue and choruses, in fact quite short, seemed to last for ever. She noted that the chorus were performing brilliantly yet again. This was, of course, home ground. The harp solo for the next scene, beautifully played, seemed to linger for hours. At last, Totti darted onto the stage searching for *Edgar*. She looked ravishing, her plaid dress setting off her shining dark hair – her own. She began the scena, *Regnava nel silenzio*, with wild beauty tinged with solemn dignity. In *Quando rapito inestasi*, the voice was rippling silver, clear as a fountain just as Detty remembered hearing it, off stage, a year ago. Now it was more complete, more certain. Her virtuosity in the repeat and the coloratura was staggering. At the end the house roared, and so it should, thought Detty. Even they haven't heard it as good as that often. The ovation should do her confidence a bit of good if it's needed.

Detty began to understand why Walt Jonah was highly regarded. Black and very handsome, they made a good-looking couple. Musically his tenor set off Totti's soprano well. It is a pity that the plot doesn't allow them to do more together, she thought. The evening went from strength to strength. Totti took the cruel intervals and demanding runs of the Mad Scene with great feeling, the confidence of a veteran and supreme skill. At its end, she folded gently to the floor, her shift falling about her like a white flower. It was a beautiful moment. The house thought so too and it was some minutes before the performance could continue. When they were allowed to go on, the story ran to its tragically heroic conclusion with Walt Jonah giving of his best.

'What about that then?' Detty said rhetorically to Marc as the curtain fell and the cheers and applause rocked the theatre.

'She's good, isn't she?'

'I told you. He's not half bad either.'

'You wouldn't think she could do that when you see her joking and laughing over a plate of pasta.'

'I don't suppose people see me as *Brünnhilde* or *Elsa* when I'm throwing snowballs or running down the towpath.'

They forced their way through the chattering crowds and round to the stage door through the still slightly chilly early May night.

'*Buona sera*, Signora O'Neill.'

'This is my husband, Flavio, we want to go and see Totti.'

'You won't be the only ones, I expect. A wonderful night for the young lady and a great night for Florence. And you were so splendid last week.'

'Thank you, Flavio,' and in an aside to Marc as they walked on, she added 'that was a bit of an afterthought.'

'Paranoia' he replied smiling.

The principal soprano's *camerino* had been cleaned up and there remained so sign of the sanguinary events of the previous week. Alessandro and Totti were locked in an embrace. He must have been in her dressing room before the curtain calls finished. Detty coughed politely and Totti started back.

'We just wanted to tell you that was absolutely fabulous. I think that they will give you the Freedom of the City to-morrow and you will deserve it. Wait until La Scala hears and you will have a 'suit' from the Met round any minute.'

Totti shook her head in a slightly dazed fashion, oddly reminiscent of the role she'd just portrayed.

'No, I mean it, Totti, *senza complimenti*, and if you want any tips about handling the Americans ring up Hank. I know he would love to hear how it went. If you're too modest, I'll tell him.'

She smiled and said rather simply.

'I'm so glad that you liked it. You are the most important people. I can trust you.'

'Liked it!' chorused Marc and Detty together 'But we must not monopolise you or you will never get out of here. Can you come to the hotel for a coffee and a grappa later or will you be too tired?'

'Of course, we'll come. I'll be singing it all night anyway correcting the mistakes.'

'From what we heard, that won't take you long,

Firmly, they left as others trooped in.

*

The *Ost Hanse Kurier* had done well. It was exactly as Liese wanted it with just a hint, not overstated, that transporting the stuff would be the weakest link. 'The medieval treasure found earlier this year at Lovets and the more recent finds in the second chamber, together with the Sacred Chalice of Zablovsk, is to be moved. Up to now it has been under the jurisdiction of the Air Force under guard at the base. All the finds however will now be transported to Königshof for detailed historical and scientific examination by local and foreign experts. The discoveries are of the most important historical interest and some are of great value individually. The highest security will be observed at the technical department of the University and, subsequently, when some of the exhibits are put on public view.'

Detty threw the paper aside and shifted restlessly in the leather armchair. For some minutes, she stared into the blazing log fire. At least Kurt Steuermann, the ex FWL landlord, had somehow been able to still get logs instead of the dreadful sulphurous local coal. For the umpteenth time, she opened the score of *Tannhäuser* mechanically going through the marked pages of *Elisabeth*'s role. Several days before, an anxious Marc had returned from Florence to Washington for a NATO meeting. Before he went, he had extracted a promise from her that she would not go on the operation to trap Pueblo. Detty, her usual reckless determination shaken by the fate of her last pregnancy, had reluctantly agreed. The operation was going to be hazardous and uncertain in the extreme and the odds were stacked against success. She had been closeted for hours with Liese and Tanya going through the main plan and the contingencies. They had brainstormed the possible snags and all three recognised that, although they had identified and planned for many, others would be unforeseen. Detty desperately wanted to be near her friends. Marc had wanted her to go to Oberdorf or home to Ireland but, as a compromise, had finally agreed that she could go to 'The Woman in Armour' and await the outcome. She, in turn, had promised to stay put at the inn.

She got up and walked through the hall to the front door. Fog, thickened by the fumes of the wretched coal from other houses around, swirled over the river. It was unusual to have fog in summer and, anyway, it usually cleared by midday but not today. She looked up gloomily at the newly arrived inn sign that had been painted for Kurt to order in England. The fog was so thick that she could hardly make out the portrait of Liese Zahnsdorf in the armour of *Bradamante*, Ariosto's Frankish warrior maiden, on the side nearest to her. She knew that her own likeness, armed, as *Brünnhilde* on the other side would be no clearer.

*

The headlamps were thrown back by the fog. For kilometre after kilometre the three artics trailed at a snail's pace down the narrow minor roads, often almost farm tracks. Liese lay huddled in a concealed space high in the roof of the third and last lorry. With five of her men, she lay on top of a case of carefully packed, but false, Bruegels and van der Goes. She knew that the lorries could get through this route as she had checked it out with a FWL transport warrant officer only two weeks before. They had reckoned, though, without the unseasonable smog, which made the difficult driving near on impossible. However, from one point of view the slow progress suited them. There was more time for the convoy to be ambushed. Her scrambled phone vibrated in the pocket of her gilet. It was police headquarters. The decoy convoy, which had travelled the main road from Lovets to Königshof, had arrived at the specially guarded security compound at Königshof University unmolested. The police Commissar on the other end of the phone sounded disappointed. Liese feigned sharing his disappointment but was secretly elated. At least this might mean that the leak about the decoy convoy had reached the right ears. With every grey, faceless kilometre they went, her anxiety grew. If they too reached Königshof by their circuitous route unmolested, the whole elaborate exercise would be a disastrous failure. It would also, she thought gloomily, be a disastrous failure, if they all got themselves shot or blown up. They had counted on their opponents' reluctance to risk damage to the uranium bearing armour, she just hoped that they were right.

A series of loud bangs sounded in front. They bumped to a halt. Good, they've gone for the tyres to block the road Liese calculated. Silently she motioned the ragamuffin crew around her to take up their machine pistols and wait. Heat and sparks pierced the darkness as the armoured back doors were cut through. Eventually, amid shouts, the rear door of the truck fell away with a clatter. She could see the drivers and the plain clothes police escort lined up with their hands over their heads. Three men in flak jackets were guarding them. She counted and they were two short. The rest, thank God, seemed unhurt. They were brave men and women. They knew that they had to surrender rapidly but even so there was no guarantee that they wouldn't be shot in the confusion. Four men, masked in balaclava helmets, climbed over the twisted remains of the armoured tail gate, and started inspecting the contents of the truck. They had hardly begun when there was a shout from in front in Livonian *plat Deutsch*:

'*Wir es gefunden haben*' [40] and the four men scuttled out of the third truck. Liese climbed cautiously down followed by her men with machine pistols ready. They had calculated that once Pueblo's men had found what they had been to seek, they would not search further. Liese had, therefore, split her thirty-strong force between the first and third trucks. They were hidden above the packing cases containing virtually worthless artefacts collected from the junk shops, theatres, and art colleges of Königshof. Only the armour in the second truck was 'genuine'. Many pieces were truly medieval from Lovets but the two modern copies were also 'genuine' and stuffed with near weapons quality uranium 235. They had worried long and hard about using the genuine article. It would however have been impossible to copy the uranium armour accurately enough to fool a detailed inspection, particularly if, and it was a big if, Pueblo was there himself to carry it out. They thought that it was unlikely that he would be there in person, unless, of course, he was so anxious that he would not trust his henchmen without personal supervision. You could not be sure. Liese scanned the masked figures and as far as she could tell none of them had the bearing and authority of Pueblo. They had assumed that he would arrange the ambush at arm's length and she was almost sure that they had been right.

She dragged her phone out of her pocket.

'OK, there is no cover except for the trucks so we shall have to rely on them. Sergei, go out by the roof opening. Climb over the cab and down the left side. Leave the two marksmen on the roof as arranged.

---

40 We've found it

We will do the same. Our party will leave through the tailgate, which is open and we can't be seen there from the bandits' present position. Fingers crossed that they don't go walkabout and just concentrate on the armour. Try not to shoot them unless there is no option. Is that clear?'

There was a low '*Jawohl, Frau Major.*'

'Let's go then.'

It went smoothly. In a few minutes, the middle truck and the bandits were silently surrounded. At a blood-curdling shout from Liese, they rushed in shouting '*Waffen herunter! Hände hoch!*'. One man tried to shoot and was picked off by one of the marksmen from the roof but the rest were so startled that they obeyed instantly.

Liese then played her part giving the impression that her party were themselves bandits from a clandestine group of ex NAS outlaws. She gave orders that the captives were to be shot. The terrified bandits were lined up and the balaclavas torn off their heads. Sure enough, Pueblo was not amongst them.

'You are police spies' screamed Liese 'Shoot the lot. They are just bait sent to catch us. The terrified men begged incoherently for their lives. At last, they found a spokesman, an unlikely terrorist; he was balding, about thirty and would have looked in place behind a bank counter. He was so frightened that he seemed unaware of his captor's gender.

'Please, *mein Herr*, we are not police spies. We only wanted to take stuff from the trucks, like you. We were sent to rob them.'

'A likely story. Who sent you then?'

Liese ostentatiously fingered the trigger of her machine pistol and pointed it threateningly at the cringing spokesman.

'A man- important – some sort of priest. He promised us money if we took the armour – just two important pieces for his museum. He said it was in criminal hands and we would be liberating it. It was those two.'

He pointed to the uranium containing armour.

'He paid us well and there was to be more when the goods were delivered.'

'Another load of lies! Why should he want armour when all around there are loads of gold, jewels. and valuable paintings?'

'I don't know but that's what we came for- he said he could sell them in Russia then we will all go to Columbia and live the life.'

She looked dubious but interested calculating that it was time to get mercenary.

'No, really, we were told we must just take the two suits of armour. If we took anything else, he would have us rubbed out. I think he would do too. He said he would know and looked at us with that funny piercing look. We had to phone him, in cipher of course once we had the armour. He said that he wouldn't be far away.'

Liese paused and appeared to be thinking hard for some moments. This was the tricky bit, the real cast of the baited hook.'

'If you are telling the truth, you can have the armour, nothing else mind, at a price and we will let you go. Get your boss man here quickly with twenty thousand euros or dollars in used notes. He has the armour; you go free and we take the rest. Can you do that? If not, you're lying and...'

She drew her hand melodramatically across her throat.

'It is the truth. I will try – I can.'

'Do it then. Tell him the truth. Say that you have been taken by another gang but they will sell the suits of armour to him. We need him here in an hour otherwise the Livonians and their joke of an army may find us. They don't survey this remote area very often.'

The spokesman dragged out a phone and encoded the message. They stood like an infernal *tableau vivante* for seeming hours, the soldiers still with their arms levelled – a waiting execution squad. Then the return signal squeaked. The spokesman frantically decoded it and then to prove his bona fides, still cringing, showed it to Liese 'Only €15,000 available. Can bring in one hour. Can you/they remain hidden from authorities? Signal position and consent. If not, then goodbye.'

'He doesn't pull any punches particularly with the "if not, goodbye" bit. Signal assent, one hour, €15,000. No tricks, no traps, no delays, or you're all dead.'

She wondered where he was and how he was going to get the money and get to them. A helicopter was the obvious means but terribly vulnerable to detection. He wasn't to know that all security forces were under strict orders not to survey the ambush route, and a wide surrounding area, in any way. She hoped her father's normally meticulous defence network had really been put on the back burner in this part of rural, southern Livonia.

The smog swirls were thinning, occasionally producing spectre shapes that vanished as soon as they appeared. The silence was ghostly except for the funereal cries of crows. Still, they waited. As the hour passed, Liese became more and more doubtful if he would really come. Then at last she heard it, uncertainly at first, then louder and louder until it became a deafening clatter. The smog hid the machine from view but it was near. Suddenly a great black shadow was directly overhead then a shattering splintering crash, spurts of flame everywhere. Her ears split, she reeled backwards everywhere roared with fire then darkness.

*

Detty had given up on *Tannhäuser*. She paced up and down the wood floored lounge, which was mercifully empty. Every now and then, she went through the door and walked for a hundred paces up and down the river embankment. She took out her mobile phone and stared at it like an Indian watching a cobra. She knew that there was no one she could call for information and that Liese would let her know how it had gone as soon as she could. It was evening now and even the early summer sun, peeping through the clearing smog, was low down the river. Her phone tinkled. She leapt. It was Marc, whose calls she normally looked forward to enormously, phoning from England wanting to know if there was any news. She snapped at him and immediately regretted it. They had a brief edgy chat. She said she would phone him as soon as there was any news.

She remained pacing uselessly and fidgety and tried to decide why. She had faced more critical situations calmly but his time was somehow different. Kurt came in and they talked about trivia for a moment. A raven flew past the window to land and toddle towards the river. The hotel phone rang. Detty took no notice; it was always ringing. A young man, whom she didn't recognise came out of the back office and approached her deferentially:

'Frau Komturin, Frau Leutnant Lobokova is on the line asking to speak to you.'

Her heart leapt. Tanya from Königshof, but why? She knew Tanya was not on the operation. Despite her dexterity with a wheelchair, her disability ruled that out. She picked up the phone trembling with a dreadful, unproven fear.

'Detty, it's Tanya. I have some terrible news. There was a crash at the site of the ambush. Apparently, all had gone well, Liese's plan had worked out better than we dared hope and Pueblo was coming. We are not sure exactly what happened but it seems that the helicopter had got too low in the smog and a rotor hit one of the trucks as it tried to land. It seems that it was probably, at least partially an accident, but anyway there was a huge explosion and…'she paused 'Liese was killed instantly'.

For a moment there was only sobbing to be heard down the line then through the sobs 'there are nineteen others dead, four more probably won't survive and of the remaining six, five are gravely wounded. Only one man, Willi Stiefens, a sergeant who was saved by being sheltered by a damaged tailgate is relatively unhurt. He signalled for help and gave me this initial report. It's still a horrible muddle but I am trying to sort it out.'

Detty realised with a shudder that, with Liese dead and Irina Malinowska's fate unknown, Tanya was de facto acting CO of the efficient but tiny Livonian intelligence unit.

'Not that it's much comfort, Detty, but we are almost sure that Pueblo's dead too – at least we think so. We are trying to get hold of a DNA record that was taken in connection with some extremely dubious crimes in Argentina years ago and also a dental record that is said to exist in Burgos. The bodies are of course burnt to a cinder but we do have some flesh and bones from the two passengers. We can assume that the man at the controls was the pilot. You don't know by any chance if Pueblo could fly helicopters because if he could we must consider the third man too?'

'I haven't an idea, Tanya, I never heard that he could.'

'Never mind it was worth asking. I must go. I haven't phoned the Hansehaus yet.'

The phone went dead.

Detty stared into the empty grate. It wouldn't sink in. Liese, her one-time commander and always her friend and strength, Liese, all woman and all heroine, was dead. Liese resourceful at The Farm. Liese tricking her way out and laughing. Liese the toast of Bratislava and at the same time a key insurgent. Liese promoted and taking her squad to a disco. Liese yelling from the Presidential box to support the footballer that she loved. She remembered Liese's greeting here on the *Interfluss* when she arrived from England, wondering if she should be there at all. She remembered seeing Liese always enthusing and encouraging her boys and girls. Now Liese, so full of life, was living no more, killed on active service it was true, but killed by a stupid, lethal accident. She realised with a start that Kurt was standing beside her coughing discreetly.

'*Entschuldigung*, Frau Komturin, but Dieter said that you had spoken on the telephone and that you looked dreadful. Is there anything that I can do? Is the baby all right? Do you need any help?'

'The baby is fine, Kurt, but I have just had some dreadful news. Major Zahnsdorf has been killed on active service, an undercover operation. As Detty finished, she remembered that Liese's portrait backed her own on the painted inn sign of 'The Woman in Armour'. Kurt was silent for some minutes. They both stared, unseeingly, at the empty hearth. Then very quietly he said:

'This is a loss that can never be replaced. She was so young and so *volllebendig*. But, but' he paused again obviously not knowing if he should go on:

'but it seems right that, if she had to die, she has died a hero's death. You two *Mädchen, ach entsculdigung, gnädige* Frau Komturin, you two Frauen, have had a special patriotism, adopted, I know, in your case and native in Frau Liese's. Special things, sometimes terrible special things, happen to outstandingly courageous patriots.'

Detty murmured to herself.

'The love of one's country…'.'

'I am sorry, Frau Komturin, I have put it badly and offended you.'

'Not at all, Kurt, what you said was true. It reminded me of an old song from the troubles in the land where I was born. But, Kurt, I should have been there, it was only the baby….'

She wept and he wept too. They needed it and Liese deserved it.

There was nothing more to do. She went to bed and tossed and wept. After first light, she finally slept exhausted for a few hours. She woke to a cruel bright, sunny dawn. Before she was fully conscious, she felt a dread weight bearing down on her soul before she remembered what had happened. She wanted to scream at the birds' loud song from a nearby tree and the fierce bright sunlight scintillating through the east-facing dormer of her room. It all seemed remote. Liese couldn't be dead, it had to be a dream, but it wasn't. Deserted by her normal resourcefulness, she couldn't decide what to do. She kept thinking that Liese, Irina Malinowska and the squad of twenty-eight others should have been back in Bialovsk that morning. But they weren't and they never would be.

Kurt offered her breakfast and to humour his solicitous distress, she accepted a cup of coffee. She remembered with a guilty start she hadn't phoned Marc. She did so at once saying flatly 'Liese has been killed with most of her squad. There was silence. Then he said only:

'I'll come as soon as I possibly can.'

She half-finished the coffee and leapt up trying to shake herself into activity. She found Kurt grimly consulting with the Chef over the following day's menus.

'Kurt, can you get me a taxi to take me to Königshof. I don't want to drive. I will leave my car here if you could look after it.'

'*Naturlich, Frau Komturin, sofort!*'

Brisk efficiency seemed to be the best antidote for grief.

The car arrived in ten minutes. In a daze, she noticed that the green and white flag of Livonia, always flying so proudly over 'The Woman in Armour' sagged at half-mast.

'*Wohin, Frau Komturin?*'

'*Hansehaus, Königshof*

*

The sun had disappeared and it was drizzling when they arrived. Mara was in the front hall waiting.

'Oh, Detty' was all that she could say then 'when you are able, father would like to speak to you.'

Nicklaus Oblov looked grey and suddenly old.

'Do you know how?' Detty asked,

'It seems to have been a pilot error. In the smog, he misjudged the distance from the field to the trucks and hit one of them with his rotor. That's not the whole story though. The explosion was far too large to be just due to the helicopter fuel. There must have been other explosives on board. Ulrich Zahnsdorf's staff are carrying out a thorough investigation. Poor chap, it must be horrible for him. Liese was their only child. You know that she was to marry her footballer in September.'

'I guessed as much.'

'One of the bandits left at their forest hideout near the ambush has been arrested and confirmed that Pueblo definitely boarded the helicopter, so I think that we can be reasonably sure that he is dead. There is supposed to be a dental record in Spain and if we can get a copy of that it would confirm it. The bodies were badly burnt but the dentition seems clear.'

By mid-morning Detty felt able to set out to visit the injured. The wounded had been brought straight to the University Hospital by helicopter. Two of the most seriously injured had died already. Irina Malinowska and one of the others were unconscious and on life support machines fighting for their lives but there was hope. Her minister father and her mother were at her bedside anxiously praying and watching the bleeping machines keeping their precious daughter alive. She floated in and out of semi consciousness. Detty held her hand and spoke to her for several minutes not knowing whether she was heard or not. She spoke of the success of the operation in spite of the casualties. Afterwards, she stepped to one side to speak to the girl's parents. She told them how much she admired their daughter's courage and how vitally necessary their mission had been, not only for Livonia but also for the peace and safety of the whole world. The Reverend Malinowski was a kindly, grave man seemingly old to be his twenty-three-year-old daughter's father.

'You know, Frau O'Neill, Irina really loved the job. Only a month ago she said to me "Papà, I wake up every morning thinking how lucky

I am. A few years ago, a girl wouldn't have been allowed to do my fascinating job. I am terrifically privileged to be doing it and have a boss like Liese Zahnsdorf. She makes every day exciting and interesting." Irina must not know yet that Liese is dead.'

'She must know sometime but I agree, not until she is stronger.'

Detty completed her tour of the wounded and pensively got a taxi back to the Hansehaus. There was a further message at the front desk that the President wanted to see her again.

'The question, Detti, is sadly about funerals. We have twenty-three dead souls, pray God no more, who have died serving this country and I am agonising about how we should honour them – appropriately and without offence.'

'What are the options?'

'I suppose private funerals only, private funerals and a remembrance service later or a full state funeral for all the dead and a Requiem later. There are personal and political problems with each choice.'

'For example?'

'Family objections and two of the dead are Lutherans.'

Plus, one of the just alive, thought Detty, her mind on Irina and her minister father. She tried to banish the thought quickly.

'They were all volunteers and from my observations, they were all proud of the FWL. I can't answer for the relatives of course but I think Liese and her comrades would have chosen a state funeral. Have you spoken to Ulrich Zahnsdorf and Liese's mother?'

'I haven't. I felt it was too soon but you were very close to Liese and I am grateful for your advice.'

'Would you like me to contact the other families and sound them out? I have no immediate commitments and I feel that I would like to do something to help. I should feel better.'

'If you could, I would appreciate it and I think that they would too.'

'In the meanwhile, I think that your staff could look at the arrangements for a state funeral with military honours because it will have to be soon.'

For the next few days, Detty did her melancholy tour of the bereaved families. She was comforted by Marc's arrival. Nicklaus arranged for them to stay at the Hansehaus, protected from the glare of publicity that would have been unavoidable in a hotel. One evening they were finishing the evening meal when the switchboard came through asking if Detty would take a call from New York. Surprised she agreed. A familiar and famous voice came over the line.

'Detty, I've only just heard the terrible news. They were all your friends. I only met Liese once but she was great. I am so sorry.' They talked for some minutes about how it all happened then diffidently he said:

'If you could do the Berlioz as a Requiem, I'll come and sing the Sanctus even if I have to welsh on a Met Gala to do it.'

'Thanks, Hank. That would be wonderful, we'll work on it.'

'Keep in touch.'

Her work was made easier by the ready acceptance by the families of a state funeral. She also touched on the subject of a memorial service and was surprised that even the Lutheran families said that they would attend a Requiem Mass. They added that they would be having services in their own churches with their own ministers to which, of course, the Catholic families would be welcome. It was sad that it took a national disaster to produce this ecumenical warmth but it was also heartwarming. A lesson for her own homeland she reflected. She took the information back to Nicklaus and was relieved when he told her that the Zahnsdorfs agreed completely.

*

Her telephone rang. It was Helge von Grunstrand:

'Detty, I need to talk to you about music for this melancholy event; would that we could be talking about the Nicklausfest. Are you at the Hansehaus? Can I come round?'

Detty was reminded of the first time they met when they all thought that they were losing the war and the National Anthem was born.

After draining several coffee pots, they had the order fixed.

The day dawned grey and misty. The band left the barracks for the short procession to the cathedral playing the Wild Swans regimental march. Somehow, they had found twenty-four-gun carriages. Each was drawn by volunteers from the FWL and carried a casket draped in the green and white flag with its gold falcon and chalice. There was not a millimetre between the ranks of Königshofers shoulder to shoulder along the pavements. An interval of muffled drums was followed by the reflective '*Im feld des Morgens früh*' arranged by Helge. He had insisted that the band should play the Irish Soldier Laddie, which eons ago they had joked about during the passing out parade. Detty reluctantly had agreed thinking the words were appropriate even if the names and the country were wrong. She had an acute pang of survivor misery as she talked about it. The gun carriages drew up in turn to the great door. The FWL guard of honour presented arms and the band struck up the National Anthem. Each group of six pallbearers, stepped forward and lifted their casket shoulder high. There were family, sweethearts, and comrades in each group. The caskets were in alphabetical order. The Zahnsdorfs had insisted that nobody should pull rank in death. As they reached the last but one casket, Liese's six stepped forward. There were David Sensky, Liese's footballer fiancé with Sergei Malinov, the Commander in Chief of the FWL, then Detty and Marc and finally Mara representing her father alongside a young soldier from the Intelligence Unit. Detty glanced at the brass plate over the remains of her friend:

Liese Maria Zahnsdorf
Ritterin Orden St Nicklaus
Major
Freiwehr Livonias

Above the plate was Liese's officer's beret with its green and white cockade that Detty remembered her wearing with such pride in Moscow. Below the plate was Liese's sword of the Order of St Nicklaus, which Detty had presented to her only a few short months before.

The service, conducted by the Cardinal Archbishop and the senior pastor, was short, ecumenical, and moving. Martina Schlerova, the lovely *Marzelline* of the year before opened the service with *Quis non posset* from Haydn's Stabat Mater

Nicklaus Oblov gave the address saying that they could never adequately acknowledge the debt that they owed to the men and women who, literally, had given their lives for the immediate safety of the country.

One of the students from the music school then sang Bach's *'Tief gebückt und voller Reue'*. Then there were prayers for the dead and the families and they were coming to the end of the service. Detty came slowly forward in her black Lanoure dress. She had thought carefully that only the best was good enough for Liese and her colleagues. She had said that she would not sing after *Lohengrin* in Florence but this was different. She owed it to Liese. But what? It was Helge who produced a wonderful answer. It was from Tippet's *A Child of Our time*. Lev Forjela, the onetime *Jacquino* started with the tenor solo *'I have no money for my bread.'* Then from her heart, Detty, grateful that with huge effort she could produce her voice steadily, sang *How can I cherish my man in such times or become a mother in a world of destruction?* The splendid Königshof chorus joined them for the spiritual *Steal away, steal away to Jesus*. She had no idea how she sounded but at least she had paid homage to her dear friend and her colleagues. It was a final fitting, non-military tribute to the young dead.

Afterwards the papers said that the city was in tears with their pregnant heroine pouring out her tribute to her dead friend but Detty remembered nothing. At the graves behind where the infamous Winterburg had been raised to the ground and replaced by a memorial garden, they halted. The band played *'Ich hatt ein Kamerade'* and spontaneously the graveside crowd burst into the words except that in the last line Detty and her companions substituted *meine guter Kameradin*. Detty muttered almost to herself 'Take her for all in all she was a friend, we shall not look upon her like again'. Nobody present there knew their Hamlet and they just gave her a puzzled glance.

Marc returned to England full of thoughts of the uselessness of politics. She went to bed early. At eleven, her telephone rang,

'Frau Komturin, I have a Herr Sensky for you.'

'Detty, you knew her so well. Can I come and talk to you?'

She didn't hesitate but told him to come and dressed again quickly. A short time later, she found herself closeted with Liese's huge, handsome, footballer, who was crying his eyes out.

'I loved her, Detti; I know everybody loved her but with us it was different. She was my fun, my laughter, and my joy.'

She found herself cradling his head in her lap while he wept. Most of the women of Livonia would envy her she thought. It wasn't like that though. He was a huge handsome baby and she cradled his head round her developing bump like a child's. It was two o'clock before he dried his tears, thanked her very properly and left. Detty wondered what the Hansehaus night porter would think. She found she really didn't care. Some things were really too important for conventions.

Detty went back to Bialovsk, had lunch with Kurt where they exchanged anecdotes of Liese and the great days of victory over the past evil. The following morning, she got into her car and drove through Poland and the Czech Republic where she spent a lonely night then to the peace of the Bayerische Wald and then Oberdorf with its friends and its late summer gold. Even music at present could give her little solace. Swelling gently, as the summer advanced, she wandered daily through the fields and trees of the *Frankenwald*, thinking of Liese and the terrible waste. She knew that she must go back to Ireland for her final antenatal care but somehow, she kept putting it off, relishing the unobtrusive care of Hildegard and Sophie.

She had however one more task to fulfil. She met the massive sad, sensitive American at the airport in Berlin. They had lunch in the *Nikolaiviertel*, where Hank's celebrity status was discreetly noticed. They then drove to Schönefeld through a golden afternoon to catch the evening flight to Königshof. Mara was at the airport incognito to greet them. She kissed Hank gratefully and thanked him for coming. Supper at the Hansehaus was a domestic Mara special, smoked eel, blinis and vodka, wild boar salmis. This was accompanied by a Brunello di Montalcino specially sent to Detty at the request of Totti by a winemaking cousin. Totti was, at this time, singing the lead in *Maria di Rohan* at Torino, to the accolades of the international press. After dinner, they toasted Liese in the 1780 Jameson that had now become an essential item for Presidential hospitality. Detty had only allowed herself token sips of the good things. The morning after, apparently none the worse for wear, Hank departed for his *general probe* with Helge and the orchestra in the Cathedral.

Detty had arranged to see the display of the Lovets treasures at half past eight before the exhibition opened to the public at ten. She had ordered a taxi and, in a few minutes, arrived at the new Königshof Exhibition Centre

At the entrance to the exhibition was an illuminated scroll, 'The operations associated with the recovery of the treasures in this exhibition, cost the lives of Major Liese Maria Zahnsdorf, Ritterin Orden St Nicklaus, and twenty-three other men and women of the *Abwehrdienst* of the *Freiwehr Livonias*, serving with her. With homage and reverence, the organising committee respectfully dedicate this exhibition to their memory.' Underneath on the plaque were the names of those who had died.

She walked round the exhibition with her attention wandering from the marvellous manuscripts, jewellery, paintings, and weapons. She growled resentfully to herself that all this was not worth her friend's life. She took herself to task for being illogical. Liese died fighting organised crime. The discovery of the Lovets treasure was merely incidental. Despite her self-reproach, her thoughts kept flying back to the dedication at the entrance.

The majesty of the Berlioz Requiem was a balm to her. As always, Helge marshalled the huge, augmented chorus and orchestra with skill filling the fine old church with glorious sound. In the Sanctus, Hank produced a pure lyric sound, truly remarkable for a tenor whose reputation rested on the dramatic roles. Nicklaus Oblov spoke briefly at the end thanking all the performers, but most particularly Hank, who had come so far to make his invaluable contribution. Hank had to leave immediately afterwards to fly back to the States for the Metropolitan gala which he had offered to sacrifice. Detty just caught him in time to add her personal thanks before she, in turn, went back to Dublin by way of Berlin. In reply to her repeated thanks, Hank's parting words were:

'The very least that I could do Detty – I'm so sorry'.

*

At her antenatal visit, her blood pressure was slightly raised and Ralph said she must rest. Her mother got wind of this and fussed over her endlessly. Sweet as it was, Detty found it rather overpowering and was glad when, a week later, the blood pressure had settled and she was allowed to go to Henley, as long as she had regular checks from the English midwife. With the arrogance of the lay person, Detty was sure that the raised blood pressure had been due to her distress over Liese's death and not related to her pregnancy. She assured Ralph, however, that she would take every precaution and if she slipped up, her fiercely protective husband would make sure that she conformed.

At all events, for the moment, everything seemed satisfactory and the English midwife confirmed that her blood pressure remained normal. She began to enjoy herself with an adored husband who came back to her almost every evening. The luxury of behaving like a regular married couple was something new and to relish. In the middle of a wet and windy August, she returned to Ballyinch to be near Ralph and the Rotunda. She took every opportunity to walk in her beloved Kildare fields but found that she got tired and her range was limited. She also usually got wet and was scolded by Peggy until she felt like a small child again. She longed for Marc's visits and tried to pass the dragging time working hard on *Tannhäuser* and her French and Italian.

Mara arrived for a few days visit at the beginning of August and Peggy was finally conscious of the status of her daughter's close friend when Detty had to find adjacent accommodation for Mara's private detectives. Recent events had meant that however hard the President's daughter had tried, she was no longer allowed abroad without two detectives. This did not, however, prevent the two women talking endlessly of the momentous events, which had shaken their lives, Detty was a few days from term when Mara left. She felt lonely as she tried to study and, unsuccessfully, help in the house.

The date came and went and the weather improved into a warm sunny August. Marc arrived with two weeks leave. It was little enough but it brought her great joy. A few days after she was due, Ralph was making threatening noises about admitting her to start the baby. She returned from seeing him feeling glum, with Marc making soothing noises, in the soft sing-song Bavarian of the old lullabies. She woke at just after four o'clock in the morning feeling strange and terrified. She remembered how she had felt in the back of the car during that dreadful captive ride. This was similar and brought it all back. She felt between her legs. No blood and dry. Another pain came and she was fully awake. She woke Marc and whispered:

'It's begun.'

He put a hand on her stomach. She pouted:

'You don't believe me, do you?'

They both laughed and at that moment, there was a stronger contraction and Marc grinned:

'You're right! Do you think that you should go in?'

'I don't know. I'll wake Da and ask him.'

She clambered out of bed and tip toed along to her parents' room. In a few minutes, she was back.

'He says no hurry but as we've got a fair way to go, he will take us in. Better to miss the morning rush, the traffic's right terrible on the N7 once you get past Rathcoole. She collected her things and the three of them left as the sun rose over Wicklow. It was a silent ride. The pains were coming every three or four minutes. Between times, Detty looked over the fields and over the Curragh. She wondered the while how Firebrand was and whether she knew that another female, her adoring mistress was embarking on this great adventure. Another stronger contraction. Would Firebrand have foals? Another contraction. She felt relieved when they arrived. The caring confidence of the midwife reassured her.

'Singer – grand' she said smiling 'you'll be knowing how to breath properly. Horse woman, not so good, they say, although I've delivered plenty from your part and, for myself, I don't see much difference.'

'I've not been on a horse much recently' gasped Detty struggling with a strong contraction.

By mid-morning, it was very hard work. Ralph came in and said she was doing splendidly. Detty gritting her teeth through another pain thought evil thoughts about cheerful men and was not the first woman to wonder what it would be like if they had to do it.

At one o'clock, she wondered whether she was made right as she panted desperately through her mask. Then sudden there was calm, broken only by the sound of Nicolas Maximilian Brian, Graf von Ritter yelling lustily at his new surroundings.

'He is greeting the world like *Brünnhilde*' whispered his father passing the baby to Detty then kissing her.

'Don't be daft' said Detty 'He's all fella, bass baritone, I should think; it's probably the baby version of '*Vollendet das ewige Werk*[41] as her son nuzzled her breast.

---

41 Completed the eternal task, Das Rheingold Sc 1

ABOUT THE AUTHOR

Sixtus Beckmesser, a character from Wagner's *Die Meistersinger*, is the pen name of Richard France.

He was, formerly, a GP and cognitive psychotherapist in Hampshire, UK. Since retirement he has enjoyed travelling round Europe and going to music festivals at home and abroad. Out of the festival season he has lived in Hampshire and the Tuscan hills making wine, book binding and writing, whilst still finding time for music in Florence, Milan, Venice, Germany and London.

He has always been interested in how people manage to survive terrible circumstances and events. This has led him to write the five books of the *Livonia* series. This is number four (five or six).